D0288272

1.

Agatha Weatherby longed to be a principal player in the drama of Life, or at very least to play the lead in the story of her own life—which was not much to ask, surely. Yet at the age of thirty-nine, she felt herself still relegated to the role of loyal sidekick, wise confidante, and catalyst in the lives of other more glamorous and charismatic people, chief among them her friend Valerie Hughes.

If Agatha had failed thus far in her quest for stardom, it was not for want of trying. With that aim in mind, beginning in childhood, she had adopted the device of narrating to herself lively accounts of her daily life and viewing herself as if through hidden cameras, creating in her head a sort of perpetual slice-of-life documentary of which she was the undisputed witty and winsome protagonist.

She was engrossed in that mental exercise one September day when she arrived at the Back Bay café where she had arranged to meet Valerie for lunch. Agatha was early. That was important; she needed to prepare the setting.

Choosing a table in the bay window, she angled her chair so that she was visible both to the passersby on Newbury Street and to the other patrons of the café. By turning her head just so, she could also get a good three-quarters view of herself, reflected in the window glass. Peeking out the corners of her eyes, she surveyed her fine Roman nose and gave her head a tiny shake in order to admire the swing of her severe black Cleopatra-cut hair. Then she blew out a sigh, checked her watch, rolled her eyes, and tapped her fingernails on the table, all this broad mime of impatience for the benefit of anyone who might be watching—just in case an attractive man, for example, might have noticed her there and mistakenly supposed she had no one to lunch with. She couldn't bear for anyone to think she was sitting there all alone without a date. And seeing her check the time might even give the man an opening for a conversation. "Is he always late?" he might ask, as a way of finding out if she had a husband, and she would feign surprise, as if she hadn't noticed him there. She would blink and arch her eyebrows— she practiced that now in the window—then she'd correct him dryly: "She. And yes, she always is." That would make him smile, and then he might try to charm her by saying something like—

"You're early again," a voice interrupted. Valerie had arrived, and in just doing so she had attracted all the attention that Agatha's elaborate pantomime had failed to draw. She swung a shopping bag onto one empty chair and slid into the other. "Do you have any idea how bad that looks?" With two quick dips of her straight, bony shoulders, she shrugged off her jacket. "Like an old lady with nothing to do but feed cats."

Agatha almost turned to give an exasperated look of *You*

see what I have to put up with? to her new friend, the man—
but remembered just in time that she'd made him up.
Sharply, she said, "I think you mean that being late on purpose in order to make an entrance is a very sad attempt to impress. It's a well-known fact that genuinely busy and important people are meticulously punctual." She smiled brightly.
"So what's in the bag?"

Valerie held up a smart black jacket with a plunging neck-
line. "Think it'll do the trick?"

Agatha fingered the material and frowned intently, her
pique forgotten. Clothes and shopping were important matters to her; she took objects and their acquisition seriously.
"Yeah. Yeah, they'll sign. They may not be sure what they're
buying, but they'll sign."

Valerie gave a short laugh, and hearing the annoyance in
it, Agatha added, "I mean, obviously, they'll be impressed by
your proposal, too."

"I know they will. Because it's brilliant. Now, come on,
let's order. I have a plane to catch tomorrow and a million
things to do before that. What'll it be? My treat." Valerie
flashed a smile at the waiter, who held out a menu to her,
right on cue.

Of the two types of lunches Valerie ate, it was hard to say
which was more irritating. Either she had something pretty
and skimpy, one of those dishes that are 93 percent orna-
mental, 7 percent edible, and which she managed to eat
without staring hungrily at Agatha's more laden plate, or else
she had an absurdly rich meal and tucked into course after
course with the gusto that looks life-embracing and sexy only
when skinny people are doing it. Somehow a heavier person packing it away never has quite the same appeal, and
Agatha couldn't eat that much without making self-conscious

jokes. Not that she was fat—no, she was not fat—but she had been fat in high school until Valerie, bless her, had taken her in hand, and now the Ghost of Fatness Past seemed to hover over Agatha, threatening to reassert itself unless she remained vigilant. It was tempting to wonder whether Valerie's slenderness might not arise from some kind of eating disorder, but Agatha didn't think so. All she could draw from Valerie on the topic was a smug, "I just listen to my body." Today Valerie's body was telling her to have a small salad, and Agatha bitterly ordered the same, but the difference was that she kept sneaking glances at the passing cake trolley. Of course she wasn't going to have any cake, but the trolley still snagged her attention each time it creaked past, causing her to lose track momentarily of their conversation.

"He wishes he were coming with me on this trip," Valerie was saying when Agatha tuned back in after a Black Forest cake had sailed by, "but he can't, of course. We worked so hard on this project together, it's ridiculous that he can't do the presentation with me. God, he's suffocating in that marriage! He says the only time he feels alive is when he's with me."

Agatha snorted contemptuously.

"Oh, come on now, Agatha. Just because it didn't work out for you doesn't mean—"

"Don't be naïve. Married men don't leave their wives."

"Of course they do. They do it every day."

"They do not. Look at me and Howard. He was—"

"We're not talking about Howard! God help me, will I never stop hearing about Howard? I mean, the name alone—*Howard*, Agatha—did that not tell you anything? I've had to put up with Howard stories for years, all throughout your affair and every day since, and I've listened because I'm such a goddamned good friend, but now you listen to me for a change. The guy was a dope, you were a dope, and that's all there is to say about Howard. And don't you dare compare him to Adam, because they have nothing whatsoever in common!"

"Except that they're both married men having affairs and not leaving their wives," Agatha finished, unruffled. "But I know it's hard to see the bigger picture when you're so involved. You're too close to make out the pattern, but someday you'll see it all in perspective."

"Oh, now that's a relief!" Valerie struggled for a breezy tone. "I appreciate your concern for me, of course, but you're wrong about Adam. It's obvious you don't know him. He's a serious and conscientious man, not the type to leave his wife and children on a whim. I wouldn't love him if he were."

"Wow, is that a hoot! I have to hand it to the guy. He's really conned you, hasn't he? Let's see, he's made it so that his *not* leaving his wife is the *reason* you love him. What a master!"

"Shut up and let me finish, would you?" The breezy tone was hard to maintain, but Valerie tried again. "I know—I'm certain—that someday he and I will make a life together, but not—"

"How do you know that? Has he actually said so? In words? Ha! You see?"

"I know he's desperately unhappy with her."

Agatha studied her poised, queenly friend, and an amusing idea came to her, a little way of paying her back for that measly salad. "If you really believe that, Valerie, if you really think he's so unhappy, then you'll do him and yourself a favor and you'll give him an ultimatum—today. 'It's me or her, buddy.' Make him choose. That's the only way to find out what's really going on between you. And damn it, it'll show him you still have some self-respect!"

"I have far too much respect for myself to give my lover an ultimatum. That's just the kind of adolescent, drama-mongering idea I would expect from you. Adam just needs a little time, and I've got plenty. I know he'll choose me in the end."

"In the end, exactly! But how far off is that? When his kids are in college? You don't have that kind of time. Or is that what you had in mind, a golden-years romance, conducted on the golf course? Or maybe you're supposed to wait for the wife to die of natural causes? Tricky, since she's so much younger than you."

"Three years," Valerie said tightly.

Agatha changed her tone from challenging to persuasive. "Think about it, Vee. This is the perfect time to do it, while you're away on this trip." Agatha was warming to the idea now, almost wishing she had thought of it in time to use it on old Howard. Not that it would have worked, but it would have gotten her out of that no-win situation faster. "Give Adam an ultimatum and just go! You'll be gone for a couple of days, right? So let him sweat. For forty-eight hours. Give him a little taste of what life's like without you. Of course"—this was the clincher, and Agatha had to stifle a laugh as she thought of it—" it would be pretty scary for you to run a risk like that."

"Oh, don't be absurd." Valerie glanced at the bill, tossed down some money, and began gathering her things.

Agatha pressed on, enjoying herself. "But if you honestly think that being with you is what he wants, you'll muster the courage and seize this chance to find out!"

Valerie glanced at her watch, appearing not to have heard. "I've got to run." As she stood up, Agatha clutched her arm. "Take the chance, Vee. Listen, why in God's name should he *ever* choose between the two of you, as long as he can have you both?"

Valerie pulled herself free. "I have a lot to do this afternoon. I appreciate that you're looking out for me, but I assure you I know Adam, and I know he loves me." She blew Agatha a quick kiss and turned to leave.

But Agatha hadn't quite finished. In a crude imitation of Adam's English accent, a voice more reminiscent of a monocled colonel in India, she boomed, "You know I love you, old girl, but it's not that simple!" Then, more loudly, after Valerie's retreating back, "She's my *wife*, gawd demmit!"

Forks froze in midair as lunchers turned at long last to look at Agatha, who, basking in their attention, demurely pretended not to notice it. She crumbled some bread and smiled to herself, feeling so gratified by the outcome of the lunch that after a moment's thought she lifted her finger and gestured for the cake trolley

Normally when Valerie peered out the window of a plane during takeoff, she felt a delicious sense of self-congratulation and superiority to the earthbound wretches who lived in the tiny houses below and circled boringly in their poky little cars. Clearly, all the dynamic, vital people were up here in the clouds, sipping champagne and plotting their next professional triumph. She never felt more confident than when she was on a business trip, and this was due in part to the excellence of her luggage and its contents, for she traveled blissfully unencumbered, with just one small leather bag neatly packed with good clothes and the finest toiletries. All very chic, very expensive, and very compact.

It was only when she was flying to a fresh project and the promise of another victory, feeling reassured by the quality of her luggage, that Valerie allowed herself to think about her dreary childhood, and then only as a measure of how far she had come. She and her mother had owned sacks and sacks of clothing, all of it unfashionable or ill-fitting, tight or bunchy or scratchy or missing a button, the wrong color or the wrong material. But they could never throw any of it away, because "it might be useful one day." Valerie's mother had had the knack of making what was actually a sufficient income feel like abject poverty, and their kind of poverty was not having too little, it was having too much—too much crap that they didn't dare throw out because they might be grateful for it someday. Some evening, if her mother wasn't too tired after work, she might get out her sewing machine and "do something with that skirt." But she was usually too tired, and even when she did alterations, they were never quite right, so Valerie had to learn to dress carefully, cleverly combining and layering to conceal the defects in her clothing. From the day that her adored father walked out on them until the day Valerie left home, she and her mother lived shackled to their junk, dragging bags and boxes of useless stuff from one rented apartment to another, lugging their bulky, humiliating poverty around with them from one New England town to another until they settled near Boston in the gray suburb of Burlington when Valerie was in high school.

There she had met funny, angry Agatha, and a lifesaving friendship had sprung up between the two girls, the one funnily dressed, the other chubby, both of them outsiders because the qualities they shared—intelligence, irreverence, originality of thought—were not qualities valued in their high school. Valerie had found her salvation in saving someone else, in the form of Agatha's Great Makeover. By dint of firm coaching and unflagging encouragement over many months, she had transformed a homely fat girl into a striking and passably slender *jolie laide*. And in gratitude Agatha had taken Valerie shopping for her first really good outfit, which Valerie had subsequently worn, with variations, nearly every day and hand-washed at night to keep it perfect. Yes, to own little, but of excellent quality, was what Valerie had craved all her life. And now, thank God...

But this particular trip was failing to produce the usual euphoria, in part because there was no first class on this busy intercity flight to Newark. After shifting restlessly in her seat, Valerie ordered champagne but found it tasted tinny. Clouds obscured the view, so there was nothing to look down on, and her fellow travelers seemed a particularly ill-favored bunch, all sniffling and coughing, with ugly mottled complexions. And was it her imagination or did the headrest cover feel slightly oily? Oh, ugh, could that oil be seeping into her clean, shiny hair? Like fog rolling in, a strange *ickiness*—no other word quite fitting the case—was settling over everything, and it was all Adam's fault, of course. Instead of soaring free, she felt anchored to the ground by a tether that was stretching uncomfortably tight the farther she got from him. "Going the wrong way" was how it felt. Scary and dangerous, hurtling at hundreds of miles per hour in the wrong direction. What a bore. He should be by her side where he belonged, and instead he was down in one of those very suburban houses she despised, with those kids and that wife of his. One of the more galling aspects of being involved with a married man was that when you were apart, *you* were alone, but *he* was not.

Valerie's spirits recovered a bit during the presentation of her project—designs for a new petrochemical factory—which went well, as expected. She was adroit and charming as always, dynamic and professional, with just a dash of sexiness she could toss in, or not, *à choix*, like a packet of condiments in an airplane meal. "Our best hustler," Masterson, the boss, always called her. An old hustler himself, he valued the ability to sell over creativity, because, "What's a good idea? I'll tell you what a good idea is—it's the one the guy just bought." The client had sent a committee of three to meet Valerie, and if she got over this hurdle, there would be a meeting the next morning with their boss, more of a formality; the real test was here. The committee consisted of a tough young woman, the type who broadcast her high personal standards by being hard to please when evaluating other people's work; a middle-aged man who didn't say much—clearly the important one; and a youngish man whose eyes wandered ceaselessly between Valerie's breasts and her thighs, like an unusually meticulous nomad scouring the same patch of sand over and over for the very best place to pitch his tent. Valerie was free to make these observations because she was becoming such an old hand at this business that the glib patter of her sales pitch did not require her full attention. "...creating a space ideally suited to your needs. The work areas are specifically designed in terms of the technological requirements of your enterprise, as well as the physical and psychological well-being of your staff. Our vision reflects your company image: progressive, approachable, and above all ecologically minded." That last was the clincher; the committee's butts shifted uneasily in their chairs, and their eyes shifted, too. Their business was anything but green, and the pretense that it was formed the cornerstone of Valerie's argument. The tough woman kept insisting it was over budget, and Valerie

responded by hammering home the green thing. The addition
of the atrium was what pushed the project over budget, but
the atrium was essential. "Envision it, the impact it will make
on your clients. Step inside and your immediate impression
is of greenery, lushness, tall trees, flowering shrubs, water
splashing in the fountain—a fresh and magical place. By
bringing Eden right into your factory, you are demonstrating
louder than any words ever could how completely your enterprise and the forces of nature are in harmony." *Take that,
ya bastards*, she added to herself. The company had had com-
plaints from local ecologists; Adam had found out about it,
and the atrium was his response. "Trees," he'd said to Valerie
with a weary wave of the hand. "Fill it with trees. It'll be a case
of 'We're green because we say so.'" And how right he had
been. The two men were sold on it, and even the woman relented with a taciturn, "Well   so long as Valvassori approves
it." The older man glanced with irritation at the younger, who
was still gaping at Valerie and who happened to be his son-
in-law. "We'll see what Valvassori has to say tomorrow." They
rose and shook Valerie's hand.

Over lunch with the son-in-law—there was no getting out
of it—Valerie explained a point of architectural layout with
the aid of her napkin, a dessert spoon, and her water glass,
being consciously charming, because pretending that Adam
was watching and making him jealous was the only way of
injecting any interest into the meal. There had been a time
when she'd considered flirting with business contacts one
of the perks of her job, when clients had provided a good
source of lovers, and this type of bantering after work had
been great fun. But now that seemed trivial at best, at worst
downright sordid. Thank God all that was over. Thank God
she was no longer "available"—an odious word. How grate-

ful she was for that, and how soul-destroying it would be to have to go back to fishing for sex and romance in pools where fish like this one swam—bottom-feeders, ghastly blind fish that dwell in the slime. She looked in disgust at his plump, freckled hand.

No hand could be more unlike Adam's—refined yet manly, like Adam himself. At first he had seemed unattainable. Always polite and charming, but reserved and removed from Valerie's sphere. His voice was what she had first loved about him, a cultured English public-school voice, saying wonderfully amusing and self-deprecating things. "Classy" was how she secretly thought of it, aware that finding things classy was itself déclassé. But to an erstwhile poor girl—well, lower middle class actually, but "poor" was gutsier—it was irresistible, and so was he: the prize, the prince for Cinderella. He had education and talent, tempered charmingly by fatherly traits: He was protective and concerned, teacherly and encouraging, sometimes disapproving and admonishing. His drooping frame, his graying temples, even his slight tendency toward fuddy-duddiness enchanted her, as they seemed to be proof of his pedigree. Once she had sensed his submerged desire for her, overcoming his reticence became an erotic experience in which she found her boldness as arousing as he did. The challenge of seducing such a man required all her skills and guile, and in the throes of frustrated longing she even made a pact: *Dear God in heaven, if you give me this man, I promise I will never ask you for another single thing.* When Adam at last succumbed, his guilty anguish intensified her sexual pleasure—as it did his own—and fueled her fiery sense of triumph.

Valerie spent the afternoon trapped in her hotel, downtown Newark being no place to go out shopping. She passed the time in her room rereading the same paragraph of a dull novel, in the gift shop buying herself trinkets that failed to raise her spirits, and wandering the halls, glancing anxiously into mirrors.

Back in her room at dusk, after a solitary drink in the bar, she sat wishing she could light a cigarette and looking at her phone. No one had called. Was there someone she could call? Agatha? To hell with Agatha. That asinine "dare" of hers—that was how Valerie viewed the idea of the ultimatum—had rankled all day, and so had Agatha's insinuation that she was afraid to do it, for as Agatha knew damned well, Valerie was brave enough to do anything...except pass up a dare. One particular line had been running through her head in Agatha's taunting voice: "Why in God's name should he *ever* choose between the two of you, as long as he can have you both?" Just another case of sour grapes, nothing to get worked up about. So. No calling anyone. Not Agatha, not Adam, not anyone. That's that. She glared at the phone. Oh, perfect. As if the day hadn't already been crammed full of adolescent humiliations, now she was going to spend the evening staring at the phone, hoping it would ring. No, to hell with that. Enough moping, thank you very much. She tapped in Adam's office number—he didn't like her to use his cell phone. It rang, once, twice, and again. Now that she had finally made up her mind to call, she was sick with worry that he wouldn't be there.

He was, but only just. When the phone began to ring, he was already on his feet, organizing papers on his desk, getting ready for the next day. His jacket was lying neatly folded over his sports bag on the chair. It was Tuesday, the day he really played squash with James after work—on Thursdays he only pretended to and went to Valerie's apartment instead for his weekly dose of sophistication and lovemaking—and James had been talking all day about the thrashing he was going to give Adam in revenge for Adam's victory the week before. Adam was so nearly out the door when his phone rang—once, twice, and again—that he considered not answering; after all, it was past six, and his workday was finished. But then it occurred to him that it might be Sophie needing him to pick something up on his way home. Ever since he'd become unfaithful to her, he'd been punctilious in small matters concerning her, so he glanced at the caller ID, ready to agree cheerfully to bring home a carton of milk. But it wasn't Sophie. He lifted the receiver on the sixth ring. "Hello, Valerie." At the sound of his mannerly English voice, its precise diction and well-modulated tone, Valerie felt a stab of longing for him.

"Well, they ate it up!" she said, her voice artificially bright. "Just like we thought. We won't know for sure until tomorrow, but my guess is we've got it in the bag, partner!"

"Ah, wonderful." Adam frowned at James, who had appeared in the doorway and was waggling his squash racket impatiently. "Well done. That's good news. Congratulations." James, first sensing Adam's discomfort and then guessing who must be on the phone, made an operatic mime of excusing himself and tiptoeing to close the door and let Adam speak in private, then grinned back at him through the glass. Embarrassed, Adam muttered, "Bravo."

"What's wrong? Is somebody there?"

"No. Not now."

"Do you miss me?" Valerie had not meant to say that, or anything resembling it, but the words were already out of her mouth. There was silence on the other end of the line as Adam gestured to James to go downstairs and wait there. He mouthed, *Five minutes*, with one hand in the air, five fingers outstretched.

"Adam," Valerie prompted. "Adam?"

James looked puzzled and mouthed back, *What?*

"Yes, of course," Adam said sharply, in exasperation with James. "Always. Keep up the good work and let me know what happens. All right, then? Speak to you tomorrow."

"Adam, wait!" The brush-off? "I just..."

"Yes?"

"I wanted to know if...you love me." What? What was she saying? Stop it, for God's sake, stop this drivel!

There was a breathy sound on the line that made Valerie stiffen; it was very like a weary sigh. She sincerely hoped that it had not been a weary sigh. "Of course I do," Adam said. But there it was in his voice: that hint of weariness.

"No, I mean...really," she said, meaning that she really, honestly needed reassurance; this wasn't just some stupid little game. To keep herself calm, she thought, *Don't worry, it's okay to miss your lover, okay to show him that you do, okay to express your insecurities. None of this is uncool, it's all right, it's natural, he'll understand.*

"What do you mean, 'really'? Come on, Valerie—you're not the 'Do you love me? Really?' type!"

There was a short silence. Then Valerie asked in a dangerously even tone, "Oh, no? What 'type' am I, then?"

"Valerie, what is the matter with you? You know I love you."

Said impatiently. Irritably.

James could lip-read well enough to catch Adam's last three words—as who cannot? He knew about their affair, of course; it was pretty hard to work in the same office and not know, so now he gave Adam a big, knowing wink. Adam's left cheek pulsated with annoyance. It was high time to wind up this tiresome call. "Look, I've got to go," he said. "Let's leave this for some other time, shall we? We'll talk when you get back."

It was his tone of voice that did it. That brisk, harassed tone, as if after a long day at work it was just too much to have to put up with the hysterical neediness of his mistress, when all he really wanted to do was get home to a nice, relaxing dinner with his two small sons and his wife. It was the long-suffering quality of it that made anger shoot through Valerie like an electrical charge, and when she spoke, her voice was low and forceful. "Oh, no. No, that won't do at all. We need to talk right now. That's why I'm calling, in fact. I've thought things over, Adam, and I've realized I'm not 'the type' to sit around waiting for you to decide who you want to spend your life with. Time's up, I'm afraid. You have to choose. Who's it going to be, Adam, your wife or me?"

"What?"

She was as shocked as he was by what she had said. She felt a queasy jolt in her stomach, as if she were careening down a roller coaster, but also that same reckless elation. She betrayed nothing of her vertigo, however, as she continued in a firm voice, "I'll be back in the office on Thursday. That gives you two days to make up your mind. During the next forty-eight hours, you can do one of two things: either tell your wife you're leaving her, then call me and tell me you've done so, or else tell your wife nothing, in which case it's all over between you and me."

"Valerie, you must be joking. This is infantile!"

"I know what I want, Adam. Now it's your turn to decide."

He opened his mouth to protest, but the line buzzed dead;

she had hung up. He sat staring at the receiver in his hand. It was no good now wishing he hadn't answered the phone.

James came back in, shifted his weight from foot to foot, cleared his throat twice, and then whacked a few imaginary squash balls in slow motion, supplying the sound of the distant crowd's roar of approval, but none of this succeeded in rousing Adam from his reverie, so at last James broke the silence with a tentative, "Trouble in paradise?"

A slender, blondish woman with her hair pulled back in a ponytail, wearing a cotton dress, flat shoes, and no makeup, made steady progress through the aisles, frowning thoughtfully as she chose a cabbage, oatmeal, some Bosc pears, fruit juice, raisins, milk, cereal, fish, piling things and more things into her cart until it was so heavy she could barely steer it. She paused over two bottles of jam and read the ingredients carefully. "No added sugar," one label promised in big letters, but in smaller letters it admitted to aspartame, which was worse. *Such an astute jam buyer*, a little voice in her head mocked, a voice she had come to think of as "the imp."

In the supermarket Sophie Dean was sometimes assailed by doubts, although about what, exactly, she would be hard pressed to say: her life, herself, something fundamental; which was puzzling, because this was, after all, the life she had chosen, with much care and forethought, in every detail. She had reflected at each fork in the road before selecting her path, her decisions had been sound, and yet sometimes she felt bewildered by the unfamiliarity of the countryside in which she now found herself.

She caught sight of her face in the reflection of a gleaming

chrome freezer and she was surprised by the ferocity of her
expression. Her four-year-old son, Hugo, wouldn't approve
at all. "Hairbrowns" was what he called eyebrows, and he
used them to gauge whether a person was good or bad. Bad
people frowned harshly, so their eyebrows were straight lines
pointing down to the bridge of their nose, whereas good people's eyebrows rose in high, perky half circles. This was true
of the illustrations in children's books, and it was also a reliable way of judging real people and their moods. "Why do
you have those hairbrowns?" he would sometimes ask his
mother when she was looking worried or angry.

Waiting in the checkout line beside her heaped cart, Sophie noticed a woman of her own age in the next line who
was buying a container of yogurt, some frilly lettuce, and a
bar of plain soap. Three things. So easy to carry that she
didn't even need a basket. She was a woman who, without
appearing disdainful of her surroundings or standing out in
any definable way, still managed to look markedly out of
place in a supermarket. Only five years ago, right up to the
time Matthew was born, it was still rare for Sophie to go into
a supermarket. When she was single, and later, her first year
with Adam, she had lived in a little studio on Marlborough
Street between Exeter and Fairfield, and she would pop into
DeLuca's for one or two things on her way home—some cau-
liflower, a carton of eggs—and then off she'd go, clipping
briskly down the street toward home, swinging her shopping
bag. Now things were very different. Living in the suburbs
meant she had to take out her car and drive a long distance,
specifically to the supermarket, not on her way to or from
anywhere, but on a trip of its own. Now she had to drag
a giant shopping cart around a chilly, fluorescent-lit cavern
and pile it high, the cart growing so unwieldy that she had to

throw her whole body into the task of moving it. Grunting and shoving, buying more food than she could push, let alone lift. It was obscene. But the alternative was worse: buying less and coming more often, thereby ruining several mornings a week instead of just one. Seized by a sudden doubt, Sophie hunted for a mirror, found one on top of a stand of sunglasses, and studied herself anxiously. She looked all right, but...But! Her suspicions were confirmed: She did not look out of place in a supermarket. Not anymore. Those days were over. What hideous process of degeneration was this, then, more insidious than aging and so much more damning? Could it be reversed? What fashion makeover, what corrective surgery, what course of psychological overhauling could be required? She pushed her groceries across the parking lot, head down, muttering to herself, struggling to keep her sidewinding cart on track to the car, and planning the rest of her day.

After a morning of domestic industry, she would drive to the Montessori school with a snack of cheese sandwiches and Bosc pears, her sons' favorite fruit. It was a warm mid-September day, so they would go straight to the park and picnic there. Hugo, the younger of the two boys, had been in school for only a couple of weeks, so this routine was still new to Sophie, as was the vertiginous freedom of having both children occupied from nine to two-thirty. Time to herself at last—or not, as it turned out. With nature's abhorrence of a vacuum, her timetable quickly filled up with other chores; the illusion of freedom vanished, and only the strangeness of separation from the children lingered. She usually got to the school early and sat by the gates, enjoying the feeling of anticipation before the bell rang and the schoolyard overflowed with shrieking children, among them her own two.

She would kneel to hug them, relishing the strength of their small arms around her neck, their flattering shouts of joy at seeing her, and their breathless accounts of the days they now spent away from her. It was the happiest moment of her day and theirs, this reunion, and thinking about it now as she toiled across the parking lot, she wondered how she could be so churlish as to resent the supermarket that supplied her children's favorite fruit.

The sight of the pears in her cart transported her to her Marlborough Street studio one rainy Sunday morning several years before. She and Adam had been sitting looking out the bay window at the garden and eating pears and Roquefort when she was reminded of a favorite poem. She found the book, opened a bottle of white wine, and he read "A Late Aubade" by Richard Wilbur aloud to her while the rain and wind dashed the blossoms off the little cherry tree out front.

Her memories were interrupted by a beggar in the parking lot asking for spare change—and then something unaccountable happened. While she was digging in her purse, her unattended shopping cart began to roll. The man took his coins, grinned toothlessly, and pointed at her cart, which had picked up a little speed, but not much. In a few quick steps, she could easily have caught and stopped it, but she didn't move. She just watched. Feeling strangely detached, she stood watching as the cart rolled across the asphalt— slowly, slowly—gaining just enough momentum to smash the left taillight when at last it crashed into her car.

Adam was sitting on the chesterfield, his eyes closed, his hands covering his head as though to shield his thoughts from scrutiny. It had not been a good day, even discounting that hysterical call from Valerie—which was no joke, he knew. It had been a taxing day of tension and conflict, with that partnership looking more unlikely all the time. And now some nonsense about a shopping trolley.

"But I don't understand. How fast was the bloody thing moving?"

"Not fast at all. That's the funny part."

"Then why didn't you stop it, for heaven's sake?"

"I don't know. The whole thing seemed...predestined."

"Christ Almighty, Sophie!" Adam felt that it was vulgar to compare his mistress and his wife, but good God, here he had on the one hand a woman pulling off a multi-million-dollar deal and, on the other, someone who couldn't even— "What good would you be in a crisis? Really, with reactions like yours, who needs danger? Through your sheer inertia, the most tri fling incident could eventually become life-threatening—given that it has all the time in the world to evolve!"

"It's very strange, I know." She handed him his drink and went into the kitchen.

At Adam's feet Matthew and Hugo were playing with toy airplanes, using part of the design in the Oriental rug as a runway and expertly re-creating with their mouths all the sounds associated with air-traffic control, takeoff, then engine failure, the triggering of the alarm system, generalized panic aboard, a forced landing in the jungle, the leading of the passengers to safety, and the subsequent explosion of the aircraft. Once the heroic crew had pulled one another to safety from the burning wreck and doused the flames, the boys wanted to play the game all over again, this time with their father as admiring spectator. There were cries of "Daddy, Daddy, look at this!" from Matthew, taken up by

Hugo, and much eager tugging at Adam, resulting in Hugo's knocking over his whiskey.

"For the love of God!"

Sophie dashed in from the kitchen, dishcloth in hand, ready to protect Adam from his offspring's exuberance and them from his indifference—well, no, not indifference; she didn't mean that. "Here we go," she said gaily, mopping whiskey off the rug. "All clean." Matthew stood by uncertainly, holding his airplane. "Matthew, honey, Daddy does want to see your planes, but not right now. He's had a hard day at the office, and he needs to rest. You can show them to him later, how about that? Now, run up and play in your room until dinner. Go on."

"Daddy never wants to play," Matthew muttered, and taking the cue from his older brother, Hugo hung his head, too, and left dragging his feet.

Adam sighed, contemplating his empty scotch glass, a symbol of all he had to put up with. Sophie looked from him to the children trudging resentfully up the stairs and frowned as she played back in her head something she had just said: "Daddy's had a hard day." Where had she dredged up a hackneyed line like that—from some obscure *Leave It to Beaver* rerun? She smiled apologetically at Adam. "They're crazy about those airplanes." When he didn't respond, she sat next to him, looked at him with concern, and stroked his hair back from his forehead. "You do look tired. Things all right at the office?" Without opening his eyes, he reached up and stopped her hand. Surprised, she took it away, then looked at his impassive face for a moment, stood up, and went back into the kitchen, raising her voice to be heard over the clanging of pots and pans. "The plumber finally showed up today. Three hours late! I was stuck in the house waiting for him. Did a pretty sloppy job. I think it's still leaking. Should I get him to come back, do you think? Or try somebody else?"

Adam massaged his forehead, his eyes resolutely closed.

"Adam? Do you think I should call the same guy back or try to get someone better?"

"Oh, for Christ's sake, can't you work it out for yourself?"

Sophie came to the doorway and looked at him in astonishment.

"I'm sorry," he said crossly. "It's just that…" He waved his hand in a broad gesture that meant a hardworking man deserved to return home to something better than toy planes and plumbers.

"No," Sophie said quietly. "I'm the one who's sorry. I look forward so much to having a grown-up to talk to, and then when you get home, I have nothing more interesting to say than, 'The plumber came.'" She laughed uncomfortably. "I don't blame you for finding it boring. I do, too. Sometimes I almost don't recognize myself, you know, in my…in my life now…as wife and mother. This funny thing happens to me sometimes, Adam. It's a mocking voice inside me, like a little imp that leaps out and jeers at me when I'm just going about my business. It happened in the supermarket this morning, and again right now when I told the kids you'd had a hard day. It's a little voice that makes fun of me for doing things that I actually want to be doing. I mean, I'm happy, really. I am happy. I don't like waiting around all day for the plumber, of course—who would? But the sink can't leak, so someone has to get the plumber here, and for the time being, while the boys are little and I'm not working, that person is me. That's how we decided to do it, and I'm glad we did. I am. But you know, I find it every bit as boring as you do, believe me. Actually, *more* than you, because I'm the one who has to do it, so..." Up to then Sophie had been addressing her speech to various corners of the room, anxiously twisting her wedding ring, but now she turned to Adam, who was leaning forward with his elbows on his knees and his hands clasped on his bowed head in an attitude of concentrated listening that gave her courage to continue on a firmer note. "So I think you could sympathize with me for having spent such a dull day doing something that was for the good of all of us, instead of reproaching me for it. I was bored—it's unfair to also make me feel boring." She smiled at him, ready to accept his apology with a careless wave of the hand, feeling more like her old self for having told him about that evil imp. Now they could laugh about it together and exorcise the demon.

When it dawned on Adam that silence had fallen over the room, he roused himself and stood up, saying, "Feel like some music?" She stared, her confidence trickling away, then returned slowly to the kitchen while the imp taunted her triumphantly: *You burbling ass! First you bore him out of his skull, then you make it worse with all that whimsical crap! Can't you just shut up if you have nothing interesting to say?*

But why reproach herself? It certainly wasn't her fault that having the plumber in wasn't interesting! What was she supposed to do—check every comment for suitability for his lordship's ears? However, it was also possible that Adam was right. It was her duty, a sacred duty to herself principally, to make her days interesting, and it could be construed as unfair to punish him with her failure to do so. Best, she thought, not to express her anger until she was sure it was justified. So instead she launched into a nervously high-spirited account of the children's doings, speaking disjointedly, but loudly enough to be heard from the kitchen, in a kind of parody of housewifely prattle that the imp enjoyed heartily.

Matthew's painting...plenty of movement...get it framed...

Barely listening, Adam searched through their music in the vain hope of discovering something new and exciting there.

...had the sniffles...took him to school...a touch of hay fever...

No. Nothing new or exciting. Stepping back from the stereo, Adam stumbled over a basket of clothes that Sophie had stashed behind an armchair. "Jesus!" he said, staggering to regain his balance. Sophie raced out of the kitchen and scooped up the basket.

"I'm sorry, darling, Milagros is off sick, and I haven't had time to do the ironing. But I will get your shirts done, I promise." They stood for a moment staring at each other; Adam looking offended by his close call with the laundry and Sophie, basket on hip, earnestly promising to iron. Then she threw back her head and laughed, a deep, healthy laugh that felt good. "Oh, Adam, my darling, isn't life rich? So full of the funny and the unexpected! Here I am, haunted by the specter of Mrs. Cleaver, begging forgiveness for the ironing! And you're standing there like the lord of the manor, looking peeved and accusing!" She leaned forward in a fresh burst of laughter and squeezed his forearm to steady herself. "Oh, honey, this is one for the annals!" After which, as far as she was concerned, the air was cleared.

The boys thundered down the stairs, now in hot argument.

"Daddy, Matthew broke my elephant!"

"I did not! It broke itself!"

"You did too! Daddy, can you fix it?"

But Sophie was on the job. "I'll do it, honey." She snapped the trunk back onto his elephant, a service she performed often, and gave both boys a quick hug before pushing them gently away. "There, all fixed, off you go." She looked tenderly at Adam. "Can I get you a fresh drink, sweetheart? Dinner will be ready in a minute." He nodded, and, exceptionally, she poured one for herself as well and sat next to him, wisely opting this time for companionable silence. Whatever troubles he was having at work, he would tell her about them in his own time and way. The first sip of her drink, a well-watered scotch, made her shudder, although not unpleasantly, raising gooseflesh on her arm. She had fallen out of the habit of drinking, first with pregnancies, then breast-feeding, then all those months of broken nights when she was too tired for anything. Gazing into the pale golden liquid, she marveled at having a drink again, just like a grown-up.

Then the boys were back, full of outrage. Hugo threw himself into Sophie's lap, spilling her drink on her dress. "Matt pushed me down!" Adam cursed and held his glass up high, out of danger.

"It's not true, Mommy! He just fell down! And he took my—"

Adam cut them off with a roar of, "Quiet! Quiet, both of you!" They stared at him round-eyed. "Not another word! Do you understand, Matthew? Hugo? I've had enough!" They crept back a bit, Hugo's mouth trembling, Matthew pale. "I've had enough," Adam repeated, quietly this time, and to Sophie, with a hint of apology in his voice.

She looked with regret at her empty glass. "It's well-engineered, isn't it? Parents are protected from becoming alcoholics by their young children knocking the drinks out of their hands." But he didn't smile, so she went on in a lower voice. "Honey, it's hard now when they're so young, but this won't last forever, and soon we'll be looking back on this time wishing they were little again." She smiled tentatively but still got no answering smile. To the boys she said, "You must be tired and hungry. Let's have some supper."

But Adam got to his feet. "I'm going out. Carry on without me. I...Just carry on without me."

When the door closed behind him, the children turned questioning eyes on their mother. "Well!" she said brightly. "Daddy had to go out. Come on, let's eat!"

Valerie had dinner alone, having dodged the son-in-law's persistent invitations to join him. Back at the hotel, she reminded herself that it was too soon to expect to hear from Adam. Unless...There was one scenario she had been playing in her head that would account for a call this early. It went like this: Adam had felt braced by her ultimatum, grateful for that little push, and he had marched straight home to have it out with his wife. Not terribly likely, perhaps. Somberly, Valerie rode the elevator up to her room, and as she was opening the door, her phone began to ring. She pawed in her bag for it, then gasped into it, "Hello? Hello?"

"So how'd it go, gorgeous?"

"Oh. Agatha. Hi. Look, can I call you back? I'm expecting a call."

"This is a call."

"But I just got in. I need to— I'll call you back, okay?"

"No, not okay. You have call-waiting. But it's nice to know you're so glad to hear from me. Listen. I'm going out tonight.

I have a hot date for once—what do you think of that? Valerie? Valerie. Vee, are you okay?"

Valerie didn't answer. Hearing the concern in her friend's voice had made her suddenly afraid of bursting into tears.

"Is something wrong?" Agatha insisted.

"No. I'm fine." She gave a shaky sigh. "Just tired. Long day. I'm not really in the mood to talk right now."

"I'm not hanging up this phone until you tell me what's wrong."

Valerie took a deep breath and said as calmly as she could, "I did it."

"Congratulations! I knew you would. Now, answer me this. Do you think they would have signed if you'd been wearing...uh, let's say...a big, hairy, hand-knitted pullover? Come on, tell the truth."

"No, I mean I told Adam. You know...to make up his mind."

"You *what*?"

"You know. I told him to choose between us. Her or me."

"Oh, my God! I can't believe you really did that!"

"What do you mean? It was your idea! 'Make him choose, give him forty-eight hours, stop wasting your life!' Remember?"

"You did that? You gave him *forty-eight hours*? *To leave his wife?*"

For a moment Valerie found herself poised at a fork in her emotional pathway. In one direction lay Stark Panic, brought on by the realization (belated) that Agatha had not been serious, had just been trying to get her goat as usual, and that Valerie had fallen into her trap, wantonly jeopardizing her love affair and possibly her entire future—in other words, Valerie had just ruined her life. In the other direction lay Defiant Anger, as in, how dare that bitch try to make a fool of her? For a moment she hung undecided, staring into the faces of both possibilities: panic and anger.

She chose anger. "What's wrong, Agatha? Don't you have the courage of your convictions? Are you all talk and no action, is that it? Well, I'm not!" It felt good, and it solved another problem: Ever since Valerie had decided to take this drastic step (or, more accurately, ever since Valerie had found herself taking this drastic step), her pride had suffered from the knowledge that the idea hadn't been hers in the first place. Feisty and daring, it was the sort of thing she normally attributed to herself. There was something lowering about merely following the advice of others, and particularly of Agatha. But here was an opportunity to appropriate the idea, and quite rightly, for who did it really belong to—the person who had idly dreamed it up or the one capable of seizing it and boldly acting upon it? "I'd always meant to do something of the kind," she said airily, "and now seemed as good a time as any."

"Well, obviously, it was the only thing to do under the circumstances," Agatha countered smoothly. "I only wish *I* had come up with the idea sooner—in time to use it on old Howard. I was just surprised to hear you'd gotten up the courage, that's all."

"Were you indeed?"

"I mean, it's not an easy thing to do. Bravo. At least this'll cut your suffering short. Better to learn the truth right away and get on with your life than screw around for years, like I did."

"Not that there was ever the remotest chance of my doing that." It had not escaped Valerie's notice that Agatha wasn't even considering the possibility that Adam might choose Valerie over his wife. Valerie would get her for that one day. "Listen, I have a big day tomorrow, and I need some sleep. So I'll let you—" But she broke off abruptly, imagining the long, lonely night ahead and thinking that under the circumstances giving her friend the brush-off wasn't in her best interest. So hey, she could be magnanimous. To hell with pride and scoring off Agatha for once. She dropped into an armchair with a sigh. "Oh, shit, Agatha, I'm scared."

It wouldn't be fair to say that Agatha gloated, but she did derive quiet satisfaction from the fittingness of Valerie's suffering for something that was entirely her own fault. It all came down to that salad; there would have been no need for revenge if only Valerie had eaten a decently caloric meal. Spooky, though. It just goes to show how great events can hinge on small ones: You order the wrong thing, you lose your man. Sobering.

"You're scared, huh?" Agatha asked, and she decided to knock it off, too. "Well, of course you are, and no wonder. Look, let's think this through. I think you've done the best thing, but we'll hash it over until you feel good about it. Or if you don't, we'll come up with something else you can do. Either way, we won't stop talking tonight until you feel okay. Okay?"

"I'm listening," Valerie said in a small voice, feeling comforted already. Then she remembered that Agatha was going out. She didn't suppose it mattered, but for form's sake she thought she should ask, "But what about your hot date?"

"You're more important right now."

Valerie snuggled up in the chair and tucked her feet under her, all ready to be calmed and reassured.

Agatha cleared her throat and assumed the tone of someone making a formal address. "Now, uh, very briefly, I would just like to begin by saying that— Check…check… testing…one…two…Is this microphone working?"

"Agatha."

Before beginning her dissertation, Agatha glanced at the clock and saw that she should really be leaving the apartment now, on her way to her date. "Fine. Okay…ah…oh, yes. Let's see, you two have been sleeping together for six months now, more or less. That's a key moment in a clandestine affair. You're probably at the pinnacle of your relationship—sexual attraction has turned into love, but familiarity has not yet bred contempt. So you had two options with Adam: to go along as you were, or to bring about a change. If you had gone along as you were, what would have happened? One: Very soon, Adam would have begun to grow comfortable with his double life, no longer tormented with guilt about the lying and betrayal involved. He would have lost that feeling of 'I can't possibly go on like this!'— which is so useful to us in forcing his hand. Two: He would have come to see you as someone willing to accept the role of the 'other woman,' and deserving nothing better. If after six months you still seem satisfied with the crumbs from the marriage feast, believe me, that's all you'll ever get. Three: As his estimation of you drops, your resentment of the situation will rise accordingly. You'll become bitchy and nagging, which will make him like you even less, which will make you even bitchier—and so you will spiral, down, down, down, down."

"But what if—"

"Quiet!" Agatha wasn't allowing interruptions, not when she was being so damned self-sacrificing. "What I conclude is that if you'd done nothing, your affair would have burned out on its own."

"But wait," Valerie insisted. "What about this—I do nothing, he sees how perfect I am for him, and in his own time, without unseemly pressure from me, he makes the adult and lifesaving decision to be with me?"

"No."

"No?"

"No. Don't forget, it's easier to stay married than to get divorced. Newton discovered that. Objects in motion stay in motion, and those at rest stay at rest, and that means that staying in a marriage is the natural thing to do. We're talking about the Energy Well here. Listen, Valerie, he would have to pack up every one of his books. Had you thought of that? All those architecture books, every one of them, he has to put them in boxes and lug them somewhere. And his other stuff—tennis rackets, high-school yearbooks, possibly some old sporting trophies—"

"Are we cleaning Adam's closet now?"

"I'm making the immensely valid point that breaking up your home and marriage is an enormous move, incredibly difficult to do, and not a thing someone is likely to undertake unless there's a real emergency. And what's more, we're dealing here with a fundamentally 'nice guy.' No, he will not, of his own accord, just walk out on his wife and two small children, definitely not." Agatha paused for effect before adding, "Not unless you make him."

By now her poor date would be standing on the street corner, looking around hopefully for her, the wind ruffling his—well, no, he didn't have enough hair for that, but still, it was awfully hard on the poor guy. Nevertheless, she plowed on dutifully.

"And that brings us to the second option. You force his hand, which is what you've done."

Nervously, Valerie began to twist a lock of hair. "Go on," she said.

"Well, basically he still thinks you're the bee's knees, and he still feels guilty about lying to his wife—probably still feels at this point that cheating on her is worse than leaving her. Deep down he agrees that he has to choose between you, so it's good you hit him with this while he still has a conscience to torment him."

Valerie's finger twirled faster around her hair. "So you figure he'll leave her?"

"No! Haven't you been listening? The chances of his leaving her are nil if you don't force his hand, and very poor even if you do. Face it, Vee, you're going to lose him. The question is, now or later, and how much will it hurt? If he's very important to you, then it's worth risking the heartbreak of losing him now, just on the infinitesimal chance that you might get him. But if he's not, then you're better off calling him back and apologizing, telling him you lost your mind, and letting things peter out of their own accord, since that way, by the time you lose him, you won't care. If you ask me, that's what you should do. The no-pain option."

"But I do want him."

"Really? I mean, really? Is he...you know...The One?"

Dear God in heaven, if you give me this man, I promise I will never ask you for another single thing. "Yes. He is."

"Oh, wow. Well, in that case you've done the right thing."

Valerie closed her eyes and savored those words for a moment. Then she snapped into action. "Right. I have a big day coming up, and I need some sleep. Call you tomorrow."

Click. The dial tone buzzed in Agatha's ear. She was an hour late for her date.

Despite Agatha's reassurances, Valerie jerked awake in the middle of the night and lay staring into the darkness of her hotel room, her heart thumping with terror at what she had done.

And the next morning she was like a person recalling with mingled horror and defiance a rash act committed during a drinking binge. She dressed and applied her makeup carefully before going down to the lobby to drink cup after cup of black coffee, just as if she had a real hangover. She was jumpy all morning, listening out for The Call that would change her life. *Call, Adam, call,* she chanted in her head. She couldn't bring herself to switch off her phone, even during her meeting with Valvassori. The question of whether or not this man would buy her plan for his factory seemed ludicrously unimportant now, and her utter indifference to the matter allowed her to deal with his hedging with impressive firmness. He was going to capitulate, she knew, but she hardly cared, which only went to prove, she thought grimly, that when the prize didn't matter to you, you won it every time, but...she couldn't bear to think what this would mean about Adam should the reverse be true. Nor could she imagine a sadder future than that of a rich and successful architect with no one to talk to when she got home. The appalling waste! Would she one day look back on this as the defining moment of her life, the day that Valvassori said yes and Adam said no, condemning her to a life of professional success and personal failure? *Oh, Adam, Adam, don't let me go to waste. Call me. Call.*

Obediently, the phone in her bag began to chirp. At first she was unable to credit it, wondering in confusion if she had somehow caused it to happen. Then she wrenched open her bag and dug frantically, but her overeager fingers were too clumsy to find the phone, so she tipped the contents out onto the table and caught the phone as it nearly skidded over the edge. "Hello? Hello?" she panted, her back turned rudely on Valvassori.

"Hi there, you daredevil. Has lover boy called yet?"

"No." Valerie had to unclench her teeth to get the word out.

"Ooh...that's too bad. Well, never mind. You're doing the right thing. Bye-ee."

Valerie's face acquired an expression that further impressed her client. She put away her phone and pointed the face at him. "Sorry about that, Mr. Valvassori. Where were we?" A few minutes later, he had bought the factory, and Valerie was almost sorry he had, now that she had equated professional gain with romantic loss. But there was one bright aspect: It gave her an excuse to call Adam—made it necessary, in fact, to call him. As her project partner, he had the right to know.

"Hi, it's me," she told him briskly, and raced on, not wanting to linger dramatically. "He bought it. Just a few last details to hammer out tomorrow morning, and then I'm coming home." She let that sit there.

"Excellent work," Adam said, nervously jovial. "Well done. The...uh...atrium. They fell for it, then?"

"Well, they hedged a little, over budget and all. But I gave them your 'in harmony with nature' line, and they didn't dare disagree."

"You pulled it off. Congratulations."

"Well...you, too. We did it together." The silence that followed sounded pathetic and pleading to her, so hesitantly she

filled it with, "Remember...please remember what I said yesterday, Adam."

"Yes." Adam frowned, because James had just poked his
head around the door to ask a question but broke off short
when he saw that Adam was on the phone, signaling, *No
problem, take your time*. James would wait.

"I love you," Valerie said.

"Me too," Adam answered quietly, and he hung up. James
grinned at him, knowing what "Me too" was in response to—
as who does not?

"I don't know what you're up to, pal," James said with a
chuckle, "but I sure hope you know what you're doing!"

Adam's left cheek pulsated.

———

That evening Adam stood in his front yard contemplating his
house and trying to summon inner calm and courage for the
task ahead: the leaving of his wife, Sophie Dean. It was a
pleasant-enough house. A family dwelling of a style that could
best be described as "rectangular." Spacious rooms, big windows, plenty of light. A practical eat-in kitchen large enough
for a living area at one end. Located in a residential area chosen for its mature trees, big gardens, and proximity to good
schools, it was a sensible place for an "upwardly mobile"
young family to live—an expression that set Adam's teeth on
edge. Not close to downtown, it was true; not, indeed, within
the city limits at all. In the suburbs, in fact. In Milton. To
put it bluntly, it was a suburban house in Milton. And that
was okay; that was no crime. Ironic, though, that the ideal-
istic young domestic architect he had once been, devoted to
the creation of ideal spaces for people to grow and develop

in, should end up living in anodyne suburbia. He and Sophie had talked about moving back into the city—to Back
Bay, if they could afford it, or the South End—when the boys
reached adolescence, but for the time being this was the practical solution. The children could ride bikes on quiet streets,
play in their own yard, and run in and out of neighbors'
houses in safety. (They had even had a puppy for a few days,
and what a mistake that had been. Another suburban dream
gone sour. The dog kept running into the street with Matthew
right behind it, not looking out for cars, risking his life to
save the dog's, until after a close call involving much squeal-
ing of brakes the puppy had been returned to its former
owner. No more pets, they decided, until Matthew's survival
instinct was stronger.) Inside, the house wasn't decorated to
their taste; they had laughed at the previous occupants' color
sense, but what was the point of redecorating with the boys
still so small and scribbling on walls? Little boys are hard on
a house. Better to save the money and give them free rein.
Of course. Viewed separately, all the decisions that added up
to Their Life were logical and sound. But put all the parts
together and...This house, for example—yes, spacious; yes,
schools; yes, pleasant, *but*...But it was a boring goddamned
suburban house that he didn't want to live in! A house that
was "perfectly good," as Valerie's mother used to say (poor
Valerie), as in "a perfectly good jacket" or "perfectly good
food," meaning that it was ill-fitting or bad-tasting, but it
would have to do. "Perfectly good" was no good at all, and
here was Adam, forty years old and living a "perfectly good"
life! Bloody ironic when you considered that he had gone to
the trouble of uprooting himself and crossing the Atlantic in
search of adventure—all to wind up in the American counter-
part of Twickenham, for God's sake!

The evening ahead seemed impossibly difficult. *Simplify your goal*, Adam told himself, *pare it down to one achievable task*. All he had to do was utter one sentence. All he had to say was, *I've fallen in love with someone else. I'm leaving.* All right, two sentences. It would take four seconds. And then it would be done. Adam walked slowly up the steps to his house, concentrating. The whole thing hinged on finding the right moment to introduce those four seconds. He pushed the door open, and Sophie was in his arms. "Oh, Adam, I thought I heard you. I've missed you so much today! I couldn't wait for you to get home. Boys, look! Daddy's home!"

"Daddy's home! Daddy's home!" they shouted eagerly.

This wasn't the moment.

After dinner he lay in the tub, staring unseeing at the ceiling for so long that Sophie called to him softly from the bedroom. "Honey, have you fallen asleep in the tub? Honey?"

"Coming." But he didn't move, just continued to stare at the ceiling. This wasn't the moment either. Damn it, why didn't she help him, give him an opening? Why couldn't she say something like, *What's the matter, darling? You seem so unlike your normal self. Are you in love with someone else? Would you like to move out—is that it?* But she was too damned tactful to pry into why he was so touchy. He groaned aloud.

Her voice wafted in sweetly from the other room. "Come to bed, sweetheart, and I'll rub your shoulders."

The Moment, he was beginning to suspect, his eyes fixed unblinkingly on the overhead light fixture, existed only in a parallel universe. There was no place in this world for that four-second announcement.

Later still, after Sophie had fallen asleep, he was sitting alone downstairs in his bathrobe, scotch in hand, when the telephone interrupted his brooding. He snatched it up after the first ring—the children were asleep!—who in the hell...? "Hello?" he said softly, and then in a harsh whisper, "*What? What in God's name are you doing calling me here? Have you gone mad?*"

Prior to placing this rash call, Valerie had been sitting curled up in her hotel room with the lights off and the curtains open, hugging her kimono around her knees for protection, looking out over the twinkling city lights and feeling like the smallest and loneliest thing in that vast panorama. Alone, unloved...and in Newark, New Jersey. She had even begun to wonder where her father was, and that was an impossibly bad sign. She had put him out of her mind years ago. Agatha was wrong, of course, about men never leaving their families. Valerie's father had. The charming, boyish father she'd worshipped had left home without a backward glance. The mystery wasn't why he had gone but how he had stuck it out for so long, until Valerie was eight. Not that her mother was a bad person. She was just...no fun. Muted, pale, tentative, round-shouldered. Everyone said that pretty, vivacious Valerie took after her father, but clearly she hadn't been attractive enough, because he had run off with a pretty woman who worked in a travel agency. At first he sent birthday presents (never money, as Valerie's mother pointed out repeatedly), but after a few years the presents stopped coming. End of story with Daddy. Valerie had no idea where he was now, whether he was still with that woman, or whether he'd had other children. Once, in a weak moment, she had tried searching for him on Google, but his name was so common that without any other clues it was hopeless. And anyway, if he were alive, wasn't it up to him to search for her? Never mind. He might have been run over crossing a street years ago. All she knew about him for certain was that he was a man who had put love first, and she had tried to console herself with that thought throughout her lonely childhood. But all that pain was behind her, she reminded herself firmly. And indecisive, weak-willed Adam was not going to force her back through the squalor of memory lane. Enough already! Defiantly, she tried his cell phone once, twice, three times, but it wasn't switched on.

She leaped up and began to stride around the room, her kimono swishing against her trim calves, glad to be moving and angry instead of curled up and miserable. If only she could talk to him! She couldn't call his home phone, of course. No, wait! Why not? Why not just call him at his god-damned house, wake everybody up, and let him know how unhappy she was, alone and cast off in a distant city, her whole future at stake? It was "against the rules" to call him at home, but whose rules? And wasn't it against the rules for him, a married man, to sleep with her in the first place, make her fall in love with him, and then jerk her around with his weak-assed inability to leave a woman that he himself said was incapable of making him happy? Wasn't it against the rules to raise her expectations and then break her heart? Why should she be the only one to respect the rules? Had her father respected the rules? There *were* no damned rules, except the ones Adam invented to protect himself and keep her at a disadvantage! Her hands shaking with self-righteous anger, Valerie swooped on the phone and punched in his home number, which she'd memorized long ago, just in case. But when he answered on the first ring, his "Hello?" sounding hushed and concerned, "It's me," was all she could say.

"*What?*" he whispered harshly. "What in God's name are you doing calling me here? Have you gone mad?"

She burst into tears.

"What if Sophie had answered the phone? What damned game are you playing now?"

"I'm so sorry, Adam! Have I ruined everything? Say I haven't, please!"

He held his hand over the receiver and cocked his head toward the upstairs, listening for signs that the telephone had woken Sophie. Nothing. He put the receiver back to his ear.

"Adam? Adam? Are you there?"

"Yes."

"I'm just so afraid you won't tell her. I'm so afraid you'll abandon me. I need you so much, Adam, and I love you so much. It's so hard for me to trust anyone. I'm always so afraid they'll let me down."

"I won't let you down."

"Oh, if only I could believe that! I know, Adam, I know how hard this is for you. Don't think I don't. Don't think I'm a monster."

"I don't think that."

"Really?" Valerie sniffed and wiped her face with the flat of her hand. "You know..." She swallowed her tears and sniffed again, and a hopeful note began to creep into her quavering voice. "You know, when you have something hard like this to do and it seems impossible...it's just like looking out the window of a train."

"What?"

"It seems like such a huge thing to do, so scary, but once you do it, it's gone. Finished! Like when you flash through a town on a train and you see all those little houses and backyards and a quick swatch of this and a quick flash of that,

and then *whoooomp!* You go into a tunnel, and when you
come out the other side, everything's different. It's a waste-
land, the town's gone, those little houses have disappeared as
if they never existed. And you don't exist for them anymore
either. Only seconds have passed, but they're already miles
and miles behind, in a different world. It'll be like that when
you tell her—really hard, but only for an instant...and then
it'll be done." Her voice wobbled again as she whispered,
"You'll be free."

"Darling, lie down now and go to sleep."

"You won't abandon me?"

"Shhh. No, I won't. Now, go to sleep."

Adam tiptoed into the bedroom. Sophie was asleep. Silly to
tiptoe when his intention was to wake her. "Sophie?" He sat
down gently on the bed and touched her hair. "Sophie?" He
couldn't bring himself to speak above a whisper. She stirred,
made a little sound, reached out and took his hand, still asleep.
Adam looked gravely at their joined hands. After a moment he
eased himself off the bed and crept out of the room.

That spring, some four months earlier, Adam and Valerie
had had the incredible good luck to be sent together on business to Paris. It was just at the time when it was becoming
clear that their sleeping together was not an aberration but
rather the beginning of a love affair. The month was May, the
city was sublime, and Adam had marveled at finding himself cast in the role of clandestine lover. He had never felt
so lucky or so daring before. Valerie had insisted they get
a few pictures of them together so she would have something to remember him by. For her long, solitary nights, she

had joked, something to slip under her pillow. Adam had felt flattered by her insistence, enough so to override his native caution, and after a delicious, boozy lovers' lunch on the Île Saint-Louis he offered no objection when she asked the waiter to snap them. She had mugged for the camera, hugging and kissing him, dissolving into laughter for the final shot, looking vibrantly happy and beautiful. Later she made copies for him. "Don't think I'm going to be the only one pining," she'd said. "You've got to sigh for me, too—otherwise it's no fun." He had been uneasy about accepting them but felt it would be ungracious or, worse, unsophisticated, to refuse them. That night he had hidden them in a book on a high shelf in his study at home, feeling like a naughty child, excited by the knowledge that Valerie's image dwelled secretly in his house, trapped between the dusty pages of an old textbook on building materials, their weight-bearing properties, and their responses to torsion and stress—something he felt fairly sure Sophie would not be dipping into. Now he retrieved the photos from the book and stood with them in his hand, looking around vaguely, wondering where to leave them...somewhere the children would not happen upon them. Then he thought of a place. He crept back up to the bedroom, eased open the drawer where his shirts were kept, slipped the photos in, and carefully slid the drawer shut again. Tomorrow when Sophie finished the ironing, she would open the drawer to put his shirts away, and then...

But his imagination balked at what would happen then.

———

"Valerie." Adam's voice was crisp and businesslike as he spoke into his office phone the next morning. He was closely shaven, immaculately dressed, keen-eyed: a man who was at last taking his destiny into his own hands. "She knows. Yes. Yes, last night."

Waves of joy rippled through Valerie. She was in a taxi on her way to the airport, having wound up the last details of the deal over breakfast. She threw back her head and laughed with sheer relief. Out the sunroof the tops of trees were zipping past, their leaves sparkling in the dappled sunlight. Gazing up at them, she vowed to remember, all her life long, the perfection and joy of that moment.

"I'll see you tonight, darling," Adam said. "We'll have dinner. Call me when you get in."

"Adam, wait!" She needed to prolong her happiness. "You're a perfect man. How could I ever have doubted you?"

"Just see to it you never do again." God, it felt good saying that!

Valerie introduced a note of concern into her voice. "How did she take it? What did she say?"

Adam frowned and fiddled with a pencil on his desk, half expecting James to appear at the door in time to witness this latest awkward exchange. The doorway was empty, but James would still serve. "I can't talk now. James is here pestering me. We'll talk this evening. Yes... Yes, me too, darling. Yes, all right. Good-bye." Adam hung up, drummed his fingers for a moment, then called his secretary. "Odette, has my wife rung this morning?... I see. Well, put her straight through, will you, when she does.... Thank you." There shouldn't be long to wait. Sophie would doubtless telephone when she...ah...found the...He cleared his throat and got on with his day's work as best he could.

Humming, Sophie whipped into the laundry room with the basket of clean, crumpled shirts in her arms. She found that the dullness of ironing was compensated for, to a degree, by the hot, clean smell of it and the satisfying steamy hiss of the iron, things she had first experienced from the low angle of childhood, gazing up at her mother while she ironed, occasionally sighing and brushing a strand of hair out of her flushed face with the back of her hand. A strong and capable woman she had seemed then, a household goddess. Her young daughter noted her perpetual busyness and fatigue with approval, savoring the grown-up importance of it.

Sophie shook out the first shirt and got started on it, doing only a passable job. Milagros, on the other hand, ironed beautifully, and, what's more, she believed in ironing. It seemed to be a moral tenet of her native Spain: Good ironing equaled clean living. (Sophie pondered this. Was that because good women ironed, or was it the act of ironing that imparted goodness to women?) In the beginning she had struggled to curb Milagros's ironing, for Milagros believed that everything needed ironing, including bath towels and underwear. "It preserves the fabric," she insisted. It was not unusual in the early days for Sophie to discover Milagros holed up in the laundry room, having raced through the other chores in order to do secret extra ironing. "If I don't iron this, it will *rot*!" In the end Sophie gave in. Milagros could iron even the oven gloves if she wanted to (and she did), because you can't give someone work to do without relinquishing some power as well, and after all, Milagros was kind to the boys, she cleaned so thoroughly that it felt like an accusation, and she made succulent chickpeas with spinach—so she could iron anything in sight.

Milagros had come to work for the Deans when Hugo was born. With a one-year-old and a newborn to take care of, Sophie was glad to have someone come in to clean and leave supper on the stove. Her mother had suggested she get help with the boys, but that was the wrong way around to Sophie's way of thinking; she'd rather take care of the children herself and have someone else wash the floor. Adam was also in favor of their raising the children themselves and not hiring others to do it. When Sophie was pregnant the first time, he had talked movingly about the importance of a heavy investment of the parents' time and attention in a child's vital early years, and Sophie agreed completely. She quit working as a freelance editor without regret in her eighth month of pregnancy, disillusioned with editing anyway—all frenzied deadlines and wrestling in solitude with other people's verbal tangles—and feeling exhilarated by the much more important task ahead. Adam earned enough for them to live on; they would simply scale their life to his income, and Sophie could work again later on, maybe at something new, maybe with people instead of words. Alternative medicine interested her, and shiatsu in particular after she had tried it for recurrent headaches. The treatment had been so successful, not only curing her headaches but making her feel well inside and out, that she had considered becoming a practitioner herself, but Adam had discouraged her, the whole thing seeming "rather fey" to him and a waste of her education. She would go back to work at something eventually, but in the meantime she pored over piles of books on childbirth and babies and toddlers and discussed them with Adam in the evenings. He was as enthusiastic as she was in those days, when it was all still theoretical. Matthew was born, and then, startlingly, when he was only five months old and Sophie was still feeling her way, she got pregnant again. Well...so much the better. More diapers, more late-night feedings, more snapping up of tiny garments, more kneeling on the bathroom floor supporting grapefruit-sized heads with one hand while splashing warm water over gyrating limbs with the other. More toys and books and bibs, more walks with the double stroller, and more first smiles, first teeth, first steps and words. In those early years, making it through each day was a challenge that sapped all Sophie's energy and resourcefulness. She kept her head down and worked. But as the boys got older, the pace relaxed and the stardust began to settle. She was able at last to look around herself, and when she did, she made an unsettling discovery: She was alone with the children. Adam had not followed her into this new phase of their adventure together. He was standing off on his own, eyeing them with a blend of wistfulness, boredom, and irritation; somehow or other he had gotten left behind. It was hard to say how it had happened. Of course, as eager future parents, snuggled in bed among their toppling towers of child-raising books, they hadn't foreseen how much his work would interfere with his fathering. It had been unrealistic to imagine that their parenting would be of equal intensity and importance. Inevitably, if he was at work all day and she was at home, the bulk of the work—and the rewards—would fall to her. Her commitment to raising their children was continuous and real; his could only be occasional and academic. She told herself regularly that as the boys grew up, he would become more involved with them. In a few years, they would have more in common, share more activities, grow closer. She reassured herself of that once again as she finished ironing the last of his shirts, and if there was a hollowish ring to it, she resolutely ignored it, not in the mood today to deal again with that mocking inner voice. Good, the sun was coming out; she could do a bit of weeding after lunch and plant those cuttings before they wilted. Then vacuum downstairs and make some little treat for after school—banana bread, must use those overripe bananas. Then get their sports clothes ready for tomorrow.

Mind buzzing, body taut, mood upbeat although slightly harassed, Sophie gave a pat to the last shirt, set down the iron, which heaved a steamy sigh of relief, switched it off, placed the shirt on top of the others in the basket, picked up the basket, nudged the light switch off with her elbow as she opened the door with her foot, leaned into the kitchen to yank two wilted dishcloths off the rail by the sink, flung them back into the dirty-clothes hamper, caught the basket as it slipped off her hip, hiked it up again, and switched on the teakettle as she passed, thinking that if she had just tea and a sandwich for lunch, she'd have time for a quick shower after the gardening—she could scrub the sink and fold the towels before she jumped in. But first she would put these shirts away. On her path through the living room, she scooped up some teddy bears—it was a rule of hers never to take a trip up or down the stairs without carrying a full load—and her step was springy as she headed down the hall to the master bedroom, the laundry basket bouncing on her hip. As she passed the boys' door, she tossed the bears into the toy box with perfect aim.

It was nearly the last action she would perform as a happily married woman.

Agatha was sitting at home in her South End apartment, typing; she wrote a style column for a middlebrow women's magazine. If she had had an audience, she would have affected to hunt and peck artistically, but as she was alone, she prosaically touch-typed. Of course, if she had had an audience, she wouldn't have been in this room to begin with, as this room was something of a shameful secret. It looked as if the owner of a large junk shop had been forced by circumstance to move into much smaller premises—furniture, boxes, and clutter defying description were stacked in dangerous tilting columns nearly reaching the ceiling, the only clear space being a narrow tunnel from door to desk. Birdcages, old bicycle wheels, baskets, antique dolls, an airplane propeller, and examples of nearly every other man-made object filled the room, remnants of Agatha's last interior-decorating phase, when she'd had one of those *horror vacui* places where "fun" objects take up every inch of table, shelf, and floor space, as well as being nailed to the walls and suspended by wires from the ceiling. There might have been a window in Agatha's study, but if so it was obscured by junk. The only light came from a large desk lamp with a thick gray base designed to look like an elephant's leg, complete with painted-on semicircular toes—awfully "fun."

Agatha was working away by the light of her elephant's leg, surrounded by teetering towers of clutter, her fingers flying unerringly over the keyboard as she thought of witty and insightful things to say about cheese boards (truly witty and insightful things; she was good at her job), when the phone began to ring in the next room. Her typing slowed until it stopped altogether, and then began the familiar struggle with the question of whether or not to answer the phone when she was working. In theory the answer was no, which was why there was no phone in her study. No, she was working, therefore she was not "at home," it being neither here nor there that her office happened to be two steps from her living room instead of across town. Whoever it was could leave a message, just as people always did when they called the house of someone who was at work. Ah, but those words: "whoever it was"! The whole problem lay there. As a woman with no husband, no boyfriend, who was dating no one and wished she were—when she had arrived so late for her date the other night, he hadn't been there, and his phone was turned off, so either he had left in a huff or he had never shown up in the first place—Agatha did not feel she could afford to leave her telephone unanswered. She heaved a theatrical sigh of annoyance meant to mask from imaginary viewers the silly, hopeful lurch of the heart that she always felt—she couldn't help it—when the phone rang. (Is this where my love story begins? Is this the pivotal moment of my life? Will I tell the story in years to come when I'm cozily married? *Well, I was sitting at my desk one day, and the phone rang. So I got up and answered it, and it was this weird guy....* All laugh, as they know full well that it turns out to be her husband, who's sitting there with them, smiling self-consciously at the frequently heard tale.)

Agatha opened the door and started across the living room blinking, her arms extended to feel her way because, in harsh contrast to the study, the living room was bright and bare, and to eyes accustomed to the dim light cast by the elephant leg, the first impression was of a featureless glare. Everything in the room was white, and the camouflage effect achieved was so successful that on first glance the room seemed to contain nothing at all. It was only as pupils narrowed to pinpricks that faint detail could be made out: One white shape could be seen to differ slightly in tone from the white of the wall behind it and eventually be identified as a sofa, and so on, until gradually several pieces of furniture could be distinguished in the room. Agatha clacked across the white floorboards in high-heeled pink bedroom slippers with puffs on the toes, a garish blaze of color in her lime-and-fuchsia bathrobe, groping her way toward the sound of the ringing until she thrust her hand into a white cube balanced nearly invisibly on a white stand and silenced the telephone within.

"Yeah?" she said belligerently into the white receiver. "Whaddaya want?" An aggressive sound was better than a timid voice cracking with hope, forlorn but brave. (And it would make the story of how she had met her husband funnier, too, in the retelling.) She waited, though, with bated breath. She hadn't looked at the caller ID to see who it was, because she was convinced that doing so could be unlucky. *Might scare him away.*

"Nice phone manner you have."

Only Valerie. Agatha could breathe again. "I happen to be in the middle of a piece due half an hour ago. I'll call you back. Bye." She made no move, however, to hang up.

"What are you writing about?" Valerie asked silkily. It was most unlike her to show any interest in Agatha's work, and immediately Agatha's suspicions were aroused. Valerie was up to something, she was sure, and indeed she was: spinning out the delicious moment before she would knock Agatha sideways with her news.

"Cheese boards. Who wants to know?"

"Oh, Agatha, you're so defensive. Don't you ever let up? Look, I have news that's going to make your day."

"Oh, yeah?" In spite of herself, Agatha felt her hopes rising ridiculously. Was this the way it would all begin? With a call from Valerie? *I've just met this guy who's perfect for you, and he's dying to meet you.*

"It's going to be the best news you've heard in a long, long time."

"Yeah?"

"Are you ready?"

"Go on."

"He's left her. Adam's marriage is over. *Finito*. He's chosen me."

"Oh." Too late Agatha remembered that Valerie was one of those people who present their personal good news as though it were cause for worldwide rejoicing.

"I knew he'd do it," Valerie purred. "I knew it. It's me he loves. Happy for me?"

"Well, yeah. Sure I am. I'm just so...stunned. When did all this happen?"

"Last night. But he only told me five minutes ago. I wanted you to be the first to know. Oh, Agatha, isn't it bliss? I mean, my love life, the whole question of my love life, that giant question mark in the sky, is resolved now for good. A happy ending! 'She got her man.' Credits roll."

And speaking of credit... "Now, you see?" Agatha said. "You see? You took a chance, you showed him you had some respect for yourself, and it paid off. Didn't I tell you?"

"I suppose you're going to say it's all thanks to you."

"Well, isn't it?"

"Then thank you, Agatha. You're a real pal, and I mean that. Come on, we've got some celebrating to do. I'm on my way home now."

"Don't you have to work?"

"The boss said I could take the day off. He likes me. Get

dolled up and meet me for a late lunch, okay? The champagne is going to flow!"

"Okay. But first I have to finish my article." Real pal that she was, Agatha felt genuinely glad that the question mark over her best friend's love life had been replaced by a drawing of a happy face, but she also felt a queer dread in her stomach, wondering if this were the beginning of a slow, inevitable rift between them, with happily partnered Valerie drifting farther and farther away from the lonesome shoreline where Agatha stood, a solitary silhouette, her hair whipping in the wind, waiting for a ship that might never come in.

"Odette? Have there been any calls? My wife or...?...I see.... Yes, I'll be in my office." It had occurred to Adam in the course of the day that the tactic of leaving photographs for Sophie to find might be considered by some to be rather...ah...He couldn't find quite the right word. But after all, he'd had no alternative, what with the impossibility of inserting those four seconds into the flow of his home life, and anyway, it was more face-saving for Sophie this way. She was bound to be taken aback, and it seemed kinder to let her adjust to the new situation without any witnesses to her initial discomfiture. More respectful of her dignity. Adam's intense frowning study of his desktop was interrupted by James, wiggling a squash racket at him from the door.

"What do you say to a game after work, buddy?" He skipped forward and mimed smashing the ball with his racket.

Adam shook his head. "No. Thank you."

"What's wrong? Afraid I'll whup you?"

"What?" Adam glanced up, distracted. "No, no squash. Thanks."

"Look at him! He's afraid of getting his English ass whupped!"

"James. Please go away."

James stopped dancing around with the racket and looked at Adam in surprise. He lowered his voice to a confidential note. "Everything okay?"

"Everything is fine."

"Yeah. Hey, Adam, if you ever want to have a beer after work and, you know, just talk about things or whatever...or just have a beer...I'd be glad to do that. You just say the word. I'd like you to know that I consider you a...a good person to have a beer with. So you just let me know, okay, buddy?"

"Thank you, James," Adam felt compelled to say.

"It's okay! What I'm here for!" With a wave he was gone, and Adam sat wondering if the day would ever come when he found himself crying in his beer and recounting the details of his personal life to James.

He ardently hoped not.

Sliding Adam's shirts into the drawer, Sophie's fingers brushed something—several things, smooth and flat, with corners. She pulled them out and frowned at them, puzzled. Photographs. She carried them to the window, her heart beginning to race. There, in the good light, she examined them slowly, one by one, over and over.

2.

Worn out by the anxious nights spent doubting Adam's courage and devotion, and lulled by the drone of the engines, Valerie dozed on the flight home, which meant she was not looking out the window as the plane came in to land. That was something of a pity, for on the patchwork below, easily visible from her vantage point, a scene was being enacted that would have interested her intensely, had she been able to interpret the events.

The plane tilts to circle, and the urban sprawl beneath is suddenly revealed, laid out like a magnificent toy town. To the south of the city lies leafy, residential Milton, where the Deans live in one of the many sugar-cube houses centered on adjacent green rectangles. The door to one of the little white houses opens, and a fair-haired figure, barely visible from this height, darts out, rushes down the thread of a path to the street, and disappears into a tiny white car, slamming its door noiselessly. This is Sophie, clutching the photographs in one hand and her bag in the other. The white car pulls away from the curb and twists slowly through the residential lanes, now and then disappearing beneath a canopy of trees. At the end of the road, it merges onto a highway, then crosses an overpass so busy with traffic that it's difficult to follow its...Oh, yes, there it is, slowing down to turn off and head across another residential neighborhood, stopping frequently at lights. Seen from such a great height, the traffic appears to move slowly, as if accompanied by the peaceful crooning sounds of a solitary child at play with his toy cars. It's hard to imagine any sense of urgency down there. No one would guess that small white car could contain so much unhappiness.

The car has reached a grid of streets flanked by modern town houses with small squares of green yard in front and longer strips of green behind, some dotted with red swing sets and slides, some not, some with patios and decks and tubs of flowers, some with laundry drying on lines, some studded with turquoise wading pools, one with a tiny brown shape moving back and forth lengthwise: a penned dog. Sophie's car stops in front of one of the houses. The car door opens. First her foot appears and then the top of her head as she gets out. She slams the door, opens a little gate, walks in, closes it, runs up the path and up three steps, then knocks on a blue door. She turns back to the car while she waits, twisting her hands, then whirls around when the door opens, and she hands something—the photographs—to a larger woman standing in the doorway. The woman opens her arms, the blond woman rushes into her embrace, and they cling to each other for a moment. Then both disappear into the house, and the little blue door closes behind them.

"Do you know her?" Marion asked, keeping her voice neutral as she refilled Sophie's coffee cup. The photos were spread out on her kitchen table, four of them, lined up in order. The first showed Adam and a slender, dark-haired woman with a fine face, both smiling politely, sitting side by side in the sunshine at a Parisian café; in the second the dark-haired woman had sprung onto Adam's lap and they were both laughing, she audaciously and he in delighted surprise; in the third they were kissing, visible only in profile, her chin tilted down, his tilted up; and in the fourth they were smiling at the photographer, cheek to cheek, her arms around his neck, his around her waist. It was a progression, like single frames chosen from a scene in a film: "Exterior – Day – Happy Couple Frolic at Sidewalk Café."

"No. I don't know her. But I know who she is." Sophie wrapped both hands around the coffee cup, one of those coarse, handmade ones that are painted unevenly a drab blue and feel thick and gritty in the mouth, the sort of cup that overpowers the weak herbal tea it usually contains. Luckily, though, this was strong coffee with hot milk. It tasted terribly good, and Sophie, feeling shaky and wounded after crying, found it safest to concentrate on small, concrete things like this cup and its contents.

"Who is she?"

"They work together. She's new. Been there about six months, I think. I saw her once... at Adam's office. We didn't talk."

"And how old are these pictures? When was Adam in Paris?"

"In May."

"Four months ago. They didn't waste much time!"

"That's the shirt I gave him for his birthday." Sophie

heaved a long, shuddering sigh. "He looks so happy." She lowered her head, and tears began to slide again down her cheeks. She let them fall.

"Oh, come on, now." Marion swept up the photos and tossed them aside. Out of a cupboard she took a bottle of pills, the prescription kind with a typed label. "Listen. As strange as this might sound to you right now, don't worry too much. I know it feels like the end of the world, but it's not. Men do this, Sophie. The classic seven-year itch, so common it's become a cliché. Even Gerald had his moment, if you can believe that. Here, take this." She shook a tablet out of the bottle and handed it with a glass of water to Sophie, who took it without question, looking into the glass like a child as she swallowed. "You'll feel better in a minute. You keep these. They're just the thing for you right now." She popped the pill bottle into Sophie's bag, lying open on the table. "Adam has done a stupid thing. All the same, he is still, deep down, a responsible and sensible man. And he loves you and the boys. *You* are his life, not"—she waved dismissively at the pictures—"not that. So here's what you do." Marion knelt on the floor and took Sophie's hands in hers. "You put these pictures back where you found them and pretend you know nothing."

Sophie pulled her hands away and stared at Marion.

"It's for the best, Sophie. I know you're in shock, and it's hard to rally, but this is a very important moment. You've got to pull yourself together and do the right thing. Your children's happiness depends on how you react now."

Sophie swallowed. "I can't pretend I don't know."

"Yes you can. Listen, the very fact that he left these pictures for you is a telling sign. All right, he had a fling, like a typical forty-year-old man. But that's all it was. If it were serious, he would confront you with it. He left these pictures like a guilty boy, as a way of clearing his conscience and begging your forgiveness. So you'll exonerate him from his crime. It was selfish of him, no doubt about that. He should never have let you know. But he did, so that's that. And now it belongs to the past. There's no sense in dwelling on anything that's in the past, because the past is by definition unchangeable." Marion was a professional counselor, and sometimes it showed. "All that matters is now. So what do you do now? Nothing. If you simply allow this to blow over, it will. Believe me."

"Blow over," Sophie repeated dully.

"Put the pictures back. He'll think you never found them. He'll sigh with relief and burn them, break off this stupid relationship, and consider it all a very close call. And that will be the end of it."

"You think?" Sophie's lips barely moved. She was feeling light-headed and as though everything were in slow motion. Those pills... what were they? She turned her head slowly on its long, long neck and felt the room dip a little, as if she were sitting suspended in a car in that fairground ride—the whirl-a-bird, it was called.... Whirlybird?

"I don't think, Sophie." Marion cocked her head to one side and smiled. "I know."

"Oh, my God. What time is it?" Sophie looked around vaguely, without any real hope of finding a clock. "I have to pick up the boys at school." She stood up, reached way down for her bag on the table, and gripped the back of the chair for balance. It was hard to remember that this was just a day like any other, with children to pick up at two-thirty. Finding the photos had winded her, like a blow to the stomach. It had hacked her day in two, chopped it like a melon, and the dripping, still-rocking halves were now alien to each other, scenes from different lives. She would never again feel as she had this morning. Without those photos she might so easily have had hundreds, thousands more days pretty much like this morning. But now she would never have even one more. And yet, across town in their school, the boys' day was still normal and whole. The bell would ring at two-thirty, and the gates would open, the same as always. The school gates didn't know that her life had just been flipped over onto its back and was kicking its little legs uselessly. *The school gates don't care*, she thought with what seemed piercing lucidity.

"Don't worry about the boys," Marion said. "I'll pick them up and keep them here for a while so you can go home and pull yourself together before Adam gets home. Come on, you look all washed out. Let's put some makeup on you."

"Makeup? What are you talking about?" Marion was coming at her with blusher in one hand and a fat little brush in the other, squinting like an artist. "No, stop that. I don't wear makeup." Sophie batted the brush to the floor and surprised herself by laughing. "If I go home looking like a clown, Adam will know something is wrong. Or maybe you should! Paint red circles on my cheeks and a bright, happy smile. Help me get into the part!" She swung her bag onto her shoulder and laughed again in confusion. "What's happening to me, Marion?" Her laughter changed abruptly to tears, and Marion enveloped her in a strong, warm hug.

At the Meritage in the Boston Harbor Hotel, Valerie and Agatha were lingering over their celebratory lunch, sipping their way more slowly through a second bottle of champagne. Agatha was tracing designs on the linen tablecloth with a sharp crust of French bread as she spoke. "I just didn't want him to jerk you around forever, that's all. Hell, look at me and Howard. Three years of my life wasted, going from 'You're the only one who understands me' to 'Can't you understand she's my wife?'"

Valerie laughed and lifted her glass in thanks to her friend, too mellowed by drink and victory to mind hearing about that no-hoper Howard and their squalid affair.

"Speaking of the wife," Agatha said, straightening up and looking interested, "how did she take it?"

"Oh, I don't know the details yet. He couldn't talk at the office. We're getting together tonight. No doubt I'll hear all about it then. But I'm sure she knew about us already, or at least suspected. She must have been half expecting this to happen. Unless she was deliberately closing her eyes."

"The way I see it, you've done her a favor. He would have kept on two-timing the pair of you for as long as he could get away with it. At least now she knows where she stands. And she knows her husband is nothing but a rotten, cheating fink." Valerie raised her eyebrows, but Agatha insisted, "From her point of view, he is. From yours he's a wonderful man, obviously, the best. But from hers he's a shit, let's face it. First he cheats on her, lies to her for months, and reneges on his marriage vows, and now he craps out on his parental duties as well and leaves her flat with two young kids. How old are they, again?"

Valerie masked her annoyance by feigning a yawn. "I don't know, Agatha. You're always asking that. They're young— three and four, four and five? What does it matter? Oh, this champagne is making me sleepy."

"The point is, now she's free to find someone who really loves her. She may even thank you for this one day. What I mean is, there's no reason *at all* for you to feel guilty about what you've done."

"And I don't."

"Right. And why should you?"

Valerie shook her finger at Agatha. "Careful, now. No sour grapes."

"Oh, come on, Vee, that's not fair."

Valerie yawned again, a real yawn this time, ruffled up her hair, and smiled. "I'd better get home for my beauty rest. Wouldn't want Adam to regret his choice." She wrinkled her nose and stretched. Then, "I don't want dessert. Do you?"

"Heavens, no."

Valerie caught the waiter's eye and smiled.

Agatha thought grumpily that it would have taken *her* ages to get his attention. She was feeling unsatisfied with the way the lunch had gone, not content for it to end just merely on this note of Valerie as the cat who ate the canary. There should be some of that, obviously, but something more as well. More thanks for her pivotal role in all this, for one thing. Come on, if it weren't for good old Agatha, none of this would ever have happened, and while she didn't like to take all the credit, what choice was there if Valerie wouldn't give it to her? And another thing: Just where did this leave her? Okay, she had solved the problem of Valerie's love life for her. (No small favor!) Now what? What about hearing from Valerie some of the old, *Well, I'm all set, now it's your turn for romance, so let's talk about you for an hour or two*? Agatha decided to get the conversation onto the right track. "So! That's you settled, living happily ever after with the man of your dreams...with just a little help from your friends. I guess it's my turn next, wouldn't you say?" There. That should launch them deep into some juicy girl talk, the luxurious kind, where you kick off your shoes and reach languidly for the bottle to top up your glasses, and you blow smoke rings and laugh huskily, and they close the restaurant around you (then jail you for smoking in public).

"Yep," Valerie said, and then to the waiter, "The bill, please." She stood up, stretched again, and smiled. "Well, now! Wasn't that fun?"

———

Adam opened the front door and listened before stepping into the house. It was strangely silent. Sophie had not called the office all day, making it impossible for him to gauge the temperature of the situation from a distance and fine-tune his farewell speech in accordance with the reigning atmosphere, as he had hoped to do. And now this ominous silence at home...But then Sophie called out cheerfully from the kitchen, "I'm in here! How was work?" in her normal way.

Something seemed to be wrong with his throat; he had to clear it a few times before he could answer cautiously, "All right." He set down his briefcase softly, as though making a noise might be dangerous, and went into the kitchen, taut and alert—all ready, he realized with shock and shame, to *duck*. This made him angry, angry at himself and at the ridiculous life he was leading that had reduced him to this slapstick role, and his anger made him glad that this farce of a home life was coming to an end, so he could recover some goddamned dignity!

Sophie was standing at the sink with her back to him. "Dinner's nearly ready. Would you like a drink?"

"I'll get it. And one for you, too."

"Thanks." She did not turn around when he came back

with drinks but nodded at the counter beside her. "Just put it there."

Adam drank deeply and studied her from behind: long neck, silky ponytail, T-shirt, apron strings dangling over her jeans, small waist, shapely bottom, black sandals. Another day he might have walked up behind her and hugged her, nestling his crotch against her bottom, kissing her neck and tickling her, making her laugh. Instead he was going to leave her. He felt no regret; the idea merely passed through his mind as a fact. With a curious detachment, he registered the fact that he was at a crossroads in his life and that his actions in the next few seconds would take him off in a new direction. He studied her back a while longer, considering that, and then he asked, "How...did your day go?"

"Oh, you know. A bit of this...and a bit of that."

If only she would stop playing games, stop faffing about in that damned sink, face him, and hear him out! But what if— Good God! It was only then that it occurred to Adam that Sophie might not be merely stalling—that it was possible she hadn't found the pictures. The blood rushed out of his stomach at the idea of having to deliver his farewell speech "cold." He dithered for a moment, then decided that the sensible thing would be to go up and see if the photos were still there. If they were gone, he would know she knew, and if they weren't...well, he'd think about that later. He muttered something to her averted face about being right back and climbed the stairs two by two.

The moment Sophie was alone, she sagged over the sink, exhausted by the effort of keeping her voice cheerful and her conversation inconsequential. She hadn't known that lying could be physically tiring. The small part of her that remained a neutral onlooker, even in this intensely trying and emotional moment, took note of that fact to ponder it later. She doubted she would be able to make it through the evening without further chemical help. But where had she left those pills of Marion's?

Adam came quietly back down the stairs holding the photographs against his thigh, unsure of how to proceed. When he stepped into the kitchen, he surprised Sophie in the act of furtively gulping down a pill. She gasped and swung around to snatch the pill bottle out of sight, and in that moment Adam registered two things: that the bottle contained some sort of prescription drug (unheard of for Sophie) and that her face was pale and blotched from crying. So she *had* found them; he hadn't been sure. She, in her brief glimpse of him, saw the photographs pressed guiltily to his leg. Pills, tears, photographs; the pretense was over.

"Where are the boys?" he asked quietly.

"At Marion's," she said, her voice coming out in a whisper. She swallowed and added in a stronger voice, "They'll be home soon." She stared at the kitchen floor, noticing the details of its pattern for the first time, an intricate geometric design. How sad—a piece of kitchen linoleum yearning to be the Alhambra.

Adam cleared his throat, and like a high diver springing from the board and hoping someone has filled the pool, he said, "Sophie, this isn't the life we wanted for ourselves. I don't know what happened, but somehow it's all gone very wrong. We have nothing to talk about anymore, nothing in common. We've come to a dead end. All we can do now is cut our losses. I'm...I'm sorry it's come to this. But we have no option." There was a stilted, rehearsed sound to all this that he was unable to avoid, and Sophie lifted her head to stare at him uncomprehendingly through the flow of trite phrases. "I'll see to it that the children don't suffer from...from this. I'll spend as much time with them as possible. And of course I'll provide for them, and for you, financially. You'll have no worries on that score." Pale and shaken, Sophie nonetheless remained dry-eyed. Heartened by how well she was taking it, Adam continued with more confidence. "What we have to do now is think of the boys. As responsible adults, we can—we must—put our own disappointment to one side and concentrate all our energy on our children and their well-being. It's important that their lives be as little disrupted as possible. They need continuity, and it's our job to see they get it: same house, same friends, same school. It goes without saying that I'll leave you the house and everything in it. I'll take only my personal belongings and half of our savings." He paused for a moment. Then, "Well...there's nothing to be gained by prolonging this. I'm...going out now. I'll be back later tonight to pack up a few things. I'll pick them up tomorrow after work. I think the best thing to tell the boys—for now—is that I'm going on a little holiday."

Incredulity moved Sophie to speak at last. "A little holiday?"

He glanced away uncomfortably. "There's no point in upsetting them unnecessarily. We can let them know gradually, over time." Then, with renewed vigor, "It's them we have to think of, Sophie. The good of the boys."

Sophie stared. "You must love her very much."

"She has nothing to do with it. If our marriage had been a success, no third person could have made any difference. The problem is us, Sophie, you and me, and this wretched automatons' life we lead. Let's not look for a scapegoat, shall we? She's beside the point."

Sophie spoke slowly, trying to work it out. "But...if that's true, why did you leave me pictures of her?"

Mercifully for Adam, the front door burst open and the boys dashed in, Matthew announcing excitedly, "Daddy, Marion has a new cat named Trudy! She has scratchy paws!" To illustrate, Hugo struck a pose with his fingers curled like claws.

Adam laid a hand on top of each boy's head. "That's wonderful, boys." To Sophie he said, "I'd better get going. Don't wait up. I'll...be back late."

Blankly, she watched him leave. Then she sank into a kitchen chair, and Matthew climbed onto her lap, chattering unheeded about Marion's cat, while Sophie grappled with the knowledge that her husband, Adam, had just left to see his lover, and she, his wife, knew it, and there was nothing to stop him, and nothing she could do about it, because all the rules had suddenly changed. Adam could walk out of the house now and have sex with someone else, while she stayed here and made dinner for the children they had decided to have together—and now all of that was somehow *all right*. Because the deal was off. There was no more agreement. His fingers had been crossed behind his back all along. "Mommy," Hugo said, "I'm hungry. What's for supper?"

The evening routine lay ahead, ineluctable. Dinner, bath, pajamas, books (half an hour's worth), then bed (kiss, kiss, door ajar, night-light on). From now on, Adam's life would be almost completely different. But her life—incredibly—would remain almost exactly the same.

Except, of course, that she would be alone.

Each time Adam stepped into Valerie's apartment, he felt himself a different man, and a man he vastly preferred: sophisticated, sexy, clever, and keen. With Valerie, Adam felt like a winner, eager to tackle new work, capable of great achievement. Her ambition was contagious, as was her real enjoyment of the spoils of hard work. That's all there was with Valerie: work and pleasure. So refreshing to live that way, so sharp and crackling!

Whereas at home...Oh, God, with Sophie, Adam felt harassed and inadequate. Work, to Valerie, meant only work on architectural projects. But work in the Dean home also included household maintenance and child care—chores of which, whether or not he actually pitched in, Adam was uncomfortably aware. The execution of such tasks was unpleasant enough; the guilty disquiet of avoiding them was more than anyone should have to bear. So discouraging to be unable to enjoy a drink after work, all because you have a nagging feeling you should be making a kite! And the less Sophie complained about shouldering most of the burden, the more of a heel he felt, which, if it is true, as some say, that we love others for how they make us feel about ourselves, was a big strike against Sophie. Her willingness and good cheer worked very much against her. Yes, work, at home, was endless and ungratifying, and as for "pleasure"...well...Jaunts had to include the children and were usually geared to them. It took forever to get out of the house, what with the lengthy packing of bags to provide against every contingency and the last-minute drinks and pees, and no sooner were they under way at last than it was time to stop again for more drinks and more pees. Progress was slow, the distance covered little, and when stock was taken at the end of the hectic, messy day, the success of the excursion was rated by such things as "the look on Matthew's face," ephemeral in the extreme in Adam's view, but sufficient satisfaction, it seemed, for Sophie. Adam would come home dropping with that peculiar kind of exhaustion one gets from moving too slowly, like being trapped in a crowd of shuffling old ladies on a long museum tour. And was the day over? No! There were still the children to catch, feed, wash, clothe, read to, and tuck in, that inexorable routine, the parents' ball and chain.

Adam sank gratefully into Valerie's sofa, noting with approval the large number of breakable or dangerous objects placed down low in this house of adults. This evening he was in the mood for listening to Bach and sipping whiskey, but the knowledge that he could, if he wanted to, suddenly dash off to a child-unfriendly place like the opera lent a tingling sense of possibility to the promise of a quiet evening at home—this last being yet another thing not to be had chez Dean. Doing something and doing nothing are the two things you can never do when you have young children. You can neither achieve anything nor relax. Days are crammed full of hectic activity yet utterly empty of worthwhile content. Adam was brooding on these matters, weighing his two lives, reassuring himself of the wisdom, the inevitability, of his decision and yet feeling ill at ease and obscurely angry. He watched Valerie poring over some architectural drawings at the table. She raked a lock of hair behind her ear and narrowed her eyes in concentration. She was still wearing the sleek black dress and stockings she'd worn to work. Her only concession to being home was that she had kicked off her shoes and messed up her hair by tugging at it while thinking. It was one of the many things Adam loved about her, that she didn't change clothes after work. She felt perfectly at ease in her elegant, sexy clothes, dressing as a matter of course in a way that for Sophie would constitute "dressing up" for a party or a rare night out. Poor old Sophie in her T-shirts and jeans, skirts and sweaters. Pretty, of course. Adam sighed and poured himself another drink. Pretty and practical. "Well scrubbed." Whereas Valerie…chic, confident, conquering. And sexy as she was, she was also refreshingly masculine, in her aggression, her ambition, her willingness to take risks, to make spur-of-the-moment decisions and shoulder the consequences. Her boldness, yes, that was attractive to Adam, but equally so was her vulnerability, the fearful child that still dwelled in her and needed his protection and reassurance. Such wonderful extremes of toughness and tenderness, so breathtakingly seductive when combined. Valerie was richly and darkly layered, with startling contrasts concealed in her depths. Sophie had no layers. Sophie was homogenized, wholesome goodness through and through, efficient, considerate, kind. Adam's eyes drifted back to Valerie, and he marveled that this sleek and complex creature was now his own. But he also felt…uneasy. No other word for it. In spite of his self-congratulatory thoughts, he was inclined this evening to brood.

Valerie looked up from her work to gaze at Adam, her prize, settled on her sofa as if he belonged there, which of course he did now. She considered his familiar face—his high, flat cheeks and long mouth, his furrowed brow and wavy hair, graying slightly—with a proprietary feeling that was new. He was looking sweetly sad and pensive, poor baby, frowning into his whiskey glass, as well he might on the night he had left his wife and children. If he had been in the mood to celebrate, he wouldn't have been the man Valerie loved. She knew better than to intrude on his thoughts with annoying babble meant to cheer him up. In a while she would go to him and they would talk quietly about the serious events taking place in their lives. Until then she would leave him to reflect and to admire her profile. She was conscious of looking rather fetching as she sat there, intent on her drawings, occasionally biting her pencil like a schoolgirl. It was not the moment to interrupt his thoughts, and, more to the point, she was busy, putting the last touches on a project that had occupied her heart as well as her mind for the past months.

She had started it a few weeks after the beginning of their affair, when she was at home alone and feeling the first twinges of the other-woman syndrome: jealousy, self-pity, and resentment. At this rate she would soon be moping about having to spend Christmas alone, the classic mistress's lament. It wasn't that Valerie felt a deep need to be the one to wash Adam's socks; on the contrary, she was alert to the dangers of numbing domestic routine, having seen its effect on her parents' marriage. She had never blamed her father for deserting them; it was her mother she despised for being so dull and dowdy that she was incapable of holding on to the man Valerie so desperately needed in her life. Nor had she resented her father's mistress; there was nothing wrong with a single woman's testing the strength of the marriage bonds of the attractive married men around her. If those bonds were solid, she would get nowhere—fair enough. And if they were flimsy, they deserved to be broken. Adam had tumbled into her arms, proof that their affair was destined. No, a guilty conscience wasn't Valerie's problem, and neither was a craving for cozy domesticity. It was simply that she wanted more.

More attention, more time, more company. At first, secrecy had had its thrills, but there was something undignified about it, and it was frankly inconvenient. The inequality of their relationship bothered her; he had another whole life away from her, whereas she had nothing that excluded him. She gave all of herself; he gave a small part. She didn't relish sinking into the role of sulking mistress, so she had set to work on a project designed to lift her spirits: sketching the dream apartment—completely imaginary and therefore unfettered by considerations of space and cost—in which she and Adam would someday live. It was crazy, she knew, but still wonderfully consoling, and the drawings served as a springboard for dozens of fantasies about their future life together. Work always cheered her up, and as the floor plans began to take shape, her enthusiasm and determination grew. It even crossed her mind that she might bring about some white magic: If the apartment she designed were good enough, Adam would leave his wife and come to live in it. It was a relief to feel she was actively helping things along, if only by voodoo. And if she could do white magic, why not black? One evening she imagined that each time she set her pencil to paper, Adam would experience another feeling of disillusionment with Sophie and his thoughts would stray longingly to her. With the aid of the magic house plans, she would loosen the grip of his present life on him and pull him, slowly but irresistibly, toward her.

So it was natural that on Adam's first evening in her house as her very own man, Valerie should turn to her house plans—now perfected in nearly every detail—and glory in their victory. During all those months, she had never mentioned them to him, partly from embarrassment, partly superstitious fear that talking about them might eradicate their power.

She tapped the pages straight and glanced through them one last time, feeling shy all of a sudden. It was a simple apartment, really; lots of daydreaming had been necessary to spin out work on it for so long. It was light and airy, mainly open plan, occupying the top two floors of some charming Back Bay building. Downstairs, the larger space included a living area, a dining area, and a kitchen, and the smaller space combined a bedroom, a dressing room, and a bathroom, all flowing together en suite. One of Valerie's convictions was that a bathroom should be a room of good size and a pleasant place to spend an evening, alone or à deux, with music and pictures and space around the large bathtub for setting down books and drinks. From the living area, a staircase led up to another open space above, this one an immense architecture studio with exposures on all four sides as well as skylights. Sitting on top of the world with views all around them, they would feel like gods, so creation would take place as a matter of course. They would each work at one end, close enough for a sense of camaraderie but distant enough not to contaminate each other's creative aura. The studio opened onto a long balcony overhanging a terrace accessible from the living space downstairs, and both looked out over the surrounding rooftops. Valerie judged the apartment to be nearly perfect in terms of spaciousness and elegance, and also practicality—built-in storage space ran along both sides of the entire length of the one interior wall. However, as an architect, Adam would also want to make some contribution, naturally enough, so she would defer to him on a couple of questions with obvious answers. Tact, it was called.

"About staircases, Adam, how do you feel about a broad, curving open tread? I think that gives such a gracious, airy feel. A staircase should be a focal point, don't you think—the spinal column of the house and all?" She smiled. "Or would you prefer something dark and cramped?"

He frowned. "What?"

"Come and look at this, darling." Here we go. Silly to be so nervous.

He stood behind her and peered at the plans. "What is this?"

"It's our ideal future home." She felt such need of his approval that it was a struggle to keep her tone casual. "What do you think?"

"It's what?"

"Our home! Where we'll live someday. You and me!" She had spoken rather sharply, so she added a little laugh.

He frowned and studied the drawings more closely while she held her breath. But far too soon, he wandered away. "We'll need a room for the boys," he said over his shoulder. "They'll be spending time with us, you know."

"Well, of course!" She struggled to hide her consternation. "I...I wanted to get your ideas on that."

"A lot of wasted space in that bathroom. Could put it there."

Oh, right, wreck the bathroom and the whole flow of movement and light, to say nothing of their privacy. And what, dared she ask, would a boys' bedroom look like? Bunk beds, plaid sheets, and dinosaur posters, perhaps?

But...this was not the moment to contradict him. "Mmm," she said, in an arcing tone that might have meant, *By golly, I guess we* could *put the boys' bedroom there!*

But then again, it might have meant anything.

———

Sophie sat, still at the kitchen table, in a state of narcotized bemusement. The children had wandered off to play, come back to inspect the kitchen for signs of dinner and, finding none, wandered away again. This had happened several times. The thought that she had to make dinner ran through her mind repeatedly, but without sparking off the least action on her part. She sat looking at the bare tabletop in dazed amazement at her inability to move. It was the first time since she had become a mother that she had sat doing nothing when something needed doing. And slowly the realization came to her that she could not do it. She could not make dinner. What was more, and this was more puzzling, she could not make herself care. *The children, my children, are hungry*, she told herself, trying to instill a sense of urgency strong enough to overcome her inertia, but instead she laughed out loud. Her weird laughter made Matthew apprehensive. He and his brother had been standing quietly at the door for some time, watching her. "Hugo's hungry," he said finally.

"Then sit down," Sophie said gaily, "and we'll eat!"

They sat and waited. "What?" Matthew asked eventually. "What is there to eat?"

"Well…we're going to…" Sophie's voice died away as she hunted for inspiration and found it. "Have a picnic! That's it, a picnic. Here's how we'll do it. You can take turns going to the fridge and taking out something you want to eat. Hugo, you go first. Anything you want, but just one thing at a time." Hesitant at first, they quickly caught on to this interesting new game, and in minutes the table was piled with food and the children were enchanted. "Okay," Sophie said. "Now we eat."

"But we don't have plates."

"We don't have forks!"

"It doesn't matter on a picnic. Look." She scooped a pickle out of a jar with her fingers and crunched it between her teeth. "See?" They did see, and they busied themselves building elaborate sandwiches while she looked on, smiling dreamily.

At bath time she knelt beside the tub and splashed them with both hands, hard, laughing. Amazed by this infringement of the rules, they splashed back until she was drenched. Then, following their long-established tradition, once the shampoo was well worked in, she twisted and shaped their lathered hair into foamy horns and held the hand mirror up so the little devils could admire themselves. It was only having horns that made hair washing bearable. Last came the anxious-making part of the bath: rinsing out the shampoo. Fearful but obedient, they tipped their heads well back, and she carefully poured water from a pitcher over their heads. The rule was that if a trickle got into their eyes, they were to shout, "Eye! Eye!" and she would shriek and fumble hastily for a towel to dab their faces, pretending to be in a panic that always made them laugh. The bath ran its normal course, ending, that evening like every other, with Hugo's solemn proclamation, "Bath is over." Then she bundled their firm, slippery, wet bodies into towels and hugged them to her tightly.

Valerie put on Mozart's *Don Giovanni* and poured herself another glass of wine. Adam's scotch was resting forgotten in his hand. She perched on the sofa and faced him, looking serious; it was time to talk.

"Darling, you're doing the right thing. I've done my homework, and the experts agree that children suffer least from divorce before the age of six. Yours are still young enough to accept what's happening as perfectly normal. Doing it now is kindest."

He glanced at his watch. "I have to get back."

"Do you have to go?" She wrapped her arms around him. "Oh, Adam, stay here tonight. I have this scary feeling that if I let you go now, something terrible will happen."

"Don't be silly," he said gently, giving her what he meant to be a brief kiss. But she held him firmly, pressing herself against him, and the kiss gave way to rather frantic and fumbling lovemaking amid the sofa cushions. Before releasing him, she whispered, "Remember. You're mine now."

Looking down at her defiant but frightened face, he felt a sudden great surge of love for her—and huge relief that he did. Having just broken up his home for this woman, he needed to feel something fierce and fiery for her that had been evading him all evening until that moment. Jubilantly, he fanned the flames by reminding himself that she had grown up in poverty—well, practically in poverty—that she'd been abandoned by her father, and that beneath her hard-boiled façade she was still a vulnerable and needy child. That was it, really; that was the difference between her and Sophie: Sophie could have a better day or a worse day, but at the core of her being she would always be "all right, really." Sophie didn't need Adam. Valerie did. It was that simple. Obviously, then, he had made the right choice; he had done what was fair.

A short while later, Adam got out of his car and stood gazing at what had been his house but mercifully no longer was: that loathsome temple to mediocrity, the fruit of a thousand soul-destroying compromises. It was little wonder he had felt diminished living there, as a creator and as a man, stifled by the banality of those surroundings. The house was in darkness. Good. There would be no late-night scenes, then, no throwing of crockery, not that he really expected such behavior from Sophie. She was above all that—and too lacking in passion. She would be saddened by his leaving, no doubt, and angry, too, as was only natural, but quickly she would come to terms with it and get on with her life. Sensible Sophie could be trusted to act with a view to what was best in the long term, and, of course, moping or making scenes could never be that. Her fundamentally life-embracing nature would protect her from prolonged unhappiness. Sophie was strong; the children were young and resilient. Adam was lucky; not all men could correct a wrong turn in their lives without creating victims. But he was managing to grasp his own happiness without jeopardizing anyone else's—a small miracle in this world of intricately entangled lives.

There was no light on in their bedroom, and peeking in, Adam saw that Sophie wasn't there. A crack of light was showing under the guest-room door. He hesitated, then decided not to knock. It was too soon, he thought, for more talk. She needed some time alone to... collect herself. So he tiptoed into the bedroom, snapped on the reading light that used to be his, and quickly filled a couple of suitcases.

Deep in shadow, on the flight of steps up to the attic, Sophie sat hugging her knees, watching him. Through the half-open door, she caught glimpses of the man who up to that day had been her husband, crossing from the closet and chest of drawers to the suitcases lying on the bed, his arms piled high, first with sweaters, then with shoes, next with a stack of those shirts she had ironed only this morning, in another life. He was methodical and thorough, she noticed, and brisk in his movements, like a sprightly traveling salesman packing for just another trip. His eager fingers sorted through the collection of objects on top of the dresser with callous haste and a disregard for her trinkets that made her catch her breath. Out of the joint tangle of personal objects that had cohabited there so peacefully for so long, he snatched his cuff links, a pile of change, his comb. In his haste he knocked over the Chanel No. 19 he had given her last Christmas, and, woundingly, he didn't set it upright again. What if the top were loose and its precious liquid were dripping away? He worked like an experienced burglar, quick and uncaring, sorting the valuables from the rubbish, his from hers, stowing his away safely and leaving hers—the fallen perfume, a limp gold chain, a bracelet, a special seashell—scattered on the dresser top, which looked dusty now that it was half bare. Two sharp snapping sounds and the first suitcase was closed—*snap, snap*. Then the other—*snap, snap*—and Adam emerged carrying all that he had looted from the place where they had slept and made love and planned and laughed and cuddled each other and their children for the past five years. He set the suitcases down in the hall and returned to the bedroom to switch off the lamp—he had always been careful about wasting electricity. Then he lifted the suitcases again with a slight grunt and carried them down, the stairs creaking under their weight. Sophie waited until she could hear him busy in his study, and then she trailed down silently after him and stood out of sight in the darkness of the sitting room across the hall, watching him cull the best books from his shelves. Now that he was farther from the bedrooms, he made more noise, tossing the chosen books into boxes with a thump. Certain books he was unsure about, so he flipped through them to decide. He became so engrossed in one that he stood reading it for a long while, lost in the text. Many minutes passed before he closed the book and returned his thoughts to the business at hand, the leaving of Sophie Dean, his wife. Looking on from her hiding place, Sophie felt amazement that he could forget what he was doing, even for a moment. Men's minds must be very different from women's; it was unthinkable that she should become distracted by a passage in a book at such a time. If she were the one packing, each object she touched would spark off memories, and no matter how determined she was on her course of action, she would feel nostalgia and regret mixing with her resolve, and it would show on her face and in every gesture. Men's brains must be more compartmentalized, containing chambers where intellectual thought did not rub up against emotion, while in women's more integrated brains, thoughts and feelings mingled promiscuously. How restful it would be to take refuge in those intellectual spaces where all emotion was forbidden entrance. Adam was emptying his desk drawers now, one by one, shifting all the contents neatly into boxes, his movements so deft they seemed rehearsed. Had he been planning this moment, then, longing for it? Concealed in the shadows, her face grave and thoughtful, Sophie continued to watch. Just to watch. It was hypnotic, gazing on ghostlike as he prized their two lives apart, and there was something numbing, too, about the speed and ease with which he dismantled what had taken years of common effort to build. With one callous sweep of his hand, down crashed their tower of blocks.

"You've got to fight fire with fire," Marion said the next day, standing with her hands on her hips at Sophie's stove, wearing Sophie's apron, and looking stalwart and buxom. She had insisted on cooking the lunch and, after much asking where things were, had managed to get something bubbling away in a pan under a lid. "Get yourself some flattering new clothes, why don't you? Let me make you an appointment with my hairdresser—my treat. He's very good."

"Are you suggesting that Adam left me because he didn't like my hair?"

"Sophie."

"Or that he'll come back if I get a new hairdo? I'm surprised at you! What's all this about makeup and...and tranquilizers? You don't believe in mood-bending prescription drugs any more than I do—and those things are hell, by the way. I'm not taking any more. Whatever happened to holistic medicine? You're a counselor, Marion—whatever happened to talking things out? At the first sign of trouble, you're running for the pharmaceuticals and the beauty parlor!"

Marion's specialty was counseling children, and she always held that her own childlessness was no impediment. *You don't need to have one*, she liked to say, *only to have been one*. "Psychology is not incompatible with a curling iron," she said now. "You're in a very awkward situation. Your husband has walked out on you, leaving you with two children that you may end up having to raise alone." She held her hand up to soften the effect of that. "That's the worst possible scenario. I don't for one minute think it's going to come to that. But you've got to face the fact that you have a rival, and she's a glamorous, seductive woman. Adam—"

"I don't care! I'm not playing competitive Barbies to get him back!"

"Listen to me. Adam will come to his senses, and he'll come back to you, but you have to help him, by remaining

calm, by minimizing the situation, and yes, by making yourself as attractive as possible. All that is hard to do, and
whatever means you can find to help you—be it prayer, eye-
liner, or drugs—you've got to use it. This is a crisis, Sophie!
It calls for any and every measure we can think of."

Sophie buried her face in her hands and rubbed her eyebrows with her fingertips. She had slept poorly in spite of
the tranquilizer, or rather because of it. She hated dreamless
sleep; it made her feel she'd been robbed. Both she and Adam
had avoided their bedroom that night, she sleeping in the
guest room and he fitfully on the chesterfield with only one
thin blanket, which he'd left there in a conspicuous show of
martyrdom. He was gone before breakfast, his suitcases and
boxes stacked neatly in his study, a note on his desk saying
he'd pick up "these last few things" that evening after work.

"He'll come back," Marion said again. "If you're understanding and indulgent, if you make it easy for him to come
back, then he will. Because deep down it's what he wants to
do."

Sophie raised her head out of her hands and frowned.
Her attention had been snagged by two words that had sent
her mind reeling off into distant and surreal realms. (Was
someone telling her to be "understanding" and "indulgent"
to Adam? No. No, surely not.) "I need to think," she said
slowly, out loud but to herself. "I need...to think."

"You'll come through this. I know you will." Marion
reached across the table to squeeze Sophie's hand. "You'll do
what's best for everyone." Then she got up and went to shake
pans, lift lids, and generally see to lunch. "It's tough for boys
to grow up without a father. If there's anything you can do to
prevent that from happening, you owe it to them to try your
damnedest."

Elbows on the table, chin in hands, eyes fixed on the wall opposite, Sophie said, "I don't know what to do." And eventually she added, "I need to think. I just…need…to think."

"You do that, honey." Marion set a steaming plate before her. "But first, eat."

———

"The water, electricity, and gas bills are deducted directly from the checking account, but the bank can make mistakes. I've caught them out more than once. Open all the bank statements as they arrive and make sure they tally with the bills. I suggest you file the bills somewhere handy so you won't have to hunt for them when the bank statements come in. Here. Keep these somewhere safe." Adam held out a stack of papers, which Sophie made no move to take from him. She merely glanced down at them, then back up at him. He went on. "If you feel you can't cope with all this, I can recommend a reliable accountant, but I do think this is something you should be able to handle on your own." Sophie continued to look at him without expression. "Oh, for Christ's sake, Sophie! I'm only trying to help. Get a grip on yourself—if only for the boys' sake."

"What you're doing now—is that for the boys' sake?"

"As a matter of fact, it is! You may not know it, but children under the age of six suffer the least in a divorce. They're still young enough to accept everything that happens as natural. That's why we have to do this now."

A dart pierced Sophie's heart as she recognized this so-called fact about children and divorce as coming not from Adam but from an evil alien source—from *her*. Adam didn't know a thing about the subject; it was *she* who had dredged this up as a way of convincing him to come away with her. How triumphantly she must have pounced on this "proof" that it would be just fine for him to abandon his children, *actually kinder to them*. Sophie felt a surge of anger so powerful that it was physically debilitating, like dizziness or nausea, and she had to lock her knees and close her eyes against it.

Adam was speaking again, with exaggerated patience, as though to a slow child. "Of course the good of our children is foremost in my mind—it has to be that way. Can't you see that we mustn't put our own problems first?"

Sophie's eyes opened again. "Adam—"

"It is essential," he ground on, "that their life continue as smoothly as possible, without upsets or interruptions. Same house, same school, same daily routine…" He paused to glance at his watch, then wound up more quickly. "We simply have to be grown up about this, Sophie, and make this transition as seamless as possible for them. So…"

If Adam had not chosen that moment to check his watch, their story might have progressed differently. But he did check it, and when Sophie noticed that small gesture and the implication of it struck her—that he had allotted a certain amount of time, and no more, for his farewell speech to her, that he had an important date to keep with *her*—she had a sudden and piercingly sweet revelation, like a single ray of sunshine bursting through pewter clouds, of what she must do. In that instant of illumination, Sophie saw the way forward. When she spoke, it was in a tone that an untrained ear might have called cheerful, or at any rate resigned.

"You know, you're absolutely right."

Adam looked surprised, then pleased.

"You've said all this about the children before, I've thought it over carefully, and I've decided that you are absolutely right...."

Adam shrugged the polite, diffident shrug of the victor. "Then you'll understand how—"

"...which is *why*"—Sophie carried on over him. She waited for him to fall silent before continuing, not loudly but with clear enunciation—"which is why...I am the one who is leaving. Not you. Me."

It was Adam's turn to stare.

At first Valerie didn't hear her phone ringing over the tune she was humming to herself as she flitted around putting the finishing touches on her scrumptious dinner for two. "Oh, the phone!" she said out loud, for such was her ebullient mood. "That'll be Adam wondering if he should stop and pick up some wine." Into the phone she trilled, "Hellooo!"

But it was Agatha's voice, flat with sincerity. "I just wanted to let you know that I'm here for you."

"What?"

"If you want to call me later, if you need to talk, I'll be here. I mean, I'm going out, but I don't want you to feel you're interrupting me. It's really no problem. Feel free to call."

"What the hell are you talking about? Adam's moving in tonight. I'm making us our very first dinner as a real couple. Ris d'agneau and artichauts farcis with a stunning little Saint-Émilion."

"That's nice. Look...Valerie...I didn't want to rain on your parade at lunch—"

"But you're going to now?"

"But the truth is, you're still on pretty thin ice. These first days after the bomb has fallen, well...There's a real danger of reconciliation."

"That's ridiculous."

"No it's not, Vee. I wish it were. I hope everything will turn out, but I just wanted to let you know that if it doesn't, you have a friend here at the other end of the line. I do have a date tonight, as I said, but it's no trouble whatsoever for me to give you any support you might need. My phone will be switched on, ready."

"Oh, for Christ's sake! Adam isn't going back to his wife. He's coming over here tonight with his things. To live here."

"In theory, yes. But he's not there yet."

"Just go on your date, Agatha!" Valerie slammed the phone down and lit a cigarette. Date, my ass! Trust that envious bitch to try to wreck her evening by putting poisonous thoughts into her head. Well, she wouldn't succeed; no insidious fears were going to start tormenting Valerie... scenes of Adam and his wife...in tearful embrace... thinking of the children...her guilt-tripping him ruthlessly... them vowing to give it a second chance...all forgiven...a fresh start...Valerie poured herself out a slug of wine and tossed it back. Oh, no—she wasn't going to start thinking about any of *that*!

Adam was still staring, and Sophie was explaining things. Her speech had none of the overly rehearsed sound of Adam's stiff little discourse, because she was putting it all into words for the first time. It came out in gushes and dribbles, now fast, now slowly, as she thought it through, her voice and rhythm growing steadily more confident. The moment of revelation had been thrilling, but equally satisfying was this leisurely ramble through the logical reasons supporting it and the discovery that her solution was in fact a nesting set of solutions within solutions, as lovely and close-fitting as rose petals. All paths, all considerations, led to this conclusion; what she found at the end of every line of reasoning was further vindication of her decision to leave.

She had begun tentatively, feeling her way. "You've just put an end to our family life, and that was the only life I had. The least you can do now is take responsibility for the children while I get back on my feet."

"But I will! I've told you I'll pay generous child support—of course I will!"

"That's not enough. I don't mean just money, I mean real responsibility. I have my whole life to rebuild. I have to go back to work. I've been wanting to change careers, and this is the obvious time to do it. You know I'm interested in shiatsu." He nodded, frowning impatiently, but she continued, unflustered. "I'll have to train to qualify as a practitioner, and I can't do it overnight. Building up a practice takes time, too. There's a lot to do, and I can't take care of the children at the same time. You're going to have to do that part. Just until I'm on my feet."

"Oh, come on, the boys are in school now. You can go to classes while they're at school and study while they're asleep. It's perfectly feasible—countless women do it."

But she shook her head calmly. "I don't want this transitional phase to last any longer than you do, believe me. I want to be settled. I'll see if there's a fast track. I'll take classes every morning if I can, but there will still be weekend seminars, retreats, evening courses. It's not compatible with child care. No, I won't be able to have them, Adam. It's out of the question."

"What are you suggesting, then? That I take them with me?"

"Not at all. I agree with everything you've said about putting the children first. You're absolutely right about their routine and how we mustn't upset it. We both agree they should stay here, in their home, but I can't afford the payments on this house. You can. So that means you stay here with them."

Adam forced a little laugh. "Oh, no. I couldn't do that, I'm afraid."

"You don't understand. I'm not asking your permission. These are the consequences of your actions—you have to assume them." The profound rightness of those words produced a surge of self-confidence in her.

"Sophie, be reasonable! I'll keep up the house payments for you. I'll put it in your name! I'll hire a nanny for when you're away...on these seminars or what have you."

"A nanny? But that would be terribly upsetting! A strange face, new habits—it's exactly what you've been saying you don't want for them! And I won't live in a house paid for by you. You'll contribute to the children's upkeep, but not mine. Try to understand, Adam—and I know it's hard, believe me—that you've just separated your life from mine. You can't support me—it would be nonsensical. What I'll do for now is rent a small apartment I can afford. And later on I'll find a place big enough for me and the children. In the meantime, they'll live here with you."

"I can't believe this! I cannot believe you would abandon your own children!"

She threw back her head and laughed at the irony of that. "They'll see a lot more of me, Adam, than they would have seen you. I'll pick them up from school every day that I can, and they'll spend all afternoon with me. I'll get Milagros to drop them off with you at suppertime. I'll speak to her—I know she'll do extra hours to help you. On weekends the children can take turns between us. And once I'm truly settled, they can come to live with me. It's the only possible arrangement—for now."

"Young children need their mother!"

"They'll have their mother! Every day! That's the beauty of it—it's the absent parent who has to be the conscientious one. The one they live with, they see as a matter of course. Anyway, Adam, the boys love you as much as they love me. They'll be happy here with you. I know you'll manage."

"Sophie, this is anger. This is anger speaking. Understandable, justifiable, but—"

"It goes without saying," she interrupted, repeating his words of the day before, "that I'll leave you the house and everything in it. I'll take only my personal belongings and half of our savings."

"We need more time to talk this over, Sophie. Please."

"Oh, now we need more time, do we? You would have left an hour ago! No, Adam, it's what you said so truly yesterday—how did that go?—oh, yes: 'We must put our own disappointment to one side and concentrate all our energy on our children and their well-being.' Well, as you can see, I'm acting on that. Let's see if you can do as much. The good of the children is foremost in your mind? Good—then you can begin by going upstairs and telling them you don't want to live with their mother anymore, and why. Don't forget to tell them why! It's not something I could do, seeing as I don't know. You never bothered to explain it to me, but I'm sure you'll do a beautiful job of it with them."

She went into the dining room and reappeared carrying her coat and handbag. "I'll be back for my things tomorrow while you're at work. Good-bye."

"Sophie, this is ridiculous. Wait! Goddamn it, what am I going to tell the children? This is serious—we've got to work it out together!"

"It's your problem, Adam. You broke up the home, you pick up the pieces."

And she was gone.

Valerie had cleared away the dinner things long ago. It was more than she could bear to see her lovely table set before two empty chairs, the poor spurned mistress's attempt at a celebration. She had finished one bottle of wine and part of another, one pack of cigarettes and part of another, and she was sitting in the dark on the floor. She'd even called Agatha for consolation but hung up when she remembered that Agatha had gone out on a date. (Agatha on a date? Would pigs be flying next?) Not that she didn't want to intrude on Agatha's date—she didn't give a shit about that—but what she didn't want was an extra witness to her humiliation, some idiot Agatha had met online listening in on half their conversation and Agatha discussing it with him afterward: *poor Valerie.* Her mascara had run, so when she brushed her tears back, it smeared, giving her sixties-style cat's eyes. Adam was so late by now that it could only mean disaster. If it were anything less, he would have called. She had thought of lots of scathing things to tell him, but by the time he did call, she was only grateful to hear his voice.

"Darling, I'm so sorry about tonight. I can't make it. She's left. Sophie's gone. It's too late for a sitter, so I have to stay with the boys. I'm stuck here tonight, I'm afraid. Had you gone to much trouble?"

"Then you...haven't made up with her?"

"What? Good Lord no, nothing like that. I told you, she's gone. She's left me! Here with the children!"

"So...what's going to happen?" Valerie was confused, but so relieved by the major news that the rest hardly seemed to matter.

"Well...I don't know. She'll come to her senses, I imagine. It's the shock, that's all. Until then we'll just have to adapt our plans a little. Nothing to worry about. I can't talk now, Valerie, the boys are asleep beside me. I'll see you at the office tomorrow. Good night, my love."

Adam hung up the phone and settled back on the chesterfield between his sleeping sons—all alone in his spacious suburban house.

"Now, hang on a minute. Let me get this straight. Do you mean to tell me that, not content to lose just your husband, you've decided to throw your house *and your children* into the bargain?"

To avoid a late-night lecture, Sophie had waited until morning to tell Marion what she had done and why. After explaining as succinctly as possible, she had sat back with her coffee and borne Marion's voluble protest patiently, her eyes straying now and then to the morning paper's classified ads, which she was searching for apartments to rent. Surreptitiously, she circled another ad: *"Seeking reliable tenant, preferably with green thumb..."* Then she continued. "I don't want the house, and I'm not losing my children. It's a question of logistics, not a melodrama. Breaking up our home wasn't my idea, you know. I'm coping the best I can."

"What did you tell the kids?"

"I didn't. I told him to."

"Sophie!"

"He told them I was visiting my mother. To buy some time. He sent me a text message last night."

"But you have to speak to them yourself! You can't—"

"I know, I know! It was very wrong of me. But it was a question of momentum. I had to *get out of that house.* I just...I'll speak to them."

"Put yourself in their place. They won't understand the complexities of why you're going or how it was really Daddy who 'made' you go by having an affair! The only thing they're going to remember, all the rest of their lives, is that Mommy left them. Why should they feel rejected by *you* when it's Adam who's to blame?"

Sophie nodded eagerly. "But don't you see? That's another reason I should be the one to go! I can make sure they *don't* feel rejected. I'll see to it that they stay right at the center of my new life. I'm not sure Adam would have taken the trouble to include them in his—or even known how to. With him it would have just been, 'Daddy's gone.' With me it'll be, 'You have two houses now!' and I can make that...fun." She smiled, and her eyes filled with tears. "Yes, fun! One of the things I've thought of, to help them feel at home in my new place, is to get them some kind of pet to keep there. So something of theirs is always with me. A little...hamster, maybe? I thought that might—"

Marion interrupted. "Sophie, you're hurt and confused, and no wonder. But moving out is a disastrous mistake. As your best friend, I can't let you throw your life away like this. So finish that coffee and go back before it's too late. You'll thank me one day."

"It's Adam who threw my life away."

"Oh, Sophie."

"And as my best friend, you should be helping me to make a new one." She felt a little uncomfortable calling Marion her best friend, although that was presumably what she had become in the three or four years they had known each other. Certainly no one else fit the description.

Marion sighed and folded her arms. "All right. It's a big mistake, but all right. Maybe this will give Adam the kick in the behind that he needs. With you gone, the foolishness of what he's done will hit him between the eyes. It may actually be the fastest way of getting him back."

But Sophie was lost in thought, barely listening. Irritated, Marion allowed a little laugh to escape her, then clapped her hand over her mouth.

After a moment Sophie asked obligingly, "What's funny?"

"Oh, nothing..." When it became clear that Sophie was not going to press her, Marion continued, "I was just thinking how silly all of this will seem, once you're safely back home."

Sophie folded her hands on the tabletop and looked at them.

"Oh, that bitch!" Agatha screeched, gulping foie gras meant for Adam the night before. "That scheming bitch! Can't he see what she's up to? My God, this is delicious!"

Valerie had summoned Agatha to her apartment after work for an emergency meeting to discuss the latest development. It was also a chance to get rid of the canapés she had so laboriously prepared the previous evening; those calories would sit better around Agatha's middle than her own. "What kind of woman would abandon her children?" she prompted.

"A ruthless, cold-blooded bitch, that's who," Agatha said with relish, licking her fingers. "A Machiavelli of the suburbs! I mean, what could be more perfectly calculated to screw up Adam's escape plans? It's brutal—but brilliant!"

"Admire her, do you?"

"Of course I do! Don't you? I mean, come on, if she weren't the enemy, you'd love this. Pass that brie, will you? Mmm, good and runny. Don't forget, Val, in these wife-and-mistress things, who's right is never a moral question, it's just a question of which one is your girlfriend. I can't get over how she just up and went like that! Imagine Adam's face! She says, 'So! You been cheatin' on me? Well, fuck you, mister, I'm outta here!' Ha, ha! I wish I'd been there!"

"Agatha?"

"Hmm?"

"Shut up."

"I'm just zooming out for the broader picture, Valerie. That's important in assessing the situation."

"The situation is obvious. She's run away, leaving her poor children behind. It's vindictive—and worse, it's cruel." Valerie paused, but Agatha was busy with the canapés, so she continued. "She doesn't give a damn how much they suffer, just so long as she can use them as a wedge to drive between Adam and me. It's typical of married women to use the kids as leverage, but I never heard of one going this far before."

Agatha swallowed, nodding, then said, "What I don't get is him. Why doesn't he fight back? He's such a wimp to put up with this."

"What do you mean? He's furious!"

"But he's letting her get away with it, isn't he? When did she leave?"

"Yesterday."

"Ha! She must be holed up at some girlfriend's house, laughing her head off, eating Danish and waiting for him to beg her to come home."

"Danish?"

"That's what housewives have, coffee and Danish, with artificial sweetener in the coffee to make up for the Danish—don't you know anything?"

"He has no idea where she is. And he hasn't tried to find out either."

"He will. And soon. And then it'll be, 'Honey, come home, I can't hack it alone, the kids are driving me nuts, you were The One all along—I see that now!' Well, you have to hand it to her. Chalk one up for the wife." She frowned intently at the hors d'oeuvres, fingers fluttering over them, not sure whether to try the smoked salmon or the shrimp next.

Valerie seized the tray and set it out of Agatha's reach. "I'm not giving Adam up. I don't care what kind of shit she pulls—he's mine now. I'm just going to have to make him see this cheap stunt for what it is."

"Fat chance. If he had any guts, she would never have gotten out the door in the first place. Forget it, Vee, she's won."

An interesting fact popped into Agatha's mind. "Hey, do you know what the Danish expression for 'being henpecked' is? They say 'under the slippers.' Isn't that bizarre?" Eyes wide, she tilted her head from side to side and fluted in a fake Danish accent, "Adam, he is under the slippers, *ja*?"

Valerie looked at her with loathing.

"Ah, me," Agatha sighed, "it all brings back visions of Howard. Speaking of which, don't forget about that vernissage next week. He might be there—the painter's a friend of his wife's—and I'll need your support to survive the ordeal."

"I don't know."

"Come on, you promised ages ago! And it'll be fun. I've heard it's the most priceless bullshit."

"I'm not as keen on bullshit as you are."

"Well, naturally not—it's how I make my living. First I look at other people's bullshit, then I come home and spin my own. Bullshit is my life. But you're my friend, so you're coming with me. Look, I don't want to face Howard and his wife alone, two against one. I mean, I don't really care anymore, and yet I do. *You* know. Come on, I need you there."

Valerie assented vaguely but, as always when Howard's name arose, her thoughts had drifted to other matters.

The atmosphere at Adam's firm was growing tenser by the day, with rumors that the new "up or out" campaign was in action. True or not, it had the effect of honing the competition among the employees, and by six o'clock everyone had had enough backbiting for one day. Before leaving the

building, James popped into Adam's empty office to use the
john there. No sooner had he gotten things under way than
he heard a furious woman's voice hissing, "...classic bitchy,
manipulative power play!" He hunched instinctively over his
open fly and at the same time turned his head awkwardly
to see what was going on out there: Valerie and Adam, and
she had him pinned against the wall. As quickly as he could,
James shook, tucked in, and zipped.

"And you don't have the wits—or the balls—to call her
bluff!"

But he wasn't quick enough. Once a hidden man has
heard a woman tell another man he has no balls, it's too late
to step out and say hi.

"Don't be vulgar," Adam said. "It's unworthy of you. And
very unattractive, believe me."

"All you have to do is refuse to play along with her."

"She's gone, Valerie; it's a fait accompli. I had thought she
might change her mind, but no. It's done. It won't be forever, though—that's the main thing. Just until she's on her
feet. And you know she's only thinking of the children's well-
being."

"Oh, how can you be so naïve? Can't you see what she's
up to? She's dumping the kids on you in order to keep us
apart."

"It's not a question of 'dumping' them on me. I'm leaving
my wife, Valerie, not my children. My children will always be
welcome wherever I live."

"Spare me the sanctimony, please. Those kids bore you,
and we both know it."

Because it contained a shameful kernel of truth, her remark angered Adam like nothing she had said so far. He grew
pale and spoke in a clipped, quiet tone of fury. "Valerie, let's

forget this whole thing. It's been a terrible mistake. I can see that now." As he turned to leave, she cried, "Adam, no!" and threw her arms around him, but he untwined them, saying, "I know I've complained to you about my children on occasion. Sometimes they annoy me, and yes, at times they even bore me. But I also love them, and I always shall. It's not something I could expect you to understand." At that she began to cry.

"Adam, I'm sorry, I'm sorry! Please don't go!" She clung to him until he felt the familiar pity and tenderness for her mingling with sexual desire and, relenting, put his arms around her. "I don't mean to be so horrible," she whispered, her wet cheek pressed to his. "I'm just so afraid of losing you, and I'm jealous...jealous of your children. I'm afraid they'll take you away from me."

He stroked her hair, murmuring, "Come now. It's all right. Shh."

"Adam, will you take me to England next summer? I want to know everything about you. I want to visit your boarding school, and see where you played, and meet your mother, and sit in your old bedroom. I want to..." She wanted to immerse herself in his past and shed her own. "I want to sit with you in a country pub and eat your favorite dish and drink your favorite drink...." And acquire his tastes and accent, and breathe his air and be far away and safely his.

Of course, he had done all that before. He had made just such a trip with Sophie, the year after they met. He had a sudden vivid recollection of her sitting by the fire in a country pub in Yorkshire on a blustery day, gazing lovingly at him over her half pint of bitter, the firelight flickering across her younger, smoother face. "Of course we'll go," he told Valerie sadly, and she nestled against his chest, feeling comforted. He led her away, and they made awkward progress down the hall, his arms around her, she still clinging to his neck.

When the coast was clear, James stepped out from his hiding place. He had just one word to say.

"Whew."

3.

Sophie lay in the bathtub squeezing hot, lavender-scented water over her shoulder with a large sponge. The bathroom was lit all around with candles, for someone—the owner and former occupant of the apartment of which she had become the "reliable, green-thumbed tenant"—had had the good idea of setting ceramic candleholders right into the tiled walls. Sophie had done all the transactions through a real-estate agent, so she had not met the owner, but Clement was the surname on the lease, and the apartment afforded some clues about him or her: a practical person (well-built shelves in all the right places), a gardener (dozens of thriving potted plants on the porch), and an aesthete (all the windows had colored glass at the top that glowed in the sunlight).

Filling the apartment with life had been Sophie's preoccupation her first evening there. She had lit candles for the motion and warmth of the flame and carried in plants, two by two, from the porch. When she was done, the effect was not the same as the soft breathing of two sleeping children, but it was enough to ensure that she slept well that first night. Clement, she decided as she drifted off, was a soulful person who had mastered the art of living alone happily, and gradually, as she lived here in Clement's house, that knowledge would be imparted to her.

On Sophie's first morning in her still-echoing apartment, Milagros had driven over with a carload of goods she had stripped out of Adam's house in indignation. Sophie had chosen a few things and asked Milagros to return the rest, which she'd done only reluctantly and after enumerating Adam's character flaws at high volume. Alone again, Sophie had arranged some books on shelves and unpacked her few clothes. Her dresses looked oddly insubstantial hanging alone in the closet instead of crowded against a man's dark suits. That first morning she stood for some time at the open closet door looking at them: her bright, skimpy dresses dangling defenseless on the nearly empty bar.

The days passed, and different aspects of Sophie's painful situation tossed up into the front of her mind like pieces of laundry thrown against the glass door of the washing machine, momentarily unique and identifiable, then churned back into the amorphous mix.

One day after school, she took the boys to a pet store, where they chose two goldfish—"No, not that one, *that* one"—and set them by the kitchen window with colored marbles half buried in the gravel to sparkle in the light and a fernlike aquatic plant to nibble on for vitamins. The fish flashed around the bowl, silver (Cloudy) and orange (Fishtag), lending more life to Sophie's home.

The children settled quickly into the new routine. Sophie still picked them up from school every day, gave them a snack, and played with them, but then Milagros took them

home for dinner and a bath before Adam tucked them in
and read to them. Their new life was not very different, and
as Sophie pointed out, the changes were all for the better:
two houses to play in now and the treat of Daddy "doing
books" every night. The fact that their parents' paths no
longer crossed did not seem to occur to them. It was all so
easy, the children appeared to accept her departure so well,
that Sophie felt almost rueful, but she was bolstered by this
proof that she and Adam—no, that *she*—had handled the situation correctly. And that was something to feel good about
at a dark time.

The first days she would glance at the clock and, out of
habit, half start up out of her chair with a gasp—only to realize with a feeling of blank surprise that nothing at all needed
doing. Her only duty was to be at the school gates at two-
thirty and the rest of the time—nothing. No questions to
answer. No tasks to perform.

She moved her head, creating ripples in the bathwater,
to look up at the ferns on the windowsill, looming greenly
through the steam in the flickering candlelight, and wonder
yet again why Clement had left all these lovely plants behind.
Must be traveling somewhere…but where? And what did
the A. R. stand for? Anthea Rose…Albert René…"A. R.
Clement," it had said on the mailbox before she turned the
card over, printed her name on the other side, and slid it back
into the slot. She hadn't wanted to throw the card away; it
was nicer like this, with their names nestling back-to-back.
She wondered if it were unhealthy to think so much about
Clement. A lonely, cast-off woman with her mind on one subject for hours and hours of each empty day…"I don't care,"
she said out loud. Her voice reverberated in the tiled room,
sounding surprisingly stern. Recently she had begun speak-

ing out loud when alone. Nothing unusual about that, except that she did it unconsciously, so she was surprised, both by the sudden sound of her voice and by the things it said—often rather harsh things. She wondered if these were signs of failing mental health: first her preoccupation with Clement, then startling herself by voicing thoughts she could not identify as her own. She tried to make herself worry about that, but it was as useless as trying to make a fist first thing in the morning; she really didn't care. Clement was a safe and pleasant place for her mind to dwell, so let it. She was all too aware that other, darker thoughts lurked out there, waiting to pounce. At night she would wake up suddenly, unable to move, paralyzed with dread, feeling a great weight pushing down on her, pressing the breath out of her. She would lie perfectly still, trapped, struggling to break the spell of horror before her chest was crushed. When at last she mustered the psychic strength to move, she would curl up tightly on her side and press her palms into her eyes to shield her mind from the black thoughts that flapped against her eyelids like bats seeking entry. She promised herself she would examine these thoughts in due course, but not now; for the time being, she must block them out and keep moving. To think might be to crumble, and she couldn't afford to do that yet.

She slid down in the bath and bent her knees so they rose, steaming, out of the bubbles, and warm water trickled into her ears, closing off all sounds except the underwater ones, which were amplified. Overhead, reflected candlelight danced on the ceiling. She counted slowly; she had been living in Clement's house for six...seven...eight days.

The classroom was cathedral-like in its height and hush, its smell of incense and the soft light drifting down from high windows. The only decoration on the cream-colored walls was a large reproduction of a sixteenth-century ink drawing entitled *The Centers of Grand Heavenly Circulation, Front and Back View*, showing a man sitting cross-legged, his centers of circulation marked and labeled with Chinese characters. The instructor was a tall, pale man named Malcolm, giving his introductory lecture to a dozen students sitting scattered about the floor on mats. "Chi is the vital life force. It enters our body from two directions: up from the earth in its yin form and down from the heavens in its yang form. When we are healthy, chi courses freely through our body along the meridians, and located along these meridians are pressure points called *tsubo*s—special places where chi can be felt and regulated. An unbalanced or stagnant chi can result in pain and illness, so our task is to unblock and equalize the flow, allowing the patient's natural healing powers to operate more efficiently."

His words produced a rare and thrilling sensation in Sophie: absolute certainty that this was where she belonged, this was what she was meant to be doing. At this precise place and time, destiny had kept its date with her. Elated, she glanced around to see if any of her classmates looked as if they might be feeling the same way. They were mostly women, mostly in their thirties, some with a shaggy, granola look, others not so much. She noticed one man who was a type she remembered from her student days: a sort of earth daddy, a man a good deal older than everyone else, with hair white and flowing, who seemed to strive for an air of having seen it all and of exuding gentle wisdom. He kept his eyes on Sophie for some time, waiting for her to glance in his direction, and when she did at last, he smiled lazily. She looked away.

Introductions followed, and out of the jumble of names and histories revealed, Sophie retained the fact that the earth daddy was named Jacob, although he invited everyone to call him Jake-O. There was an earnest, bony fellow named Anthony, much given to speaking with one long index finger held in the air, and a laughing woman with black corkscrew curls, named Rose. There was also an intriguingly self-contained, rather languid young woman, quite tall, whose name sounded like Elle or El, although it turned out to be, as she put it in her lazy drawl, "Just the letter L."

Another person in the room, sitting cross-legged on a mat and smiling quietly, made no particular impression on Sophie that first morning.

Marion came over that afternoon with a big, hairy cactus as a housewarming present. "Didn't you used to have one of these?" she asked, handing it over with a grunt.

"Oh, Marion, I love it! Yes, I did, but Adam hated it so much I gave it away. Now I feel it's come back to me, a vestige of my former life. You couldn't have chosen a more fitting present. Thank you."

"Well! Quite a nice place you've got here," Marion said, looking around. "Very tidy, of course!" She laughed, but Sophie perceived the sting in that remark, because she knew that Marion found tidiness—along with thinness—suspect. "How much are you paying?" Her eyebrows shot up at the amount Sophie named. "Really! In Jamaica Plain?"

It was true it was more than she had planned to pay, and

the apartment wasn't really big enough, the second bed-room being hardly adequate as a treatment room, but the place had felt right to her, and that was what mattered. Even in the confusion of those first days, she had had the wisdom to recognize that this was not a time for penny-pinching or roughing it in grim surroundings. "It's the going rate, more or less," she said. "Don't forget, JP is an up-and-coming area. And I like it, its diversity. People from all over, families of all kinds ... It has no associations for me either, and that's important for a fresh start. And there's a playground for the boys just across the street," she added, arranging the tea tray, "so that clinched it." She pushed open the glass door to the porch with her foot and carried out the tray. "Come and look at the best part! We'll have our tea out here if it's not too cold for you." The porch was as big as the kitchen, lined with plants on three sides and overlooking gray rooftops, with the tips of the trees in the park creating a leafy green patch among the jumble of chimneys, satellite dishes, and old TV antennas. Birds swooped overhead; the air was cool and quiet. Sophie set the tray on the table and poured out the tea, chattering about her landlord or -lady, and how lucky she had been to get into her shiatsu course after someone dropped out at the last minute. Marion didn't look terribly interested in speculations about this Clement person or in the rundown of Sophie's classmates. "But what about you?" she put in when she could. "How are *you*?"

Sophie felt suitably deflated. "Well, I miss the boys, espe-cially at night when it's time for books. I love tucking them in." Marion pressed her eyes closed in sympathy as Sophie continued. "On the other hand, there's a lot I don't miss. I don't miss cooking or housework or ... or helping Lydia with that play group. God, I was sick of that! It's only now that I realize how sick of it I really was."

"You've stopped doing the play group?"

"Yes, I called Lydia and told her I have other things to do now."

"She must have been disappointed." When Sophie shrugged, Marion insisted, "But you loved that play group!"

"I did once. But there's a time for everything, and my days as an exemplary suburban housewife have drawn to a close." Sophie sipped her tea, surprised by the bitterness of her remark.

"Now, that's just bravado—or rather it's just you being brave." Marion allowed a little silence to fall before her next question. "Do you hear from Adam?"

"He calls when he can't find things around the house. Yesterday it was the boys' vaccination certificates. One thing I hated about marriage—and I really did hate it, this isn't sour grapes—was his asking me where things were all the time. Now he's walked out on me, and he still expects me to find things!"

"It's just an excuse to talk to you."

"I don't think so. I think he has a lot of nerve. I told him not to call anymore. Milagros can pass on any messages. Or he can e-mail or text me. I don't want to hear his voice anymore. It's too upsetting."

"That's only natural. But what I hope for you both—Adam, too—is that this crisis will serve as a springboard to a healthier relationship. I'm sure, Sophie, that if you meet this challenge head-on, you'll come through it more united than ever."

Sophie eyed her friend. "Oh, yes? You feel it in your bones, do you? No, Marion, listen to me. Nobody, not me and certainly not you, can possibly know what's going to happen. So do me a favor and take that crystal ball of yours and..."

Marion looked so offended that Sophie laughed.

"And put it away safely! Now let's forget it. Do you feel like going to the movies tonight? There's a new French one at Kendall Square. Agnès Jaoui."

"I can't. It's my night out with Gerald. The first Thursday of every month is our standing date. With crazy schedules like ours, we have to make a date if we want to see each other!" She laughed, then grew earnest. "We needed the time together, so we worked on making it." Sophie nodded; she knew all about the work Marion and Gerald did on their relationship. It was Marion's belief that relationships required continual hard work, and this had always puzzled Sophie, for it seemed to her that if it took so much effort, surely that was a sign of fundamental incompatibility. But with Marion there was the sense that to simply get along well with someone like-minded was morally inferior to "working at it" with a less suitable person. Marion's relationships with her parents and siblings were also the uneasy result of years of diligent work; in fact, no relationship came easily to her, which was probably why she had chosen counseling as her profession. "I'm sorry I can't go to the movies with you," Marion said. "It would have been good for you to get out."

"Oh, I'll go. I have to get back in the habit of going out alone, and the movies are a good place to begin. It's dark, so no one notices you're alone, and you can't talk anyway, so...Or wait, in the Phoenix I saw a painting exhibition I could go to. That would be more daring—or do I need to work up to that? You know, I used to like going out alone. At first going out with Adam seemed like being in a bubble. We brought our own world with us wherever we went. When you're alone, the world can encroach, and that can be scary, but it can be good."

Marion laughed. "Maybe. But I don't think you'll find many women who wouldn't prefer to be escorted by an attentive man, given the choice." As she stood to leave, her eye fell on a basket of toys. "Oh, that's nice," she said, pointing. "Makes them feel more at home here."

"They *are* at home here," Sophie said firmly, and as she closed the door, she reflected that in the old days she would never have told Marion to put away her crystal ball. It was quite freeing, speaking her mind, and new to her, for she had been raised to believe that hurting other people's feelings must be avoided at any cost. Of course, Marion had never seemed quite so domineering before, but maybe that was unfair. Marion was a good person, no doubt about that— a member of Greenpeace and Amnesty International, for heaven's sake. They had met at a neighborhood meeting of mothers interested in forming a play group, and although Sophie hadn't intended to participate in running it, Marion, as its organizer (*You don't need to have one, only to have been one*), had teamed her up with Lydia and somehow talked her into it. So instead of a rest, Sophie had gotten even more work, but it had been fun, too, in its way. In the days when she was a weary, sometimes uncertain mother of two babies, Marion's energy and confidence had been reassuring. It was only now that unflattering terms like "steamroller" flitted through her mind, but she told herself that was ungrateful. Marion's determination to patch up Sophie's marriage sprang from wholesome professional zeal and not from...well, envy of Sophie's newfound freedom was how it sometimes felt, but that was ridiculous, of course. After all, Sophie was only free because she had been discarded.

"Discarded" was one of the words that came to her at night when she lay in bed, unable to move.

But that was not a line of thought to pursue. As she did many times each day, by an act of will requiring an actual physical effort, Sophie redirected her thoughts onto pleasanter lines. It was nearly two-thirty, the magical hour, the one safe anchor point in her day, time to see the children. She yanked her jacket off a hook and ran down the stairs, remembering that she had promised to take them to the aquarium to see the seals. And that night she had a stack of reading to do for class, so there would be little time for moping, which meant she could probably make it through another day, running just ahead of the rising waters. She knew she couldn't hold off her feelings forever and that sometime soon her emotional floodgates would open and all the misery and fury she had suppressed since the morning she found the photographs would come sweeping over her. She recognized the inevitability of the deluge that must one day engulf her, but she dreaded its violence and re-assured herself with the thought that as long as nothing happened *today*—and she was learning to think in terms of the present—she would be all right.

Adam was kneeling on the floor of his study, unpacking his books and returning them to their shelves in order both alpha-betical and according to subject, dusting as he went with the aid of a soft rag he had finally found in a plastic bag under the sink (God forbid that he should call Sophie and ask her a simple question like where she kept the rags!), wiping first the empty shelves and then each book as he put it away, all shockingly filthy—what did they pay Milagros for? It was a disheartening—and yes, humiliating—task that he had put off doing for as long as he still clung to the dwindling hope that Sophie would return. Well, at least the boys were asleep, that much he could be thankful for; they wouldn't be interrupting him with a thousand questions or running off with his books or, worse yet, "helping." He had learned that any task involving the organization of a large number of small objects could not be performed in the presence of his children. Wiping his rag over a study of Greek temples, Adam thought ruefully of how this dreary unpacking compared to the carefree way he had flung these books into these same boxes only—what was it?—nine, ten, eleven days ago. Could that be right? Had his life changed so utterly in only eleven days?

Other men left their families. Other men packed their bags and walked away. How was it that he, Adam Dean, found himself, eleven days after his supposed departure in his one great bid for freedom and happiness, a prisoner in suburbia, shackled to his children, on his knees, *dusting with a soft cloth*?

And now Sophie had moved into an apartment of some kind. He couldn't gather much from the boys' garbled account except that they were enthusiastic about it. Fine. They would be spending the weekend there, which would give him a chance to catch up on some of the work that had been piling up since Sophie left and he could no longer work late at the office, because he had to be home with the boys. A nice, quiet weekend at home—oh, the bliss of having the boys gone; he could almost whimper with gratitude. But there was Valerie, of course. She might not think much of his working all weekend when they had hardly seen each other since Sophie left—so annoying, how "since Sophie left" had become his time reference for everything! They had managed lunch a few times, not particularly successfully. She was so...*wrathful* about Sophie's departure. It was fatiguing. It was all very fatiguing. Feisty Valerie, his battle maiden. Interesting how the qualities that first attracted one in a lover could be the very ones that...Well, he loved her. That was the point. He loved her, and he had succeeded in making her the woman of his life, so he could take heart. The fact that he would be living in this house a bit longer than he had expected was neither here nor there. To persevere calmly—that was the key now.

It was Sophie's reaction that he couldn't get over. So extreme! And in retrospect he couldn't help finding something suspicious about the alacrity—there was no other word, "eagerness" possibly overstating the case—with which she had left. It was insulting. Almost as if she were jumping at any excuse to go. Taking advantage of him. Using him.

Adam rose to his feet, dusted his hands off, and surveyed his work grimly. Then he stacked the empty boxes into a cut pile and carried them out on his way to hunt for the vacuum cleaner.

That evening Sophie did the brave thing and opted for the painting exhibition, forgoing the dark safety of the movie theater. But she found that a painting exhibition is in fact another good place to go when you're alone and feeling shy, as the people there don't notice each other, not because they're engrossed in the paintings, which are beside the point, but because they're all too busy showing off. Sophie weaved her way through the gallery, plastic cup of tepid white wine in hand, studying the crowd with interest. There were the usual beards, black clothes, and swinging earrings, but most inter-esting were the identical expressions on every face, of hunted self-importance, as though in dread of being spotted and hounded by the paparazzi. Each imagined that all eyes in the room were upon him, and since none of them looked at one another, pretending to be too busy or too deep in thought, no one was ever disabused of this. In such a self-conscious crowd, it was impossible to tell who the true star of the evening was, the painter himself. But that was nice, So-phie decided; that way the glory was shared out—thanks to their egotism and determined mutual disregard, they could all be stars for a night. As for the paintings . . . well, they were the usual huge gray canvases with black and brown slashes and the odd splotch of red.

Agatha had guessed that no friend of Howard's wife could paint his way out of a paper bag, but still the unrelieved banality of the work rankled, although not half so much as the fact that Valerie had backed out of coming at the last minute, claiming she had too much work. "Somebody's ass is going to get canned, and it's not going to be mine," she had said, the traitor. So Agatha was left facing the possibility of encountering her ex-lover and his wife by herself, and it was exhausting, simultaneously scanning the crowd (without appearing to) for the once beloved now dreaded shape of Howard, while taking care to look animated and carefree, in case he spotted her first, and getting enough wine down her throat to bolster herself against this eventuality. After a nerve-racking hour of this, it became evident that he wasn't going to come after all, but by that time it was too late to relax, or to stay sober, and Agatha, ensconced by the drinks table in desultory conversation with a hawk-eyed gallery owner, re-flected sourly that even after all this time Howard was still managing to ruin her life. Not in big ways anymore, to be sure, but in little ways.

"Oh, sorry!" Sophie turned to apologize to the woman she had just bumped into and saw that she was a sort of Cleopatra look-alike, with jet-black hair that fell to her jaw and a severe wall of bangs cut high over her arching, plucked eyebrows, wearing heavy cat's-eye makeup and a dress made of shiny bits of mosaic, like armor. On further consideration, what she looked like was not so much an ancient Egyptian as an extra in a sixties movie about ancient Egypt.

"Don't worry about it," Agatha said, and then, seeing that the blond woman was about to refill her glass with warm chardonnay, she added, "Psst! Don't drink that weasel pee! Over here!" From beneath the table, she lifted out a bottle of chilled champagne and filled both their glasses.

"A secret supply," Sophie said. "Thank you."

"You go to enough of these things, you learn the tricks. Cheers." Agatha knocked her glass right back, and after a moment's hesitation Sophie did the same. Agatha laughed and refilled their glasses.

Behind them a pompous voice began to hold forth. "It is my opinion," it said, loudly enough for others to hear, "that he was uniquely his own man."

Agatha raised her eyebrows gleefully at Sophie, who smiled back.

"I can't agree," countered another voice. "But I do think that he lived very much in his own time—perhaps more so than any other artist *of* his time. Or ours, for that matter." The men nodded gravely and lifted their drinks to pursed lips, while the two women subsided into giggles, Agatha supporting herself for a moment on Sophie's arm. It was then that she spotted Howard and his wife weaving toward her through the crowd, his bald head glinting, her red lips parted in the toothy silent scream that was her party smile. Agatha ducked behind Sophie. "Oh, my God, hide me! Be my human shield!"

"Who is it?"

"My ex-lover and his wife!"

"Does she know about you?"

"Yes!"

"Will she claw your eyes out?"

"Worse! She'll condescend!" Sophie turned toward the crowd and positioned herself in a wide stance with one hand on her hip, allowing Agatha maximum room to crouch behind her and pivot her slowly for protection as the couple passed. When they had gone Agatha straightened up and blew out a sigh. "She's still dining out on how understanding she was about our affair. She'd give her eyeteeth for another chance to be nice to me, the bloodthirsty bitch."

Sophie laughed. "Don't tell me 'the crisis served as a springboard to a healthier relationship'?"

"I'm afraid it did," Agatha said bitterly. Then, "You're a real pal. Thanks." And she gulped thirstily from her glass.

Sophie studied this rattled, champagne-guzzling, B-movie Cleopatra of an ex–other woman and smiled at the irony of finding herself a collaborator in the enemy camp. "It was a pleasure," she said, lifting her glass in farewell, and as she drifted away, she found to her surprise that she meant it.

The hawk-eyed gallery owner touched Agatha's arm and lifted his chin toward Sophie's departing back. "Who's the Romy Schneider look-alike?"

Agatha watched the blond ponytail retreat into the crowd and shrugged. "No idea."

The next morning in shiatsu class, Malcolm paired Sophie with a lithe, dark man named Henry for practice on the Heart channel (a Fire channel, yin), and she went first, placing her "mother hand" comfortingly on his chest while her "child hand" worked down the channel—one hand stable, one hand moving, starting in the axilla, going along the underside of the arm, across the elbow, down the inner forearm to the edge of the hand, and ending at the nail of the little finger. She concentrated on finding the correct heart points and using her weight to lean into her thumb instead of just pushing with it. At the point on his wrist called "Mind Door," he murmured appreciatively, and when it was his turn to work on her, she also noticed how good pressure felt there. His hands were strong, and after he had finished, she lay for a moment enjoying the tingling feeling along her arms. When she opened her eyes, he was smiling down at her, his teeth looking very white in his dark, lively face. He suggested they have lunch together.

"Did you not come to class the first days?" Sophie asked him as they scooted their chairs up to a wobbly table at a vegetarian place around the corner. "I didn't see you."

"I was there," he said. "And I saw you."

"It's funny I don't remember."

"No, not really. I do it on purpose. I don't like to bowl people over with my charm. I prefer it to sort of sneak up on them."

They ordered salads, and he ate hungrily, chatting about his upbringing (in France mainly, by his American mother and in the absence of his Pakistani father, who had returned to an arranged marriage in Pakistan shortly after Henry's birth) and his travels (through Asia and Malaysia), pausing in his story only to swap the vase of flowers on their table for another that he liked better. When he had finished eating, he pushed his plate away and said, "Ah, that was good. I feel good now."

"I'm glad." Sophie moved her fork around her own plate without much interest.

"Eat your olives, they're good for the skin." He mimed patting under his chin to firm it up.

Obediently, she speared an olive, and as she was eating it, he startled her by throwing his arms open wide and saying, "I feel so good! Don't you? Don't you feel good?"

"Ah...probably not as good as you."

"I'm sorry. Is something wrong with your food?"

"No, my salad is—" Abruptly, she stopped talking. Staring into her variegated lettuce, she found she could not utter another word. Her throat had closed. Her heart was thumping. And something was coming.... Something was looming up before her.... Something was drawing nearer.

"What's wrong? An olive pit?"

"No," she whispered, with what felt like her last breath of air ever.

"Can I get you something?" He leaned closer, his forehead creased in concern. "Water?"

Sophie waved her hand no, meaning, *No sympathy! Don't show me any sympathy!*—because she knew that it would bring the huge thing closer. But she couldn't get the words out. She squeezed her eyes shut.

He studied her pale face and closed his hand lightly over hers. "Is there someone you'd like me to call? Your husband?"

With that the floodgates gave way. Sophie opened her eyes and stared blankly at the approaching tsunami. In a flat voice, she said, "I don't have a husband. He left me a few days ago for another woman." With a detached part of her mind, she realized she had never said those words out loud before. "My husband is gone." And then it smacked into her, that great wall of black water, and knocked her, churning, to the very bottom of the sea, swirling down into the grit.

Of all the places, she wondered between sobs, *why here? Why now?* She fumbled in her bag, too blinded by tears to find a tissue. "I'll do that," Henry said, and she felt him take the bag from her and then press a tissue into her hand. She cried hard, like Matthew when he fell down the stairs. People must be staring, she knew, but there was nothing she could do about that. She jammed the soggy tissue against her face with both hands and sobbed, rocking back and forth rhythmically. After a time her rocking slowed, and finally it stopped. She opened her bleary eyes and saw Henry watching her with kindness, smiling a little, apparently completely at ease. "You cry with your whole body," he said. "I would like to do that. Next time I'll remember to cry like you."

She smiled in a watery way and whispered, "Thank you." She cleared her throat, blew her nose, drew a shuddering breath, wiped her eyes, and looked away for a while, out the window, until her vision cleared and she felt, although still fragile, very calm. Then she said, "My stomach hurts. Like I've been kicked." And she laughed weakly. "Ow!"

"You have been kicked," he said, "and shit upon. Your husband has kicked you and shit upon you." Startled, she lifted a hand to protest, but he carried on. "He's done everything in his power to make you feel bad, and so you do. But you won't feel bad forever. Something will happen to give you the *switch*." He snapped his fingers as he said it. "You know? The *switch*?" Snapping his fingers again. "And then you'll be fine."

Sophie looked for solace in his words, but she was perplexed, feeling she ought to thank him, or apologize—but for what in either case? "The…switch?" she managed to ask, but she wasn't up to snapping her fingers. She would cry again soon, she knew.

"The switch." He snapped again; it seemed to be obligatory. "The switch can be anything. It clicks your mind into a new groove, it jumps you onto another track. Look, I'm going to give you the switch right now. Not the big switch, just a little switch. Come on, come with me." He stood up and gave her his hand. She stood, too, on shaky legs.

"Where are we going?"

"Swimming."

"Oh, no…"

"It's the perfect place to cry. Think of it. You can fill the pool with tears, and the more you cry, the saltier the water becomes. The saltier the water is, the better you float, so in the end your own sadness buoys you up. Come on. We're going swimming."

"I really can't. I have to pick up my children from school at two-thirty. They spend every afternoon with me. But…I…" She started to say she would like to do it another time, but she wasn't sure that was true, and anyway she was crying again and couldn't speak.

"Cry," he said. "You go ahead and cry." And he led her out of the restaurant, still holding her hand.

———

It was only after she was able to cry that Sophie could bring herself to remember the early years with Adam, and with the merciless acuity of hindsight even those happy memories now seemed tainted with a foreshadowing of doom. Adam Dean, the handsome graduate student from England studying architecture at Harvard, met by Sophie Szabo, just finishing her master's in English literature, at that long-ago party in Cambridge...Both reserved, both tentative, they had embarked on a courtship characterized by its silences—silences that at the time Sophie had taken as proof of their profound compatibility but that now, knowing what she knew, seemed a sinister portent. He was enchanted by her simplicity and kindness, finding in her the antithesis of his sarcastic, gin-drinking mother. He saw something prototypically American in Sophie, a sort of prairie woman: wise, capable, and strong, with great purity of spirit. She found his reticence restful and intriguing. He had declared his love in a way that charmed her: by giving her a present of a fine old volume of John Donne's poetry with a white silk bookmark placed at the poem "Lovers Infinitenesse." (He had been worried at the time about the presence on the periphery of Sophie's life of another suitor: a man devoted to her, but from whom he had nothing to fear, had he but known it, this man being that type of genuinely wonderful person, beloved by all, whom no one wants to marry.) Sophie could still recite the poem from memory. It ended:

> *Love's riddles are, that though thy heart depart,*
> *It stayes at home, and thou with losing savest it:*
> *But wee will have a way more liberall,*
> *Than changing hearts, to joyne them, so wee shall*
> *Be one, and one another's All.*

...One, and one another's all.

At first glance Agatha and Valerie appeared to be hovering in midair, two gravity-defying splashes of color suspended against a backdrop of dazzling white. But in fact they were sitting in Agatha's white front room on her white sofa near a window covered by a white rice-paper shade and surrounded by—nothing.

"I can't let you do it," Agatha was saying. "Not this. Uh-uh."

"I'm not asking for your permission." Valerie lit a cigarette and looked around, squinting against the glare, for some-where, anywhere, to set her cigarettes and lighter: a table, a chair, a . . . a goddamned surface of some kind! But no. Testily, she tossed it all on the floor.

Agatha watched her friend's lighter skid to a halt, then continued. "You, stuck out in Milton? How long do you think you'd last out there? One day tops, and then you'd be biting off the wallpaper—which would be beige and tex-tured, by the way. They call it 'oatmeal.'"

"I'm not going to let that woman outmaneuver me."

"Unless you're trying to get back to your suburban roots—is that it? Missing good old Burlington? Ask yourself some tough questions, Valerie. Are you really strong enough to live with Laura Ashley curtains? Come on, let's do a little creative visualization together. You come home after a hard day's work and have to pick your way over cheap toys scattered on the carpet—the washable nylon kind of carpet, Valerie. Slightly sticky?"

"If Adam won't fight her, I will!"

"In the kitchen you find, about halfway up the wall, one of those decorative bands of tiles featuring a row of teakettles alternated with pepper mills, like this: teakettle, pepper mill, teakettle, pepper mill, teakettle, pep— Are you seeing this with me?"

"She's banking on keeping Adam and me apart. It's like you said, her whole plan hinges on him struggling with the kids in that house alone, until finally he gives up and asks her to come back—which is why I'm not going to play along!"

"Potpourri," Agatha mused. "I bet you'll find wooden bowls of potpourri everywhere, with perky ribbons tied around them. That's my bet. Dishes of seashells in the bathroom. Decorative pinecones?" A look of alarm crossed her face. "*Ducks?*"

"Once she finds out I'm cozily installed with Adam in her suburban dream home, sharing the housework and helping him raise her golden-haired babes, she'll come tearing back, screaming like a hellcat, to reclaim her house and kids. It'll work. I know it will."

"And the kids! Oh, Valerie, the kids! I'd forgotten the kids. This is suicidal! My God, Valerie, listen to me— *suburban life will crush you like a turd under the wheel of an oxcart.*"

Valerie had been cupping her hand under her lengthening cigarette ash for some time, craning around in vain for an ashtray. "This minimalist shit has got to go! I bet you have a secret room somewhere, exploding with junk. What do I do with the ash—eat it?" She tried to flick the ash toward the window and nearly made it. Cursing, she jammed the cigarette into her mouth so she could brush her dress off with both hands, and the smoke curled into her eyes, stinging them. With a cry of irritation, she jumped up and fumbled behind the white shade until she managed to yank the window open and hurl the butt outside. Then she slammed the window closed, muttering, "...going fucking snow-blind!"

Agatha watched it all dispassionately. "Put it on record," she said, "that I don't think you'll last a week out there. You'll be stabbing your veins with the fondue forks."

"Agatha, do you know how often Adam and I have had sex since she left? We hardly ever see each other, and when we do, we fight. Our relationship is falling apart. Her goddamned plan is working! This is not idle theorizing I'm engaging in here, this is fact. Listen to me—I am losing Adam! We have to act quickly!"

Agatha looked at her friend's tense white face and shook her head sadly. "That bitch," she moaned, "oh, that bitch. To think she has brought you so low."

Valerie waited.

And sure enough, Agatha straightened up, all briskness and efficiency. "Okay! If this is the sorry state things have come to, so be it. Now!" She rubbed her hands together. "A thing worth doing is worth doing well. First off, we need to hire a damned good nanny. Someone's got to keep those kids away from you, even if it's only for the day or two it takes for the wife to come running back. Plus, it'll show Adam you mean business."

"So you think it'll work? If I move in, she'll come back?"

"Of course. What woman wouldn't be driven mad by her usurper occupying her very bed? The question is, will you survive out there till then? That's why we need the nanny. Hang on." Agatha left and came back with her laptop, smirking. "What should we look under—animal trainers?"

Valerie gave her a long, appraising look, and when she spoke, it was calmly. "I wonder, Agatha, if you'll ever reach the level of maturity necessary to keep you from trying to score cheap laughs off my personal problems. I'm running the risk of losing the man I love, and that's a serious matter for me."

"Oh, Christ, Valerie. I know it is—"

"Then please grow up."

"And I'm helping you, aren't I? Jesus, I'm always helping you! All we ever talk about is you."

"Agatha, I know that your own private life doesn't have much content and that you use frivolity to mask its emptiness, but it's inappropriate in a case like mine. That's all I'm saying."

"What do you know about my life? For all you know, I could be involved in a passionate romance at this very moment. How would you ever find out? You never even ask me how I am! It's just installment after installment of The Valerie Show, which I'm sorry to say is *not* a serious drama but just a farce in need of a few jokes to make it palatable."

Silence followed as Agatha frowned at her computer screen and Valerie looked stonily out the window, or rather *at* the window, as it was completely blocked by the white shade. Sparring was intrinsic to their friendship; it invigorated them, and playing off each other for laughs was a trick they had learned in high school. But there was no audience now, and their irritation, while real, was only mild. Neither wanted hostilities to spiral. The question was how to back down without loss of face.

In the end Valerie made the peace, which was only fair, as she had started the argument. "Let's look under lion tamers," she said.

Agatha smiled. "Okay." It was strangely fun lying on the carpet together compiling a list of nannies. It was an engrossing task, and an unusual one for two childless women, which added a sense of novelty to their mission. "Hey, we haven't had so much fun together since the junior prom, have we, Vee?" Agatha chuckled, remembering, and Valerie hummed agreement in a distracted way.

The junior prom had marked their entrance into high-school society, their transition from dowdy nobodies to notorious rebels, admired by a few and hated by many, but hatred was okay; as attention-seeking teenagers, it was indifference they couldn't bear. Agatha had been sunk in despair at not being asked to the prom, not asked by anyone, knowing of course that it didn't really matter but feeling painfully humiliated all the same, because the whole problem with high school is that even though you know it doesn't matter, it does. She had moped, ranted, and even cried until Valerie took the situation in hand. It wasn't hard. She bought a tuxedo from the Salvation Army, forced her mother to do some proper alterations for once on that old sewing machine of hers, got her hair cut like James Dean, put on a pair of sunglasses, and took Agatha to the prom as her date, "Angelo." They stole the show, dancing a nearly pornographic tango together (exhaustively rehearsed beforehand in Agatha's bedroom) until Angelo's identity was discovered, exciting much homophobic indignation and culminating in the unprecedented honor of being asked to leave the prom. Their reputations were made. The prank was seen as free-spirited by some, as depraved by others, but at any rate "Val 'n' Ag" never again had to suffer the ignominy of anonymity. From that first achievement, it had been just a short step to the fake IDs that got them into the Rat in Kenmore Square on Saturday nights to see Lou Miami and the Kozmetix—the very pinnacle of the high life. For all this, Agatha had been profoundly grateful to Valerie. And still was.

"Remember Lou Miami, Vee? I love Boston. Why is it that we Bostonians always feel we have to justify ourselves for not living in New York? Did you know that in New York City for every unmarried man there are something like twelve point three unmarried women? Think of it—what if you ended up being the 'point three'? I'm glad I stayed right here. And I know why *you* never moved."

"Because I'm such a zealous Red Sox fan?" Valerie asked, intent on her task, eyes on the screen. "Here's one. Ready to take this number?"

"You never moved to New York because you prefer to be a big fish in a small pond, that's why."

"Her name is Miss Amelia Eldridge," Valerie said. "Sounds too good to be true."

"It could be a nom de guerre," Agatha said, reaching for her phone. "Let's find out."

Sophie lay low for the next few days, ailing in spirit. She pared down what she must do to the bare essentials: attend class and play with her children. The rest of the time she stayed in bed with a pot of herbal tea and a stack of novels. What she did mostly was cry—cry as she had never done before. Even with her mind on a book, her eyes would fill with tears until the print got blurry and she had to blink to clear her vision until her eyes filled up again. There was no resisting it; she let the tears fall and imagined them washing away her sadness and anger. This weeping was healthy and cleansing, she told herself. She was undergoing a water cure of sorts, her body acting as a spa.

Henry took her swimming, as he had promised, in a pool

at a gym near their school. At first she was reluctant to go, envisioning the usual dank and chlorine-reeking indoor pool, but it turned out to be warm and bright, with one wall made all of glass—a tall poplar visible through it—and a vaulted translucent ceiling, and she found swimming so soothing that she didn't need to top up the pool with salty tears for extra buoyancy. She swam slowly, concentrating on the rhythmic movements of her arms and legs and the silky feeling of gliding through the water. When she got tired, she dawdled on the ropes idly, gazing at the sun sparkling on the water, thinking of nothing.

At home she avoided the telephone, opened no letters or e-mails, and went to bed as soon as Milagros had picked up the children at six. There she cried some more, reminding herself that this was her weeping cure and that teardrop by teardrop she was washing her spirit clean of the poison Adam had poured into it.

Messages stacked up on the answering machine. The light blinked continually, menacing her fragile calm until one afternoon, tired at last of being bullied, she decided to listen to them all with her finger poised on the "erase" button, ready to eliminate anything upsetting.

"*Sophie, it's Marion. How are you, hon? I—*" That caring, professional voice...Erase.

A hang-up. Adam? Erase.

"*Sophie, what in heaven's name is—*" Her mother's voice, taut with anxiety. Or annoyance. Erase.

"*Hellooo, Patricia here. Look, darling, I've just spoken to Adam, and—*" The low, throaty English drawl of Adam's mother. Let him deal with her, now and forever. Erase.

Another hang-up. Adam again? Calling to beg her forgiveness? Or because he couldn't find the toilet brush.

"Sophie, it's Lydia! My God, I've just—" Erase.

There seemed no end to these messages from friends and neighbors, sounding concerned or reproachful, or simply curious.

"Sophie?"

"Sophie!"

"Soph—"

Each time she heard her name, she punched the "erase" button. The only person she needed to respond to was her mother, who must have called Adam's house and heard God-knows-what from him. But talking to her mother required adopting an upbeat, reassuring tone that she wouldn't be able to sustain. Luckily, it was Wednesday, so her mother would be busy all day with her volunteer work, and Sophie felt she could just muster the energy to leave a short message. She dialed, composing herself for the emotional lie, and when the answering machine beeped, her eyebrows leaped up and her eyes widened as she spoke in tones of practiced cheerfulness. "Hello! It's Sophie calling to say that the children and I are just fine, so please don't worry about us. I'll call you in a few days. In the meantime take good care of yourselves! Love to you both! Bye!" Her face sagged as she lowered the receiver, duty done. She stood for a moment looking with distaste at the phone, the one vulnerable point in her fortress. On the bottom of it was a switch for silencing the ringer, so she did that, but she still didn't feel safe. Reaching down, she unplugged the phone from the wall, then lifted the receiver experimentally and smiled when she heard nothing. There. Then she switched off her cell phone. Now no one at all could reach her for any reason whatsoever, which was just fine. After all, what was the worst that could happen? One of the children could have a fatal accident and call in vain for her with his dying breath? She plugged the phone back in, turned the ringer up loud, went into her bedroom, and wept.

By Friday morning, after five and a half days of the weeping cure, she was feeling as she often did after a fever: light-headed and weak, but beautifully calm. The children were coming for the weekend. *It will be all right*, she told herself. *I'll move slowly and gently, and it will be all right.* Now then, what to do. Food. Must buy food for the children. When she was ready to go out, she stood uncertainly at the door, hands pressed flat against her jacket pockets as she stopped to think if she had everything, feeling she must be leaving something important behind. But no. Her money, keys, and phone were all she needed, and they fit in her pockets. No need for a bag. How odd it was, being able to walk out of the house so easily. A single woman again. She locked the door behind her and went bravely down the stairs.

Courage was what Valerie prayed for aloud the next morning when Adam pulled up in front of his house and she got her first look at her new suburban love nest. She gazed at it with comic dismay while Adam got her bag out of the trunk. "It's awfully good of you to do this," he said, leading her up the path. He pointed down at the flagstones. "I hope you're admiring the crazy paving," he added jauntily, trying to show he was on her side.

"The what?" she asked, frowning down at the path.

"Crazy paving...you know...irregular flagstones laid in that random pattern. The emblem of suburbia, I should have thought. What do you call it here?"

"I wouldn't know."

He fumbled with the keys before managing to get the front door open.

"If you ever needed proof of my love, this is it," Valerie said with a rueful laugh as she stepped over the threshold. Well...no potpourri immediately in evidence anyway, and no perky ribbons. It was a little better than Agatha had predicted (no "oatmeal"), but not a lot: banana-yellow walls with the bottom three feet scuffed and scribbled on. "Can you assure me again this is only temporary?"

"Of course. Of course." He followed her eyes to the defaced walls and laughed awkwardly. "I know it isn't what we had in mind, darling, but we'll be all right here for a few months. Come in and look around. The boys are with Sophie this weekend. I thought it would be best if you settled in while they were away. I've told them, of course, that you were coming to live with us, so it wouldn't come as a shock."

"Oh, yeah? The wicked stepmother, eh? Did they scream blue murder?"

"Not at all. They didn't even seem particularly interested. I'm not sure how much all this means at their age. Go on, take a look around and get acquainted with the house...such as it is." Time had inured him somewhat to the place, but he dreaded to think how it must look through her eyes.

Gingerly, Valerie strolled from room to room. Well, there were no ducks, and no tiles in the kitchen with teakettles on them. Oh. But there was a dish of seashells in the bathroom—good old Agatha. At least it was tidy; the toys were in baskets. No sticky nylon carpets. Still, it was a little like living in a nursery school. "I can't understand the phenomenon of the suburbs at all. Why does anybody choose to live out here?"

Adam cleared his throat. "There are certain advantages for children."

"Oh, God, of course, I forgot. 'Nice, quiet streets where kids can ride their bikes.'" She made a mocking face and laughed.

"Yes. That's it."

There was a short silence. Then she said, "It's only now, darling, seeing this, that I can really appreciate how unhappy you've been. It breaks my heart to think of you here." She took him in her arms.

"And now you've come to share my martyrdom." He smiled. "Only one bag? You travel light."

She smiled back. "Always. I can bring things from home as I need them." She didn't tell him that if everything went according to plan, they would both be living in her apartment before the week was out. She hadn't bothered to share all the aspects of her plan with him—for example, that she fully expected, by moving in, to drive Sophie back home. She'd just said it was the only way they could spend any time together during this interim while Sophie got settled, presenting it as a sacrifice she was willing to make, and he had been suitably grateful. "How did Sophie take the news of my moving in?" she asked, as casually as she could, running her finger along a kitchen cabinet. Simulated knotty pine; Agatha must be told.

Adam frowned. This was a gray area on his conscience. It would have been better, he couldn't help but feel, to have let Sophie know beforehand, but it had all happened so damned quickly. Valerie had only suggested the idea the day before, and she'd been so keen, and it was so good of her, and so convenient for him in so many ways.... Perhaps the boys would break the news to her. Yes, that might be quite the best way, come to think of it. He cleared his throat again before saying, "I haven't actually spoken to her."

"Oh, Adam!"

"She doesn't like me to call, prefers me to write, and there just hasn't been the time. I'm awfully busy in the evenings, you know. Milagros is showing me the ropes with the boys, and it's quite a to-do. There's the bath, and they get soap in their eyes and shout, 'Eye! Eye!'" He sighed, remembering. "Then there's reading, then glasses of water and whatnot."

"Call her right now. To hell with writing—she's just being obstructive. You owe it to her, Adam. This is something she has a right to know."

"Is it? I don't think she cares what goes on here."

That would be very bad news indeed, if true, but Valerie recognized it as the type of thing a man feeling guilty or self-pitying chooses to think. "Of course she cares! It's her house, her furniture, her...her curtains...her..." There was something else that was hers, but what? Oh, yes. "Her children!"

"What does it matter what she thinks, anyway?" Adam said, his guilty feelings giving way suddenly to self-righteousness. "She left without so much as a backward glance, obliging me to stay here, so now it's only fair that I should live with whomever I choose!" He felt better for having reasoned that out, and it was a line he could take with Sophie, should the need arise. He smiled at Valerie. "She can't throw you out, darling. Is that what you're worried about?"

Valerie didn't smile back. "No, it's just that...I won't feel comfortable living here if it's...underhanded. I want everything to be aboveboard. It's only fair, to her and to me."

He put his arms around her. "That's very good of you. I'll tell you what, I'll e-mail her this evening. Will that do?"

Valerie nodded, then followed him up the stairs, where he opened the door to the spare room, saying, "I thought we could sleep here."

She leaned in and looked around. "Hmm. It's got all the charm of a roadside motel. Isn't there a better room somewhere?" And she went down the hall opening doors—the boys' room, the bathroom—until she came to the master bedroom. "Ah, here we are!" She wandered around appraisingly, parted the curtains and peered out, fingered the objects on the dresser—all his now—and slid open a closet door. Women's clothes still hung there. She sat on the bed with a bounce, testing the springs. "Yes, this will do." Adam was still standing in the doorway, his head bowed. "What's wrong?" she asked.

"Not here," he said.

"Why not here? Why shouldn't we have the best room?" Then, more softly, she said, "Come here," and lay back and held out her arms to him. "I'm not going to live in a haunted house, Adam. We have ghosts to dispel. I'm your woman now. Come here and make love to me."

Excitement overcame his reluctance, and in the course of their lovemaking it struck him fleetingly how strange it was to see short, dark hair splayed out on Sophie's pillow, and afterward, as they sat in the kitchen, Valerie wearing one of his shirts as a robe, belted with one of his ties, he marveled again at how exotic and thrillingly out of place she looked, lounging there with one bare knee resting on the edge of Sophie's well-scrubbed pine table. But...

"Valerie, I don't want us to use that room again. It isn't a question of ghosts, it's me. I want to make a new start, with you, in a room all our own. It's the least we deserve."

She shrugged, then sipped her coffee and grimaced. "Remind me to bring over my espresso maker."

"We have all weekend to ourselves," he said. "I thought I might catch up on a little work. If that's all right."

"Fine. I have to work, too. Hey, it's sort of fun playing house, isn't it? Even here. Oh, by the way, I have a surprise for you." She lowered her knee from the table and leaned forward excitedly. "I've managed to get hold of this fantastic English nanny, and she has agreed to live in. It wasn't easy finding someone at such short notice, let me tell you. And get this—her name is Amelia Eldridge. Honest to God. Isn't that great? It'll bring back your childhood."

"Oh, no, Valerie, that was kind of you, but no. Milagros will do for the time being."

"But this is a fully qualified professional from a top agency. Isn't Milagros just a cleaning lady?"

"The children love her. She's very kind, very dear to us."

"But we need someone for nights and weekends."

"She can baby-sit sometimes, and Sophie has them every other weekend. No, it's out of the question. The whole point of our arrangement—mine with Sophie, I mean—was to upset their routine as little as possible. A nanny would be a disruption. Adjusting to you will be enough for now. Believe me, we'll be all right. Perhaps in the future…"

In the future, Valerie thought, they wouldn't be seeing enough of Adam's children to warrant a nanny, but aloud she said, "Then what about having this Milagros person live in?" God, what a name.

He shook his head. "She has a family of her own. We'll be fine. Truly."

"Adam, I want to make one thing clear to you. I do not intend to wipe a single nose while I'm here. That is not part of our deal. I've come to darkest suburbia to help you out, but I do not wipe children—not their noses, not their asses, not their chins. Like some cleaners don't do windows? Me, I don't wipe."

"You won't need to. They're my children, and I'm perfectly capable of looking after them."

They eyed each other frostily for a moment, and then she defused the situation by laughing. "You have no idea what you're letting yourself in for, believe me." Seeing that he wasn't mollified, she squeezed his hand. "But I guess Daddy knows best! Okay, you win, but I won't throw away Miss Eldridge's number. In fact, I'll keep it under my pillow, just in case we need to call in the middle of the night." He managed a smile, and she stood up and stretched. "Where's the phone? I'll order some Japanese food. Then we can get to work."

"Oh…I…" Adam coughed. "I'm afraid you'll find they won't deliver this far out."

Valerie covered her face with her hand and groaned, but then she laughed again. "Okay. Since we're playing house anyway, I'll just go and cook us something delicious. And you know, my love," she added, taking him in her arms, "I really am happy to be here with you. Don't let my tough-gal act fool you. You're the best thing that's happened to me."

So Adam got a foretaste of his new life after all. He spent the weekend alternating long stretches of fruitful work with spells of torrid lovemaking: the life of a sophisticated professional man—at last.

His e-mail to Sophie did not get written.

"Can we feed the fish? Can we?"

"Okay. Hang on a minute." Sophie followed the boys into

the kitchen, her arms full of the balls, bats, and skates they had brought to the park. She dumped the things down and picked up the container of fish food.

"Here we are. Now...we open it up...and..." She was kneeling on the floor about to deal out perfectly fair and equal portions of fish food when the phone rang. "Oh, no," she groaned.

"We can do it," Matthew said eagerly. "You go."

Somewhat mistrustfully, she handed over the food. "Remember, just a tiny pinch each, or the fish will get sick." Shrugging off her coat, she picked up the phone. "Hello?"

"Sophie, at last!" her mother said. "What on earth has been going on over there? I spoke to Adam, and he gave me this number. You haven't really moved out, have you?"

"Hello, Mother. Boys, it's Granny! The boys are spending the weekend with me, and we're feeding the fish just now. Careful now, boys, not too much! Would you like to speak to your grandma?"

They would not.

"Your father and I have been so worried, Sophie!"

"I'm sorry to hear that. You mustn't be. Everything's fine. I know I should have been in touch earlier, but there's been so much to do, and I wanted to get settled before I spoke to you. So you wouldn't worry."

"But you haven't left Adam, have you?"

"Yes. Or rather no. He's the one who...Listen, Mother, I'm sorry, but I can't talk right now. I'm busy with the boys, you understand?"

"I understand perfectly that you don't want to speak in front of them."

"That's it exactly. I'll call you back, all right? As soon—"

"So I'll do the talking, and you just listen. Now, my darling, whatever quarrel you two have had, just remember that communication is the key to married life...." Sophie sighed, turned her back to the boys, and listened, fiddling with the phone cord.

The boys were devoting all their attention to the delicate job of not overfeeding the fish. Each sprinkled in one pinch of food, but— "They still look hungry," Hugo said after watching them closely. He tried to shake in just a tiny bit more from the jar, but— "Uh-oh."

He turned alarmed eyes on his elder brother, but Matthew reassured him, "It can be their lunch *and* dinner." He stirred the water vigorously with his finger to try to get rid of the telltale covering of fish flakes on the surface, but they only swirled down and around, like the flakes in a snow globe. Cloudy and Fishtag darted this way and that, confused by such riches. Hugo stole a guilty glance at Sophie, who was off the phone now, frowning out the window and moving her lips. He eased off his chair, walked over, and took her hand.

"Why do you have those hairbrowns, Mommy?" he asked.

"What?" she said.

He glanced back at the fishbowl, where the excess food still clouded the water. "Let's go water the plants," he said, steering her toward the porch.

Matthew followed them out, and she used the hose to refill their watering cans as they made the rounds of the plants, looking important and spilling a little water with each step. Later they sat at the table eating sandwiches and drinking juice in contented silence. It had been a satisfying weekend, now drawing to a close.

"I like your house, Mommy," Hugo said eventually.

"I'm glad, honey. It's your house, too, you know."

"We have two houses," Matthew said patiently to Hugo.

"Mommy's and Daddy's." He looked at his mother for praise, and she smiled at him.

Hugo drank some juice, then: "Daddy's girlfriend is coming to live in Daddy's house. Her name is Valerie."

Sophie stared at him. "You mean she's coming to visit, don't you, darling?"

"No," Matthew answered for his brother, "she's coming to live with us. Daddy said." He took another sandwich. "Is she nice, Mommy?"

Sophie's heart began to race. "Well...I...I don't know. But if Daddy likes her...she must be...quite...okay." Not an inspired performance, but this was ad lib and she was struggling. And then she realized they must have gotten it wrong. It couldn't be true; Adam couldn't be taking such an enormous step without consulting her. They'd overheard something and misconstrued it. It had to be that.

"*I* know," Matthew said slowly in an I-have-an-idea voice. "We could play..." He paused for suspense, and the tactic worked wonderfully well on Hugo, who became round-eyed with expectation. "Hide-and-seek!"

"Yes!" Hugo leaped in the air. "You be 'it,' Mommy!"

Here was further proof, if she needed it. Sophie put her hand over her eyes and started counting aloud. If a strange woman were really moving into their home, they would have more on their minds than hide-and-seek, surely.

"...seventeen, eighteen, nineteen..." She could almost laugh now at the shock she had felt at the news, like a body blow knocking the wind out of her.

She could almost laugh, but not quite.

Confirmation of the news that Valerie had moved in came at breakfast on Monday morning, when after long and insistent ringing of the doorbell, Milagros burst into Sophie's apartment, breathless with indignation and from climbing the stairs, to announce that she had quit her job. "I'm sorry for you," she said to Sophie, accepting a cup of coffee, "and I'm sorry for the boys, but I will not work in that house! I told him. I told him, I will not work for a *fulana*!" Milagros spoke triumphantly, but her hand trembled when she lifted the cup to her lips.

"And that's it? He just let you go?" Sophie's voice was barely a whisper.

"What could he do? *¡Qué poca vergüenza!* Those poor boys! I'm never going back to that house, I tell you, I *refuse* to work—"

But a loud crash interrupted her. Sophie had hurled her coffee cup to the floor.

"Hypocritical bastard!" Sophie spat the words out. "What about not upsetting the children, eh? Not changing their routine? Or doesn't *replacing me* count as a change in their lives?" It was no longer Milagros she had before her, but Adam himself, pale and speechless. She had pushed past his secretary into his office, and now he crouched, half risen out of his chair, staring in shock at a woman so transformed by anger that he could barely recognize her as his wife. "What about the fucking good of the fucking children now?" Her words resonated down the hall. *There's some mistake*, he thought, *Sophie doesn't say "fuck."* Out of the corner of his eye, he saw Odette tiptoe up and close his door, and he felt

grateful to her. In a voice gravelly with rage, Sophie continued, "In spite of every cowardly, traitorous thing you've
done to me, I still thought—I really did—that although you
were a sadly inadequate human being and a shit of a husband, at least—and I consoled myself with this thought—
at least you really did care what happened to our children.
But it's perfectly clear now that all you care about is fucking
that woman, and if our bed is the easiest place to fuck her,
then fine, you'll fuck her in our bed—and to hell with the
children and all that pious bullshit you gave me about not upsetting their lives! Adam, how dare you? How *dare* you bring
a stranger into their home without consulting me first?"

There was no doubt about it: Sophie had lost all sight of
the fact that she didn't say "fuck." Adam managed to find his
voice. "But that's why I didn't hire a nanny! I was thinking of
them!"

"A *nanny*? I'm talking about the woman in our bed! Or
did you think they wouldn't notice it wasn't me?"

"Sophie, I never—"

She pointed menacingly into his face. "The first thing
you're going to do, you son of a bitch, is get down on your
knees and beg Milagros to come back."

"I'll speak to her."

"You'll *crawl* to her, if that's what it takes. You'll get her
back under any terms she cares to name."

The staccato sound of their voices, one higher, one lower,
continued for some time through the closed door, while
Odette nervously shuffled and reshuffled the papers on her
desk, trying to catch what was being said without actually *listening in*. Word of what was happening had spread quickly,
and more than one colleague had found reason to drift out
into the corridor, where looks of concern were exchanged, as

well as twitching smiles. Then Adam's door flew open, and Odette ducked instinctively as Sophie tore back out. James pressed himself against the wall as she charged by, trying to catch her eye with a sympathetic glance, but she swept past him and out, brushing a tear from her cheek and slamming the door. A couple of sheets of paper fluttered to the floor, mute casualties of her wifely wrath. James watched them settle, then stooped and gathered them up.

When Sophie's departing shadow had rippled past her translucent office door, Valerie pounced on her phone. "Our lit-tle plan is work-ing!" she trilled to Agatha. "Guess who just blew out of here like a bat out of hell?...Yep, the irate little wife herself! Now she's speeding back to pack up her aprons and oven gloves, and soon she'll come swooping down, screeching, all sharp talons and beak, to reclaim her nest and chicks. And welcome to them!" Valerie swiveled back and forth in her chair girlishly. "Well, I guess I'd better go and console whatever's left of Adam. Bye now!" She hung up, laughing, and spun herself once all the way around in her chair in exuberance. Then she stood, smoothed her skirt, and arranged her face into a suitably sympathetic expression for Adam. "So undignified...How awful for you..." She stifled another laugh.

Valerie and Agatha had been right to assume they would goad Sophie into action, but they miscalculated the direction that action would take. Instead of packing oven gloves, Sophie began divorce proceedings. Sitting in the lawyer's office on a slippery leather chair, she maintained an expression of polite concentration while he ground out routine legal phrases, but her mind was on other matters: lawyers' offices, the graveyard of human hopes and aspirations. Marriages, business partnerships, so many dreams and projects, created with enthusiasm and mutual trust, came to an end here. When communication and the ability to problem-solve failed, the losers took refuge in these gleaming chrome-and-leather offices and sat listening to statements like this one: "Divorce is no-fault in the Commonwealth of Massachusetts. Either spouse may commence divorce proceedings whenever he or she feels that there has been an irretrievable breakdown of the marriage relationship. So-called grounds for divorce— e.g., adultery, mental cruelty, abandonment, et cetera—are not part of the law governing dissolution of marriage in this jurisdiction."

Riding down in the elevator, clicking past the floors, the terms "irretrievable breakdown" and "no-fault" echoed in Sophie's head. So everything boiled down to that: It was over, and it was nobody's fault. That was knowable, was it? And by that stranger? Going up in the elevator, Sophie had still been a married woman, just. Coming down, she was no longer married, nor yet divorced, but cut adrift in a gray no-man's-land of pending paperwork. The thought depressed her, and the fact that there was still a legal bond uniting her to Adam made her feel vulnerable, as though it were a channel through which he could continue to hurt her—a sort of umbilical cord transferring pain instead of nourishment. If only it could be severed immediately, she would be safe. "I'm no longer married," she said in a loud, clear voice, just before the elevator doors rolled open. She stepped out and crossed the polished floor of the lobby. "I'm no longer married," she said more quietly, mindful of the people brushing past her. Outside, she stood at the top of the broad flight of stone steps and said again into the wind, in a firm but neutral tone, "I am not married." She listened carefully to the sound of that, testing it for truth. But no, it lacked conviction. She went down the steps, twisting her wedding ring automatically, unhappily, and looked up and down the street, feeling at a loss. How to continue the day...? What time was it, anyway? Eleven-thirty. Only eleven-thirty? Go home, go to class, eat lunch; all were equally unthinkable. People crisscrossed in front of Sophie and behind her, creating one diamond-shaped island of irresoluteness in a mesh of busy lines. She peered into their faces as they hurried by, hoping for a clue of where to go and what to do, but their faces were closed, their steps quick and purposeful, as if to remind her that the whole busy world does not grind to a halt all because one man has left one woman. Only eleven-thirty, and she was standing utterly alone and purposeless on a windy sidewalk. She took three hesitant steps forward, then stopped and drifted three steps back. A man bumped into her and growled. She was in the way. She was in everyone's way! She looked down at the pavement and saw a candy wrapper jammed in a crack. Unable to take her eyes off it, with rising panic, she realized she had nothing to do and nowhere to go. Any step, this way or that way, was equally absurd and pointless. A lanky teenaged boy bumped into her, knocking her handbag off her shoulder. Catching the strap in the crook of her arm, she scurried into the shelter of a storefront, out of the stream of pedestrians, and stared at the window display. With relief she noticed another woman looking at it, too, studying the contents critically with narrowed eyes, moving her lips as she made some calculation. Sophie inched closer to her, then closer still, hoping the woman would speak, comment on the display, include Sophie in her life for just a moment, acknowledge that she, too, had a right to be on the sidewalk. Sophie lifted her eyes shyly, prepared to speak first if the woman would not—but the woman had gone. Sophie looked back to the vast shop window and saw her reflection on its surface, in pale outline only, without detail, her hair blowing across a dark oval that should have been her face.

With a stab of certainty, she knew then that it would be impossible to get through the day as if nothing unusual had happened. There was no conceivable way she could pick up her children today and play with them as if everything were okay, smiling bravely while they prattled on about "Daddy's girlfriend." Enough of being a tower of strength! Enough of Sophie, the good sport, the model mother, doing her duty and then...doing her duty some more. "I'm not having a good day," she whispered to her featureless image in the window, and then again, with greater conviction, "This is not a good day." It was then that she noticed, also reflected in the window, a neon sign spelling "Budweiser" backwards. She turned and saw the blacked-out front of a dingy bar across the street. A place to go. Clutching her bag to her chest, she dashed through the traffic and hurled herself against the heavy door and into the bar.

Darkness, reeking beer fumes, plaintive country music: a mistake. She stood disconcerted. *Never mind, just leave again.* She turned, then stopped dead. If she left, she'd be outside again. Out there with that candy wrapper.

The bartender looked up, his bottom lids drooping like a St. Bernard's, showing the red below. "Yeah?" he said.

Uh-oh. She'd been spotted. Now it would be rude to leave. "Oh, hello. I'll...I'll...I'll have a..." And that was that. She could think of nothing more to say. There were no more words in her mind.

"Want some time to think it over?" the bartender said at last. It looked like she was teetering, about to take a swan dive off the wagon.

"Beer!" came a shrill voice from the end of the bar. Peering through the gloom, Sophie made out a red-haired woman of sixty or so who slid off her stool and ambled up to her. "I think the word you're after is 'beer.' " She smiled, showing drinker's teeth. "Mind if I sit down?"

Sophie made a polite gesture, and they perched on stools side by side. For a time the woman sang along in a high, cracked voice to the country song on the jukebox. Then she broke off abruptly and said, "Is it safe to say you're not having a good day?"

"Ye-es," Sophie said cautiously. "It's safe to say that."

"Want to talk about it?"

"Not really."

"Fine." She got back to her song: "You Picked a Fine Time to Leave Me, Lucille."

But on the other hand, why not? "Well, actually..." Sophie began, and the woman fell silent. "Actually, I don't mind. It's this. My husband left me for another woman three weeks ago, and now she's moved into our old house, and she lives there with my children, and I feel very angry about that."

The woman nodded and leaned toward Sophie. "You know what?" she said.

"What?"

She leaned closer still, and when she spoke, it was slowly and with emphasis. "It's...not...important."

"Oh." The woman must be drunker than she looked.

"I mean, it stinks and it sucks and everything else, but for all that you're mad and hurt and filled with anguish, there's a little corner of you that doesn't give a shit. Not really."

"Oh. Well. I have to say I'm...having difficulty locating that corner."

"Ah, but it's there! And sometimes, just for a rest, you need to get into that place and stay there for a little while. You know what I mean? Okay, so he's an asshole, no doubt about it. But...it's...not...important."

"Hmm," Sophie said neutrally.

"So! You get yourself into that place, and if you don't mind, I'll join you there! It's nice and cozy there, warm and dry." The woman giggled, then screeched, "April fresh and dry as a bone!" Sophie smiled uncertainly, but the woman reached out and shook her hand. "My name's Liz, and I'd like to buy you a beer."

"I'm Sophie. And...well, yes, all right. Thank you."

"Billy," Liz snapped. Evidently their relationship did not require much small talk.

The beers came, and Liz raised her glass high. "To that special place," she said, "where you don't give a *shit*." It sounded like a dangerous toast to Sophie, but she lifted her glass, and when she had finished her beer, she ordered two more, as was only polite, before bidding Liz farewell.

Back outside on the sidewalk, feeling a little dizzy and flinching like a vampire in the harsh daylight, Sophie fished out her phone and made two brief calls. The first was to Marion, asking her to pick up the children at school and play with them until six, then deliver them to their father's. The second was to Milagros, telling her that Adam would probably be calling to apologize and asking her to please take her job back, if he did. And so that afternoon at four o'clock, Matthew and Hugo were at Marion's house finger-painting, and Milagros was shrewdly negotiating with Adam the terms under which she would allow herself to be reemployed by him. And Sophie…

In rapid succession she pictured all the things she might conceivably do with her afternoon: seek counseling, pour out her heart to a friend, meditate, lunch, or shop in Copley Place. Have a massage, a run, a nap, a swim. Go to the Gardner Museum or the MFA. She could even don an assortment of trash bags (a small one as a turban, a larger one as a tunic) and go sweep Boylston Street as a sort of reincarnation of the famous Bag Man, then run back to the bar, her plastic garments flapping, and tell Liz to set 'em up again. She closed her eyes and pressed them with her fingertips in an effort to think what, what, what she wanted to do. And then the answer came: nothing. She wanted nothing, nothingness. Not to feel, not to think. To shed her sad and weary self and sit in the dark, engulfed in something else. Her soul's only desire, Sophie realized, was to gaze hour after hour at a big screen in an empty theater.

Such bathos, she thought. *My life falls apart—so I go to the movies.*

She saw four films that day and night, starting with the excellent Agnès Jaoui. All the films were foreign and subtitled, all of them transported her completely as she watched, rapt and wide-eyed, like a child greedy for bedtime stories. Her thoughts spun out in ever-widening circles as she walked home from the Coolidge Corner Theater that night, muttering to herself, reenacting certain scenes from the films and inventing others: the things that should have happened, but hadn't. Her evening had achieved its purpose. She had succeeded in bombarding her senses with alien sights, sounds, and stories until she had drummed herself temporarily out of being and she could consider her own plight with a sort of numbed indifference.

4.

$\mathcal{A}$t midday the students were draped around the shiatsu classroom in various poses: one sitting cross-legged on the floor, rolling her head in gentle circles; another lying flat, her legs propped against the wall; another resting her head on a friend's lap. Most of them were also eating some form of lunch involving thermoses of soup, sandwiches with leafy bits poking out, and pieces of fruit held in the hand and studied with frowning concentration between bites. Occupying roughly the center of the composition was Jake—or Cob, as Rose preferred to call him, favoring the second half of his name—his white hair fluffed out magnificently, seated with his legs well apart, one hand gripping his knee and the other stroking his beard with a satisfied air. It was he who eventually broke the silence, delivering a monologue that felt like the sort of set piece used in theatrical auditions.

"Change…" he began, shaking his head with amusement. "Change…" He forced out a chuckle. "Oh, if only…if only we could accept the fact that change is the rule rather than the exception..." He sighed; then, his voice soft and earnest: "we'd all find life a whole lot easier." He slapped his thigh softly and emitted another low laugh.

L looked up from her stoneware crock of greens, her fork, trailing bean sprouts, poised in midair, and gave Jacob an unreadable look. She was the one, Sophie suspected, most likely to fall for the avuncular charms of the old earth daddy, and he seemed to think so, too, for he smiled and addressed the rest of his discourse directly to her. "It's normal for human beings, their lives and their relationships, to be in constant motion—that's how life is. Nothing stands still! The earth turns, the seasons turn, the constellations shift in the sky...." This last was accompanied by expressive hand motions and a face radiant with childlike wonder. "Constant change is the norm—not an aberration. Not the tragedy, not the crisis that we make it out to be. Change is growth. Change is health. All the trouble begins when, out of fear, people try to lock themselves and others into static roles." Clenched fists, wincing. "That's not right, that's not nature. If something's not moving, not changing, not flowing, that means it's blocked, it's stuck—it's sick."

"So we can depend on nothing and no one?" Sophie asked sharply, wary of getting into a discussion with Jake-O but annoyed enough to be drawn in anyway.

"No!" Jacob turned to her, a triumphant gleam in his eye. "We can depend on everything and everyone—to change! To evolve! That is the beauty of it."

"Not all changes are beautiful."

"No, some are very painful, but we must embrace them— as proof of life."

"No." Sophie shook her head and set down her apple. "No. There's no obligation to embrace anything. To acknowledge and act in consequence, yes. To embrace, no. And there's nothing unnatural about wanting some consistency in your life. The seasons you mention, the constellations—they move in a known, predictable cycle. They're perfectly reliable."

Anthony joined in, his finger raised. "Yes! I was going to say that there seems to be some confusion here between motion and change. Real change wouldn't be day following night, but rather the day the sun doesn't rise! And every time that has happened, during eclipses, people have freaked out pretty hard. It seems pointless to blame them for that."

Jacob spoke gently. "I'm not suggesting we blame anyone for anything." He turned to L for support, but she was back to munching her greens. "I'm just making the valid point that we must not fear and reject change, when change is the very essence of life."

L set down her empty bowl and spoke. "I think what Jacob is getting at here"—she raised her eyes to him, and he smiled at her gratefully—"is that he's trying to come up with a theory that will do away with the concept of responsibility." His face fell as she continued. "He means it's okay to let people down. It's healthy, even." They glared at each other, and Sophie wondered what was going on between them, because something obviously was.

"Yes, it can be okay!" he said. "Of course it can be! It depends on a thousand—no, a million!—circumstances, great and small, and how they all mesh together and the intricate pattern they form!"

Sophie actually snorted. "So life is just a wonderful, constantly shifting kaleidoscope—"

He pointed at her. "That's a very good way of putting it!"

"And expecting anyone to be dutiful or dependable or loyal is ridiculous and pathetic. Is that it?"

"No. Duty exists, and so does responsibility, but their nature is also constantly shifting. Take the case of a parent and child. The parent's duty to the child is always changing. When she's little, you have to tie her shoes, but soon you won't need to. Here, too, is constant change."

"Here, too, is a fucking cop-out," L said, her eyes resting on him.

Anthony cleared his throat. "Again, I think, Jacob, if I may say so, that you're taking an example of a natural cycle—a child growing up, the changing of the seasons—while I think some of us here are talking about change as a *breaking* of those natural rhythms. The day the sun doesn't rise..."

"The day a parent walks out on you."

"Or a partner does."

"The day someone you always thought loved you punches you right in the face!" This last was from Rose, and it produced consternation in the room.

"Your husband?" a sympathetic voice inquired.

"My sister! Last Christmas!"

"Yes, yes! Some changes are tough!" Jacob raised his voice to take the floor again. "I acknowledge that. But there's a value, in troubled times, to recognizing that change is life...and life is change!"

"Do you really think so, Jacob?" Henry said, suddenly joining the conversation. "Let's take Rose's case. Her sister's just slugged her, and she's sitting there with her brand-new black eye. Do you really think that as she holds a lump of raw meat to her face, she is consoled by the thought 'Life is change'?"

After class Henry and Sophie walked partway home together, he pushing his bike along the sidewalk, she still fuming. "It's easy to say change is wonderful when your own life is on an even keel, but when you've just been 'changed' for another woman, you have quite a different take on the whole thing, believe me. That Jacob is such a jerk."

"He is a jerk. But he's right, too. Always remember, my dear—jerks can be right. Life is change. Look at you, changed for a different woman. Well, all you can do is let this new event flow into the stream of your life."

"Henry!"

"It's true. You can't dam it up. What's her name?"

"Her name?" Sophie spoke with careful neutrality to conceal the revulsion she felt pronouncing it out loud. "Valerie."

But he noticed and said loyally, "Bad name. But the point is, your children won't be happy until they can feel free to like Valerie, even love her."

She thought about that. "Okay. So?"

"So you have to help them do that."

"Oh, come on, surely not! Why is every damned thing my job? It's up to her to make herself lovable!"

"That too, but that comes later. The first step has to come from you. You have to give them permission to love her."

She covered her eyes. "Good God, what next?"

"What? Don't you see what I mean?"

"Yes, I see. I see and I agree. It just seems to be asking an awful lot. All this being mature and putting the children's welfare first really takes it out of a person."

"What's the man's name?"

"What man?"

"Her boyfriend. Your children's father."

"My husband?"

He shrugged.

"Adam. I'm sure I've told you that before."

"Adam! Now that really *is* an ugly name." He mouthed it a couple of times, his face crumpled with distaste.

She laughed. "You know, it's amazing to me how you can be so wise one minute and so childish the next."

"Yes. Actually, Sophie, that's something you love about me. And don't you forget it." He caught her hand and gave it a surprising kiss in the palm. Then he flung his leg over his bike and cycled away.

———

Valerie was lying on the chesterfield after dinner, a magazine in her hand and several others piled on the floor beside her, but she was finding it difficult to concentrate because of Matthew and Hugo, who were not running around the room or shouting, but sitting quite still in armchairs, knees together, hands in laps, looking at her intently.

Casting about for a subject of conversation that might interest her, Matthew at last hit upon: "I have a fish at Mommy's house." But she wasn't listening. "Valerie. Valerie." He repeated her name politely until she lowered her magazine. "I have a fish at Mommy's house. His name is Cloudy. Hugo has a fish, too. It's named Fishtag."

Valerie wondered if one were really expected to respond to conversational gambits like this one. Surely not. What could a person say that wouldn't sound cruelly sarcastic? *How interesting?* No, he'd see straight through that—kindest just to let it drop.

"At Mommy's house there's a *roof deck,*" Hugo offered, pronouncing the words importantly. "It has plants, and it's *beau*-ti-ful."

"Fancy that." With some bitterness Valerie remembered the double terraces of the dream apartment she had designed for herself and Adam. A very long time ago, it seemed.

"Time for bed, boys," Adam said, coming in from the kitchen.

From behind his back, Hugo produced his elephant and its detached trunk, which he handed to Valerie. "Can you fix this?"

Without glancing at the pieces, she passed them to Adam, who snapped the trunk back on and returned the toy to Hugo, who beamed to see it whole again.

"Come on," Adam said. "Let's go up and get your pajamas on."

"No bath?" Matthew asked.

"Oh, yes, of course. Bath, then pajamas, then books, then bed. That's right, isn't it?" They nodded, and Adam felt a touch of pride at his mastery of new skills—and something else, too: He was beginning to draw comfort from this evening routine of theirs.

After they'd gone upstairs, Valerie drifted over to the table and surveyed the unappetizing remains of that night's supper: lima beans spilled off the edge of the boys' plates, chicken in congealing gravy, Hugo's fork with two lima beans speared onto it standing upright in his water glass. Adam's plate was still half full. She finished the wine, had a quick cigarette on the patio, then wandered around the living room, waiting for Adam. What a bore these evenings were. She looked at her watch, feeling rather left out. She could hear the boys begging Adam for one more book, and she realized it was stupid of her to mope down there alone. She went to the bookshelf, chose a thick volume, and climbed the stairs with a straight back, lightly shaking the hair from her forehead.

"But we're not sleepy," Matthew was saying. "Just one more, Daddy?"

"Please, Daddy?" Hugo chimed in.

"I've got a story for you," Valerie announced in silky tones from the door, and the three of them turned in surprise. She pulled the book out from behind her back and sat down on Hugo's bed. "Once upon a time," she pretended to read, "there was a prince who lived in a very big house. It was just about the fanciest house in the whole kingdom." She turned the book—one on French architecture—to show them all a photograph of Versailles. The boys' eyes widened, and Adam smiled at her, thoroughly charmed. She smiled back demurely and continued. "But there were too many mirrors, so one day the prince decided to move, and guess where he went next?" As she hunted for another picture to show them, Valerie was aware of a strange feeling of contentment, there in the center of that admiring, all-male circle.

Sophie's earlier feelings of fright and desolation gave way to anger, causing her to sleep poorly for a couple of weeks. Even asleep she thrashed in bed with such fury that she woke herself up, and then she would fling off the covers and pace the apartment, ranting aloud until she got cold and had to jump back in bed, where she lay for hours, awake and wrathful.

That continued until she took out a three-month membership at the swimming pool and began to swim every day before shiatsu—Henry's idea. She swam steadily for an hour, thinking only about her body sliding through the water and her breathing, feeling the air circulating in and out of her. After her shower she burst out of the gym doors and set off for school with a spring in her step, her damp hair flopping in rhythm with her stride, feeling strong and well oiled—feeling, actually, the way she used to before she'd had children. She was becoming herself again, she thought, going around the spiral once more, but this time one coil up, where the view was better.

Her nights were spent studying, and she was becoming increasingly engrossed in shiatsu. Some of its tenets made sense to her instinctively, and it was gratifying to see those confirmed, but even more interesting were the things she found counterintuitive, because they required her to think again, and to think in new ways.

The only difficult time of day now was early evening, after the children had gone back to Adam's and before she was ready to settle down to her books, when she was beset by restlessness and longing. That was when she felt most keenly that something was missing in her life, at that hour when couples meet at home and compare notes of the day, sympathize over hardships, and laugh at silly things. To bridge that lonely spell, she began taking evening walks around the neighborhood, but she felt conspicuous in her solitude. She wandered, flotsam on the human tide, through random streets, stiff with self-consciousness and yearning for the safety of the apartment she had fled, where at least she was shielded from critical eyes and her fundamental pointlessness was her secret. But, of course, waiting for her back at home were the very conditions that had driven her out in the first place.

It was a problem, until one day she stumbled, literally, onto the solution in the stairway of her building. The lights had gone off on the automatic timer, and in the dark she stepped on something that squealed, making her scramble for the switch. It was a dog, small and frisky. The door of the ground-floor apartment opened a crack, closed again, a chain rattled, then the door opened wide and a musical old voice said, "Oh, there you are, Bertie. I couldn't think where you'd gone. Come in." But the dog preferred to dance around the hall, making feints for the street door, and Sophie began chatting with his owner, a woman in her nineties (as she announced proudly and repeatedly), who wore striking makeup, somewhat shakily applied, her hair piled up in a mound of silver curls, and strings of costume jewelry tinkling on her bosom. ("Do call me Dorina, please. You can't imagine how sad it is when there's no one left to use your first name.") The upshot of their conversation, the one golden nugget of useful information that so often emerges in the course of dutiful small talk, was that Bertie was sadly in need of exercise that Dorina could no longer give him, so Sophie offered to take him along on her evening walks, and Bertie made all the difference. No one anchored securely to the earth's surface by a sturdy dog straining on a leash can be accused of drifting aimlessly. Sophie's shyness disappeared as Bertie pulled her along, yanking her to a halt when he stopped without warning to smell some dark corner and pee just a measured bit, then trotted on again, full of some busy unknown agenda. She let herself be swept through the darkening streets to the South End, until the thought of home would spring into her mind, glowing and attractive, and they would turn back. Then she would return Bertie to Dorina and climb the stairs feeling that she had done all three of them a favor and eager to get to her books.

Week followed week throughout the fall, until one day after school, about two months after she had left Adam's house, the boys presented her with that most touching of autumnal child-crafted gifts: drawings of turkeys using the outline of a small hand for the bird's body, the thumb serving as neck and the other fingers as plumage, all nicely colored in. She stuck the pictures on her refrigerator with magnets and felt a pang whenever she glanced at those innocent reminders of the great American family celebration.

———

Marion admired the turkey drawings when she came over with a sack of hand-me-downs from her nephews for the boys. She shook the clothes out on the sofa and folded them into neat piles while she talked, occasionally holding up an article for Sophie's admiration. Her topic was the usual one: "Now Adam's relationship with this woman will have to run its course and die a natural death, which could take years. I'll never understand why you left! You've been so weirdly passive in all this! Your husband seems to be tired of you, so you obligingly melt out of his life. (Isn't this shirt cute?) It's unnatural to be so acquiescent! If you ask me, your parents have a lot to answer for. That mother of yours and the way she mishandled that whole thing..." She flashed Sophie a red sweater for approval.

"You mean Patrick?" Sophie asked, nodding about the sweater.

"Yes, Patrick! The way she allowed him to dominate your childhood and how you've kept such a tight lid on your feelings all your life that you can't even—"

"Marion, Marion." Sophie held up her hand. "I don't want to have this conversation. I know all about Patrick and how he affected my upbringing—I'm the one who told you about it, remember? But that's just the way it is. And if it's made me into a boring and repressed Girl Scout, then I accept that."

Patrick was Sophie's severely physically and mentally handicapped older brother, who had occupied all their mother's attention and caused their father to retreat into himself, so that she had grown up with a distant and melancholy father and a mother so overtaxed that she couldn't cope with another single thing, including Sophie. The emotional larder of the household was depleted before Sophie arrived; nothing was left, because Patrick had taken her share along with his, and gulped down the lives of both parents as well. Even as a child, Sophie knew it was unfair to think that way. Poor Patrick, it wasn't his fault that he needed and took so much. It wasn't her mother's fault that she was tired, or her father's fault that he was sad; it was just the way things were. And as a result Sophie grew up stoical and self-reliant, careful not to add her weight to the family's already heavy burden, like someone who didn't dare to stand on the ground but must, with tremendous effort, hover in the air just above it. She grew up mature and competent beyond her years, but her achievements went largely unnoticed at home. If she made straight A's, it was only natural; there was nothing wrong with her. Who knew what Patrick might have achieved if he had had her luck? Luck was an important concept in that house. Patrick had been unlucky; therefore his parents had been, too. Sophie alone had been granted that haphazard favor: born pretty, athletic, and intelligent, through no merit of her own. So she received her rewards without rejoicing in them, as a matter of course. "We can leave Patrick and my mother out of it," she said now to Marion. "As far as I'm concerned, when love is over, so is marriage. That's all."

Marion held up a pair of dark blue overalls. "If human relations were that clear-cut, I'd be out of a job. (How about these?) The reason I'm a counselor is that I happen to believe that human relationships are the most important things we have in this life and they're worth salvaging. (Aren't these cute?)"

"I think relationships mutate. And the wise person moves with them. (Very cute.)" The task of trying to put Marion firmly in her place while showing gratitude for her generous gift was starting to make Sophie bad-tempered.

"Why jump to the conclusion that Adam doesn't love you? This affair of his—it might have been just physical attraction or a cry for help."

"A cry for help!" Sophie laughed. "Then he shouldn't have torpedoed the lifeboat! And I'm getting sick of this 'just physical attraction' crap. What is 'just' about physical attraction? It's a complex matter, and supremely important, the proof being that marriages are based on it and it's how we all get conceived. So come on, now, let's drop it. Any plans for Thanksgiving?"

"We're going to my mother's. Who are the kids spending it with?"

"Milagros."

"Ooh."

"Now, stop it. There's nothing sad about that. They love her, she invited them, and they're delighted to go, so let's not lay on the violins."

Marion relented somewhat after that, but a few days later Sophie got a similarly irritating visit from Lydia, the woman she used to help with the play group. Lydia was divorced, and she lived with her children out in the sticks—that was how Sophie now thought of Adam's neighborhood. Having gotten Sophie's address from Marion, Lydia dropped by unexpectedly one afternoon. Somewhat warily, Sophie invited her in and put on the kettle for tea.

"I've been through it all, you poor thing. You don't need to tell me, I've been there!" In her nervousness Lydia was almost shouting, one arm out of her coat, the other still in, her hair flopping in her face. "What a cute place you've got here! Wow, am I jealous!" She launched straight into a long account of her own breakup, creating frequent openings for Sophie to offer some tidbit of her own as corroboration, but Sophie held steadfastly to the role of listener. "Well, that's a man for you, every time," Lydia wound up at last, rather lamely. "But I suppose I don't need to tell you that, right? I guess you've been through pretty much the same thing with Adam? Men are such bastards. I mean, aren't they? Childish, selfish, fickle, vain!" She yelped with laughter.

"The difficult part comes now," Sophie said composedly, "trying to be good separated parents. One relationship is dead, but the other, more important one is not. He's still their darling daddy and still my partner in child raising—still my co-worker in the most important job of our lives."

Lydia nodded, looking disappointed that it was all going to be so tame. Then, "I've noticed—I mean, everyone's noticed—Adam has the kids, doesn't he? It's sort of an unusual arrangement, isn't it? Not that I see anything wrong with the father having them!"

Sophie waited, aware that Lydia was on a fact-finding mission.

"Not at all!" Lydia continued. "All power to him—and to you, too!" She gulped some tea, then frowned seriously. "So are they going to stay with him permanently? Is that what you've decided?"

"Just for the time being, while I'm getting my life straightened out. It seemed like the easiest way to handle things at first."

"Oh, sure! Yeah…" Lydia cast about for something to say. "You're lucky to have a man who's willing and able to do that."

"I am," Sophie said with some surprise. "I am lucky that way."

"I mean, Trey would never have taken the kids, are you kidding? Of course"—she flashed a smile and closed in on the target—"Adam has help with yours.…"

"Milagros, yes. She's wonderful." But from Lydia's sly yet eager face, Sophie saw that she did not mean Milagros at all, and she felt a flash of anger at Lydia's prurience. But the important thing was to squelch speculation that might get back to the children. So, "Oh, you must mean Valerie," she said collectedly.

"Valerie?" Eyebrows high.

"Adam's partner is named Valerie."

"Oh! Oh, ye-es, maybe I *have* seen someone around.…"

"She's also wonderful with the children," Sophie invented. "She studied child psychology, and she's done internships in children's hospitals and monitored foster families. She worked in an orphanage in Trinidad, and she also set up a hugely successful children's puppet theater in Guatemala. So she's really perfect for the job."

Confused by this detailed résumé, Lydia could only murmur, "How marvelous," and take mental note of a possible new helper for the play group.

"Very," Sophie said firmly. She held a smile on Lydia for a moment, then rose, giving her thighs a single slap, in the accepted manner of a polite hostess about to throw someone out of her house.

"You know what?" Sophie asked Henry the next day before class. They were doing the chi gong exercise called "Turn to Catch the Moon" used to loosen the spine and warm up the kidneys. "It's all becoming clear to me. I didn't know it, but I actually hated my old life and the people in it. I was just being a good sport. I think that's why Adam left me, too. Because I was too good a sport. That's interesting, don't you think? I mean, getting expelled from the game *because* you played by the rules?"

Raising his arms as he rotated his torso, Henry exhaled before saying, "The only way I can keep track of it all is by thinking of it as some kind of board game. Adam starts to move out, but no, you block his move. You move out instead, into your apartment. Adam moves back into his house. Then—hop, hop—*she* moves into *your* old place. Gosh, I wonder who's going to move into whose house next!"

Sophie broke her stance and faced him. "It doesn't feel like a game to me."

He lowered his arms. "Don't worry, Sophie, the switch is on its way. One day you'll get the switch."

"Oh, right. The switch. Aren't you going to snap your fingers?"

"Okay, sourpuss. One day you'll get the *switch*." Snapping his fingers that time. "It'll click your mind into a new groove and jump you onto another track—and not a moment too soon, my friend."

———

At last the children were warm and dry, in pajamas and robes and slippers, their hair combed and neatly parted, trooping down the hall, ready for supper. As they passed the bathroom, Adam glanced in and winced. Clothes in heaps, towels strewn everywhere, bath toys languishing in the dying foam—it was a mess best left to Milagros. He started down the hall again. Then—no, damn it, Milagros had enough to do! He turned back and began to tidy the bathroom briskly. The new deal that Milagros had cut with him was...well, it was okay. She worked fewer hours now, but for the same pay. Fair enough. She was due for a raise, so fine. Now she arrived in the afternoon, cleaned the house (although she didn't touch any article belonging to Valerie), and made supper, then drove to Sophie's to pick up the boys, brought them home, and played with them until either Valerie or Adam got home from work. Then she left, after a few friendly words with Adam, if he were home first, wordlessly if it were Valerie. She no longer stayed to do the bath, give the boys supper, and put them to bed. All of that had become Adam's job, and why shouldn't it be? He was happy to do it, really. It was the only chance he got to spend any time with his children during the week. Valerie didn't help, because...well, why should she? They weren't her kids, and nobody expected it of her. And who needed her help, anyway? Adam could manage fine. He even knew how to make horns now out of shampoo lather. Speaking of which—before leaving the bathroom, he thought to set a clean towel handy on the edge of the tub, ready for "Eye! Eye!" tomorrow night, and he felt pleased with his foresight.

In the living room, he found Valerie sitting in his chair, drink in hand, listening to Chopin and frowning over some papers from her briefcase. "You're home early!" he said in what he hoped could pass for a jocular tone. She'd been working late every night that week, sometimes appearing in time for supper but more often not until the boys were in bed, when he was too tired to sit down at the table again with her. She glanced up, saw a weary man with wet sleeves and a dirty towel slung over his shoulder, and laughed.

"You're a regular Mrs. Dainty! Ever read those stories? They're collector's items. Agatha adores them. *'Busy, busy, busy!' tut-tutted Mrs. Dainty, flicking her feather duster over the mantel'* ...? No? Doesn't ring a bell? She was a superb housekeeper." She lifted her glass to him in tribute and turned back to her work.

"Where are the boys?" he asked after a silence. "It's their suppertime."

She didn't respond for a beat or two, unable to tear her eyes from the page in her hand. "Hmm, what?" she managed at last.

"The boys. Their whereabouts."

"Oh ..." She still wasn't looking at him.

He waited, his left cheek pulsating slightly.

At last she looked up and read his expression. "I'm sorry, Adam. I would have come back earlier to lend you a hand, but they're really turning the screws at work. New clients." She shrugged apologetically.

Yes. Yes, Adam knew that. He worked there too. He, too, should have stayed for the "not obligatory, but you'd better be there if you value your job" cocktail party with the new clients. But someone had to be with the children; Milagros needed to get home by seven.

With the tiniest flutter of a martyred sigh, Valerie set her work aside. Then she smiled bravely and asked with good cheer, "What's for dinner?" Adam studied her face closely but found not a trace of irony there as she added heartily, in a way possibly meant to be flattering to him, "I'm starving!"

The greatest challenge is learning to separate the Lousy Husband from the Beloved Father, but it is essential to your children's well-being and self-esteem that you do so. Remember, the fact that their father was a poor husband is no concern of theirs. Your ex-husband may very well be a jerk, but your children's father is a precious person, and you owe it to them to treat him with respect.

Sophie lowered her magazine (which had fallen open to an article on divorce, as all magazines seemed to these days), shut her eyes, and raised her face to the December sunshine filtering through the bare branches overhanging the bench where she was sitting in the park across the street from her house. Through her closed eyelids, she could see the shifts from light to dark as the branches stirred, and she felt lulled by the sounds of the wind and of children playing, her own two distinguishable among them. *Moments like these are all that matter in life*, she thought, and she was wondering dreamily why it's so difficult to remember that when she was disturbed by a cool shadow falling across her face and a voice saying, "Hi."

She opened her eyes and saw a woman with short-cropped reddish hair backlit by the setting sun, standing with her hands in the pockets of her sweatshirt, her head tilted to one side. "Hi," Sophie answered.

"I'm not sure you're aware of it," the woman said, shifting her weight and her head to the other side, "but you enjoy something of a cult status in this playground."

Sophie shaded her eyes against the slanting sun to get a better look. "I do?"

"You do. Mind if I sit down?"

She sat, and Sophie was able to see her face at last: finely chiseled nose, small green eyes, thin mobile mouth. "Local legend has it that when your husband left you, you moved into a penthouse and hired his girlfriend to look after your children."

Sophie stared, then laughed. "What? But I don't know a soul here!"

The woman continued. "That doesn't matter. You are the heroine of every divorced and single mother here, which is most of us. Please don't tell me it's not true—we would all be devastated."

Sophie smiled. "Then I'll just say that, like most rumors, it has a grain of truth to it—"

"Thank God!"

"But my husband's lover is not actually in my employ."

"I'm sorry to hear that. Maybe I won't tell the others—if that's okay with you."

"Fine by me." They smiled at each other, and then Sophie asked, "Do you know my name—or just my life story?"

"Just your story, I'm afraid. I'm Florence. Flo."

"Sophie."

"I know your kids, from seeing you here. Matt and Hugo, right?"

Sophie nodded. "You have kids, too?"

"No. I just hang around playgrounds trying to pick up single mothers." Florence burst out laughing. "Sure I do. Those are my two over there on the merry-go-round. The wild-looking kid with the blond hair, that's my girl, Josie. And the little boy in the yellow overalls is Emerson."

Sophie smiled. "They're beautiful."

"Thank you. So are yours." Florence returned the smile, stretched her legs out, and leaned back on the bench. "Aren't we lucky to have them?"

Sophie's heart twisted. "Oh, *aren't* we?" She laughed, and tears sprang into her eyes.

"Hey," Florence said quietly. "It's okay."

Florence also lived across from the park, perpendicular to Sophie's, in a tall, ramshackle town house that she called the Life Boat, "because there are only women and children aboard, and it's saved all our lives." Three families lived there, each one headed by a woman on her own. Jean, the owner of the house, covered her mortgage with the rent paid to her by the other two, Mercy and Florence. They shared the kitchen and the living room on the ground floor. The second floor, with two large bedrooms and a bathroom, was Mercy's; the third floor, with the same setup, was Florence's; and Jean and her daughter had the top floor. There were five children in all, and the three working mothers juggled child care with jobs and social schedules, usually taking turns caring for the children but occasionally hiring someone jointly. It was a system that worked, and Jean was its inventor. She was a professional woman, neither rich nor poor, who on nearing forty still hadn't met "the right man" but wanted to have a child. Raising one on her own seemed too lonely to her, for both mother and child, and too difficult logistically and financially. She didn't want to put her baby in day care, and she couldn't afford a nanny, and anyway the idea of having her child raised by someone paid to do it rankled. So on her thirty-ninth birthday, over a solitary bottle of wine, Jean dreamed up the Life Boat. And soon after, she bought a suitable house, got pregnant, and found two single mothers, Carmen and Sylvia—predecessors to Mercy and Florence—to share the new place with her. They both assisted at the birth of Jean's daughter, Eliza. Carmen moved away when she fell in love (to be replaced by Mercy), and Sylvia eventually went back to New Zealand. That was when Florence moved in. "The key to the Life Boat's success," she explained to Sophie with the enthusiasm of the recent convert, "is the beautiful number three. Two women sharing a house wouldn't work—it would be too intense, too much like a marriage, and logistically much tougher than three. With two people it's either 'my way or your way'—a power struggle. And what happens if one moves out? The other's stuck, and her life falls apart. But with three there's a team dynamic. Three is a stable number. A three-legged stool doesn't wobble—Jean told me that. And if one woman moves out for any reason, the household can keep ticking while a replacement is found. On the other hand, more than three would be too chaotic and you'd lose that family feeling. Three is perfect. Three is the key. It's a magic number, actually, if you think about it—the Trinity and all that."

No fathers made an appearance on the Life Boat. Mercy was divorced, and her two kids saw their father only once a year. Eliza had no contact with her father. And Florence? Sophie asked her about Emerson and Josie's father.

"Fathers," Florence corrected.

"Oh."

"Sperm donors."

"Oh!"

"Except they delivered the sperm in person. Cheaper that way. And more fun—marginally."

"Oh, I see! And are they...involved in the children's lives?"

"No. And it couldn't matter less. A child needs a father like a fish needs a hole in the head."

"You think so?"

"Look, a child needs loving, caring adults, that's for sure, but it doesn't matter a damn who they are. They certainly don't need to be attached to the sperm sac, that's just biological supremacy. You know it's only called a 'nuclear family' because it blows up. But that doesn't happen in a Life Boat. Think about it—it's the family model of the future! More stable than a couple, more fun than being alone, with more laughs, more free time, more money, *and* our children always in good hands. It's ideal. Darwin himself would have approved."

"What if you met your perfect partner? Can partners move in?"

"No. That's a rule of ours. No couples. It ruins the dynamic. If we want to live with a lover, then we have to go. Life Boats are for single mothers and children only."

"Well, I must say, I'm intrigued."

"Great. Come over and visit whenever you like."

"Thanks very much. I'll do that sometime."

But as it turned out, their friendship was cemented the very next day. Sophie was once again reading a magazine, glancing up so often to keep an eye on the boys at the swings that she kept losing her place on the page. It wasn't a very interesting article—entitled "Coping Alone," wouldn't you know—but it must have held her attention for longer than she thought, because when she looked up again, the swings were empty, and a quick scan of the playground revealed nothing either. Panic surged, and she was already on her feet when she spotted Hugo squatting next to a parked car and peering beneath it. She started toward him, feeling relief until she saw that he was speaking to someone under the car, someone who could only be Matthew and who, since no part of him was showing, must have crawled under from the other side— the street side, the dangerous traffic side. "Matthew!" she shouted, running toward them now, banging her thigh on a fender as she barged between two parked cars and out into the street. All she could see of him were his legs poking out from beneath the car, where he was lying on his stomach, apparently trying to reach something. Then she saw the car coming. A car was coming, and in its path lay Matthew's little red-corduroy-clad legs. The driver had her head down, not looking at the road, fiddling with something, *not looking*. Sophie stood with her eyes locked on the driver as the car bore down on her son, her mind like molasses, thinking slowly, word by emphatic word: *She doesn't see him.* But Sophie didn't move. She stood stock-still.

It was in a distant, dreamlike way that she registered a shout from somewhere, then someone hurling herself toward the car and smacking its hood in warning. There was a squeal of brakes, the driver was flung forward against her seat belt, the car rocked to a stop just before the little red legs, and the driver got out to help Florence—for it was Florence who had leaped into the street—pull Matthew out from under the parked car. He was clutching a clawing kitten. "I saved him! He was scared of that big dog, but I saved him!" Sophie observed the events as though at one remove. Numbly, she hugged Matthew and witnessed the driver's departure. Dimly, she heard Florence say, "Hey, people freeze up. It can happen to anyone." She submitted to Florence's reassuring hug, gazing impassively ahead, seeing nothing there but her own inadequacy.

"So tell all!" Agatha said eagerly. "I've been dying to hear how you're coping over there. You've been awfully cagey about it. Out in *Milton*, if memory serves?" She leaned toward Valerie, eyes shining with anticipation. "Come on, confess, it's hell on earth, isn't it?"

"Not at all," Valerie said airily. "It's going quite well." But she was fishing for a cigarette.

"You can't smoke in here," Agatha reminded her. The two friends were sitting again at the window table in their favorite Newbury Street café, but today the cake trolley held no special appeal for Agatha, nor did the waiter, who was the petulant Mediterranean type she sometimes liked. So invigorating to desire neither chocolate nor Italians!

"It's going very well," Valerie repeated, lifting her chin resolutely.

Right, Agatha thought, *so this is how she's going to play it—the lofty princess. Fine. We'll see who can wear who down.* "But the kids are monsters, right?"

"No, they're not, surprisingly. They're pretty sweet, really."

"Oh. Well, what's the interior like?"

"No kettles or potpourri, I'm afraid." Agatha groaned with disappointment, so Valerie added generously, "But there's plenty of crazy paving on the patio."

Agatha perked up a little. "What's that?"

"Nothing less than the emblem of suburbia, according to Adam. It's when they lay out flagstones of different sizes—"

"Oh, yeah, any old which way," Agatha finished in a bored voice. "I know. Anything else?"

"The walls are banana yellow and scribbled on," Valerie offered, but Agatha was still looking glum, so she got to the point. "Look, the house is uninspiring, to say the least, and the kids are kids, but..." She smiled secretly, as if at an inner vision. "But Adam is won-der-ful. So tender and loving. It's such a relief for him to have me there. He's so grateful. You know, I think in the long run this experience—"

"Hang on—is there a barbecue grill over there?"

"A what? Yes."

Agatha chuckled knowingly; now they were getting some-where. "Is it 'themed' in any way? I mean, is it shaped like anything special—the Leaning Tower of Pisa, maybe? A fairy grotto?"

"It's just a plain grill," Valerie said in a hard voice, "and I don't think it's ever been used. Adam is *not* the kind of man you'll find in the backyard wearing a chef's hat and a funny apron, so you can just wipe that picture right out of your sick little mind."

But Agatha continued to smirk, making it a struggle for Valerie to regain her tone of gentle reverie. "I think this experi-ence has served to bring us closer. Now I can really understand what he was going through when we met, and one day, when all this is over, when the mother is home again with the kids and we're in our own place, I think we'll look back on this as—"

"Oh, *that* day! I know the day you mean. As part of the celebrations that day, pigs are scheduled to fly and hell to freeze over."

"What?"

"Valerie, that wife is not coming back! Why the hell should she? She has her independence, her career, probably even a lover by now. She's gone! And you're stuck in her old life! That's the ugly reality, so you'd better start coming to grips with it."

"But isn't a mother supposed to miss her kids, for Christ's sake?"

"Not when she sees them every day. What could be better? Valerie, let's face it. One, she is never coming back to that house. Two, she is not going to want those kids back—ever! She's as free as the air, and you, Valerie, *you*—are screwed."

"You're just trying to provoke me."

"You and Adam may in fact move out of that house some-time—I'm not saying you won't—but you'd better look for a three-bedroom, because those kids are coming with you. Take it from me."

"Oh, right. But you're also the one who said she would come screaming back home if I moved in. Remember that?"

"That's because you misled me into thinking she was a boring housewife who ate Danish, but she's not like that at all. She's Fannie Farmer meets Shiva the Destroyer. You never stood a chance against her."

"Oh, no? Well, I've got her husband."

"Hey, what's the name of that order of monks that used to go release captive Christians from the Moors and offer themselves as hostages in their place?"

"Piss off, Agatha."

"I think Pedro Nolasco was their founder. Thirteenth century? Ring a bell?"

"I said go to hell!"

"Okay, okay. We'll talk about something else. Would you like to hear what's going on in my life? Hey, that would make a change, wouldn't it? Gosh, I wonder how people find out that kind of thing about one another....Oh, I know! It's, 'Hi, Agatha! *How are you?*' Would you like to try asking me that?"

"No. But here's something to cheer you up. Listen to this." Valerie spoke in a suspenseful voice, enunciating carefully. "A couple of days ago, I received a telephone call from the very bowels of hell. It was a fiend in human form asking if I wanted to volunteer—wait for it, Agatha—at the local *play group*. Something involving the manufacture of *puppets*." Valerie saw with satisfaction that her words had struck their target. "So there you are," she said modestly, "and I hope that's made your day."

Sophie sat cross-legged on the ground, fretfully ripping up handfuls of dried grass. The sky hung lifelessly overhead, a uniform gray. It was chilly but windless, and her mood matched the dreary scene. Henry was lying on his back beside her, resting his head on her book bag and pulling withered leaves thoughtfully off a twig. He studied the bald stick for a moment, then tossed it away, picked up a new twig, and began to pull off its leaves. "You never noticed your husband was unhappy?" he asked.

"It's not my job to read his mind. It's up to him to put his thoughts and feelings into words."

"Some people aren't good at that."

"I guess not!"

He picked up another little branch and spun it between his fingers. "Do you still love him?" He rolled over, propped himself up on his elbows, and plucked off the dead leaves, one by one.

She sighed and ripped up more grass.

He plucked the last leaf and tossed away the stick with annoyance. "These twigs are starting to piss me off. They keep telling me you don't love me, and I'm almost sure that's not true. You don't have a daisy on you, do you? We'll get to the bottom of this."

She frowned, in no mood for jokes.

"You know, he chose you to be his wife, but he does have the right to unchoose you."

"He does?"

"Yes, he does. He can change his mind. That's his right."

"Oh, I see. So actually you think like Jacob. With his beautiful, constantly changing, nothing's-my-fault universe."

"We all have a right to change our mind. Your husband did it in a bad way, I agree. But try to separate what he did from how he did it."

"Oh, these pearls of truth!" she said angrily, hurling double handfuls of grass at him. " 'Separate what he did from how he did it.... Separate the bad husband from the good father.... Life is change.' I am sick to death of these slogans, these smug nuggets of advice, these...these turds of wisdom! Why does nobody understand they do not help? They do not console!"

"Get up," Henry ordered, rising and pulling her to her feet.

"What are you doing?"

"I'm sick of it, too. I'm sick of dispensing truth like some guru to a self-obsessed, ill-tempered woman." Sophie stared as he flung her jacket at her. "Put it on. We're going."

"Where?"

"Dancing. Hurry up."

"Dancing?" But he was already striding away across the grass. "Let's go!" he called over his shoulder, and without looking back he held his hand out behind him, ready to grasp hers. She watched his retreating back for a moment, then picked up her coat and books and ran to catch up with him, ignoring his outstretched hand.

"What a beautiful place!" Henry said about eight hours later, stepping into Sophie's apartment. He busied himself with examining things and exclaiming over them, while Sophie smiled proudly, swaying just a little. It *was* a beautiful place...really an exceptionally beautiful place. Clement— Sophie started to explain about the marvelous, mysterious Clement, but then they were too sleepy, and then they were in bed, with Sophie nestling half dressed in Henry's arms. "Go to sleep," he said, tucking her head under his chin, and then they were asleep.

But she woke up a few hours later with her ears ringing from the music in the bar and a sour taste in her mouth. Something had woken her, but what? Uh-oh, it was the room. Moving. Her sleep-blurred thought was that some careless disc jockey had left her apartment spinning on his turntable. Such negligence...it shouldn't be allowed. She pulled herself up onto one elbow, and the room gave a sickening lurch. Shakily, she reached out to the bedside table to drink some water that she couldn't remember leaving there and found it exceedingly good. Things were stiller now, barely turning. She guessed the turntable had been switched off at last, and it was just a matter of time before the apartment would wind down to a complete stop. Comforted, she slept again.

When she woke, the sky was pale, she felt calm, and her mind was blank. Then the picture of the evening filled it- self in: dinner in the North End, drinking, talking, laughing, dancing on Lansdowne Street, "cold tea" in Chinatown (beer in a teapot), apartment spinning, delicious water. She turned to look at Henry sleeping beside her, darkly handsome against the white sheets, and she was struck for the first time by what a shapely mouth he had, yet her stomach was leaden with dread. She eased herself out of bed, fished around for some clean clothes, and tiptoed away for a shower. When she came back out, her hair dripping, thirsty for tea, she found him standing fully dressed in the kitchen.

"Oh, good morning," she said, glancing away. "Would you like some tea?"

He shook his head. "Come here."

She walked over, eyes down, and let him take hold of her hand.

"Listen to me, Sophie. You have some problems right now, but I'm not one of them." He pressed her hand and released it. She nodded, not lifting her eyes until she heard the front door close behind him.

"Can you imagine a more perfect thing to say?" Sophie enthused to Marion the next day, making a note in Marion's file of the treatment she had just recieved: a bolstering of the Earth channels in order to calm Fire. Sophie had begun treating all her friends as part of a one-hundred-hour project Malcolm had assigned. She needed to work on twenty-five people four times each, keeping good records of every session, noting their symptoms, her diagnosis, her treatment, and its results, in order to prove she could follow a case through in a coherent manner. Viewing friends in terms of shiatsu was enlightening. Marion, for example, seemed less annoying now that Sophie could see her as just a case of too much yang in the pericardium. "Think of it," she said, still kneeling beside Marion, clutching the file folder to her chest. 'You have some problems, but I'm not one of them.'"

Marion stirred on the futon and opened her eyes. "Sounds a bit peevish to me. That felt great!"

"Oh, you don't know him! He's too bighearted for that. He really is the most...intriguing person."

"It was decent of him not to take advantage anyway."

"Take advantage!" Sophie laughed. "What are you talking about? I'm not a schoolgirl, I'm a thirty-six-year-old mother of two."

Marion propped herself up on her elbow. "I mean of the situation. You're on the rebound, Sophie. It was wise of him not to get involved with you. Wise fellow."

"Oh, I suppose so." That sobered Sophie, and the joy had gone out of her when she continued. "I'm glad we didn't make love, because on some primitive level—God knows it doesn't make any sense—I still feel linked to Adam."

Marion nodded. "Trust this animal instinct of yours. The body knows best, and yours is telling you that Adam is the only man for you."

And the worst thing about it, Sophie thought, *is that she might be right.* Just as compulsive liars sometimes tell the truth and monkeys occasionally do type Shakespeare's plays, it wasn't impossible for Marion to give sound advice.

But Florence's take on the situation was quite different. When she heard about it after her shiatsu (calm Wood, disperse and tonify Metal), she leaped up from the futon and began to pace Sophie's kitchen. "If you can't have sex with good-looking people who turn up in your bed, you might as well be dead. You know that."

"I still feel bound to Adam. And it makes me furious! He

doesn't give a damn about me, and yet all I could think when I saw Henry asleep by my side was, 'Thank God I haven't been unfaithful to Adam.' Unfaithful to Adam! What could be more pathetic? What am I going to do?"

"How's the divorce coming along?"

"Slowly. But a handful of legal papers isn't going to change how I feel."

"No, I know. Papers are worthless. A friend of mine got divorced from this guy, and he was taking it really hard, so she said, 'Look, what is marriage, anyway? Only a piece of paper.' And he said, 'No. What's only a piece of paper *is the divorce.*' "

Sophie groaned. "Don't."

"But he's right in a way. Bureaucracy isn't going to do the job. You need a sharp, gleaming knife—or a rusty hacksaw! You know, we don't have nearly enough ritual left in modern life, and human beings need ritual to help them through tough times. I bet you I could devise a ceremony to sever that bond for good."

Sophie felt a twinge of foreboding. "Time is a great healer," she said faintly.

"No, time is too slow. We need a fast, efficient ritual, and since our society doesn't provide one, we'll just have to invent our own. How about if I perform an exorcism to free you of this man once and for all? And firebomb those last guilt feelings so you can enjoy a robust sex life?"

"No, that's okay."

"I think it could be really therapeutic."

"Thanks anyway."

"What's the guy's name? At least I can send him killer thought waves."

"Adam."

"You're joking. The first man. The original asshole." Florence continued to pace the kitchen floor, thinking hard. "I've got it! How about if we just slap him around some?"

"Look, Florence, how can I explain this?" Sophie put her hands over her eyes and looked inward. "I have a gigantic boulder of anger blocking the entrance to the cave I dwell in—that's what it feels like. The light and the air are blocked out, I can't breathe, I can't move. I'm trapped in the darkness behind this massive lump of stone."

"Dynamite. You need dynamite. Look, have you ever told him what a shit he really is? I bet you haven't, you're so well brought up."

"I went to his office one day....But it seemed like the charge went off in my hands. I got more hurt in the explosion than he did. This time I want to be under cover when I push down the plunger."

"Now we're getting somewhere. You need to express your anger, and you want to do it from a safe distance. Then I think you should write him a letter. It may sound tame, but it doesn't need to be. Sit down here with a pen and paper after I leave and think of every last thing you'd like to tell that bastard. You know, if you don't get this poison out of your system, you'll end up with irritable bowel syndrome, to say nothing of cancer. Suppressed rage is dangerous stuff. So you transfer it all onto paper and protect your health."

"But wouldn't that be just another worthless piece of paper?"

"Not if you write to kill. Think of your pen as a knife and plunge it into his body again and again, like those crimes you read about: 'Six Hundred Stab Wounds, Face Mutilated Beyond Recognition.' You're not going to send the letter. It's just to purge your psyche, so you can really cut loose—make it so they'll need dental records to find out who he was."

Sophie swallowed. "I could try, I guess."

"Great. I'll leave you to it."

Letter writing as an alternative to irritable bowel syndrome was new to Sophie. She wrote hesitantly at first, with lots of crossing out, but then more rapidly, muttering to herself with increasing heat until she felt like a surfer riding a huge wave of anger, exhilarated. She used lots of paper, circling the good phrases that emerged and transferring them onto fresh sheets. As the letter took shape, its tone evolved from red-hot to white-hot. Then a deceptive coolness began to appear on the surface, and she fostered that until she produced a double-burn effect: first the scorch of the icy exterior, then a searing plunge into the molten iron at the heart—at which point she took a deserved break.

She made tea for herself and sandwiches for the boys, then checked the clock. Nearly time to go get them. She sat down again to reread with as much neutrality as she could muster. She pursed her lips thoughtfully when she came to the end. Fat. The thing was chubby. She crossed out half the text and reread. That was it; two hours' work had resulted in one concise but thrillingly wounding paragraph. She recopied it neatly and slid the final draft into an envelope, which she was about to seal when a happy thought occurred to her. Digging around in the bathroom, she at last found what she was looking for and slipped it into the envelope as well. A hokey touch, a bit of self-indulgence, but it made her smile, and that was all that mattered. She licked the envelope, addressed it in a confident hand, and propped it up in plain sight. It looked magnificent. She felt better then, and suddenly very hungry. Leaning against the kitchen counter, she gazed peacefully over the rooftops while she ate one of the sandwiches she'd made for her sons. It tasted unusually good. Delicious, in fact.

Children at the seashore know that when you dig a hole in the wet, packed sand, the sea rushes in to fill it up. Something similar happens with cruelty and kindness in the human heart. Having devoted the afternoon to inflicting pain on Adam, Sophie was suffused with warm feelings for the rest of humanity, which allowed her to go ahead and do the important thing she had been meaning to do for days, just as soon as she could screw up the courage. Hugo gave her an opening by asking whether he and Matthew had to kiss Valerie. "She gets lipstick on us. It's yucky and hard to rub off."

She knelt and put her arms around them. "You don't have to kiss her if you don't want to. But she's only trying to be nice, so you could try being nice, too. You know, Valerie is part of your family now, and she doesn't have any children of her own, so it's lucky for her to have you two, ready made."

"When are you coming home, Mommy?" Hugo asked.

"I am home, baby, and so are you. This house is yours and Matthew's and mine, you know that. Valerie lives with you at Daddy's house, because Daddy likes her and wants her to live there. And that's okay. People should live wherever they want, with whomever they like. Don't you think?"

Hugo nodded, but Matthew asked, "Doesn't Daddy like you?"

This was the key moment, and Sophie was equal to it, managing to produce a happy-sounding laugh. "Of course he does, baby! I've told you before—we just want our own houses, that's all." She knew that made sense to Matthew, who sometimes wished he had his own room. She looked at Hugo, but he had drifted over to the fishbowl, humming.

"Can I feed Fishtag?" he asked.

Topic closed, goal accomplished, permission granted to love Daddy's girlfriend. Feeling rather light-headed with the selflessness of her mission, Sophie glanced at the letter for moral support and caught her breath in surprise. The envelope was actually glowing, lit by a slanting ray of late-afternoon sunshine.

Christmas was not the ordeal Sophie had feared. The children spent Christmas Eve at her house and Christmas Day at Adam's, ferried between the two by Marion, who came to Sophie's house with Gerald for eggnog on Christmas morning and dropped the children off at Adam's on her way home. The boys showed no signs of distress, only delight at having two trees and two sets of presents. They came to her again for New Year's Eve, their father rightly supposing that she had no plans for the evening, and she devised an early celebration involving sparklers on the porch and the presentation of two picture calendars: forest animals for Matthew, sea creatures for Hugo. Matthew used the squares of January to hop farm animals across in a board game he invented, and Hugo colored his squares in, both of them lying on the rug in their pajamas and humming contentedly while Sophie reviewed the system of diagnosis based on the correct balance of the Five Elements. For some time she pondered the characteristics of Metal: the season fall, the flavor pungent, the lungs, the large intestine, the color white, and weeping—wondering if Metal were not perhaps the dominant element in her mother...or in Adam. Then she went over the notes she had taken in class before Christmas.

One sentence leaped from the page, written in block letters. She had asked Malcolm if there were a particular *tsubo* that helped a person to cope with change. He had frowned and said he couldn't think of one exactly like that, but the question was an interesting one because—and this is what Sophie had written in capital letters and underlined—*"The ability to accept change is a pretty good definition of health."*

Well, what do you know? Old Jake-O was right.

Sophie and the boys wished Dorina a happy New Year when they stopped at her door to pick up Bertie and bring him with them to the park. The boys were devoted to the dog and considered him as good as their own; in Sophie's view he was all the better for not being theirs.

The park was teeming with children playing with scooters and bikes and remote-controlled cars, squeezing the last bit of newness out of their Christmas presents. "Now, remember, Matthew, if Bertie runs off, just let him go. He can take care of himself. You just keep yourself safe." *Because we all know I can't come to your rescue,* she added unhappily to herself. "Murderously ineffectual" was the term she had come up with one sleepless night, to describe herself.

Matthew promised, and he and Hugo raced off to the slide with Bertie yapping at their heels. Someone called Sophie's name. It was Florence, sitting with her West Indian housemate, Mercy, a large woman with good carriage and a don't-mess-with-me voice, whom Sophie had come to like very much on her two or three visits to the Life Boat.

"—and Darwin has got nothing to do with it!" Mercy was saying.

"Well, it's *my* natural selection," Florence said stubbornly.

"Hi, Flo," Sophie said, joining them. "Hi, Mercy. Happy New Year."

Mercy nodded. "Happy New Year. I've been telling Florence here that I don't like that stupid name she thought up for our house—the Life Boat! It's riddled with negative connotations, like we'd be drowning without it or like our real ship sank and this is only a temporary measure—like we're floating around waiting to be saved! I don't know about Florence, but living as we do is my *first* choice."

"Okay, then you think of a name, smart aleck," Florence said. "But it has to be evocative of women and children. Go on, I'm waiting."

"I got one for you—'*home*.'" Mercy stood up. "I'm going home. To make some ginger beer. Nice to see you, Sophie. Rachida, Malik, come on! Emerson, where's Josie?" She set off gracefully across the park in search of her flock, her head held high.

"So did you write the letter?" Florence asked when they were alone.

"I did."

"Wow, I wish I could see it."

"Too personal, I think."

"No, I don't mean read it, just see it. Behold it. Touch it. See if it burns!"

"Well, I've got it here." Sophie pulled it out of her bag. "I had it on the shelf in the kitchen, and, Florence, I swear, it was as if light shone from it. It lit up the whole room! Then I started carrying it with me, for company, like a fetish. Does that sound deranged? Here it is. My juju."

"Ow!" Florence tossed the envelope from hand to hand,

yelping. "Red-hot!" Then she winced and mimed sucking blood from her finger. "And it cuts to the bone!"

Sophie laughed. "I'm proud of it, actually. Short but to the point."

"And heavy! I think it may contain some type of occult artifact."

"That would be telling."

"All ready for the exorcism ritual, then? Here we go. Shut your eyes."

"No need, Flo. I'm feeling better."

"No you're not. Don't ruin my fun. Now, tell me one thing. Did you change your name when you got married?"

"Yes."

"Obscene custom. To what?"

"Dean."

"And now you've gone back to your real name?"

"Yes."

"Good. That makes it easier. Now, shut your eyes and concentrate. Go on, I'll keep an eye on the kids, I promise. I'm going to do some chanting." She began to hum tonelessly but broke off to say, "The fact that this ritual is ridiculous in no way undermines its effectiveness—you do see that, don't you?" Then she got back to her chanting, which went on so long that Sophie relaxed, quite lulled, and eventually she became aware that words were emerging from the sound: "Leav-ing So-phie Dean…Leav-ing So-phie Dean…" Florence fell silent, then whispered, "And now for the final stage of the ritual. Are you ready to shed your shackles?" Sophie nodded, her eyes still closed, and Florence said very softly, her lips brushing Sophie's cheek, "Then bid your married self adieu." Sophie was considering what it would feel like to really do that when she heard the crunching sound of Florence's tennis shoes sprinting away across the gravel, followed by a metallic creaking sound like a—

Sophie's eyes flew open. "No!"

Too late. Florence crammed the letter into the mailbox, and the metal jaws clanged shut. The letter was gone.

Florence sauntered back holding her hands up, palms out, to stave off reproaches. "Sorry, Soph. It had to be done. Happy New Year."

Desperately, Sophie tried to recall what the letter said, but the words fled from her memory like cockroaches scattering when the light is turned on. "Florence, you had no right! That was very, very wrong!"

"I know. But listen. An unmailed letter is a useless piece of paper. A mailed letter is a rusty hacksaw."

"I can't even remember what I wrote!"

"Who cares what you wrote? You flushed the shit out of your system and returned it to sender. What could be more fair? Now forget it. Fuck him. What's your real name?"

Sophie was still staring at the mailbox. "At least it didn't have a stamp on it."

"It does now. Have stamps, will travel." Florence fished a crumpled roll of stamps out of her back pocket and held them up. "I stuck on five to make sure. Been carrying them for days. I was just afraid you wouldn't address it, but you did. See how your subconscious—"

"You had no right to do that," Sophie said again.

"Listen to me! What's your real name?"

"Szabo."

"Oh, wow, Sophie Szabo? It's like an actress of the silent screen. Some luscious vamp with a cigarette holder and a gravelly foreign accent, just dripping with sexiness. Sophie Szabo..."

Now forget it. Fuck him. What's your real name? Sophie switched her gaze from the mailbox to Florence. "Yes," she said at last. "It is a good name. I like it, too."

———

Adam wheeled his shopping cart down the fruit-and-vegetable aisle with an air of calm efficiency. He'd become so familiar with the layout of the supermarket that he could draw up his shopping list in the order the items appeared in the store—a minor achievement, but one he was proud of, for it should enable him to wheel his cart through just once, getting everything in one pass, and then proceed straight to checkout. No doubling back for forgotten items or time-consuming trolling of the aisles—in theory, anyway. In prac-tice, the perfect once-only sweep through the store had yet to be achieved, but the attempt to do it lent a certain sporting challenge to these Saturday mornings. Adam had also de vised a way of keeping the boys reasonably amused while he shopped, by applying a nautical theme to the task: The cart was a boat, Hugo the captain, and Matthew the nimble first mate. Adam contented himself with the role of simple seaman, navigating the vessel through the waterways and reading the items off the list. First Mate Matthew raced up and down the aisles fetching things, then handed them to Captain Hugo, who "stowed them in the hold." It was a somewhat cumbersome system, but better than the alterna-tive: boredom and bickering.

Matthew came running up to the cart carrying a net bag of avocados not on Adam's list. "Hang on, son. Isn't that a stowaway?" The truth be told, the game was rather fun.

"They're for Valerie. She likes them."

"That's very thoughtful. All right, give them to the captain." And Matthew passed them to Hugo, who threw them into the cart with a force that made Adam wince. "Let's see, now, what next? Think you can find"—he scanned the list for something not too heavy, too breakable, or too far away— "some kitchen sponges? Yellow on one side, green on the other?" Matthew dashed away, and Adam looked with pleasure at the avocados, clear indicators of how well the boys had accepted Valerie's presence in the house and proof that he and Valerie were handling the situation correctly. Matthew came running back and tossed the sponges to Hugo, who dropped them into the cart listlessly. "I'm hungry," he said. "Can we have these?" He pointed to some cookies in garish packaging.

"Hungry? You, too, Matt? All right. But no biscuits. We'll get something better." Adam wheeled the cart quickly to the delicatessen counter, which meant backtracking and ruining yet another week's attempt, but it was in a good cause: He had learned that tears followed swiftly upon the first announcement of hunger. Mercifully, there was no line. He ordered half a pound of sliced ham, two of the slices to be rolled up and given to the boys to eat right away. While they ate, a woman who had been watching them flashed a smile at Adam. "That's a good trick, Daddy. I'll remember that one!" In her cart sat a large, glassy-eyed toddler. Adam smiled distantly and made his getaway. Single mothers were the natural hazard of these Saturday mornings, and this woman was definitely giving off the lonely/deserving/brave aura of a single mother. In all his years as a bachelor, he had never been as sought after as he was now, in the company of his children, at any frozen-food counter or swing set, but as sorry as he felt for these women—and God knew he could sympathize!—

their neediness repelled him and made him all the more grateful for self-reliant and unencumbered Valerie.

"Daddy, Hugo won't say 'Aye-aye!'" Matthew complained.

"I'm the captain," Hugo said darkly.

"You still have to say 'Aye-aye.' Everybody has to say 'Aye-aye' on a ship. Right, Daddy?"

Hugo shook his head, looking thunderous.

Time to distract them. "Listen, sailors, do you know how to dance the hornpipe?" Adam began to execute some hops, arms crossed, knees out, singing softly, "Toodle-oot, toot, toot. Toddle-oodle, toot, toodle-oodle...." Matthew watched in rapt admiration.

"Ah, *excuse* me, please!" came a loud, impatient male voice from behind them. "I'd like to get past, if that's okay with you *old tars*?" Adam was blocking the aisle.

"Certainly." Adam stood to one side, his color rising.

"Again!" Hugo demanded.

"Not just now, dear."

"Again!" The checkout line was long; they needed amusing; there was nothing for it. Adam fixed his eyes on the far wall to mask his embarrassment and kept his footwork as discreet as possible. It was a red-letter day for the supermarket imp.

"Matthew's doing very well," his teacher told Sophie, "as I told his dad just before Christmas break. I guess you know he came in to talk to me?"

"You called Adam in for a talk?"

"No, no. He made the appointment. He just wanted to

see how the boys were getting on—you know, check their progress. He met with Hugo's teacher as well." She smiled reassuringly. "Don't worry, both boys are doing fine. They seem to be handling your separation very well. I don't know what you're doing, but whatever it is, don't stop—it's working!"

"I'm glad." Something else occurred to Sophie. "Was it Matthew who told you about our separation?"

"No, his father. He came in—oh, back in October. When the...events...were still recent."

"Oh, yes. Fine. Thank you." The events. Sophie moved off, her smile fading, feeling that Adam had upstaged her. She should have told the boys' teachers herself, of course she should have. But it hadn't even occurred to her back at that frantic time. Adam never used to go to meetings with teachers, not even the once-a-year official ones, and now here he was checking up regularly on the boys' progress. Well, well.

"An indifferent father..." Hadn't she called him that in her letter? Sometimes stray phrases from the letter wafted into her mind, but she resolutely pushed them aside. *Now forget it. Fuck him. What's your real name?* She was going to put that letter right out of her mind.

———————

"I know I didn't throw away the original," she said, rooting through her desk. "Just tell me what you think of it. Now, where...? Here it is!" She passed the page, blackened with cross-outs, to Henry, who was sitting at the kitchen table eating grapes. "Be honest, now."

He stood up, stretched, and took the letter. "You're sure you want me to read this?"

"I value your opinion. More than anyone's." With a slight shock, she realized that was true. More than *anyone's*. She began to feel a little odd. There was something about the way he was standing there, with his weight on one leg, one hand on his hip, in the other hand the letter...something about the way the light was striking his serious face...his mouth...

"Hmm," he said when he had finished reading. "Mean."

Sophie's ears were full of a rushing sound. "Mean?" she asked faintly.

"It's a mean letter."

"Oh!" She pressed her hand to her sternum with a gasp, her eyes squeezed shut.

"What's wrong?"

"It's nothing." She was bent forward now, though, and pressing her hand harder into her chest. "I just felt a..." She exhaled through her mouth before continuing. "A sudden stab of love for you." She breathed out again slowly, her eyes still closed, and when she opened them, he was studying her gravely.

"Is that so?"

She gasped and leaned forward in a fresh spasm. "No, stop it," she whispered. "It hurts."

He put his arms around her, and she kept very still, her face pressed to his shirt, feeling his heart beat against her cheek. The sound seemed to come from a long way inside him, and she pictured the valves opening and closing to the rhythm of the pulsation, like frilly sea creatures tossed in the waves.

The letter lay forgotten, facedown on the floor.

Adam was at that moment drawing his own much neater copy from its envelope. He had not wanted to read it at home, for reasons he didn't care to examine, so he'd brought it to work that morning but put off opening it all day—why, again, he didn't care to look into. Something to do with the strange bulkiness of the envelope, perhaps, or the long row of stamps, slapped on crooked and upside down. Strange. Valerie had already gone home, assuming that he had, too, when she got no response to her light tap on his door. Around him the building had grown quiet as everyone left, and still Adam had hesitated. At last he ripped open the envelope, and as he pulled out the single sheet of paper, something else slipped out and dropped into his lap: a mirror, the small, round kind women use for putting on lipstick. With a sense of foreboding, he unfolded the sheet of paper and scanned the short paragraph written in Sophie's once-so-familiar handwriting. The words "failed," "mediocre," and "faithless" leaped out at him at once, making his heart pound. In vain his eyes sought somewhere they could land without pain, but the whole thing was studded with thorns: "pitiably," "indifferent," "inadequacy." When he came to the end, he could feel the blood throbbing in his face. He began at the top again, slowly this time, reading every line:

Adam,

There can be no happiness for you. A man who cannot read his soul and communicate what he finds there will never find contentment. You are a small man, a failed man: an indifferent father, a mediocre worker, a faithless lover. The only grand and exalted things about you are your pitiably unrealistic expectations of yourself, which serve only to dwarf your rare achievements.

Nothing will ever make you acceptable to yourself. You will continue to run, and dodge, and hide from your own inadequacy until there is nowhere left to go, and finally you will die knowing you have wasted the gift of life.

Sophie

Adam turned the mirror over in his hands, then held it up and peered in. Reflected there he saw one worried eye.

"Where's Mr. Dean?" Valerie asked when she got home, shaking out her umbrella. Milagros and the boys were sitting at the kitchen table, Milagros already in her raincoat. The boys looked at each other and climbed down from their chairs.

"He called to say he's running late," Milagros said, rising to go. "I can't wait." She picked up her bag, wrinkled her nose at the boys, and strode away, her lips pursed.

"Oh, great," Valerie said when the door slammed. "Just great." Then she noticed that the boys were standing rather formally side by side in front of her. "What's up with you two?"

"Aren't you going to kiss us?" Matthew asked.

"We don't mind the lipstick," Hugo said, and Matthew shot him a warning glance.

"Oh!" Disconcerted, Valerie dipped down and gave them each a quick peck, realizing guiltily that it would never have occurred to her to kiss them unless Adam were in the room. They turned away and began surreptitiously to scrub their cheeks.

"Oh, I see what you mean!" she said with a laugh. "It's supposed to be no-smudge, so you don't leave telltale traces on anybody's collar. But I guess it's not, eh?"

"We don't mind very much," Matthew said.

"I have an idea. How about if I just give you those insincere, actressy air kisses to either side of your head? Then I won't touch you at all. Look, it's kind of fun. You do it at the same time I do, see? We just brush cheeks, and instead of kissing we say, 'Mwah! Mwah!' in this really fake way, and then we both shout, '*Dar*-ling!' Come on, let's try it."

Shy but willing, they rehearsed this exchange until they had it down and all three of them were giggling. Then Valerie lost interest.

"That's enough," she snapped after the thirtieth repetition, just as it was really getting to be fun. She poured herself some wine and dropped into a chair at the kitchen table. "Now, run off and play. I have work to do." With a sigh they went into the living room, but something they found there brought them right back. Matthew came in looking grave, followed by Hugo, looking doubly so. Silently, Matthew extended his hand. In it he held gingerly between thumb and forefinger, like something he hardly dared to touch, a packet of her cigarettes.

"Oh! Thanks." Embarrassed, she stuffed them in her bag.

"Smoking makes your insides black," Matthew said. "Then you get sick."

"Is that what they tell you in school?"

He nodded. Hugo, too.

"Well, it's perfectly true. Smoking is bad, so don't you ever do it."

Matthew moved closer and put his hand on her arm. "I don't want you to get sick." Hugo squeezed in on her other side, and she sat between their solemn upturned faces, unsure what to say.

Then Matthew asked, "Can you read us that book again?"

"What book?"

"About the prince in the palace."

"Yes!" Hugo's face lit up, remembering. "But it wasn't fancy enough, so he went to another house and another and another!"

"Oh, right. That one. Well. After that there was a recession in the property market, and he went broke and ended up sleeping in a cardboard box. The End."

Matthew hung his head, and Hugo said in a barely audible voice, "I wanted to see the pictures."

Oh, God. All you want to do is a little work, and you're going to be fired if you don't, but if they're going to be so pathetic about it, *all right*. Let's see now...something fun to do with kids when it's raining... "I know," she said brightly. "Let's make a cake!"

"Well, you know how it goes," Valerie related to Agatha from her office the next morning, ruffling her hair idly with the hand not holding the phone. "You start out all serious with a recipe book in front of you, and the next thing you know, you're slinging cake batter, the kitchen's a mess, everybody's screaming with laughter—and then big, bad Adam comes home. Fee, fie, foe, fum. 'What the blazes is going on in here?' I explain, and you know what he says to me? In his tight-lipped English way, he says, 'Two children in this house are quite enough!' Can you believe that? Talk about a stick up the ass."

What Valerie didn't know was that the boys had found her performance heroic. They thought her immensely brave for facing their angry father, and they were deeply grateful to her for taking all the blame.

"I can't win, that's clear," she continued. "If I do nothing with the kids, he acts like a martyr. If I play with them, he gets furious and insults me. It's a loser's game." There was silence. "Agatha, are you there?"

"Mmm." Agatha was sitting in her cluttered study, clenching the phone to her shoulder with her chin, hands on the keyboard, eyes on the screen. She had an article to send off in half an hour. There are limits to how much a person still owes someone for befriending her in high school when she was plump and taking her to a prom. Or, put another way, exactly how fat would you need to have been to still be indebted to that person twenty-three years later?

"I mean, to call me a *child*, just because out of the goodness of my heart I was amusing his kids when I should have been working! And where was he, you ask? I'll tell you where he was—walking the streets! In the rain. Alone, or so he says. But I'll bet he was kissing the boss's ass behind my back, sucking up with that partnership in mind." She raked her hair with her fingers so it stood in the air and pursed her lips poutily at herself in the mirror across from her desk, like a model in a hairdressing magazine.

There was a fresh silence, which, when it filtered through to her attention, Agatha filled with a vague, "Oh, yeah. Well, I think parents are like that."

Whatever the hell *that* meant! "Agatha, are you even listening to me? I'm in this whole goddamned mess because of you. 'Give him an ultimatum,' you said. I've been such a fool. What kind of a jackass would take advice from a loser like you?"

That got Agatha's attention nicely. She was never *that* fat. "Hey, I never told you to move into his house. This is all your own fault. You're just pissed off because home wrecking isn't turning out to be as easy as you thought it would be."

"*What?*"

"And you know what? I'm glad it's not easy. I'm glad that destroying other people's lives isn't a cinch. Now let me ask you one thing. Did you clean up that kitchen?"

"What?"

"Did you scrape the cake batter back off the walls?"

"No!"

"I knew it. Don't you see you're nothing but a spoiled brat? No wonder he misses living with a grown-up." She had to shout over Valerie to get the next part in. "And another thing, you manipulative creep—*you* didn't have a date for that prom either! It's taken me twenty-three years to figure it out, but I've figured it out at last! You pretended you were doing it all for my benefit in order to make me feel indebted to you, but no one had invited you to the prom either! In your own way, Valerie, *you were just as fat as I was!*"

Valerie leaped to her feet. "I think I understand, Agatha," she said crisply, beginning to pace her office. "This is where all your bottled-up envy of me comes spewing forth at last, after years and years of secretly hating me. It's Plain Jane's Revenge Hour! You failed to get Howard to leave his wife, so now home wrecking is evil. Okay, I can follow your reasoning, no problem. But what I'd like to know is, who are *you* to talk about grown-ups? You, the eternal adolescent, the pathetic *poseur*, all affectation! You have to go *as* someone, because you *are* no one. You've got no *life*, only a life*style*. You know, Agatha, if only you could become a real person one day, then maybe you—"

But a thin, sustained note cut in on the line. Agatha had hung up. Fine! Valerie snapped her phone shut. It was high time to get that envious bitch out of her life anyway. It never pays to have insecure girlfriends; sooner or later they knife you in the back. Friendship can only flourish among equals!

What a day. Valerie toyed gloomily with her phone, wondering what a girl could do when she had quarreled with her lover and now her best friend was history. Easy: take solace in her work. Work. Work her way up and out of trouble, just as she'd always done, leaving all the tiny envious people behind, choking on her dust.

She called Masterson and asked if he was free to talk over some doubts she had about the new project she was presenting. He invited her to lunch, and she accepted.

Agatha chuckled after she hung up on Valerie. She got up and stretched and went to the mirror. Adjusting her bangs, she was struck by two things: one, that she was looking rather attractive, flushed and bright-eyed after the battle, and two, that there was nothing second-rate about the role of catalyst. How could she ever have thought so? Transformer, bewitcher, Agatha Weatherby remodeled the lives of those she met; in the wake of her passage, all were transfigured—as poor old Valerie had good reason to know! Agatha frowned at her reflection, seeking just the right word to describe what she saw, and her brow cleared when she found it: *an enchantress.*

Serenely, she returned to her article.

James popped his head around Adam's door near the end of the day. "Looks like you were right, pal. They didn't renew Harris's contract. He's out on his ass. I'm getting kind of worried."

"Don't. They're just cutting fat off the top. He wasn't worth what they were paying him. You're all right. You're the best technician in the firm, and everyone knows it."

James excelled at making the engineering interface that fit the electricity, plumbing, and security needs smoothly and economically into the images of whichever partner was titular architect of the project—not a glamorous role, perhaps, but bloody useful, and Adam greatly admired his work and dedication.

"Well, Adam, you're our great 'idea man.' That petrochemical project ought to safeguard your job...for a while anyway. 'We're green because we say so!' That was a good 'un!"

"I hope you're right. Otherwise I've sold my soul for nothing."

James laughed and turned to go. "Well, I just thought you'd want to hear the latest."

"Thanks. Oh, James? Ah...I was wondering....Are you free for a drink after work?"

"Sure." James looked a little puzzled by Adam's air of constraint. "See you around six, then."

He left, and Adam frowned deeply at his desktop to cover the embarrassment he felt. There was nothing wrong with asking James to have a drink after work. They always had one after a squash game, so why did he feel embarrassed about it now? Well, because a drink after squash is to quench thirst, and a normal drink after work is to talk shop, but tonight Adam wanted to talk—*not* shop, just talk. To *talk*-talk, as teenaged girls might put it, he thought with distaste. And that was certainly new to his experience.

In Adam's view, conversation between men could have several perfectly acceptable tones—jocular, whimsical, challenging, thoughtful—and deal with many subjects—work, politics, travel, history, the arts. But the one objectionable tone was earnestness—the comment "Rather an *earnest* sort of fellow, I thought," was not anything one wanted said about oneself—and the subject to avoid at all costs was, of course, one's private life. Thus far Adam had never had any impulse to deliver impassioned monologues on the topic of his love life. He was discreet almost to a fault—all right, to a fault—and he found that particularly American tendency to gush intimate biographical detail to others a comical and repellent one.

And yet here he was. He and James were on their second beer, and they had exhausted all possible shop talk about downsizing. They sipped in silence, Adam trying to ignore the feeling that a large black question mark was hovering cartoon-style over their table, trying to pretend that the air was not reverberating with James's carefully unspoken question—*So what was it you wanted to talk to me about?*—and that this was just a restful silence, such as two people who know each other well and who are tired after a long day can share.

"So!" James said after a while. And that didn't make things any better, the fresh silence sitting even more heavily than the earlier one. He guffawed loudly, then drank deeply. "Hey, should I ask them to put your beer in the microwave for you?" He hooted again, slapping the bar top, and Adam smiled patiently at the old joke. The only fact that many Americans seemed to know about the British Isles was that beer there was drunk at room temperature. Hardly a week went by that Adam was not teased about warm beer.

"Actually, lager in Britain is served cold," he said eventually. He felt that the task of easing gracefully into the conversation was beyond him; it would have to be straight in or nothing. Quietly, he said, "I never thought Sophie would leave the children."

But the change of gears was too fast for James, and it caught him off balance. Still in nervous, hearty mode, he replied too loudly, practically a shout: "Well, I bet she never thought you'd leave her!" His eager look invited Adam to join him in a big laugh, but that didn't happen. Too late, he slammed his own gearshift into low, saying with ponderous gravity, "Oh...yeah...it's...Yeah." He fingered a beer mat, frowning so hard that Adam doubted he could see anything. "It's...I...I never met Sophie, but..." A little time passed. "But Valerie's...quite a woman."

"She is," Adam said, and James's shoulders slumped with relief. "She doesn't feel really comfortable with the children, naturally enough. But she does her best with them. She tries, she really does." A "but" floated unspoken in the air.

"Yeah, well, kids are..." James began, but he seemed to run into another snag. "Marriage...it's tough—not that I'm an expert! And with kids, too, it's...well, it's..."

"It's tough," Adam finished for him briskly. "You're quite right. Women, marriage, kids—it's all tough. Drink to that?" He lifted his glass and drank, feeling humiliated that James had had to point out the obvious: that sniveling about one's personal life was not the thing to do—as Adam knew damned well.

It could have ended like that, with Adam's timid attempt to confide thwarted by James, the hint taken by Adam, and their relationship remaining on the same footing as before, no harm done. But James spoke again. "Look, Adam, I..."

Adam tried to wave his words away, but there was no deterring James now.

"I don't know anything about marriage, and not a lot about women—half the time I'm not even seeing anyone. I don't have children, so I'm not much good there either. But I do realize you've been going through a difficult time, and if there's any way I could help you, I would like to. Now, I *have* spent some time with my nephews—not a lot, but some— and I'm pretty sure that I could cope with your boys for an evening or a Saturday or whatever. I could figure out some way of keeping them occupied. At the very least, they'd be safe with me, you could be sure of that. And I'd be happy to do it. I mean that."

Adam blinked as he registered the touching fact that James was offering to baby-sit. His first thought was to laugh it off with a defensive joke, but he resisted that, and bravely he said only, "Thank you, James."

Usually Milagros double-parked outside Sophie's apartment and rang the bell, and Sophie brought the boys down for her to take back to their father's house. But sometimes, when she had time to spare and she could find a parking space, Milagros came upstairs for a chat.

The boys were playing industriously out on the porch, bundled up against the cold, constructing forts out of sofa cushions, dismayed at first when the fort walls kept falling over, then incorporating that into the game—earthquake! Build the fort again! Sophie smiled at them from the kitchen window as she poured out tea for her guest. They called each other Mila and Sophie now. Formality between them had ended along with the Deans' marriage, and anyway, Milagros worked for Adam now, so their relationship as boss and employee was over. After her ritual complaint about the traffic, which, when bad, could double the twenty-five minutes it usually took her from Milton, Milagros turned to her favorite topic: Valerie.

"Always with the cigarette in the mouth. Like this on the patio." Milagros waved two fingers stiffly in the air, lips pursed, miming smoking. "No ashtray, no. Just throws the butts on the ground—*¡toma ya!* Well, what are you going to do? The woman is a pig."

"I hope she doesn't smoke in the house?" Sophie asked, and when Milagros shook her head almost regretfully, she insisted, "It's a bad example for the boys. Why does Adam put up with it?"

Milagros snorted in a way that left no doubt as to the ineffectualness of Mr. Dean in that household, but all she said was, "He's too busy doing all the work. She does nothing of nothing. Except make coffee in her fancy machine." She rose with a grunt and went to the door to call to the boys, "Come on, time to go," countering their wails of protest with, "We got cushions at home," and then she said to Sophie, "That house is a disaster, a big mess every day. But I don't touch her garbage. I just clean up after the boys. And I put away Mr. Dean's things, of course."

However, that wasn't exactly true. That very morning there had been something of Mr. Dean's that Milagros had not put away: a few papers she had come across, handwritten attempts at a letter to Sophie, three sheets in all. Each said "*Sophie*" at the top of the page, followed by a sentence or two that was scribbled out but still legible if you really tried, and Milagros figured that Valerie would. Milagros had found these efforts abandoned in plain sight in Adam's trash can, lying uncrumpled on the top, where anyone could read them without even going to the trouble of smoothing them out. And somehow or other, they had wound up on the side table where Valerie usually set her wineglass after work. "Come on, boys! I said you can play that at home!" Milagros allowed herself a small smile. Her job had its satisfactions.

When Adam got home that evening after his talk with James, he found Valerie sitting as usual with a glass of wine in her hand and her work spread out on the chesterfield. The house was quiet.

"Good evening," she said in a controlled voice that sounded very nearly pleasant. Adam, at any rate, didn't notice anything unusual about it. "Late again, my goodness," she went on. "That makes two nights in a row. More walking in the rain alone?"

There was a slight emphasis on the word "alone" that Adam also missed. "I had a drink with James tonight, actually," he replied. "Are the kids upstairs?"

"Fast asleep. Fed, bathed, read to, and tucked in."

"Oh, thanks, Valerie." He sighed and dropped into a chair. "Thanks."

"It wasn't part of our agreement, but I had no choice. You weren't here to do it, and I have stacks of work to do, so... We need that nanny, Adam. Badly."

He grunted in that way men have, indicating neither agreement nor disagreement, but merely that they want the topic to go away.

"So how was James—it was James you were with, wasn't it?"

"He's fine. He's a good fellow, James."

"If not terribly bright."

"He is bright, actually. And he's a good, solid architect. A fine draftsman."

"Hmm. I guess his buildings don't actually fall down."

"And he's unpretentious."

"Yes. Well, I suppose he'd have to be, really."

Silence. "I think I'll go soak in a hot bath," Adam said.

"Good idea." She let him turn toward the stairs before adding, "But before you go, perhaps you could explain why you left these unfinished letters to your ex-wife lying around for me to find? I mean, I understand perfectly that it's an act of nonverbal hostility—that's no problem. My only question is, why?"

"What?" He looked alarmed.

"It's the ineloquence of them that's so pathetic, like a lovesick schoolboy—" 'Sophie' ... 'Sophie' ... 'Sophie,' " she read, waving the sheets in the air as she flipped through them. " 'I hardly know where to begin. ...' Well, that's obvious. Maybe if you can't tell her what's on your mind, you'd better tell me. What's going on, Adam?"

"You have no right to read my private correspondence."

"Then why do you shove it under my nose?"

"I'd hardly call it that!" Adam had not thought Valerie the type to root through wastepaper baskets.

"What is this, Adam? An attempt at reconciliation?"

"This is outrageous!"

"Spit it out."

"If you must know, I was working on a reply to a letter I received from her."

"I see. How long have you been corresponding in secret?"

"Don't be ridiculous. She's only written this once. But I have every right to correspond with her. She's the mother of my children."

"But you're not writing about the children, are you? Because if you were, you *would* 'know where to begin'!"

"Valerie, let me make it clear to you that I will never seek your permission to contact my wife. We have our children in common, and that means we will be in touch frequently and for the rest of our lives. That's a simple fact. Your feelings about it are irrelevant."

"How you thrill me when you talk tough. Fact number one: This is not your wife. You left her for me, remember? Fact number two: It is to me that you owe allegiance, honesty, and loyalty. And writing love letters to another woman is none of the fucking above."

"It wasn't a love letter." Adam sat down and began to massage his temples. Occasionally Valerie's bellicose quality, initially so attractive to him, wearied him deeply, and a vision of Sophie as he had first conceived of her would flash through his mind—that soothing, peaceable woman, her face to the prairie wind, apron strings and loose hair streaming behind her. Trite, of course, to view them like that: the hawk and the dove. And inaccurate! The new Sophie was nothing if not pugnacious. "She wrote me a... a venomous letter. I was quite taken aback. Astonishing, really, the sheer force of her hatred. I had no idea."

A little hope flickered in Valerie. "I guess she's angry about my being here. Regrets leaving? Wants to come back?"

"No, no." Adam gave a bitter laugh. "Not at all. If anything, I think she's grateful to me for leaving her."

"Oh, wonderful. Just fucking wonderful."

"Imagine what a poor time of it women had back in the days when marriage meant 'security.' What could be less secure than marriage? Imagine gambling everything, even the roof over your head and the food on your table, on your ability to get along with one man—and he with you. It's insanely risky."

The park was covered with snow, already dirty, and the children were playing with plastic sleds, or trying to, the lack of hills proving a drawback. Sophie was sitting hunched against the cold, her hands tucked muff-style into her sleeves. She turned to look at Florence on the bench beside her, but the edge of her hood was in the way. "Brr!" was all she replied.

"But you're doing things right," Florence continued. "You get a lover, great, you move him in. It goes sour, fine, you chuck him out. All the important elements of your life— your house, your kids, your work—are still in place and rock solid. Now, that's what I call security. Always be in a position where you can change the lock on the front door. 'Change the locks!'—that was my mother's battle cry."

"Why? What was your father like?"

"No idea. I'm a third-generation single mother. Fathers don't run in our family."

"Then who was she changing the locks on?"

"Boyfriends. She always used to tell my sister and me that if we ever lived with a man and he took to drink or violence or religion or whatever, we should change the locks right away. No fooling around with second chances and hollow promises."

"Is that what happened to your father? He came home one day and he was locked out?"

"I don't know. I don't know anything about him. Or want to."

"Isn't it natural to be curious?"

"As far as I'm concerned, I sprang full-blown from my mother's loins. The same as Josie and Emerson sprang from mine."

"Hmm. I don't know. It's all very defensive, this image of being barricaded in, changing the locks.... It's not really attractive to me. I still cling to the romantic idea of finding a traveling partner for the voyage through life"—she laughed self-consciously—"in spite of everything."

"I'm not against romance, you understand. I'm just against the package deal. I believe I can create my own setup, perfectly suited to me. I want a life that's made to measure and sewn by hand, with each element carefully chosen by me and for me. I don't want that plastic life that comes in a kit and you just snap it together."

"A married life, straight off the hanger," Sophie said, feeling suddenly weary and sad. "I guess that's what I had—from the ready-to-wear line." She roused herself. "But you would never set up house with any man because it's too risky. Is that right?"

"It's not that I never would, but I'd have to think about it ver-y care-fully. And it wouldn't have to be a man either, although it could be. A brief footnote here, Sophie, on my sexual orientation—I wouldn't reject a perfect life partner simply because she happened to be a woman. I vote for the candidate, not the party."

Sophie thought about it. "That's lucky, really. It doubles your chances of finding your perfect partner, doesn't it?"

"It should."

Sophie shivered and tucked her chin deeper into her coat

collar. Florence seemed impervious to the cold, sitting casually with her legs stretched out before her and her hands in her pockets, scanning the park. "Actually, I told you a lie back then," she said after a while. "It isn't true that I never, ever wondered about my father. When I was a kid, you know...but why dwell? I decided on a line years ago, and I'm sticking to it." And before Sophie could say anything, "Hey, take a look. What's going on with your kids?" Over near the merry-go-round, Matthew and Hugo were giving each other air kisses and exclaiming, "*Dar*-ling, mwah, mwah!" in affected tones.

A car horn tooted; it was Milagros behind the wheel, ready to take the boys home. "Come on, boys!" Sophie called. "Where in heaven's name did you learn to do that?" She shot an inquiring look at Milagros, who shook her head sourly.

"Valerie showed us. It's so she doesn't get lipstick on us. You do it, too, Mommy! Mwah, mwah, *dar*-ling!"

"I'll see you tomorrow, angels. Bye-bye." Sophie watched the car pull away, feeling odd. So Valerie was fun. And inventive. Well, she would have to be an interesting person; look at all Adam had done for her—and given up for her. It hurt Sophie to think about that, but jealousy wasn't the odd feeling; she was used to that. The odd feeling was a curious little pocket of gladness. Somewhere deep within her, Sophie was glad that Valerie was fun. Only for the boys' sake, of course, not for Adam's, and it made her feel rather left out as well, so it was hardly a Pauline conversion, but still she was, definitely, just a tiny bit glad. And there was a delicious restfulness in that feeling. Through that narrow porthole, she could foresee oceans of peace.

Sophie wasn't able to put a name to this moment, but

Henry could have. And he would have snapped his fingers as he said it.

———

A bird sang, the only sound in the Sunday-morning quiet. Cold winter sunlight shone in the stained-glass window, casting an oblong pool of color onto the wooden floorboards and partway up the wall. In a bowl on the windowsill some blue hyacinths had opened early, fooled by the warmth of the radiator, and their sweet smell was heavy in the air. Clement's house had never been more pleasing to all the senses, Sophie thought as, through the open bedroom door, she watched Henry stride around the kitchen, deftly opening the correct cupboards and drawers, finding things without asking, managing to be at ease without seeming proprietary, a guest in her house, but a competent one.

She was sitting up in bed, her legs crossed, the crumpled white sheet over her lap, ready to receive the breakfast tray when he brought it. She studied his muscular back and buttocks as he reached for plates and glasses and rinsed out the teapot, moving in that proud, happy way men have when they first walk around a woman's house naked. He turned, and through the doorway he tossed her an orange, which she caught. They had been lovers for three days.

"You know, I think I've got the switch," she said, peeling the orange.

"Yes, you have," he said, busy with the teaspoons.

"Was it making love with you that gave it to me?"

"No." He came in carrying the laden tray, which she took on her lap while he climbed into bed beside her. "I was waiting for you to get it first."

"That was considerate of you."

"Yes. Considerate *to* me, above all."

"How so?"

"So you would be thinking only of me. I didn't want anyone else on your mind, not while we were making love. Afterward, of course…" He shrugged and passed her a cup of tea. "Does that sound possessive?"

"No." She sipped. "I think everyone feels that way. It's part of why sexual infidelity is so painful—finding out there was a ghost in your bed. And while he was making love to you, his mind was…elsewhere. You know, when we make love, I think of geometric shapes."

"Do you?" He smiled. "How scholarly!"

"I feel that mysterious geometric equations are resolving themselves."

"Well then, listen to this." He whispered sexily in her ear. "In a right triangle, the square of the hypotenuse is equal to the sum of the square…of the *two sides.*"

It had all begun very simply with a knock on the door. She had opened it, and there he was, standing there smiling. For a moment she stared, wondering if she had willed him to her door. Then he held out his arms, and she rushed into them without a word. It was Friday, Adam's weekend with the boys, and she'd meant to pick them up at school as usual and keep them until he got home from work, but as two-thirty drew near, she saw that it wouldn't be possible after all. She reached out of bed for the phone, started to call Marion, thought better of it, called Florence instead, made some arrangements, and then, miraculously, she was free for two more days.

"Why did you come over here on Friday anyway?" she asked, lying in his arms after breakfast.

"To make love to you."

"Only that? You didn't have an excuse ready, in case?"

"No." He kissed her palm and held it against his chest until he dropped off to sleep again, but she stayed awake, watching the patch of colored sunlight creep across the wall and onto the bedspread.

It was the first day of the Chinese New Year.

5.

*S*ophie had just locked her door, ready to set off for school, when the telephone started ringing inside the apartment. Keys in hand, she stood wondering whether to answer it and decided no, she was already gone, or as good as gone. It wouldn't be Henry, as they were about to see each other in class. Whoever it was could leave a message or call her cell phone. But the phone continued to ring plaintively. It could be Milagros, something about the children, and she was still home, really. No, gone. Home. Gone. The children. Yes, okay, home! She unlocked the door with clumsy haste and dashed back in. Now that she'd made up her mind to answer, the idea that it might stop ringing was unbearable. She scooped up the receiver and gasped "Hello!" She listened anxiously for the toneless hum that would mean she was too late and the caller had hung up. But no, there was silence, it was all right, someone was there.

"Sophie, I received some papers from your lawyer this morning."

For a moment she couldn't place the voice, and when she did, it came as a surprise that Adam still existed in this world. He seemed to belong to the remote past, or a parallel universe, but here he was, saying, "Sophie? Sophie, are you there?"

She cleared her throat. "Yes. Hello, Adam." The words felt odd in her mouth. She said no more, marveling at the strangeness.

He misunderstood her silence. "I know you asked me not to call, but we need to get together to talk about this. I don't seem to have the time that you have for letter writing."

Oh. The letter. She'd forgotten all about it. She'd also forgotten that she'd asked him not to call. It had been a long time since she'd heard his voice. Months.

"I'd like to get together today. There are a few points we need to discuss."

"Oh."

"It's too complicated to talk about over the phone, but it won't take long. Can you make it this evening?"

"I suppose so."

"Six o'clock?"

"Can it be later?"

"It could be, but I don't want to inconvenience Milagros."

Milagros! Her first impulse was to say, *Do you know Milagros, too?* It was weird hearing someone else say that name, but of course Adam saw Milagros every day, the same as she did. Milagros was Adam's, too—as were the *children*, come to that. Yet it seemed an amazing coincidence. Sophie pulled herself together and agreed to meet him at six at a wine bar across from the Pru, not somewhere they'd ever been together. Obviously, he had given this some thought, choosing a neutral place with no associations. But as she walked to school, her sense of wonder wore off and she began to feel annoyed at herself for being so passive. He had no right calling her in the first place, much less ordering her around. *Be at this place at this time.* The nerve. And all she had said was, "Okay."

"It looks like he's finally ready to talk," Henry said when she told him. They were sitting outside on a wall during the morning break, drinking tea from a thermos. She sat cross-legged, facing his profile, and he sat with his legs dangling, sometimes straightening his right leg, then relaxing it and letting his heel bounce to a halt against the wall.

"I don't think going over a divorce settlement counts as talking," she said.

"Then it's an excuse to see you. To see how you are. He's probably concerned about you."

"How unbearably condescending."

"It could be genuine. Put yourself in his position. What if you had left him for another man? You'd be concerned about him."

"So I'm supposed to show him I'm okay so he needn't feel guilty? Talk about self-serving."

Henry laughed. "Maybe all he wants is to talk about the divorce. Don't condemn him yet."

But Sophie was angry. "Wouldn't it make you angry, Henry? Doesn't anything make you angry? Or are you so understanding that you can justify anything, in any situation?"

He answered mildly, "No, not everything. I can't justify a woman's screaming at me and spilling hot tea on me, all because she's nervous about speaking to her ex-husband."

"Oh, I'm sorry," she said, mopping the spill on his leg. "It just seemed like you were trying to defend him." She frowned, dabbing at his leg over and over with a tissue. "And I suppose... I suppose..."

He moved his leg away. "You suppose what?"

"I'm ashamed to admit this, but I will anyway. I suppose I expected you... not to be glad I was going to see him tonight. But you don't seem to care a bit. In fact, you're taking his side, and I guess I expected you to... mind. A little."

"To be jealous, you mean?" he said with surprise, and he laughed again.

Sophie listened carefully to his laugh, hoping to detect something defensive in it, but alas, it was purely good-natured. Annoyed in spite of herself, she said, "I don't think I'll see him after all. It'll only upset me—it already has. He's just being lazy. He can write down perfectly well any objections he has to the settlement. There's no need for this meeting, and I'm not going to play along. Now, how do I cancel? Or do I just stand him up?"

"You have to get used to talking to him sometime."

"Why? We lead separate lives."

"Come on. Once you have a child with someone, that's it. You're bound together for life."

"But that's exactly what I don't want!"

"It doesn't matter what you want. You're fellow parents, so you need to have the lines of communication open. He's like Milagros, or the boys' teachers, only more important, because he's more important to them."

"Are you a family counselor or something? This seems to roll off your tongue."

He smiled. "It's not an uncommon problem. You're not the first to go through this, or the last, believe it or not. You have to see their father. The first time is the hardest. The second time is the second-hardest, and so on. Soon you'll be able to meet him normally, like the butcher, the baker, or the candlestick maker, and that's the goal. He'll be like a female friend. Like Milagros."

"Adam is like the candlestick maker," she repeated, trying to convince herself. "He's my co–child raiser. We have to interact easily and frequently. Adam is like a female friend."

"That's it. And because you've already dreaded this first meeting so much, you can be pretty sure it'll go smoothly. You've done all your suffering in advance."

Henry was nearly right about that, Sophie thought after seeing Adam. Right enough to say, if you were rounding things off, that he was right. But if you were nitpicking and counting every little thought and emotion, then you'd have to say he was not entirely right—there were teeny twinges of suffering during the meeting, and the ghost aura of "husband" wafted once or twice over Adam's otherwise curiously alien form.

He looks old, was the first thing she thought when she sat down opposite him. Had he changed, or was she used now to looking at Henry's lineless face? Adam looked gray and creased and stooped—altogether less threatening than the image of him she had built in her mind. Not an ogre, just a tired, middle-aged man.

"You look very nice," he said formally, thinking that she looked younger and harder, more jagged, somehow. She used to be soft and smooth.

She glanced around the wine bar to get her bearings: bland and generic, so featureless as to defy description.

"Thank you. So do you. What did you want to talk about?" She hadn't meant to be so curt, but once she'd blurted that out, she felt exhilarated and realized that this was the way she wanted to conduct the meeting: brusquely. Up to then she hadn't known what tone to take. In mental rehearsals of how the interview would go, she had drawn a blank. She noted with satisfaction that he was taken aback by her abruptness and trying to hide it by busying himself with some papers in his briefcase, and she recognized in herself a desire to hurt him, which surprised her, but wasn't displeasing. "I'm sorry to rush you," she said, "but I'm meeting someone. I want to hear you out, of course, but I can't be late, so let's be quick." She smiled glacially, marveling inside at what she had said. Was she going to tell him about Henry, then? She hadn't thought of it until now—and even now she wasn't sure.

"Of course." Flustered, he flipped through the papers, unable to find what he was looking for. "I just want to discuss the division of our property. The house, of course, will go to you—"

She laid her hand over his papers, trapping them on the table. "I don't want it."

"Maybe not now, but—"

"I mean it. Why don't you keep it and buy me out? Or if you don't want it either, put it on the market."

"Sophie, it's the boys' home." The note of reproach in his voice lent acidity to hers.

"But not mine. You've made very sure of that."

"Don't be silly. Of course you should have it. It's yours by right."

"Why? Because convention has it that abandoned wives get the house? To assuage their husbands' guilt or compensate for it? That house is contaminated. It stinks of deceit and treachery." Adam struggled to mask the alarm he felt with a gesture merely impatient, but she saw his fear and thrilled at

it as she went on, now in a gentler tone. "What I'm trying
to say, Adam, is that if it weren't for the cowardly, dishonest
way you did it, I suppose I could thank you for ending our
marriage. Because now, instead of being a bored but brave
little housewife with a cheating husband, I'm using my brain
again, learning to do fulfilling new work, living in a place I
love, and sharing my time with a man who cares about me.
A man who speaks! A man I can talk to and laugh with, who
views the world in refreshing ways and broadens my vision
with his, as I broaden his with mine." From the queasy look
on Adam's face, she knew that this waxing-lyrical stuff was
good, and she gushed on. "Life with him is a larger thing
than life alone. Life with you was narrower. We had just a
tiny crack of a life, a vertical slit in a castle wall. We had
pared down two complete lives to just the part we had in
common. With him I have my whole life to myself again, and
I also share his. This is what life in a couple was meant to
be, Adam—a life doubled, not a life halved." She paused,
breathless, and reached forward to squeeze his hand. "Anyway," she said, fakely shy, "thank you."

He withdrew his hand. "Who is he?"

"The children haven't met him yet," she went on, freshly
inspired. "I thought they needed time to adjust to our separation first. I thought it would be unfair, even damaging, to
introduce them too soon. Eventually I'll let them know that
'Mommy has a friend.'" Adam winced, as she had known he
would. "And I'll leave it up to them to ask to meet him. Their
natural curiosity will bring them around to it"—she cocked
her head and smiled—"in their own good time."

"This...man. Is it anyone I know?"

"No." She checked her watch and started girlishly. "Oh,
I've got to run." She jumped up and, planting both hands on

the table, leaned over him in a commanding position. "Let me know about the house, if you want to buy me out or sell."

He continued to stare at the door long after it had closed behind her.

———

Later, as Adam walked up his garden path—crazy-paved, to be sure—he was greeted by strains of Van Halen pouring out of the house. Inside, the music was deafening. Valerie was lounging on the chesterfield, surrounded by all her usual clutter, directing the boys in how to play air guitar, which they were doing frenziedly, tossing their heads back and forth until their hair stood on end.

"Babe, look at this! It's priceless!" Valerie shouted to him over the music. "Now drop to your knees! You got it, Hugo! Don't forget your fingering! Matthew, head back, screw up your face! Adam, I think I have a Mary Poppins streak in me after all!"

"I doubt that very much." He crossed the room and switched off the music. The boys and Valerie wailed with disappointment.

"Oh, what a party pooper you are! Okay now, boys. Time to go backstage." They groped their way dizzily down the hall, Valerie calling after them, "And check out the groupies!"

Adam poured himself a drink. "I saw Sophie today," he said.

Valerie felt a prickle of fear that she covered with a light tone. "Oh, yeah? She stirred up more fun at the office?"

"No. We got together after work to discuss the settlement."

"I see." So it had been planned in advance, and she hadn't been told. "Well, the sooner you settle it, the sooner we'll be out of here. Did she say when she'll be reclaiming the house?"

He took a drink. "She's not coming back. She's all set up in her new life—with some man, apparently."

"Fine. Then we'll sell and move on."

"I'm not sure I want to move the boys. This is their home."

"Hey, either she moves back in here with them or we sell up and the kids go live with Mom and her fancy man. It's that simple."

"He doesn't live with her! At least I didn't get that impression." He frowned into his glass, and the lines from Donne came to him:

> *But if in thy heart, since, there be or shall,*
> *New love created hee, by other men,*
> *Which have their stocks intire, and can in teares,*
> *In sighs, in oathes, and letters outbid mee,*
> *This new love may beget new feares—*

Watching his face, something hardened in Valerie. "Oh Christ, Adam, you're jealous! Of all the pathetic—"

"I am not selling this house! It would be the last straw for the boys. They need some sort of stability in their lives, and since their mother's carrying on with...God only knows who...that stable base has got to be me. Me and this house, their home."

Valerie looked at him in silence, her anger trickling away. "This isn't how it's supposed to be, Adam. This isn't how it goes."

"What are you talking about?"

"You. You don't have a clue, do you? You haven't seen the storyboard. Let me talk you through it. We open on an unhappily married man. He meets his true love. He leaves his wife and children and lives with her happily ever after. That's the end. There's no more about the wife. She drops out of his life. That's the end of the kids, too. Oh, sure, there are birthday presents and Christmas, but that's it, Adam. And in my case there wasn't even that. When Daddy left, he was gone. Off into the sunset with the woman he loved. And that's how it's supposed to be. When a thing's over, it's over. My father had the guts—the courage!—to make a clean break. But you, Adam..." Tears started into her eyes. "You are so weak and cowardly that you drag your old life around after you like a goldfish trailing shit."

"Is that what this is all about? Your childhood and some childish wish for revenge? For Christ's sake, Valerie, grow up. There is no storyboard. No rules. This isn't a game."

"There does seem to be one rule: No matter what, Valerie gets the shit end of the stick. When she was the kid, nobody gave a fuck about the kid. But now that she's the other woman, guess who nobody gives a fuck about? Huh? Take a wild guess who nobody gives a fuck about, once again!"

"I don't have time for this. It's all been a mistake, your moving in here."

"I'll say it was a mistake! You son of a bitch!"

The boys had appeared silently at the doorway, drawn by the sound of angry voices, and they watched with wide eyes as Valerie shouted, "I gave up everything to come here and help you—my apartment, my social life, my friends, everything—to be here with you, because you asked me to! I've done my best with the children, Adam, I really have! I've done everything I can to make this work, and you just...you just…" She dropped her arms to her sides and burst into tears.

Matthew came forward bravely. "Daddy, don't be mean to Valerie!" He stepped between them, and Hugo followed, wrapping his arms protectively around Valerie's leg.

"I never asked you to move in," Adam said. "It was you who insisted."

"Bastard!" Valerie sobbed.

"Stop it, Daddy!"

Valerie knelt and put her arms around the children. The three clung together, all in tears now, and Adam looked down at the weeping group with a sense of unreality.

Valerie went back to her own apartment to sleep that night. And the next morning Milagros didn't show up, so after waiting nearly an hour, Adam dropped the boys off at school himself, making them late and himself very late, which was a pity, because there was an important meeting that morning to discuss the firm's "future trends." He peeked in through the glass doors of the conference room and saw that everyone was there. Of course. James was leaning back in his chair, fiddling with a pen and frowning, obviously in disagreement with what was being said by Masterson, who was holding forth with that exaggerated look of concern that always meant he was shafting the staff. Then Valerie spoke, and when she finished, there was laughter and a ripple of applause. Masterson smiled, said something to which she riposted, and there was more laughter. Adam couldn't make out the words through the glass, only their tones of voice. He checked his watch. He was an hour and a half late. An air of restlessness signaled that the meeting was about to break up. To go in now would only draw attention to his absence, so he decided to wait where he was. Sure enough, people began to sweep up papers and tap them into piles. James got up, stretched, and yawned. The meeting was over. The boss walked over to Valerie, took her arm, and said something to her. She hesitated, glanced at Adam through the glass door, then smiled at Masterson and shook her head, gently disengaging herself. Adam and his boss exchanged a hostile glance, and then Adam opened the door and walked in.

"Adam!" Masterson said with false heartiness. "We missed you!"

"I got held up," Adam said. "Unavoidable, I'm afraid."

"Ah, well. If it was unavoidable, then it couldn't very well have been avoided, could it?" Masterson creased his face at Adam, more baring his teeth than smiling, then nodded amiably to Valerie and turned away.

"What happened to you?" she asked when they were alone.

"Milagros was late. What did he want with you?"

"Just to continue our discussion over lunch."

"And will you?"

"I told him I couldn't make it today."

"Another day, then?"

"Possibly. What's wrong with you? You were crazy to miss this meeting! Everyone noticed."

"What are you suggesting? That I should have left the children at home alone? To burn alive if the house caught fire? Or so that the first social worker to walk by could have them taken into foster care? When I say that Milagros was late, I shouldn't need to say anything else. To one who understands the details of my home life, that explanation is complete in itself. Need I really say it again? I will if I must: *Milagros was late!*"

She tossed her head in annoyance, and he continued, "Anyway. It seems you were brilliant, as always." She looked to see if he were being sarcastic, but his face had softened.

"It's because I knew you were there, listening. I kept looking at the door, hoping you'd come, and I saw you the minute you got here. I wanted to show off for you. I'm sorry about last night."

"No, I'm the one who's sorry. Let's get out of here." He took her elbow in a proprietary gesture and steered her toward the door. In his office they kissed. "I've been thinking about what you said...about giving up your social life," Adam said into her hair.

"Forget what I said," she murmured.

"No, you were right. I was thinking—why don't we have some people over for dinner? I'd like to meet some of your friends. It might be fun, make a change. What do you say?"

She lifted her face to his. "Whatever you want, darling," she whispered, and they kissed again.

A dinner party? Hmm. A dinner party...Okay, a dinner party! Back in her office, Valerie spun girlishly on her swivel chair and automatically, as she had done so many times recently, reached for her cell phone and punched "1," her speed dial for Agatha, before she remembered to hang up again. It was a reflex: Something happened in her life; she punched "1." Without that ritual she felt unsettled, as if things couldn't become fully real until she had hashed them over with Agatha, but it was a lazy habit, she told herself, and a good thing they were on the outs. It was high time she got back into the healthy habit of thinking for herself, and not always aloud. They hadn't spoken since their fight a couple of weeks ago, or was it three already? Ages anyway. At first Valerie had been sure Agatha would call to apologize, but as time passed, she realized that Agatha was pouting and trying to make Valerie call first. Well, to hell with that. If they never spoke again, whose loss would it be? Agatha would come to her senses. Valerie could win any waiting game. The days went by, and she checked her answering machine, her voice mail, her e-mail—nothing. What insults exactly had they hurled at each other, anyway? Agatha had called her a home wrecker, and then what? Valerie had retaliated in some way, obviously, something about... oh, yes, about being a poseur and not having a personality. The unadulterated truth, of course—but mean, too. Well, of course it was mean—they were fighting, for God's sake!

Valerie yanked open a drawer and took out a piece of paper. It was all very annoying, but she had to forget it and get on with more important things, like planning this dinner party. But of course that was exactly it. She needed Agatha in order to work out the menu, the guest list, everything. These details required intense discussion. And Agatha was a star when it came to food presentation.

That was a thought. If Valerie didn't invite Agatha, who would do the cooking? Now, under the pressure of necessity, her old determination not to give in and be the first to call gave way to an eagerness to prove that she was the less childish of the two, the bigger person. She pounced on her phone and punched "1."

"Pron-to!" Agatha trilled. A new affectation. But one Valerie was equal to.

"Ciao, ragazza," she purred. *"É tanto che non ci si vede. Come stai?"*

"Valerie, hi! I was going to call you! Wait a minute, is my Italian failing me, or did you actually ask me how I am?"

"I said *'Come stai?'* all right." Despite everything, it was great hearing Agatha's voice again. Valerie had missed her.

"Molto bene, wow! This is one for the records! We should speak Italian more often. Look, how are you? I've been meaning to call, but I've been so busy." (Sure, Agatha, sure.) "I've been away the last couple of weekends." (Yeah, right.) "How's Adam?"

Valerie could detect no mockery in the question. It sounded disconcertingly transparent and friendly, as indeed Agatha's whole tone had been thus far. Not a trace of ill will. Funny. "We're just fine," she said smoothly. "In fact, we're having a little dinner party. Want to come?"

"Sure. When?"

"Next Friday. You'll get to feast your eyes on my suburban paradise at last."

"Oh, damn, I'm sorry, I can't make it. Does it have to be Friday? Is the date set?"

No, it wasn't. Any weekend Sophie had the kids would do, but Valerie wasn't about to change the day just to suit Agatha. There are limits to how magnanimous one can be, especially when dealing with someone this willful and manipulative. " 'Fraid so," she cooed. "It was a good time for everyone else." Let her think she'd been invited last.

"Oh, what a pity. Nuts." She didn't sound incapacitated by disappointment, though. "Well, maybe another time. I'd love to see your place, and meet the kids, too." How condescending that sounded, and how very much more insulting than just saying frankly, *Your life is a sickening bore*. But even more unsettling was Agatha's marked lack of bitchiness. Either her acting had improved, which was unlikely, or she was truly not engaging in any kind of battle, and if so, how humiliating for Valerie to be fighting alone! Furthermore, it was clear that Agatha was not going to lift a finger to help with this party. It was a bitter double blow.

"Sure, we'll do that. Well, I'll be seeing you, then."

"Bye, Valerie, and have a great party. I'll be dying to hear all about it." Again, pure lighthearted friendliness. Valerie hung up scowling, then smoothed her facial expression and got busy inviting the other guests.

The reason Milagros had been late to Adam's was that her car was acting up, and the following day she called Sophie from the garage to say she wouldn't be able to pick up the boys that afternoon and bring them home, unless she came in a taxi—should she do that? No need, Sophie said. She would run them back, not to worry. It made her realize how fortunate she had been all this time to have Milagros as go-between, but she felt no trepidation about dropping them off at his house just this once. It would only be a matter of seeing them safely in the door and vanishing; she wouldn't even need to look at him. So that afternoon she walked up the path to his house holding a son's hand in each of hers and keeping her eyes down, which forced her to notice the flagstones. Adam had once mentioned the British name for that pattern—now, what was it? At the door she lifted the brass knocker and tapped briskly.

"Mommy, can you tie my shoe?" Hugo asked, and she bent down to oblige. She was making the first "bunny ear" when the door opened, and so it was that for one unearthly moment Sophie found herself kneeling at the stiletto-heeled feet of her husband's mistress. She rose slowly, her eyes traveling up Valerie's silky legs, her chic black dress, her slender waist, her full breasts, her graceful neck, and coming to rest on her face, framed by gamine-cut tousled black hair, the eyes narrowed, the pouty lips holding an unlit cigarette, and in her fist a lighter, her thumb poised on the top. "Good-bye, Mommy!" The boys kissed Sophie's cheek, then air-kissed Valerie, mwah, mwah, and ran inside. Valerie's thumb spun the wheel on the lighter, and she lit her cigarette, inhaling deeply.

Then she exhaled.

The two women eyed each other, the one in jeans and a ponytail, the other in black, smoking. *Young,* was Valerie's first thought. *Spooky,* was Sophie's—who would want to come home every night to Morticia Addams? Then she remembered who: her husband.

"I hope you don't smoke in front of the children," she said.

"I smoke outside," Valerie answered. "Alone." She flicked her ash. "Except for the garden gnomes."

"Good," Sophie said. "Because they love you, Valerie. And they worry about your health."

Valerie studied her for a moment, then laughed. "Nice one."

She watched Sophie turn and walk back down the path. Back down the crazy paving, back to the city, back to her roof deck and her brand-new lover.

The great thing about Henry was that he chatted easily and everything interested him, so he would give the same careful consideration to a discussion of beauty products or throw pillows as he would to a philosophical or political debate. He was a good vegetarian cook, and he repaired broken household items swiftly, improvising tools and materials. As a lover he was spirited and skillful, and he cuddled superbly. In short, he managed to combine the fun and exuberance of a girlfriend with the seriousness and sexiness of a boyfriend, making him so balanced and capable a person that beside him other men seemed incomplete.

He lived in a big house in East Cambridge shared by five housemates, a mixture of artisans and alternative-medicine practitioners in their thirties and forties who all got along well together. About his family, Sophie knew that his American-born mother had remarried in France and that a half brother lived in Paris. There was little contact between the three, and none at all with Henry's father in Pakistan, married and with many children, for whom Henry and his mother could be only a distant memory.

"Do you speak French, then?" Sophie asked him once.

"*Mais oui, bien sûr.* I have a whole other life as *Henri.*"

It had been a long time since Sophie had told a lover when her birthday was, or what music she liked, or where she grew up, and her feelings about it were mixed. It was refreshing to begin anew, but it was also saddening to find herself back at that stage. It seemed impoverished to have no well of knowledge of each other to draw upon, no shared experiences or memories, and it was strange to share a bed with a man who knew nothing about her children. But meeting someone new is an opportunity to reinvent oneself, or at least to present the latest version, and as Sophie talked about herself, she made a conscious effort to not merely repeat the supposed "facts" but to ascertain whether they were still true, and modify them if needed. It was not always easy to describe her tastes or goals; she was a moving target, and moving faster of late.

In the course of describing her childhood, it was inevitable that she should tell him about her brother, Patrick. "Every family has some problem, big or small, and ours was Patrick."

Henry nodded, and Sophie went on. "One day when I was eight, I came home from school and found my mother crying because she was worried about what would happen to Patrick after she was 'gone.' It was the first time she had talked about her death, and I was scared. Scared for myself! But the question was Patrick, not me, so I pretended to be calm. I said that because I was two years younger, I would live two years longer, and that meant I'd be able to take care of him his whole life long. She said I was very sweet, but when I grew up, I wouldn't feel that way. I'd have my own life, maybe children, and I'd change my mind. But I swore to her I would take care of him no matter what. And she hugged me and told me I was the best little girl in the world."

Henry cleared his throat. "That's sickening."

Sophie shrugged.

"And will you?" he asked.

"What?"

"Take care of him."

"Oh, no. He died when I was thirteen. In his sleep. He had serious health problems of just about every kind. My mother went into a decline, of course. She was depressed for a couple of years, very withdrawn. My father and I just...And then eventually she sort of...woke up. And started volunteering with associations that give a break to the parents of handicapped children. And she became just as busy with her charity work as she had ever been with my brother. So I didn't see any more of her after his death than before." She laughed, then added, "She does do good work."

"Is he why you decided to become a healer?"

"Oh. I don't know."

"To help people like him?"

"I guess so. And people like my parents. And me."

There was a sudden loud knock on the door.

They started and stared at each other with round eyes. Sophie felt an irrational knee jerk of guilt—caught with her lover!—before she put it aside. It was Thursday afternoon, the boys were still in school, she and Henry were decently dressed, just finishing a late lunch; there was nothing to fear or apologize for. All the same, she tiptoed to the door and peeked through the peephole, then turned and made a laughing grimace at Henry. He shrugged to ask, *Who is it?* She straightened her shoulders, lifted her head, smiled, and threw the door open. "Marion! Come in, what a surprise! We're just finishing lunch. Would you like some coffee?"

"I hope I'm not intruding. It's been so long since I've heard from you that I thought I'd—" The sight of Henry brought her to a stop. "Why, hello! You must be Henry. I'm Marion."

"Why don't you two go outside?" Sophie said. "It's warm enough in the sun. I'll be right out." So Marion had come over to snoop, and she'd hit the jackpot. Watching through the kitchen window while she made the coffee, Sophie noticed that Henry had the look of a man who had just gotten out of bed after making love, which he was, and she supposed she must look like that, too. It wouldn't have escaped Marion, who was self-consciously running her hand through her hair, a habit she had in the presence of attractive men.

"Here we are!" Sophie said, stepping outside with the tray.

"I won't stay," Henry said. "Nice meeting you, Marion. Sophie, I'll see you tomorrow. And this weekend at the retreat."

"But that's next weekend."

"No, this. They changed it. Didn't you see the notice?"

"No." Sophie looked at Henry with consternation. "But I have the children this weekend. What will I do?"

Marion was grateful for an entry into the conversation. "I'm sure Adam will take the boys. Just give him a call."

To Henry, Sophie said, "Yes, that's what I'll have to do. I hope it'll be okay."

"Of course it will!" Marion said, and, smiling at Henry, she added, "Adam is a devoted father."

"Yes, but the point is, he may have plans," Sophie insisted.

"I'll see you tomorrow, then, Sophie," Henry said.

She walked him to the door, where she made a face about Marion, and they laughed silently like children. He kissed her and left, and she was still smiling when she came back outside.

"He's very attractive," Marion said. "I feel a little jealous. No, really, I mean it!"

Sophie took a sip from her cup and asked, "How are things with you these days?"

"Not as interesting as they are with you. It's no small thing to have regained your sexual freedom, you know. No small thing at all. Tell me, are you in love with him?"

"You know, I don't think in those terms. I don't think I

could fall in love again so soon. But he's good for me. He sees things in a different light. He's very insightful—and so much fun!"

"I'm happy for you, I really am. But be discreet—you'll never get Adam back if he finds out you have a lover."

"He knows. And he has a lover, too, Marion, and he's happy with her, so there's no problem. Not all relationships can be salvaged. Or deserve to be."

"Ah, maybe not, but it's knowing which ones, isn't it? Well, the children seem to like her, that's for sure. They came over to play the other day, did they tell you?"

"No. That was nice of you."

"Well, I hadn't seen them for ages...." When no apology was forthcoming, she continued. "All they could talk about was Valerie this and Valerie that."

"I'm glad they're taking to her. Henry was so right. He told me I had to give them permission to love her. Isn't that an interesting concept? So I did, and as you can see, it's working. The funny thing is, it's made *me* feel better. I did it for them, but I'm reaping the benefits, too. I didn't expect that. What goes around comes around, eh?"

"How does he know so much about all this?"

"What do you mean?"

"Henry. Is he divorced?"

"No. He's just...wonderfully wise about human relationships."

"I see. Lucky Henry. And lucky you!"

"Yes. Very lucky." And at that moment she knew, with sudden certainty, that her friendship with Marion belonged to her old life, back in the suburbs with Adam, on top of a tall pile of oven gloves and play groups and loaded shopping carts and other obsolete paraphernalia from that era. Our friendships, it struck her, need regular pruning and dead-heading, the same as our flowering plants.

———

Tension was in the air, more pungent than the smells of cooking, as the two women vied for supremacy in the cluttered kitchen, each grimly set on her own task, each hotly resentful of the other's interference. Valerie was running late, looking fraught, stirring a sauce. Milagros, with lips pursed hard and eyelids at half-mast, was clearing a space on the table for the boys' supper.

"I told you to give it to them in their room!" Valerie said.

"Mr. Dean said they could eat in here."

"Mr. Dean is not doing the cooking. Get that stuff off the table and take it upstairs. Now."

Milagros turned, her fists on her hips, her nose bunched up, her eyes now just slits. "I take my orders from Mr. Dean."

Valerie threw the whisk into the pan and whirled around to stare in disbelief at the source of this impertinence. Talk about the last straw! First Agatha refuses to come and cook, then Adam springs the news on her that the children are going to be there, because Sophie changed her plans at the last minute, and now the hired help comes over all fat and insubordinate. "Sorry. Let me get this straight. Did you say you're not taking orders from me?"

"That's right."

"Oh, yes? Then it can only be for one reason—because you are fucking fired! Get your surly ass out of this house! Right now. Go. Go!"

Milagros's eyes widened in indignation, but she drew herself up proudly as she left the kitchen, calling over her shoulder, "Then you better set two more plates at your fancy dinner!"

Adam, on his way into the kitchen carrying bottles of wine, overheard her parting remark and smiled at Valerie. "Are the children joining us? How nice of you, darling."

The front door slammed with a violence that rocked the house—Adam's clue that something was wrong. "What...?"

"I just fired Milagros."

"What? You can't do that!"

"Why the hell did you tell her the boys could eat in here?"

"I thought they could join in the celebrations a little before bed."

"And how am I supposed to get a decent meal together in an underequipped, shittily laid-out kitchen, full of screaming kids?"

"Relax, darling, you're doing a marvelous job."

"I am not! This sauce is stick—" The doorbell rang, long and loud, and she wailed with dismay. "Oh, shit, shit, shit!"

"I'll get it," he said, but at the kitchen door he met the two boys coming in for their supper, already in pajamas, their damp hair neatly combed.

"Where's Mila?" Matthew asked. "Is it suppertime yet?"

"Get out!" Valerie ordered them. "Go back upstairs right now!"

"Valerie!" Adam's admonishment was interrupted by the doorbell again.

"For the love of God, Adam, just give them something in their room, will you? I'll get the goddamned door!" Valerie tore off her apron, raked her fingers through her hair, composed her face, and strode out of the kitchen to get on with the job of showing her friends how happy she was in her new life.

Ann leaned toward Adam during the cheese course and said in low tones, "It's so nice meeting you at last. We've been hearing rapturous accounts."

Oh, shut up, Ann, Valerie thought. The evening was not going well. First there had been introductions and drinks and nervous chat, with Valerie painfully aware of the eyes of her sophisticated friends darting over the detestable house and feeling childishly obliged to jeer at it before they could. To avoid the bleak silence that was a perpetual threat, everyone launched gamely into the kind of insipid small talk that a pack of suburban halfwits might engage in, as though the atmosphere of the house were stronger than all their personalities combined, reducing them, regardless of background, education, or inclination, into a mob of backyard blockheads huddled around the grill. *It's not old houses that are haunted,* Valerie mused as she drank, *it's new ones.* An old house has been mellowed by generations of cultured inhabitancy, but here mediocrity seeps from the walls straight into the soul, like the poisonous gases released by new plastic.

In the end, she had invited only two couples: Ann and Jeremy (he was also English), and Nick and Sara—both blissfully childless and relatively affable. All the same, Jeremy had been drinking enough to become aggressive, and Ann was slapping it back, too, and spoiling for mischief, by the look of her. But Nick and Sara seemed milder than usual—possibly they were just bored—and Sara was drinking only water. Interesting. Perhaps it was one of her new fads; she was prone to them.

Valerie turned to smile at Adam and radiate some of that "happy couple" vibe she was so anxious for her guests to pick up on, but his place at the table was empty. Again. All evening he'd been up and down the stairs, attending to the boys' endless requests for water, more stories, night-lights, and whatever else they could think of to ruin the evening. And each time he trudged up or down, it struck Valerie that something about him wasn't quite right. His...aura. Or something. It's funny how even people we love can look kind of...well, not ugly, exactly. "Fuddy-duddy" was the word that drifted into her mind. Vaguely she recalled finding something sexy about that once upon a time—but just what had that been?

Her uneasy reverie was interrupted by a hard prod from Ann, an annoying habit she had when drinking. "...the maternal streak in you!" she wound up in a shriek.

"What?" Valerie asked testily, rubbing her arm.

Laughter around the table. Then Nick said, "Stop daydreaming in class, Valerie. We're talking about children. You know—short people who talk in high voices? Sound familiar?"

Great, Valerie thought, *talking about kids, are we? All that's left now is "how to keep the barbecue from smoking" and we're off and running.*

"I was saying I thought there must be a hidden maternal streak in you," Ann said with twinkling eyes. Valerie made a bored face, and Ann turned to Adam, who had just slipped back into his chair. "Valerie never seemed like much of a child person, and yet here she is! It just goes to show how broadening a new relationship can be."

"And how multifaceted I am," Valerie said, smiling at Adam.

Sara leaned forward and spoke earnestly. "It's juggling career and child care that's so complicated, though, isn't it? I mean, it's okay for you now, Valerie, but when you get that partnership, you won't even be human by the time you get home. And to have to face children in that condition..."

"Partnership?" Adam asked Valerie. "What's this?"

A brief silence.

"Well, there's nothing to tell, or I would have, of course," Valerie said in an annoyed tone directed at Sara, who was suddenly very busy with the food on her plate. "You know what Masterson's like. He's been tossing ideas around."

"Has he made you an offer?"

"Not exactly." Adam raised his eyebrows, and she improvised. "I mean, he never comes right out and says things, does he?" And rather a lame improvisation it was, too, in Adam's view.

"Oh, don't you hate that?" Sara said, eager to make amends. "I really hate that! People who don't...you know, come right out and *say* things!" She looked around the table for help, but no one thought she deserved any, so she had to struggle on alone. "But back to the child-care thing...How can parents give the best of themselves, which is surely what any child deserves, at the end of a long day when they're exhausted? That's what I can't figure out."

"They can't," Ann said. "Either you do a shit job of one thing or a shit job of the other, or if you're *really* energetic and organized, you do a shit job of both."

"But there's got to be a way," Sara protested. "It seems awfully unfair that women have to choose between children and work when men don't."

Adam cleared his throat. "Actually, men have to choose as well. Most choose their careers without even realizing they've made the choice. How many fathers are really involved in their children's lives? I mean intimately—to the extent of knowing when they need bigger socks or what their favorite word is that week. I know it wasn't until...until I found myself alone with the children that I really—"

"Alone!" Valerie put in with a mock pout. "Thanks very much!"

"But who cares about socks?" Ann said. "What about education? What about emotional well-being? The fulfillment of personal potential? To hell with socks! It's the big issues that matter, not the boring domestic details. Aggrandizing them is just a way of fobbing them off on the women who are obliged to deal with them."

"Ah! But the details are *not* boring, and that's the surprise! It only appears that way from the outside."

"It certainly does," Jeremy muttered, tipping more wine into his glass, but Adam continued.

"A child's life is made up of hundreds of these small details and, like the pieces of a mosaic, they *are* what forms the larger picture. There *are* no big pieces, no larger issues—that's what I'm realizing. What's big—and complex and fascinating—are the patterns formed by all the tiny pieces. There's no such thing as 'education,' there are just many little things learned in the course of many days. And when you're on the inside, there with your child, you can see the patterns gradually taking shape, and it's exciting. It really is."

Nick had been listening closely and nodding along. "So if you ignore the little pieces, you lose the big picture," he said. "Interesting."

"Oh, that sounds so right!" Sara said. "I don't know a thing about it, but that sounds so right. My God, how complicated it all is, but what an adventure! It must be, I mean." She laughed awkwardly.

"Are you planning to have children one day?" Adam asked.

She shrugged wide-eyed at Nick, who nodded his consent. "Well, we weren't going to tell anyone until the trimester was up, but...the baby's due in September."

As far as Valerie was concerned, Sara's blushing announcement sounded the death knell to an already agonizing evening, since when people say they're expecting a baby, social mores demand—even of fairly rude people—that certain questions be asked, to the ruination of the conversation. Have you thought of a name? Is it a girl or a boy? The pros and cons of knowing the sex beforehand...Valerie clenched her teeth on a series of yawns. Ultrasound scans, natural childbirth, sleep deprivation...Valerie drank without looking up. The glowing star of the evening was supposed to have been *she*, their damned hostess. The whole point of this gathering had been to reveal herself to her friends in her new role, appearing as quick-minded and dazzling as ever, but newly mellowed and enriched by love, a blossom open at last to its fullest. And instead dippy Sara was stealing the limelight with her Mother of the Race act. It was only after the advantages of breast-feeding had been exhausted as a topic that it dawned on Sara that she might be monopolizing the conversation, and although she did eventually say, "Now, that's enough baby talk. Let's talk about something else, for heaven's sake!" and, resurfacing, Jeremy did cry, "Hear, hear!" and the subject did finally change to film and the latest box-office hit, but it all came too late to save the evening for Valerie. She sat chin in hand, her mind adrift, while Adam said, "He's a trivial man. He can't help it. The people and issues that interest him are trivial. In his films couples bicker, malcontents whine for effortless fame and loveless sex—all excellent stuff for comedy, of course. But that's why his dramas can never be other than shallow and dull."

"Chronically superficial…" Sara mused aloud, shaking her head sadly. "Is a person just born that way, do you think?"

That snapped Valerie out of it. "As opposed to what, Sara—an accident in the workplace?"

"For the love of God, the man is funny!" Jeremy protested. "A little respect! He's the comic genius of our times. I say leave the deep stuff to the fellas who can't tell a joke."

"Is there any reason comedy can't be art? We usually consider it a lesser achievement than serious drama, but does it need to be? I mean, is there anything intrinsically—" But Ann's question was not destined to be answered that evening.

"Speak of the devil!" Sara interrupted apropos of nothing, and she nodded toward the stairway, where the two boys were crouched, peeking owl-eyed through the banister. "Aren't they cute?"

"They're usually very well behaved," Valerie said, eyeing Adam. "Perhaps they sense that just for once the evening is not intended to revolve around them."

"I'll put them back to bed," Adam said, rising, but Sara was out of her chair first. "No, I'll go! I'd like to. It'll be more effective if a stranger does it. And I need the practice!" She ran up the stairs, shooing the boys ahead of her, looking for all the world like a little mother hen already. Nick smiled after her in a slack, "Isn't she wonderful?" way that made Ann and Valerie queasy.

"Well, I don't know about all this claptrap to do with working mothers and the rest of it," Jeremy said with disgust. "I don't see what all the fuss is about. Women used to just have children and get on with it. Work if your husband's poor, don't work if he's rich." He pointed his glass at Adam. "I'll tell you who's got it right, though—your wife. Go ahead and have the little nippers, then hand 'em over to some other gal to raise. Brilliant! That's the way to do it, if you ask me."

"No one is asking you," his wife said tightly.

"Oh, come on, it's obvious. She's got the best of both worlds. As free as the wind, but with her genes safely in the pool. And I'm afraid you, Valerie, have got it just exactly wrong. Raising someone else's kiddos—where's the mileage in that? All the dirty work and no Darwinian success. I suppose it's the old biological-clock business. You left it too long, and this was the best you could do so late in the day, eh? Oh, well. Bad luck." He lifted his glass and drank, seeming to take Valerie's misfortunes pretty well, all in all.

Valerie and Adam spoke at the same time.

"I am not raising these children!"

"Sophie is an excellent mother!"

Stung that he had leaped to Sophie's defense instead of her own, Valerie continued hotly, as much for his benefit as for Jeremy's. "I am not a surrogate mother to Adam's children. This is a temporary arrangement. If I wanted children, which I emphatically do not, I would have my own."

"All right, all right." Jeremy held up his hands. "Keep your wig on."

"The situation here, Jeremy," Valerie continued through her teeth, "is obviously beyond your understanding."

"Like so many things," his wife hissed at him.

Valerie stood and glared at her guests. "Coffee?"

At last they were gone. Valerie was craving a real cigarette after hours of barely sustaining herself on furtive puffs out on the patio between courses. Now she stood on the front step smoking deeply, blowing strong jets of white smoke into the darkness. Adam came back downstairs and frowned at the open door.

"Are they finally asleep?" she asked.

"Nearly." He began clearing the last things off the table.

"Leave that for Milagros."

"You sacked her, remember?"

"I wish you'd cleaned up your personal life before you got me involved in it."

"You didn't give me the chance."

"Dad-dy!" came a call from upstairs.

"Oh, I'll go! I'll take care of this once and for all!" Valerie flicked her cigarette into the darkness and marched up the stairs. At the sound of her footsteps, the boys raced back to bed, and when she got there, they were pretending to sleep, their eyelids fluttering in a telltale way. She sat on the edge of Hugo's bed. "Okay, you two. Sleep. And I mean it." Absentmindedly, she picked up the elephant from the bedside table and snapped on its trunk.

Hugo opened his eyes. "Thank you. Can we have a story?" No response. "I'm thirsty." Nothing.

Matthew sniffed the air. "You smell like fire. If you smoke, you can get sick. My teacher said."

"Go to sleep," Valerie said.

"Smoking is bad," Matthew whispered.

"Shh. Quiet now."

Hugo whispered, too. "You look very fierce with those hairbrowns."

She sighed. "No, not fierce. Just tired, Hugo. Very tired."

"I'm glad you're not mad," Hugo said, "because Mommy said we should be nice to you."

"She did?"

"Yes. Because you're in our family now."

She said nothing.

"You *are* in our family now. Aren't you?" Matthew asked.

She rose and went to the door. "Time to sleep."

"Aren't you?" Matthew insisted, his voice anxious. "Valerie?"

She stopped, her hand on the doorframe, then came back to give them a kiss. On the forehead—first Hugo, then Matthew. She touched Matthew's cheek. "Sweet dreams, you two."

Adam finished clearing up the dining room, then set the kitchen table for breakfast, keeping an eye out for Valerie. When she didn't come back down, he went up and found her in their room, her half-filled suitcase lying open on the bed, her drawers and closet gaping. She was packing, but with more theatricality than firm intention. When he appeared in the doorway, she whirled around, clutching a red silk scarf in one hand, and locked her eyes on his in a challenge. Matthew's voice drifted down the hall, once, twice, and then Hugo joined in the familiar two-note call: "Dad-dy!" Valerie held Adam with her eyes, willing him to stay with her, supplication in her face, but also a warning. For a moment neither moved. "Daddy?" Matthew's voice was uncertain and vulnerable. Adam straightened up. "Coming!" he called, and with a level look at Valerie he went to attend to his sons.

She hurled the balled-up silk scarf at him, but it was too diaphanous to make a good missile. It faltered partway in the air, then fluttered down like a sigh into her suitcase, forming a puddle of scarlet.

She resumed her packing, this time in earnest.

After lunch on the first day of the retreat, Sophie and L were stretched out on the stiff winter grass, the cold from the ground seeping through their coats into their backs but the sunshine warm on their faces, talking with their eyes closed in the lazy way of people lying in the sun. "What I love is that 'two hands feel like one' thing. Isn't that wild? And yesterday Malcolm did this amazing thing to me. He put his hand on my *hara*, and he said, 'Our edges are blurry, and blurrier after treatment. I want you to think about where my hand is. Is it on you, under you, where?' I was just thinking that was a stupid question when I went, 'Hey, where *is* that hand?' And you know what? It was *inside* me. Inside my stomach. Then it floated back up to the surface and stayed there. You know how he always says to take your hand off gently at the end, to not break contact abruptly? Well, I could still feel his hand on me, but when I opened my eyes—Sophie, get this—*he was all the way across the room!*" L sighed. "Shiatsu's so cool."

"Mmm," Sophie agreed. The sun was making dreamy colored patterns inside her eyelids.

"I love how tactile it is. All that pushing and pressing...and pulling..."

"And palming. P-words, mostly."

"Yeah."

A shadow fell over Sophie, and she opened her eyes to see the earth daddy looking down at her with annoyance.

"Go away, please," L said serenely, her eyes still closed.

The shadow withdrew, and the warm sun spilled over Sophie's face again. "I think he wanted to be alone with you," she said, unzipping her jacket and loosening her scarf. It was hot, lying down sheltered from the breeze.

"Let him want."

"Poor guy. He's old enough to be your father."

"He is my father."

"Oh!" Sophie sat up, cross-legged, and shielded her eyes to look at L. "Really?"

L rolled onto her side and propped her chin on her hand before adding, "In the biological sense, anyway."

"And all this time I thought he was an old lech trying to seduce you!"

"He's that, too, in a way. He cleared off when I was little, leaving me to raise my mother alone. Then about six months ago, he suddenly showed up, doing this hip, 'more a long-lost friend than a father' routine. I told him thanks, I already had friends. So he signed up for this course, just to be with me. And try to impress me—he's been a practitioner for years. Kind of sad, isn't it?"

"Well...sometimes it's better late than never. Sometimes not."

"Oh, I'm going to forgive him, obviously. I'm not going to waste psychic energy on hating the guy." She yawned. "I'm just unloading a little resentment on him first, is all."

Sophie laughed. "I like you, L. Tell me something: Why is your name just L?"

"Oh, you know. I thought it would be cool and lackadaisical of me to have only one letter. Sort of in keeping, don't you think?"

"And I liked that throwaway line about raising your mother."

"Oh, yeah? You liked that?" L couldn't help smiling.

As is typical of these things, the retreat was proving to be more of a chance for everyone to "hang out" together—and the organizers to collect their fees—than a serious academic occasion, but the sheer number of hours spent practicing and swapping tips was beneficial, and so was the concentration on *hara* diagnosis: learning to glean information about the organs and channels by palpating the abdomen—"listening with your fingers," Malcolm called it.

They were staying in a monastery set in extensive, dreary grounds and sleeping two or three to a room, Sophie sharing with L and Rose. The meals were plain and vegetarian, the heating minimal, the decoration suitably austere. To Rose, a mother of three, it all seemed great fun—no cooking, no responsibilities. A year before, Sophie might have felt the same way, but now she was freer at home than here, and that was a very heartening thought. Henry was in another wing with the men, and Sophie didn't get a chance to speak to him alone until Sunday morning, when they took a walk together. It had rained all night, the sky was as dark as evening, and the soggy earth squelched beneath their feet.

"I'm going to Seattle on Wednesday," he said. "I don't know for how long. I got a cheap one-way ticket. I go every year in March for Arianne's birthday. I'm looking forward to seeing the Pacific again. I miss it."

"Wait," Sophie said. She stopped walking. "What?"

He stopped, too. "What?"

She attempted a little laugh. "You're going to Seattle, one way, in three days, for you don't know how long? Do I dare ask who Arianne is?"

"Arianne," he said, trying to jog her memory. "Arianne, my daughter. She'll be twelve. Can you help me think of a nice present for her?"

Sophie could hear the blood pumping in her ears. "You have a daughter?"

"I've told you about her."

"No."

"Really? Well, I have a daughter, nearly twelve years old, named Arianne, who lives in Seattle. I visit her every spring. When she's a little older, I'd like her to spend summers here with me. Shall I describe her? She's chiaroscuro, very extreme, all tears or laughter. She has tremendous energy, but when it's used up, she collapses. She could have yang excess and insufficient yin, I've been thinking."

"And...this daughter of yours...," Sophie tried to ask lightly, "does she have a mother?"

"Are you sure we've never talked about this?"

"Very sure."

"Well, it's hard to believe, but maybe you're right. It is true, you know, that we've talked mostly about you." He pulled a reproachful face, then smiled. "Well, Arianne's mother is named Ming Li, and she's from Taipei. We were lovers in our twenties, and she got pregnant, by accident we thought then, but now I know it was divine intervention. We didn't want to live together, but we both wanted the baby, so she was born, and..." He shrugged. "Arianne's the best thing in my life, as I'm sure you understand."

"Yes." Sophie focused past him. "Yes. I guess what I don't understand is how you neglected to mention to me the existence of the best thing in your life."

He looked at her closely. "Are you angry?"

"It never occurred to you, Henry, in all our talks about parents and children and separation and lovers, to tell me that you had a child, too? It never once crossed your mind that I had a right to know about your child and lover in Seattle?"

"A right to know? What are you talking about?"

"A right to know. You know all about me, my children, my husband—I haven't kept anything from you."

"Did you ever ask me if I had a child? No. You've monopolized the conversation since we met, and now you're reproaching me for it!" He laughed, looking incredulous.

"Nice try, Henry, but it's not going to work. And anyway, you...you insensitive *boor*—"

"Boor?"

"I've been standing here hoping that you would contradict me about your having a lover in Seattle, but it's not happening. So what is?"

"Did you call me a boor?"

"Are you still involved with your child's mother?"

"Of course I am. She's my child's mother."

"You sleep with her?"

"What kind of a question is that? Sometimes yes, sometimes no. It depends on how we feel, obvi—"

She slapped him across the face. It made a loud crack, louder than she would have imagined; she had never slapped anyone before. Her palm stung. They stared at each other in shock. Then she was gone, splashing across the sodden grass.

———

"It's all over. Finished. That's the end," Milagros announced gravely the next afternoon.

Sophie, who had been thinking just that, asked in a startled way, "What do you mean?"

Milagros pointed at the boys playing on the rug and gestured that she didn't want them to hear, then launched into a long explanatory mime involving much gesticulation, face making, and the emphatic mouthing of words. All very expressive—but of what?

"I'm sorry, Mila. I didn't get any of that."

"The *fulana*. Is gone."

Sophie sank into a chair and listened to Milagros's impassioned account of the weekend's events, beginning with the outrage of her dismissal Friday night and ending with her victorious return that very morning, in response to Adam's pleas, to a house that no longer contained a single one of her enemy's possessions. "Not one cigarette butt! Mr. Dean has cleaned all. He's sleeping in your old room again, too," she added with a significant nod.

But Sophie held up her hands and shook her head, like one who did not wish to know where Adam was sleeping or had been sleeping. (So they hadn't been using the old room—good.)

"So she kicks me out, eh? She fires me. Ha! Look who goes in the end!" To this triumphant refrain, in several variations, Milagros returned regularly.

"Maybe it was just a quarrel," Sophie said finally. "Maybe she'll be back."

"I don't think so." Milagros leaned closer and announced in a stage whisper, "She took her coffee machine."

The two woman looked at each other solemnly, then their faces lit up with smiles.

Henry called Sophie the night before he left for Seattle, and they had a brief, wary exchange.

She apologized for slapping him.

He promised to send her a postcard.

She wished him a nice trip.

The big news at Adam's office was that the partnership had gone to Valerie. Most people said they'd known it all along. Some thought she deserved it, others thought she got it only because she was a woman, and others because she was a woman sleeping with the boss. This last group was subdivided into those who thought she'd been sleeping with the boss all along (and cheating on Adam) in order to secure the partnership and those who thought she was only now granting him that favor, having wisely held off until she had the prize safely in hand, making the affair the payoff rather than the partnership—a question of who put out first. Yet others claimed there was no affair at all; it was merely the invention of poor losers. What was undeniable was that the partnership was hers, and certainly Masterson did seem to have a more sprightly air about him. It was also an indisputable fact that Adam did not come in to work for three days and that Valerie, swanning around in what appeared to be an entirely new wardrobe, didn't seem to know or care where he was. All of that was true, but the connection, if any, between those facts was anyone's guess.

And Adam? Only James knew where he was, and he wasn't telling. James knew that Hugo was ill with the flu, running a high temperature, and that although Milagros had offered to stay with him, the boy wanted his father, so Adam had brought his work home to do as best he could by Hugo's bedside, amid storybooks and trays for the invalid. He phoned James at the office a couple of times a day, "to touch base," he said, although a woman might have called it "just to talk."

"It's interesting that it's me Hugo wants, not his mother."

"Yeah. Well…"

"I am now what the books call 'his main care provider'—

an antiseptic term, isn't it?—so I suppose it's only natural, but still, I admit I'm touched. Last night while I was sitting with him, it occurred to me that the next time he's ill, he may not need or want me. He may have outgrown this phase. This may be the only time in his life that he really needs me by his side, and I feel so privileged, so thankful to be here. I could so easily not have been, you know."

"I know. Yeah. It's—"

"In the big picture, what does it matter if I turn in a project a few days late, compared to the importance of being with my sick child, if by being here I can alleviate his suffering?"

"Absolutely. Um...I guess Masterson's starting to feel a little jumpy, though. He's been poking his head in here looking for you. I told him you were working from home—and right on schedule!"

"Well, I'm not."

"Come in on Saturday and catch up, why don't you?"

"Can't. It's my weekend with the boys."

"I'll take the boys for the day. If Hugo's better, I mean."

"Oh, I couldn't do that."

"Don't trust me, huh?" James forced a little chuckle, but Adam sensed he was hurt.

"No, that's not it. Actually...well, actually that would be wonderful. In fact, I can't think of anything I could use more."

"Okay, then!"

"All right!"

"Consider it done."

"It's awfully good of you."

"No trouble, pal."

Adam put in a good work session on Saturday and nearly caught up. When he got home in the evening, his eyes and neck muscles tired from the long hours at his desk, he was greeted by a scene of peaceful domesticity. James was reading the newspaper, and at his feet the boys were building a Lego tower. They jumped up and ran to their father, shouting, "*¿Cómo te llamas, Papá? ¿Cómo te llamas?*"

"Ah...let's see...*Llama Adam*? I'm afraid I did French at school."

"No, Daddy! That's not it! You're supposed to say, '*Me llamo Adam.*' And I say, '*Me llamo Matthew,*' and Hugo says—"

"I want to say it! *Me llamo Hugo.*"

"Why, this is marvelous, James. One day in your company and they're bilingual."

James shrugged modestly. "Oh, I brought over some beginner's Spanish CDs I had hanging around the house—just a last-minute idea. They seemed to enjoy it, though."

"Milagros speaks Spanish," Matthew told the men. "In the car, when she's mad at the other cars. She shouts!"

"I'll bet she does," James said, laughing.

"Daddy," Hugo said, "we ate chili for lunch, like cowboys."

"There's more if you'd like," James said to Adam. "Hungry?"

"Starving. James, I'm amazed—"

But James raised his hand to interrupt Adam, because Matthew had grabbed a stick and started twirling it over his head. "Now, Matt, what did we decide about the sticks? Do you remember?"

"Not in the house," he said reluctantly.

"That's right. And so?"

"Come on, Hugo!" Hugo took his stick, too, and they ran outside.

"I'm very impressed," Adam said, handing James a beer. "I'm discovering new facets of you—teacher, cook, disciplinarian."

"Oh, I know all about kids. I know what makes them tick."

"You do?"

"Sure. I used to be one."

Adam laughed and opened a beer for himself. "It should be like that, shouldn't it? We should all understand children instinctively. Why do we lose that, I wonder?"

A couple of hours later, the boys were asleep, James had reheated the chili for supper, Adam had made a fire in the fireplace, and they had switched to scotch. A ways into the bottle, they started grumbling about work. They discussed Valerie's partnership and its probable consequences, which led to sketching contingency plans of their own. Adam confided that he sometimes wished he had just a one-man shop, helping people design the houses they wanted and could afford. "Let's make it a two-man shop," James said, "and I'll work out affordable ways of running those houses on renewable energy." Warmed by fire, whiskey, and friendship, they grew enthusiastic as they fleshed out ideas that seemed more and more feasible. Then, after the crescendo of excitement passed, there came a lull in the shop talk, and as the whiskey mellowed them, talk turned to more personal matters.

James, who had been gazing into the flames, suddenly threw back his head and laughed. "I just remembered. I made a real hit with my new neighbor this morning. She just moved in—beautiful girl—anyway, she knocks on the door to ask if I can help her move some stuff, then have lunch with her, but I tell her I can't, I'm baby-sitting for a friend of mine. A single father. She was so impressed! You should have seen her face. It was a study, all the emotions that passed across it. First it gets all soft and awed, like, '*What a caring human being,*' and then it hardens into this other look: '*This one's* mine!' Man, this baby-sitting line is perfect for picking up women."

"Yes, but will they let you go again?"

"That's the trouble."

"Not interested in marriage?"

"Not really. You know how the center of the pork chop is the best because there's no fat and no bone and it comes away in a nice little circle? And how in the center of a watermelon there's no seeds? You can just twirl your spoon around and come away with a perfect spoonful of melon and no pits? Well, that's how I feel about the beginning of affairs. The beginning's the best part—no bones, no fat, no seeds. I'd rather have a life of just pure beginnings, if I could. I mean, I'll eat a whole pork chop if I have to, of course I will, but if there's a choice, I'd rather just eat those circles. Come on, wouldn't anybody? And in love affairs, once I get into the seedy part, it just seems more sensible to start on a fresh melon." He sighed and looked at the flames for a moment before adding, "It's a sign of gross immaturity, as any number of women I've dated would be pleased to tell you."

"I'm sure they would."

"So...ah...is that what happened with Valerie? You guys hit the seeds?"

"And the gristle. And the tendons."

"Yep."

There was silence around the fire, and then James sought

to lighten the atmosphere by the simple means of saying in an upbeat tone, "Oh, well!"

Adam refilled their glasses a trifle unsteadily. "As you say...oh, well." They drank in silence. Then, with irritation, Adam said, "I just didn't *understand* before about the children. I simply didn't *know*. How could I be expected to? It's a well-known fact that other people's children are boring, and Matthew and Hugo were somebody else's—my wife's! I wasn't involved on a day-to-day basis. Do you know I could hardly *tell them apart*? They were just a sort of a...*an amorphous underaged mass*. I wasn't—" He broke off. "Well, there's a lot I understand now that I didn't before. A lot."

James cleared his throat. "You want her back, don't you? Sophie."

Adam didn't answer.

"Well then, get her back. You can do it. Woo her! You did it once, you can do it again."

"What do you want me to tell her? 'Valerie's gone. You can come back now'? Or how about 'I didn't get the partnership, my job's hanging by a thread, so why not come back and support us all'? I can't do it, James. And anyway, she's...she's involved with...someone."

"Oh. Oh, I didn't know." James nodded and took a drink. "Oh, right."

"A man," Adam clarified, brooding. The knowledge that Sophie had a lover sickened him. The fact that he had also had one—that Sophie, in fact, had one only *because* he had had one—was immaterial. In one's own case, the breaking of conjugal vows is the result of a thousand mitigating circumstances and the necessary expression of one's more complex sexuality. In a spouse it's depravity.

"A guy, huh?" James nodded some more. Drank and

sighed. Then, with renewed energy, "But so what? What does it matter? She can dump him, sure she can! Win her back, Adam! Tell her, 'I love you, I fucked up, give me another chance'—women go for that stuff!"

Adam raised his somewhat bleary eyes to James's glowing ones and studied them for a moment, turning over in his mind the possibility of what his friend was suggesting. But the immensity of it crushed him. "No," he said thickly. "No."

It's unusual for ideas conceived in drunkenness to sound good in sobriety, but that was the case with the plan to win Sophie back. In the light of day, Adam's fears were paler and James's encouragement sounded less like mindless cheer-leading and more like common sense, to such an extent that Thursday afternoon Adam left the office early and stationed himself outside the shiatsu school, waiting for Sophie to appear. It was Milagros, looking hopeful, who had informed him of the time and place.

Adam stood outside the building for some time, checking his watch occasionally, correcting his posture now and then, moving his lips in silent rehearsal, and looking generally, he trusted, at ease and inconspicuous. At last people began to spill out the door—a pretty scruffy-looking bunch on the whole—among them Sophie, wearing her backpack, tossing her loose hair, and laughing, walking arm in arm with a tall girl. *She's like a child*, he thought, with a painful wrench of longing. And the irony of it struck him: It had taken his leaving his wife to make her into the kind of woman he would never leave. She stopped short when she saw him, pulling L to a halt, and the smile drained from her face.

"We need to talk," he said briskly, to cover his nervousness. "We need to decide what to do about the children."

"Why is it 'we' again all of a sudden?"

"Ohhh-kaaay, friends," L said, disengaging her arm. "I guess I'll be heading off."

"The boys ask about you all the time. They ask when you're coming home. They need their mother."

"They have their mother!"

L leaned forward and smiled. "Nice meeting you, Mr. Sophie. By-eee!"

Sophie didn't notice her friend's departure. "I've been here for them all along. I've made sure of that! The children are fine. Don't try to use them as leverage."

He opened his mouth to answer angrily but thought better of it. "Let's not quarrel, Sophie. Let's just try to concentrate on our job as parents. The boys don't understand why you won't come home now that Valerie's gone. Matthew's having nightmares. Last night he dreamed he was running, and getting longer and thinner until he was afraid he would break. Hugo wet the bed. He comes in to sleep with me most nights. I'm worried about them, Sophie. And I thought you might be, too."

"Well, of course I'm sorry to hear you've screwed up their lives again. But I don't see that it's my responsibility—or even in my power—to sort out your love life."

He looked at her helplessly. "Never mind, then. I shouldn't have come." As she watched him walk away, her feeling of triumph faded into uneasiness. She was half inclined to run and catch up with him and say something. But she couldn't think what, so she just watched him go.

"I'm kind of sorry Valerie's gone, to tell the truth," Sophie announced to Florence and Jean, "although I never thought I'd say that." She and Florence were sitting at the long oak table in the kitchen of the Life Boat, a homey room crammed with interesting artifacts like collages and lumpy pottery made by the children. Jean was at the sink scrubbing vegetables for supper. Upstairs, all the children were playing and Mercy was resting after her shiatsu session (work Water channels to dispel fears). Sophie was practicing on all three women of the household (Jean: disperse Gallbladder and tonify Heart), and finding them remarkably receptive. She continued: "I'd gotten used to the idea of her, and the boys liked her, which is so important. Who knows what'll happen now? A brand-new woman for them to deal with, maybe with kids of her own this time and all the complications of that. Or just a constant stream of strange women tramping through their house."

"You really think Adam's up to that?" Florence asked.

"I have no idea. Also—I don't know how to explain this, but…if Adam left me for the love of his life, that's one thing. But if he left me for a casual relationship that was going to end a few months later, that's even more humiliating."

"Why look at it that way?" Florence said brightly. "Why not view it as conclusive proof that the guy's relationship-challenged and have a good laugh at the bastard? *I* think it's funny."

"Hmm. You know, it was strange seeing him—this serious man, dressed in a suit, standing there in the street, holding a briefcase—and to think, 'This is my husband.' He still is technically, on paper."

"On toilet paper," Florence corrected. "Well, whatever comes next, new stepmothers or whatever, you'll deal with that when it happens. No point thinking about it now. How's Henry?"

"Henry is in Seattle with his twelve-year-old child and her mother."

Florence's mouth dropped open, and Jean spun around from the sink with a gasp. "Can you rewind that, please, and play it again?"

So Sophie told the story, in a flat, weary tone. She had turned it all over so often in her head—wondering who was right and who was wrong and whether she could feel justified in being so angry or just guilty about being so uptight—that the whole question had lost first its sting, then its urgency, and finally even its interest. It was worn out, cold, and flat, so that's how she told it, winding up, "I just don't have the energy anymore to wonder what he's doing, or if he's coming back, or anything else." She lifted her arm and let it drop again. "I'm just not up to the old 'We're all free spirits' and 'No one owns anyone' stuff. Call me old-fashioned, but I don't like my lovers to grab surprise children out of a hat, complete with mothers that they do or do not sleep with, according to how they feel. Maybe it's just me."

"No one owns anyone, Sophie, all the same," Jean said from the sink. "He's right about that. A relationship based on exclusivity and possessiveness will never allow the freedom to explore life and grow in consequence."

"Oh, really? Well. That's something to think about, certainly."

Jean laughed and pulled out the stopper, making the sink gurgle while she peeled off the rubber gloves she always wore to wash dishes. The brand name of these made-in-China gloves was Chrysanthemum Elite, and they were a great joke in the Life Boat.

"I'm sorry, Jean," Sophie said. "What you're saying may be true—probably is true—but to me it's just words. A string of syllables."

"At least he didn't lie," Florence pointed out. "He never said he didn't have a kid. He just didn't mention her until there was a good reason to, and then you blew up at him. I think I'm on his side here, strange to say."

"Fine." Sophie waved her hand carelessly. "Be on his side. You're probably right, both of you. I just don't see the point of floating through life with a casual partner, taking pleasure where you find it, no promises, no game plan. It all seems pointless to me. Vacuous."

But Florence shook her finger in warning. "Watch out for promises. Mercy says the scariest words she ever heard were 'I will love you forever.' He's back in St. John, but she still gets up at night to double-check that the doors are locked."

"Human relations can't be pinned down and labeled like butterfly specimens," Jean said. "You can define a moment in a relationship, but that's all, and by the time that moment's defined, it's already in the past. You can't even pin down 'now,' much less anything to come. And that's not an opinion, Sophie, that's a fact." Jean had been shaking the Chrysanthemum Elites for emphasis as she spoke. Mesmerized, Sophie's eyes followed the flapping rubber gloves.

"I guess I'm not very sophisticated," she managed to say at last.

That night Sophie had a marvelous dream. She was in Seattle, or what was supposed to be Seattle, although it looked more like Egypt, and all the street signs were in Arabic. Henry was there, laughing and asking, "Have you got the switch?" His eyes were shining, his presence like a strong light. She felt piercing love for him. A girl with long black braids threw herself into Sophie's arms. "Mama!" Sophie stared into the dark, beaming face in confusion until realization flooded her. This was her own darling daughter! The daughter she'd had years ago with Henry! How could she have *forgotten* her? "Oh, my sweetheart, my darling girl!" Sophie woke up filled with joy, quickly followed by an aching sense of loss.

"I don't understand it," James said, shaking his head. "I just don't understand it. You go to her, cap in hand, you pour out your heart, and all she says is 'Fuck off'?"

"More or less," Adam said. "She doesn't actually say 'fuck.'" Then he remembered. "Or rather, she didn't used to. Now..." He shook his head.

"Let me understand this. You told her how much you love her, you begged her for a second chance, you promised you wouldn't stray again, so help you God—and it had no effect whatsoever?"

"Actually, we talked more about the children."

James groaned.

"I told her the boys missed her—"

"You didn't!"

"But it just sounded like blackmail. The whole thing was a mistake. I should never have gone. I've made a complete ass of myself."

"She must be a real tough nut. Most women can't resist a guy on his knees. If only to drive their knee into his nose."

Adam lowered his eyes and began to fiddle with a pencil.

"Hey, wait just a minute here," James said. "You did tell her you loved her, didn't you?"

"It wasn't that sort of moment."

"Oh, no? Oh, no? You want your wife back, but that's not the moment to tell her you love her?"

"I told her Matthew was having nightmares."

"Hey, that's romantic! Is that the only reason you want her back—for the kids?"

Adam frowned at the pencil.

"Adam, do you love her or not? If *I* can't tell, and I'm your friend, how is she supposed to know, especially after all the shit you've pulled? No wonder she tells you to fuck off, buddy—I would, too. You have to learn to express yourself, say things out loud. Like this, look." Odette passed the glass door and glanced in just as James was saying with all the sincerity he wished Adam had been capable of, "I love you. And I want you back." Her eyes bulged and she shot down the hall bursting with the news. "Now, go back and do it again," James said. "And this time do it right."

"I'm afraid amateur theatricals are not in my line."

"It's not amateur theatricals when you mean it."

Later that morning Adam crossed Valerie in the hall. She lowered her eyes and might have walked on without speaking, but he said, "I haven't had a chance to congratulate you."

"I was the best person for the job. They needed someone brave and decisive."

"I agree. Congratulations." He turned to go, but she caught his sleeve.

"Hang on. I'm sorry. It's all this gossip in the office—it's making me defensive."

"Don't pay attention. It's just envy."

"Thanks. Things all right with you?"

"Yes. Thanks."

"Good."

Odette, who had been hovering, interrupted them then. "Mr. Masterson wants to see you," she told Adam, avoiding his eye.

"Now?"

"Before the end of the day." She gave a quick smile, more like a wince, and scurried away.

"What's this about, do you know?" Adam asked Valerie. But she lifted her shoulders in a shrug.

Back at her desk, Valerie dropped her face into her hands and stayed that way for a time, massaging her eyebrows. Then she straightened up and watched her fingers tap on her desktop. She caught her lower lip beneath her upper teeth in a pensive way. Biting her lip was a new habit, but with teeth and lips like hers, it wasn't unattractive. She took a deep breath, shook the hair from her eyes, and jabbed "1" on her cell phone. And, in a voice artificially bright, "Are you sitting down? Get ready for the craziest piece of gossip ever! Office rumor has it that Adam is already consoling himself in someone else's arms."

The punching of "1" on her cell phone had become a habit again. The night she left Adam's house and moved back to her own cold apartment, she had debated calling Agatha and trying to patch things up but decided against it—too humiliating to call when her love life had just fallen apart. But when Masterson had given her the good news, she hadn't hesitated. It was bang "1" and "Celebration time! I'm finished with Adam, I'm out of the 'burbs, and I've just been made partner! So is it your place or mine?" The champagne cork had flown into the air in Agatha's living room, and Valerie had prattled away all evening, determined to present both her promotion and the end of her affair as personal triumphs, which Agatha had kindly allowed her to do unchallenged. (If Valerie had been attentive to her surroundings, she would have noticed that Agatha's apartment had changed. There were a few objects in it now—a book, a plant, a teacup—standing out garishly from the white background like a handful of flowers strewn on the snow. And Agatha was looking different, too, softer somehow, her hair paler and floppier. But Valerie didn't notice.) And ever since then, the two friends had been back in touch, although it was always Valerie now who called Agatha—naturally so, Valerie thought, as she was always the one with news. Like now. "You'll never guess who it is, so save your breath. Are you ready? James Mackay! Adam's squash buddy. And half these idiots in the office actually believe it! Now, is that a riot or what?"

Agatha, hard at work on an article due in ninety minutes, thought it was more "what."

The boys were becoming difficult, there was no denying it. They quarreled and fought, Hugo was sucking his thumb again, and Matthew was distant and glum. Sophie did her best to keep their spirits up, but she was deeply irritated that once again Adam's sex life, or this time his lack of one, was making things hard for the children and therefore for her.

"Don't you want to water your plants?" she asked Matthew, who was sitting on the floor with his arms crossed. Hugo was out on the porch overwatering his. Matthew shook his head.

"Are you feeling okay?"

He shrugged without looking at her. She put her hand on his forehead, but he pushed it off.

"What's wrong, honey?"

"Can we come and live here with Daddy?"

"Oh, honey..." She pulled him up onto her lap. "This house is too small for that. It's better to stay in the big house for now." He turned his face away.

Hugo had come in and was listening, too. "Valerie left," he said.

"Do you miss her?"

"I don't know. Daddy's sad now."

"I guess he misses her," Sophie said.

"No, he doesn't want Valerie," Matthew said firmly. "Daddy wants you."

Hugo agreed. "Daddy wants you."

They looked at her, waiting.

At such a moment, it's hard to clap your hands together and suggest a game of hide-and-seek, but that's what Sophie did, and if Matthew sulked a little at first at being brushed off like this, soon they were both absorbed in the game. But Sophie wondered how they had gotten the idea that Adam wanted her back. It would be enraging if he were moping and playing the victim. But most likely the children had made it up, assigning their own wishes to him in order to give them more weight.

Just when Sophie was beginning to think Henry might be back from Seattle soon—and working hard to keep her mind off it—a postcard came from him. She pulled it out of the mailbox with the message side up, so she read that first. It took no time. Scrawled on it were the words "*Bracing sea air! Wondrous for the complexion!*" She frowned and tossed the card in the trash, but then it occurred to her that the picture on the other side might have a significance that would make up for the thinness of the text, so she fished it back out and turned it over. Yachts. Moored somewhere. Possibly the dullest postcard on sale in Seattle.

There was no doubt about it: Henry was a lightweight. Well, a man whose only preoccupation was "switching"…She should have known. It was all over. He was reunited with the mother of his child, and Sophie would never see him again. By clinging to the dimmest possible view, she hoped to protect herself from disappointment— or maybe even tip the scales in her favor somehow, as if hoping were unlucky, so banishing hope might improve her odds. But, of course, trying to trick fate like that could only be doubly unlucky. So best to forget the whole thing. Just forget it.

On Thursday, Milagros let herself into the Deans' house as usual with her key. She cleaned the kitchen and bathrooms as usual and dusted and vacuumed the living room, but when she flung open the door to Mr. Dean's study, she let out a startled yelp.

"Mr. Dean! You scared me! What are you doing here?" He was wearing a sweatshirt and shapeless corduroys, and the room was a mess, with books piled on the floor and the furniture shoved every which way. His head was bent over a drawing at his architect's table, and it wasn't until he had finished tracing a line that he looked up and smiled. "I've been fired. So I'll be working at home, for the time being, anyway." He was unshaven, and on his feet were a pair of holey bedroom slippers.

"Fired! You don't look too worried about it."

"I'm not." He stood up and stretched. "Like some coffee?"

Milagros sat stiffly at the table while he made and served the coffee with the loquaciousness special to the solitary worker-from-home. "It's wonderful working from home," he confided. "My mornings are so different, you can't imagine. It used to be hellish, getting their breakfast, my coffee, their hair combed, my tie....I was always shouting at them to hurry and pulling on their arms. Now there's no rush. I attend only to them until they're safely at school, and then I come back and deal with myself. No tension this way. No boss either, and no colleagues. This is the life! And, of course, I don't need to wear a suit, so you don't have to bother with ironing my shirts—that's good news, isn't it? Have one?" He held out a plate of oatmeal cookies. "I made them myself."

He sensed he was failing to put her at ease. It was with an air of recognizing the signs of incipient mental breakdown that she said, "I prefer to iron some shirts all the same, Mr. Dean. You'll need another job."

"No doubt. Eventually. But I'm in no hurry, I have to say. Ah...Milagros?"

"Yes, Mr. Dean?"

"I don't want Sophie to know just yet that I've lost my job. It would only worry her, and..." *And sound like more black-mail*, he finished to himself. To say nothing of making him seem utterly pathetic, losing first wife, then lover, now job.

"It's nothing to do with me," she protested, raising her hands to mean that keeping secrets wasn't part of her job. But he misunderstood her. "Oh, thank you. I really appreciate that. It's only for a little while, until I'm set up elsewhere. And I'm working on a project—a sort of surprise for her. I won't show it to her until it's finished."

"A surprise for Sophie," Milagros repeated slowly. "Okay. I am a tomb." Which Adam took to mean that she would hold her tongue for a bit and wait to see what happened.

———

But Sophie did find out about Adam's losing his job, that very night when she got home from walking Bertie. She was grateful again for her dog walking now that Henry was gone, which made her realize how close she was to being lonely, really. Henry had shielded her from it for a while, but loneliness had been there beside her all along, waiting to repossess her—the empty apartment, the ticking clock, only her books for company, and hardly any phone calls now except for the odd one from her mother, sounding peeved ("disappointed" was her word) that Sophie had still not managed to patch up her marital problems when she, her mother, had so many worries of her own. "I know. It's inconsiderate of me, isn't it?" Sophie had said once, startling herself. But her mother appeared not to have noticed.

Sophie had left Bertie in Dorina's apartment and started

up the stairs when she stopped short, her heart hammering. Sitting on the first-floor landing was a strange man.

"I'm sorry, Sophie. Didn't mean to scare you. I wasn't sure which apartment was yours," he said, standing up. "I'm James. James Mackay. I work with Adam. Pleased to meet you." He smiled nervously and held out his hand, which she didn't shake, so he raised it in an awkward wave.

Sophie thought she recognized him vaguely. "Is Adam all right?" she asked.

"Well, no. Not really. He got fired. He wasn't going to tell you about it."

"Fired? Why on earth would they fire him?"

"Oh, different reasons. Downsizing, for one. And he was late a lot, and he missed meetings. Missed whole days sometimes, what with taking care of the boys."

"Oh. I didn't know."

"No, he didn't want you to know."

"Then why are you telling me? Are you implying I'm to blame?"

"No! Not at all. It's just because..." He drew a breath. "Because Adam's basically a good guy. He knows he's made mistakes, of course, lots of them. But his heart is in the right place." She crossed her arms and leaned against the wall, waiting. "The problem is...that not everybody is good at using words. Adam's not. He may not always be able to say what's on his mind, but...but that doesn't mean he's not..." He grew flustered by the impatience he read in Sophie's body language. "What I mean is that the ability to use words...or rather the inability to use words..."

"Is a trait the two of you share," she finished for him. *I like being mean*, she marveled to herself once again. "Did Adam send you here?"

"Oh, God, no. He'd be furious if he knew."

"Then how did you know where I live?"

"Oh, I got it out of him. I told him I was going to pick the kids up here tomorrow. I baby-sit them sometimes."

"You do?" A complete stranger to her—oh, the indignities of being a separated parent.

"Look, Sophie, I see now that I shouldn't have come, but since I'm here, I might as well go ahead and make a *complete* fool of myself. What I came to say is that Adam is a good guy and he's changed. Taking care of the boys has really opened his eyes, to a lot of things. He misses you. But he can't tell you that because he's ashamed. That's all. Now I'll go. And excuse me for butting in."

He started down the stairs, but she stopped him. "He may very well miss me now, James. I can believe that. But he would never have missed me if he had been allowed to leave the children with me and start a new life with Valerie. That's the truth."

James could only shake his head. "I'll see you tomorrow," he mumbled.

"Tomorrow?"

"It's true that I'm coming to pick up the kids. I'm taking them to a movie."

"Oh."

"Bye, then." He nodded and left.

Just when it seemed to Sophie that everyone was ganging up on her—Adam, her mother, the boys, and now this James—Matthew's teacher took her aside to show her some of his drawings.

"Take a look," she said, passing them over. "You see how everything's divided?"

Sophie studied them—mostly pictures of houses standing in gardens with trees on either side, the whole thing divided vertically into two halves. But there was also one of a child with a double profile looking both ways at once. "I see what you mean."

"It looks like something might be upsetting him. Can you think what it could be? This is classic parents-splitting-up stuff, but he seemed to be taking your separation so well. Both boys did."

"Their father's new relationship also ended recently," Sophie said—with a tiny amount of relish, she was surprised to note. "His girlfriend moved out about a month ago. The boys were quite fond of her."

"Okay, that could be it, then. It's actually pretty common for a second breakup to be more upsetting for the children than the first."

"But why? I mean, surely..."

"Well, children are adaptable, but only up to a point. One divorce and the kids weather the storm, new partners come onto the scene and the kids cope with that, too, but now what? A second relationship breaks down, and they start to think, 'Are people going to be coming and going continually?' They can't accept that. What's happening now is that Matthew's feeling your separation all over again, and that's what the dividing lines are about: 'Mommy's house, Daddy's house—and where do I fit in?'"

"How infuriating," Sophie said after a silence. "How infuriating that something I have no control over should affect them so much, and affect even my relationship with them. It's not fair! But then, what is?" She laughed angrily.

The teacher shrugged apologetically. "This is only a temporary setback. Don't worry too much about it. They're well adjusted, confident little boys, and they'll come through this fine. Just so long as you and their father are there for them, that's all that matters."

"Could I take these?" Sophie asked, touching the drawings.

"Sure."

Sophie sat alone that night in her apartment, feeling sad about the two-faced child in Matthew's drawing. She poured herself a glass of wine and remembered what Henry had said about how someday Adam would seem like just another girlfriend, how he was her Number-One Helpmate in raising the children, and how in order to do a good job of it, they would have to learn to work together smoothly. That included helping each other out when they needed it. And Adam needed help now. He was going through a hard time...he'd lost Valerie, lost his job...and he needed to see these pictures of Matthew's. When the glass was empty, Sophie reached for the phone and dialed his number calmly, her face relaxed into a magnanimous expression.

"Hello! Sophie, is that you?" There was a lot of background noise, music and chattering people, bursts of laughter—a party. He was having a party. "Yes, I'd love to get together!" he shouted. "Yes, whenever you want! Fine! Okay, I shall look forward to it!" There was another great gust of laughter, a woman's, cut short by the hanging up of the phone. Sophie looked around her silent, empty apartment and felt a lump of anger forming in her stomach. She regretted bitterly having arranged to meet him.

Then Dorina fell down and broke her hip. A silly accident. She slipped on a rubber toy of Bertie's, invisible against the pattern of the Persian rug, and lay there for hours before the cleaning lady found her and called an ambulance. The first day that she was allowed visitors in the hospital, Sophie brought her a photograph of Bertie and pinned it to the wall by her bed. Dorina was vague and disoriented, but delighted with the photograph and anxious for news of her pet. "If anything should happen to me," she said in a trembling voice, "will you take Bertie? I worry about him so."

Sophie took Dorina's hand and held it firmly. "I will. That's a promise. I'll take Bertie, and I'll give him a happy home for the rest of his life."

"Oh, thank you, darling. You have no idea...." Dorina closed her eyes and rested.

On her way out, Sophie remembered reading that old women who break a hip often die within a year—and she wondered how long dogs live.

The trip to the hospital made Sophie a little late for her meeting with Adam, which was all to the good, since it allowed her no time to fret or grow nervous. She had chosen as the most appropriate venue for their talk the bar downtown near her lawyer's, the place where she had drunk with the old barfly some six months before, on the day she had started divorce proceedings. When she stepped inside now, she had to pause and touch her brow, momentarily overcome by stale beer fumes. "You Picked a Fine Time to Leave Me, Lucille" was playing on the jukebox again—or still. The bartender looked up with the same St. Bernard eyes, wiping the bar top slowly with what was probably the same rag, quite possibly unrinsed since her last visit. This was a place where time stood still. Sophie's redheaded drinking partner wasn't there, but Adam was, sitting in a corner, looking around uncertainly in the gloom. Sophie swung her backpack down onto a chair and told him the story of Dorina and the dog, almost as if he were a just another person in her life.

"The boys will be delighted," he said. "About the dog, I mean. Not the... accident, naturally." He was less at ease than she was and looking interestingly different—unshaven and scruffy, like a cartoon caricature of an unemployed man. The funny thing was, he looked better like that. Not younger exactly, but... looser.

"Hey, does that imp in the supermarket ever taunt you?" she asked on impulse.

"What?"

"Nothing. Anyway, look. Here are some pictures Matthew drew. Look at this one especially." She passed over the stack, the double-faced one on top.

She watched as he fished for his glasses, put them on, and inspected the pictures carefully. When he got to the end, he began again, his eyes moving all over the page, taking in the details. In the old days, how happy she would have been to see him pay such attention to the boys' artwork. "Very nice," he used to say, without looking, when they held up their drawings for his approval.

"It seems you were right that they are upset," she said.

"Well, it's good they're expressing it, anyway," he said at last. Then he set the drawings aside and drew some papers of his own out of a folder. "Take a look at these," he said, passing them over in turn. It was what he had been working on for days at home, the surprise he had mentioned to Milagros.

They were the floor plans of a house. "But what does this...?"

"Just take a look," he said. "Please."

After living with an architect for nearly ten years, she was adept at reading floor plans. It was a house with three entrances: a central one to a large open-plan eating/cooking/living area and one to each of two discrete apartments on either end of the house. Each apartment was divided into a front and a back room, with a bathroom between them. The one on the east end had a second floor, also divided into two rooms. The west apartment had only the ground floor, its upstairs being part of the main house, comprising three bedrooms with two bathrooms between them. The attic was a big playroom lit by skylights with storage space all the way around under the eaves, built-in bookshelves and cupboards.

"So it's sort of a triplex?" Sophie asked, pointing to the end wings. "And these are to rent out? Or granny apartments?"

"No, I'd thought of those as independent work spaces. Offices, if you like. Each with a reception area in front and a work area in back. This is a family house designed for a professional couple who both work at home."

"Oh, I see." She nodded, then pointed to the east office. "Why is this one larger than the other one? With two floors?"

"Well, that's in case one person would like more privacy. The upper floor could serve as a bedroom and separate living space, even, away from the main house."

She passed the plans back to him. "Nice. And expensive."

"Not so expensive, really. It would cost more than a traditional family house, certainly, but much less than three distinct spaces, a residence and two offices. I...I've decided to put our house on the market after all."

"Fine."

"Yes. I've come to agree with you that it's haunted."

"By Valerie, then, I take it," she couldn't resist saying. "You felt no need to sell it after I left."

"No. No, not by...Valerie." It was still hard for him to say the name in his wife's presence. "That's all over, and I think it's a relief to both of us that it is. No, I suppose I feel that the house has been a witness to too much foolishness on my part." She said nothing, and to fill the silence he added, "And I'd just as soon get out from under that mortgage."

"Oh, yes. I heard you lost your job."

"You did?"

He looked annoyed, and to stop him from asking how she knew, she asked quickly, "What happened?"

"Oh, the usual sort of thing. They needed to cut the executive budget, and it suited the boss—and maybe Valerie, too, I don't know—that I should be the one to go. It's not serious. My severance pay will last awhile, and I'm not sorry to be out of there, to tell the truth. I never really wanted that job in the first place. But it was flattering to be headhunted by such a big firm....It seemed too good to pass up. Isn't that funny— that a job can be so 'good' you're forced to take it, like it or not? I suppose I didn't dare *not* take it—that was really it. It was cowardice, the kind of cowardice that society approves of, the kind that comes labeled as 'ambition' or 'being a good provider.'" He waved dismissively. "Anyway, it's over."

"Is it true the boys were part of the reason you were fired?"

"Let's just say that management wasn't very tolerant of my situation—but then, since when is management understanding of the demands of parenting?" He gave a bitter laugh that struck Sophie as completely new.

"So are you job hunting now?"

"A bit. I'm studying several possibilities. But for the time being, I'm working at home and enjoying it immensely. I've been working on these." He gestured at the house plans. "And I'm finding it very absorbing. It's designed for an independent couple, both self-employed and home-based, who share equally in the task of child raising—just some ideas I had, you know. Traditional family houses haven't really responded to changing needs and work habits. More people are working from home, but the kitchen table won't do, and I'm finding that just an office doesn't really do the job either. My study at home is just about all right when the children are at school, but it's far from ideal even then. I need a space to receive clients, and there's a psychological benefit to separating work from home—that idea of getting up and going to the office, leaving domestic concerns behind.... The professionals in this house share the central living area, but they have private space, too, for their work, obviously, but also for themselves and that's important as well. However—and this is what I think is clever—the living and work spaces aren't completely separate either. Take a look at this. Between the house and the offices on either side are these covered patios. They provide light, of course, and an important sound barrier, but see how I've aligned the French windows across from one another? That means I could be working at my desk and by just raising my eyes I could glance through the patio and see what the boys were getting up to in the main room. Isn't that a nice touch? I haven't felt so enthusiastic about a project for years. And I have to say, I'm quite pleased with how it's turned out." He paused. "Do you like it?"

She nodded, looking at it again. "Who commissioned it?"

"Commissioned it? No one. It's an idea of my own. I'd forgotten what it felt like, developing my own ideas. Creating good, affordable living spaces... This is why I wanted to be an architect in the first place. Domestic architecture doesn't have the prestige, of course, but so what? What I enjoy is designing places where all types of people can live and thrive. Does that sound sentimental? I suppose it does." He grew self-conscious and said awkwardly, "I can't afford to build this house right now, of course, but if we get a good price on the old house and things sort themselves out with my work...maybe..." He looked at her in a mute appeal.

"What?" she asked in alarm, but she was beginning to understand.

"I wish you'd take these home with you and look them over. If you have time, that is." He slid them gently toward her across the table. "I'd like to get your feedback. And please feel free to make any modifications that occur to you."

She trapped the papers under her palm. "Why?"

He lowered his eyes and didn't reply.

"Adam, I'm not an architect. Why should I look at these?"

Still nothing.

"I see." She sighed deeply and settled her eyes on him. "Adam, you wooed me by giving me a book of poetry— you left it up to John Donne to tell me you loved me. The way you announced to me that you had a mistress was by hiding photographs of her for me to find. I learned that our marriage was over when you put a water bill in my hand. Now you're scooting house plans across a table at me and I'm supposed to understand that you want me to move back in with you. Another wordless exchange of paper. Well, it's not good enough. It's just not good enough. This isn't how relationships are conducted. We humans differ from the beasts in that we have a very effective form of communication at our disposal. It's called speech, and I suggest, for the good of your future relationships, that you begin to use it."

She rose to go, but he caught her hand. "No, stay. Please. I do want to talk. Really." She sank back into her chair, and for the next twenty minutes or so, Adam spoke.

"In some ways it was a perceptual problem—or maybe not, maybe that's just a way to describe it. I confused what's real and matters with what's superficial and doesn't. They got switched in my mind. Like a foolish boy in a fairy tale who gets bamboozled at the marketplace and swaps something simple and valuable for something gaudy and worthless. It was like an enchantment, a blindness, and now that I can see again, really see again, I can't imagine how it happened. I feel it must have been someone else...but I wake up each morning to the fact that you're gone, and that means it's real. I did that. Yet I don't wish to undo it—not if going back means returning to that blindness. I've gained some things as precious to me as the ones I've lost, and I try to console myself with that. I used to be nothing. Sham husband, sham father, even sham architect, just a neurotic man unable to face his own mediocrity. Now I'm a true father, but I'm no longer a husband of any sort. And I want to be one, Sophie. I want to be a real husband. I yearn for the chance."

He paused. She could feel his eyes on her face, but she didn't raise hers from the tabletop, where she was twisting her glass to create wet interlocking rings.

He continued. "But if it turns out that the price I have to pay for becoming a true father is ceasing to be a husband, then I'll try to accept the exchange gratefully. I came so close to losing our children, to never understanding the magic of them, or of my role with them. Even now it frightens me to think of it. I'm so thankful I woke up in time, before they were grown and gone and their father was just a scarecrow, a suit stuffed with straw, propped up lifelessly in their memory. This is what life is, what real life is—children, love, satisfying work. This has nothing to do with mediocrity. It's excellence, the ultimate success, the noblest human goal. The specter of mediocrity, Sophie—what terrors does it hold, after all? I'm a healthy man, thank God, and I'm lucky enough to earn my living doing the work I like best—twice blessed already. And I love my children, and I love my wife—because you are still my wife. I can still say that for a few more days, so I will. If all this is mediocrity, then bring it on, for the love of God! Bring it on! I embrace mediocrity!"

A short silence followed, which Sophie broke by saying gently, "I don't think you're mediocre. I'd say you have a long way to go before you achieve mediocrity."

He burst out laughing. "Oh, Sophie! Sophie, you've changed! And I've changed. How I wish I could show you that. I wish you'd give me the chance, my love."

She picked up the floor plans, tapped them into a neat square, and held them in her hands pensively. Then she passed them back to him. "No," she said.

"I accept that, of course. I have no choice."

She said nothing.

"You can't forgive me, is that it? I know I have no right to ask, but I'd like very much to know."

"Forgive you? I don't know. I only know that I've lost a lot of respect for you—although I've gained some, too, elsewhere. But what I've lost completely is trust in you. I don't mean that I don't trust you with the children—I do. But I don't trust you with me. And I don't think trust can be mended once it's broken. It isn't something like metal that you can weld together smoothly so the break is invisible. It's more like a plate, and no matter how tightly you glue it back together, the crack will always show—and harbor germs. I can't conceive of a worthwhile relationship where respect and trust are lacking. Can you?"

"No. Quite. Well...thank you for telling me."

It was typical of him to take it like that—in a quiet "manly" way, hurt but polite, the long-suffering hero, Sophie thought angrily. She said, "I would also like to say that I'm stunned by the fact that I seem to play no part in your thinking. Here is the scenario you're suggesting: Man has midlife crisis, man leaves wife, man sorts out his priorities, snaps his fingers, and wife runs back. As though she's been on hold all this time, suspended in...in *aspic* while not in use. You don't seem to understand that I've moved on since I left your house. I have a new life, new friends, a new profession, and a new lover, as I think I recall telling you, and I am very, very happy. Does all this count for nothing in your plan? Do you seriously think I would drop everything and run back to you, simply because you've come to terms with your own mediocrity? You are monstrously self-centered, egotistical, and self-referential beyond belief, and yet, as I can see by the hurt expression on your face and the self-pitying things you've been saying here, you actually consider yourself a bit of a *victim* in all this. And a rather attractive one!" She raised her hand to her forehead as if overcome by dizziness. "It's nauseating. It's literally making me feel unwell."

She was turning to go, but he dared to stop her again. "I'll think about everything you've said, Sophie, but we do need to do something about the boys. I'll put the house on the market right away and look for something to rent—but where? It would be ideal for them if we could move close to you. But are you going to stay where you are? Milagros told me it was quite small, and you might need somewhere bigger. It would be silly for us to move near you and then for you to move away. That's why I need to know what you decide to do. Will you keep me in the picture?"

She nodded curtly, afraid suddenly of bursting into tears, desperate to get away from him, and racked by the feeling that it was all such a terrible pity and a sickening waste.

"I'm sure, Sophie," he said gravely, "that we can come up with a solution that will suit everyone."

It sounded like a threat. She nodded and fled.

6.

It was early April, muddy and still cold, but Florence was celebrating the arrival of spring by wearing her softball cap and glove to the park. Sophie told her that Adam was looking for somewhere to rent, closer to her, and Florence listened, her eyes resting thoughtfully on Bertie, frisking at their feet.

"We-ell, let's see. If Bertie's owner downstairs kicked the bucket, Adam could move in there," she said practically, popping the gum she was chewing. "Great solution for the kids. They could just run up and down the stairs. It would be like all living together, except you're not."

For a moment Sophie's heart leaped up. Sleeping under the same roof as the children again, with them free to see her whenever they liked and in perfect safety—but... "And Adam and I bumping into each other's lovers on the stairs? Too close for comfort, I think. And it might be the thin edge of the wedge, in and out of each other's apartments. I'd end up cooking the boys dinner down at his place some evening, and then what—washing his dishes? No, I don't think so.

Definitely not." She stooped to pat the dog's nose. "Anyway, we don't want Dorina to die, do we, Bertie? No plan for happiness can succeed if it's built on someone else's heartbreak. Even a dog's."

"It was just an idea. You know, I'm surprised he didn't ask you to move back in with him." Florence chucked her softball into her glove a couple of times and smiled. "I'd sure want you back if you were mine."

Sophie didn't tell her he had actually suggested it, in his roundabout way. It made her uncomfortable to think about that. "Forgiveness" was a word that passed uneasily through her thoughts. It was a fat word, a rancid word that smelled of sickly sanctity, a word used for scolding and manipulating people who have been mistreated. A con man's word. First someone offends us, and then, as if that weren't enough of an outrage, we're asked to reach deep into our depleted emotional reserves and dredge up forgiveness. Of course it's unwise to harbor hatred and anger after we're wronged— that's common sense. Resentment festers inside us and produces harmful poisons, so it's in our own best interest to let it go, and we can accomplish that through a philosophical process. But why take this outlandish second step and also forgive? Why must we reassure the transgressor that it's "all right," when it's not? Wiping the offender's conscience clean is not the duty of the offended. It wasn't difficult to guess which of the two sides, sinner or sinned against, had invented the concept of forgiveness.

———

Doubtful about what to do next, disillusioned with Henry and feeling under mounting pressure to give Adam another chance, Sophie discovered the next day that the very last person she wanted to see had left a message on her answering machine saying she would be downtown on errands and could she stop in for a cup of tea? It seemed not only intrusive but impertinent of Marion to call, when Sophie had decided weeks ago that she'd outgrown her and her my-size-fits-all advice. But, of course, when a person decides to weed her social garden of friends and acquaintants, the unwanted plants don't know it, and for some time they continue to re-seed themselves. Sophie picked up the telephone reluctantly and braced herself for the sound of Marion's voice, dreading having to field all the alternative suggestions Marion would bombard her with when Sophie begged off. No, not Thursday, not Friday either, Saturday's no good because... until Sophie would run out of excuses and finally cave in under Marion's insistence. Sophie had braced herself to call back when it struck her, quite simply, that she didn't have to do it. There was no need to explain anything. And certainly no obligation to expose herself to Marion's heavy artillery, then dance around dodging bullets as best she could until finally one lodged in her chest. So instead of returning the call, she erased the message. Magic. One touch and Marion was gone.

Two days later another message came: *"Human relationships are not expendable, and that goes for our friendship. I miss you, Sophie! If something's wrong between us, let's talk about it. I'm your friend, not a piece of Kleenex! Not something you can just—"* She erased that as well. But Marion was not a piece of Kleenex, it was true, so Sophie opened her cell phone and tapped out a message: MARION, I NEED TO TAKE A STEP BACK AND LOOSEN THE TIES A LITTLE. THANKS FOR UNDERSTANDING. The reply came straight back: I UNDERSTAND COMPLETELY. TAKE ALL THE

TIME YOU NEED. But later in the week came a loud, frantic message that Sophie had to listen to twice before figuring out it was from Lydia, the former play-group collaborator, inviting her, between shrieks of strained laughter, to a garden party (*"Bring your um-brel-la!"*). Sophie suspected that Marion had put Lydia up to it, and Marion would be there, too, ready to waylay her. Zip, she erased that message as well, feeling decidedly lighthearted. The gardening metaphor was good, she thought, because it's also by thinning out invasive plants that we provide the light, space, and nutrients for new plants to thrive. Time now to cultivate a welcome bloom. After dashing off an e-mail to Lydia, thanking her and declining, claiming that she was too busy studying for her shiatsu exam to accept any social engagements, Sophie invited L to dinner.

"So, like, I may regret it, but I'm going to give it a try. Why not?" L's father, the earth daddy—Sophie tried to remember to call him Jacob now—had invited L to set up shop in the alternative-health-care center where he worked. There was an unoccupied room, and he had asked if she would like to hang her shingle there—once she passed her exam and got a shingle, that is. "I mean, it's not like it'll be just him and me, because that would be way too intense. There's a dozen practitioners there, so it might be cool. Anyway, if it sucks, I can leave, right? And I have to start somewhere."

"It sounds great, L. I bet there'll be a good atmosphere."

"And there's another thing, you know? I can tell that Jacob feels like it's this big compensatory act, helping me set up my practice. And I'm, like, if I don't allow him to do something for me, to relieve his conscience in some way, he's going to keep following me around like this sad-eyed puppy dog. I want him to feel like, you know, we're *even* now."

"Does it seem like a fair trade-off to you?"

"Well, let me think about that." She pretended to consider, her finger under her chin. "Let's see. On the one hand, he abandons me at the age of four to a drug-addict mother, but on the other hand, twenty years later, he helps me unroll my futon. Hmm. No, it's not a fair trade-off. But nothing could be. It's really just so he'll cut me some space and at the same time be free to, you know, do whatever he needs to do, 'cause I feel like this whole father-daughter/karmic-debt routine is blocking his growth. And for me, basically, it's a pain in the ass."

"It's amazing how unresentful you are."

"Actually, it's selfishness. Self-preservation or whatever. My time is too precious, and anyway, look at the guy— emotionally he's three years old. So he didn't act like a responsible adult? Well, no shit. That was never one of his possibilities."

"Doesn't it make you wonder what your mother saw in him?"

"Uh, no. No, it doesn't." L lifted her chin and raked her hair back from her face. "You'd be asking that question the other way around if you'd ever met my mother."

"Oh, L..." Sophie laughed, but reluctantly. L's childhood made her sad.

"And he wants to subsidize my rent for the first year, so you see this is a cold and ruthless financial calculation on my part, too. It's lucky for me, really, that he's such a fool, and guilt-ridden to boot. If I play him right, I can spin out the free rent to two years. You know, 'Oh, I can't afford to pay yet, Jake-O! I'm still finding my way!' " L laughed, and Sophie felt a twinge of sympathy for Jacob.

"What about you?" L asked. "Where are you going to set up when you're licensed, So?" She'd taken to calling Sophie "So," perhaps on the theory that cool people don't need more than a syllable's worth of name—and of course the coolest of all get by with just a letter.

"I'll work right here. Come and look." Sophie led her to the treatment room, and L lingered on the way, looking at things and touching them.

"Your apartment's fantastic. Is all this stuff yours?"

"No, some of it belongs to Clement, the landlord or -lady, I don't know which. Clement is my guardian angel. When I first moved in especially, it was as if Clement had prepared this haven just for me."

"Cool."

"Look, here it is. My workroom. Not very big, but it's nice and quiet at least. And light." She pointed to the stained glass in the top of the arched window. "When the sun shines through there, it's gorgeous. It looks like heaps of jewels spilled on the floor."

"Wow." L gazed at the floor, imagining that. Then, "You're going to work from home?"

"Yes, that was the plan. Why?"

"There are a lot of wackos around."

"Oh, I don't . . . Do you really think it's dangerous?"

"No doubt about it. This is America, So. Come on, weirdos are, like, our major crop. For export *and* domestic consumption." Sophie's carefully woven plans began to unravel as L continued. "Basically it's, do you really want strange men coming into your house? You know what 'massage' means to a lot of idiots out there. And from the client's point of view, would you feel good about lying down in a stranger's house and closing your eyes? The anonymity of a clinic and all that, it's more reassuring. And for you, too—if there's any trouble, you have people close by."

Sophie felt utterly deflated. "Of course you're right. I see that. What I don't see is how I failed to think of it before. I flatter myself that I'm such a good organizer, and then...I don't know what I was thinking. I guess I'd imagined mainly women coming in...."

"Well, of course a lot of women practitioners won't treat men at all, but hey, there are some pretty weird women out there, too—don't underestimate your own sex."

"I just hadn't counted on paying two rents, is the thing. What if I accept only women clients who come to me with a referral?"

L shrugged. "It might be hard to make a living that way. You'd miss out on a lot of clients who might be legit." Then, seeing that Sophie was upset, "On the other hand, sure. Women clients only, referred to you, all by word of mouth—why not? For starters, anyway. Hey, it'll work out, don't worry. It's like a game of bagatelle, right? *All* the pretty glass marbles are going to roll into their places!"

"What's bagatelle?"

"It's a game where...*all* the pretty glass marbles roll into their places!" Having made Sophie laugh, L changed the subject. "Can I see the rest of your apartment? I love seeing people's houses. I'm really nosy that way."

"Sure. But there's not much more to see."

"I think it's fascinating how the spaces we live in shape our lives, you know? The exterior shapes the interior, so if we change our living space, we change the life we lead inside it. It's like..."

"Adam believes that, too. He told me he wants to design houses where people can 'live and thrive.'"

"That's it, exactly! I'd love to see his work. I wonder if I should have studied architecture.... Co tells me I'm a natural, though. At shiatsu."

"Co?"

"Malcolm. We're having a scene—I can never resist that mentor/acolyte thing, and I've always maintained that all knowledge is sexually transmitted, like gonorrhea. *And* I need a good grade...." She read Sophie's face and laughed. "I'm an opportunist, So! What do you expect? That's what happens to kids like me—we become survivors. Co tells me I have a good touch. He's the one with the touch, though—wow. Get this." She dropped her voice. "This is a man whose hand can reach inside you from across the room—right? Now...imagine having *sex* with him." After a pause she continued. "This is such a cool place. Can I see your bedroom? Sophie? Sophie."

But Sophie was staring ahead unseeing, wrestling with troubling images of sex with a dismantled—or very stretchy—man. "What? Oh, yes." She showed the bedroom and finally the bathroom, which brought a cry of joy from L. "Look at that amazing tub! There's only a shower at my place. Oh, and pretty seashells! Do you think I could take a bath? Would you mind?"

"You mean now? Sure, go right ahead. There are plenty of essential oils and things. Use everything!"

"Oh, and candles, too. This is going to be bliss."

And so the evening ended with them sitting out on the porch, L wrapped up in Sophie's terry-cloth robe, her long hair wet and her skin gleaming, smelling of soaps and oils from her bath and of the joint she had rolled, both of them chatting until late, pondering the mysteries of the Triple Burner meridian, drinking wine and laughing and watching the moon arc across the sky on the same path the sun had blazed that morning. To Sophie it seemed to be a model dinner party. They should all be like this.

She felt more jaded about it the next morning, however. She had a slight hangover, the bathtub was dirty, there were wet towels on the floor—amazing how fast one lost the taste for picking up after others—and she had agreed to let L copy her class notes to study for the exam. L had asked politely enough, and Sophie had said yes; in fact, she'd practically forced them on L—so why did Sophie feel manipulated? When the doorbell rang, she assumed it was L, back for the many things she'd forgotten—her books, her earrings, a scarf, a bag of apples—but when she opened the door—

"Hi." It was Henry, all smiles.

Lying in his arms after making love, tracing his profile with her finger, she found it hard to remember what she had objected to about his trip or why she had been upset that he had a child. It was marvelous that he had a child—unthinkable that he should not. All the same, it was time to talk.

She waited until they got up to make brunch. "Adam's selling the house, Henry. He wants to move closer to me, for the boys' sake."

He nodded and turned on the coffee grinder. She winced until its gritty screeching was finished, waiting for some comment, but none came. "Do you think that's a good idea?" she prompted.

He looked at her in surprise. "Do *I* think it's a good idea?"

She felt irritation but spoke lightly. "Yes."

"Do *you* think it's a good idea?"

"I want to know what you think."

"But I don't…" He shrugged.

"You have an opinion—you must. Does it seem like a good idea for Adam to move into my neighborhood? Just say yes or no."

"How can I, when I don't know how you feel about it?"

"But I'm asking how you feel."

"Well, I guess it would be more convenient for you."

"That's a thought, not a feeling."

He began to slice a pineapple. "I have no feeling about it, Sophie. If you mean am I jealous, no. As I understand it, you prefer me to him. If you don't, you should tell me."

Sophie brought out the question that had been tormenting her. "What if all this were merely a sort of sabbatical, Henry, and my marriage were meant to resume now?"

"In any case, it wouldn't matter to me where he lives."

"You know…calm is one thing. Callousness is another."

"What? I don't care where he lives, Sophie. How could I possibly care what address he has?"

"What if he moved in here?"

"But that's cheating."

"It's not! It's the whole point!"

"It's cheating because then the issue becomes who he lives with, not where he lives. I didn't say I didn't care who he lived with, only where."

"So you do?"

"What?"

"Care if he lives with me!"

"Is that what you want?"

Sophie dropped her face into her hands.

"Listen," he said. "Do you want to go back to your husband?"

Her reply was a muffled no, followed by a sentence that was longish and mournful-sounding, but too indistinct to make out.

He pulled her hands gently away from her face. "What was that?"

She lifted her face and met his eyes, feeling suddenly calm. "I guess, Henry," she said finally, "that I need more of a game plan than this. You, me, us, and what's going on. What are we, Henry? Friends who sleep together, or lovers, or a couple, or what? What's the plan here?"

"Plan? There's no plan. Just tell me this. Are you happy with me?"

It had the sound of a trick question. "Ye-es," she said cautiously, but when she realized how rude that much hesitation sounded, she added, "Yes, of course I am. Very happy."

"I am too. That's all that needs to be said. I don't care to assign a word to this. You think a label will be some kind of refuge, but I think it'll be a cage."

"But what are we moving toward? What are we hoping to do together one day? I need a game plan—a flexible game plan, of course, but I need some kind of structure and not just this nebulous…" She made big vague gestures to fill in for the words she couldn't find.

"You need a game plan. Okay, how about this? Our game plan is to have no game plan."

"No," she said sternly. "That won't do. Because no game plan is no game plan, and I just said I needed one."

"All right, then, listen to this. We're both happy, so we continue as we are, until you or I, or both of us, want a change of some kind, and then a change will come about. I don't need to say that what kind of a change is unknowable—we might split up, have a baby, or whatever. There's no point in trying to throw words at the future—it's senseless, just tossing pebbles down a well. I don't like promises. They're hot air, usually used as persuasion, usually for gain. But listen. Right now—the future is unknowable, agreed?—but *right now* I'm willing to try to bring about, or adapt myself to, any changes that become necessary or desirable. And that's as much as any person can honestly say to another. If I were to tell you I'll never leave you, that might turn out to be a lie. It's crazy to think that a fabric of lies is going to serve you as a safety net. I won't lie to you, not even to make you happy. I refuse."

But Sophie's mind had snagged on something a ways back. " 'We might split up,' " she echoed dully, " 'have a baby...*or whatever.*' You're calling that a plan?"

"Or whatever, yes," he said crisply. "That's all I can offer, because that's all there is. Anyone who offers you more is lying, as you saw very clearly with your husband. Think of it, I'm offering you all there is—everything in the world."

"And nothing."

"Of course. And nothing. That's thrown in, too. Everything, including nothing."

"So—sorry—just to sum up: You're saying you'll stick around until you don't feel like it anymore. Is that right?"

He smiled tenderly. "Well, of *course* I will! Won't you?"

"Oh, Henry, Henry." She clutched her hair with both hands and laughed. "Maybe we'd better call this thing off."

He studied her face. "Well, all right," he said at last.

" '*All right*'? Just '*all right*'?"

"Well, of course it's all right, if it's what you want. How could it not be all right?"

"You see? You see? This is proof to me that nothing's going on here."

He slid the pineapple off the cutting board onto a plate and set down the knife. "All right."

"Please don't say 'all right' anymore."

"I won't. And I'll go." He wiped his hands on a towel and faced her. "But first I want you to agree with me that the reason you no longer want us to be lovers is that I refuse to promise the unpromisable. Do you agree that's the case?"

"Yes, yes. Henry, look, I don't doubt you're right—about everything. Why *should* I need a label? I know that everyone has to play it by ear....I know there's no other way, really. But I don't know how to function like this. Remember, just a short time ago I was still a suburban housewife, trudging around supermarkets, smashing my shopping cart into my car. I'm changing, and fast, but this is still too..." She made circles with her hands again, searching for that elusive word. "For me. Maybe one day I'll be more..." She dropped her arms to her sides and shrugged. "Maybe not."

He took her face between his hands and kissed her. "Until the day this is no longer too...and you're more..., then." They smiled at each other. "Come on, breakfast is ready."

"I like you more than anyone," she said, pouring the coffee.

He flicked open his napkin. "I know."

They ate peacefully, and when he had gone, she sat for a time listening to the new quality of the silence in her apartment.

Over the next days, two letters from Europe appeared in Sophie's mailbox. The first was addressed to Miss Szabo in an even, sloping hand, and the sender was A. R. Clement. Her heart beat faster as she fingered the thick, creamy envelope, wondering what her guardian angel had to say to her. She decided to savor the suspense until she was sitting comfortably in front of a cup of cappuccino, and then she opened the envelope and unfolded the one expensive sheet of writing paper inside. She read quickly first, then again slowly, her excitement draining away. It was merely a nicely worded query as to whether Miss Szabo thought she would be renewing her lease, recognizing, of course, that she was under no obligation to decide so soon. But if by any chance she had already made up her mind, Clement would be glad to know, as some future plans would be contingent upon Miss Szabo's decision. That was all. There was no clue as to the writer's sex, the handwriting indicating a good education and an appreciation of beauty, but not gender. Age? Well, probably not young; the grammar was too good. The return address was Abruzzi; Clement was in Italy, traveling or living. And it seemed that now even Clement was pressuring her to make up her mind about where to live.

The second letter came from Felicia, her former mother-in-law in Kent, mocking her lack of sophistication and her puritanical attitude and telling her to forgive the poor boy, who had been naughty, certainly, but boys will be boys, and really we love them all the more for that—a letter so spectacularly vile that it deserved to be preserved and studied by teams of learned professors, but instead it wound up in an anonymous municipal trash can. A pity, really. Sophie counted the people who would like her to move back in with Adam: Adam, Adam's mother, Sophie's mother, Milagros probably, Marion certainly.... Not that it mattered what other people wanted, of course. Or did it—when those people were Matthew and Hugo?

"But your marriage is not Matthew's and Hugo's business," Florence said, drinking lemonade at Sophie's. "You don't need your children's permission to divorce—that's not how it works."

Sophie sighed. "I know. But here's another factor. They can't sleep on the sofa bed in my kitchen forever."

"What do you mean?"

"They'll need their own room eventually. I've only got two bedrooms, and the workroom is essential. I have to start making a living soon—I'm using up my savings fast. I guess I just need a bigger apartment. It's ridiculous, but I feel so attached to this place. Irrationally so. I have to move, though, and that's that. Find a nice big place with room for everything." Adam's floor plans flashed into her mind—her independent work space, the boys playing happily, glimpsed through the French windows across the courtyard, the sense of wholeness and safety that would give. She could fill the patios with plants....

"Hey!" Florence shrieked suddenly, making Sophie jump. "Look!" She pointed at the glass of lemonade Sophie had just raised to her lips. "My God, would you look at that!" The cork coaster that Sophie had set down to protect the table had adhered to the condensation on the bottom of the glass. "You have achieved bevel-meter! That's what it's called when the coaster sticks to the glass like that—bevel-meter."

"And is this a"—Sophie hunted for the right phrasing— "a recognized scientific phenomenon?"

"You ever been to Boise, Idaho? A bar called 'Humpin' Hannah's?'"

"I...don't think so."

"That's where the achievement of bevel-meter first received formal recognition. Of course it'd been happening to people for years, but it wasn't until late one night in 'Humpin' Hannah's' that the three morphemes—beverage, level, and meter—came together to form the term we use today. There are purists who measure the distance the coaster travels before it becomes unstuck and falls—that's the 'meter' part—but I call that pedantic. The point is, it's called bevel-meter, and it's a real achievement! This calls for about a million beers!"

About half a million beers later, during the drinking of which Florence also achieved bevel-meter, twice, Sophie confessed that Adam had asked her to come back and that she'd been seriously considering it. "Oh, Flo, what if these last months have just been a kind of time-out, and now my married life is meant to begin again? The same only better, having learned from our mistakes, forging a new and more equal relationship based on mutual blah, blah, blah? Isn't that the conclusion the mature, responsible mother of two would draw? It's not the conclusion I *want* to draw, but there it is!"

Florence's reaction was not what Sophie would have predicted. "Well, I'm glad to hear he wants you back. He'd be crazy if he didn't," she said, lifting her beer bottle to her lips. "What does Henry think about it?"

"Henry?" Sophie was evasive. "Does that matter? Isn't it only what I want that counts?"

"God, Sophie, do you really need to ask that? Of course— jeez! I'm just curious."

"Oh. Well. Henry doesn't give advice, really. He thinks

it's all up to me. I just have to look into my heart and I'll make the right decision." She made a face. "And he's right of course. He always is."

"I know he can't advise you, that's obvious. What I meant was, how does he feel about this?"

"Oh"—Sophie tossed one hand up carelessly—"that I couldn't tell you. I don't completely *get* Henry. He likes me, I know, but everything for him is kind of loose and easy. People are free, they don't belong to each other, and when you love someone, you just want them to be happy, whatever that takes. He says there's no such thing as a wrong decision, and people are free to change their minds—that kind of thing. He's so well adjusted that he doesn't really count. He said it himself, he's not one of my problems."

"I think I like Henry!"

"Yeah," Sophie agreed listlessly, "he's great. But I need to feel firmer ice beneath my feet so I can, you know, *stride out*."

"Hey, you strode out with Adam, and you still plunged into subzero waters." Florence swallowed some beer, then added angrily, striking the table with her fist, "And bobbed back up like a seal with a fish in your mouth!"

"I know, I know." Sophie sighed. Then, with renewed energy, "But meanwhile I have to figure out where to live! In a bigger apartment, with Adam in his dream house, by myself, or with the boys. Or would it be unfair now to take them away from Adam. Or *what*? Where? Whither? Whence?" She laid her head on her forearms on the table and moaned. "I'm like a cub reporter, shouting my WH-words to the heavens." She lifted her head. "Remember that in grade school? A good newspaper report had to cover the answers to all the WH-words?"

"Yeah. I think 'whither' and 'whence' are archaic, though."

Florence screwed the tops off two more bottles of beer and passed one to Sophie. "Here, Scoop, bottoms up. What about living at Henry's place?"

Sophie picked at the label on the bottle. "Not an option." Then she closed her eyes and slumped, suddenly remembering something else. "Oh, and I forgot to tell you. To top it all off, get this—L told me it's dangerous to work from home. So all my plans crumble. If I can't work from home, what good is a bigger place? What good is anything? Oh, God, I can't believe that all this time has passed since Adam and I split up, seven long months, and here I am right back at the beginning with nothing settled, my whole life up in the air all over again. I wish that damned Valerie had never moved out. First she screws up my life by taking Adam, then she screws it up all over again by dumping him. Do you realize that my entire life is dictated by my husband's lover, a woman I don't even know? How surreal is that?"

But what about having your entire life dictated by your husband's lover's *best friend*—the dissolution of your marriage set into motion by her casually, what's more, as the result of a petty dietary rivalry? And if Sophie had known that a few months before, at that vernissage, she had actually drunk a friendly glass of champagne with that meddler-at-two-removes in her affairs—and quite *liked* her—she would have been certain of Dalí's hand in the matter.

Sensing that things were starting to deteriorate, Florence took control of the situation. "Okay, Sophie, listen. I have no idea what you should do, but..." She paused dramatically and took a swig of beer to prolong the suspense. "But I will tell you a rule that will help you to solve problems—any problem, big or small—all your life long. Now, listen carefully." Holding one finger in the air, she spoke slowly and emphatically, making audible quotation marks around her words. "One problem is only a problem. But two problems are already pointing to a solution." She held her arms out and beamed. "So there you go!"

"Wait. Say it again?" Sophie screwed her face up in an effort to understand through the haze of beer.

Florence obliged, in the same clear, lilting voice. "One problem is only a problem. But two problems are already pointing to a solution."

"No." Sophie shook her head. "No, I don't get it."

"Yes you do. Just think about it. It means that you're lucky if you have more than one problem. Because multiple problems sort of intermingle...and snag on each other...and where they intersect..." Florence ground to a halt. "Well, *you* know," she finished off testily. "Don't make me pick at it. This kind of thing makes less and less sense the more you— Just let it bob on your brain waves for a while until it sinks in. Think of it: an idea bobbing gently, up and down, on the waves of your brain, until eventually it's accepted and it flutters slooow-ly, slooow-ly down, and it's absorbed into the calm blue sea of your understanding."

Sophie followed this explanation with a frown. When it was over, she blinked. "Florence, do you understand what the saying means?"

"Uh...not really. It's a pearl that was passed on to me, but I could never make heads or tails of it, to be honest."

"Oh. I see." Sophie picked up her beer and opened her mouth to drink from it but spilled it down her shirt when Florence grabbed her arm, yelling, "You've achieved bevel-meter again!"

Indeed, the coaster was firmly affixed to the bottom of her raised bottle. While Sophie's mind clawed for the possible implications of this, Florence tossed her head back with satisfaction and stretched her arms wide. "Oh, Sophie, it's bevel-meter again. And by God, it's an achievement!"

———

The boys had been behaving badly all morning. They'd woken up fractious, bickered through breakfast, and then Sophie had brought them over to the park to play with their kites—a foolish move, since twisting kite strings and fickle winds can blacken tempers even on a good day. After numerous mishaps with the kites, hostilities between them reached such a pitch that Sophie made them sit and be quiet. They leaned their bottoms against the bench, keeping both feet on the ground, a minimum of conforming to the rule that they must sit. They scowled darkly, Matthew into the distance, Hugo at the knotted string in his hands. They frowned with the intensity of young children that is lost in later life: frowned with their whole bodies. Sophie resisted the urge to laugh at their thundercloud faces. Five minutes crept by, and she gave a curt nod to indicate that time was up. A bit more silence followed, broken by Hugo. "Mommy, why did Valerie go away? Were we bad?"

Matthew looked anxious, sensing that this was not a thing to ask but eager to hear the answer, happy to ride on the coattails of his younger brother's indiscretion.

Interesting they should bring this up now—revealing the cause of their bad behavior, or clever manipulation, or a bit of both. She put an arm around each of them. "No, not at all. That's not why she went." Damn Adam for not explaining this! "She went because she and Daddy didn't want to live together anymore. They changed their minds, and that's okay. It's not because of you. She does like you—very much."

"We were nice to her," Hugo admitted.

"I'm sure you were."

"And now we want you to come back."

She sighed and hugged them closer, propping her chin on Hugo's head, her eyes resting straight ahead on a white point across the park, her mind on the two small bundles of unhappiness in her arms. Just one word from her would transform their lives. One word and they would be leaping with joy. She could make it all right, if only she would. To possess such power over them and yet not use it to make them happy—could that ever be justified? While she sat wondering, the point of white she had been gazing at resolved itself into a sign on one of the houses across the way, a skinny three-story house with high weeds in the garden.

The sign said FOR RENT.

One problem is only a problem, but two problems are already pointing to a solution. The next morning Sophie phoned the real-estate agent named on the sign and asked some questions, and later she made a long, tentative call to Adam. Next she left a brief message for Henry. Lastly she wrote a polite reply to Clement in Abruzzi.

In just forty-five minutes, she set all their lives on a new course.

On her way out to mail Clement's letter, she stopped to ask if Bertie would like to come along, and Dorina said yes. The old woman was looking frailer since her accident, but still beautifully turned out, with her silver hair swept up in combs. She brightened when she saw the address on the envelope in Sophie's hand. "Oh, how nice!"

Sophie pressed the letter against her leg, feeling a surge of panic. Of course Dorina knew Clement; they used to be neighbors. But it was imperative that—

"You've written to my dear, dear fri—"

"No!" Sophie shouted, and she clapped her hands over her ears. A graceless action, but it was all she could think of to cut off Dorina in time. Dorina started, Bertie barked, Sophie blushed.

"I'm sorry I startled you," Sophie said, lowering her hands. "It's just that Clement is...very special to me, and I...don't want to know anything about Clement, nothing at all, because..." She was about to grind to an embarrassed halt when she realized that there was no reason not to tell the simple truth, so she wound up unapologetically, "Because to me Clement is a magical beneficent spirit who could only be diminished by becoming a real person."

"Oh! Well..." Dorina touched the necklaces at her bosom. "How eccentric of you, darling. But who am I to talk? A woman who dresses for dinner *en tête-à-tête* with a dog!"

"I don't really need Clement now, not like in the beginning. But...Well, you just never know."

"Don't worry, you'll learn nothing from me. I believe firmly that mystery should be respected. All this meddling—it's just plain hubris! I *detest* detective novels, don't you?"

Back in her apartment, Sophie stood with her hands on her hips surveying her treatment room with a touch of regret for what now would never be.

Well, no point in putting it off. Packing again, and so soon. Filling cardboard boxes. Dumping out drawers and finding that one rubber band, that one bent paper clip, the one small coin, and the one rolling marble that inhabit the backs of drawers all over the planet. She worked methodically, dismantling everything that she had assembled so recently, and with such hopes. Down came the charts, down came the books, the candles, the music. She left the futon for last and knelt for a moment amid the boxes and bare shelves to run her hand lovingly over it. Then she gave it a pat and rolled it up.

May Day was moving day. Sophie ripped open a box of books, watching Adam out of the corner of her eye. He was staring dazedly into boxes he'd packed himself only days before, as though he had never seen any of their contents before. "James, give me a hand, will you?" he said. "We need to clear some space in here."

"Sure thing." James stacked three large boxes marked KITCHEN on top of one another and carried them down the hall, giving Sophie a wink as he passed. He was being friendly to her, too friendly, she thought, as if he felt she needed reassurance that he hadn't usurped her place. He had been very helpful to Adam throughout the move, she knew. He, Adam, and Milagros had worked together packing up the old house, and the boys had helped, too, mainly by riding empty boxes down the stairs and vetoing the giving away of any toys. Now, at the unpacking stage, they all functioned together as a slick team, with Sophie the odd man out, unsure where things went, that well-intentioned but not terribly useful outsider who lends a hand at such times.

"What you got there?" Milagros asked James fiercely as he came into the kitchen. He nudged a flap open with his chin and peered into the top box.

"Pans, looks like."

"There by the stove. Now, get out of here." He laughed and left her to it. She was arranging the kitchen the way she'd always wished the old kitchen were arranged—like hers at home. And why shouldn't she, Sophie reasoned—she did lots of the cooking, and would continue to.

Back in the living room, Adam was eyeing the chesterfield doubtfully.

"You want to try it under the window?" James asked.

"Do you mind?" Adam looked apologetic.

"Hell no! We can't see what it looks like till we try it."

Milagros had already unpacked the bathroom boxes, again according to a private system, so when Hugo asked for a washcloth to make a superhero cape for one of his teddy bears, Sophie reached automatically into the top drawer of the wicker commode, but there weren't any there. She had to hunt until she found one hanging on the back of the bathroom door. Not a very convenient place for it, she couldn't help thinking, out of the children's reach like that. But that was all right.

The men squatted at either end of the chesterfield and chose their handholds. "Got it?" James asked, and Adam nodded. Together they straightened their knees and lifted as if it were weightless. The times Sophie had moved it with Adam, it had been all she could do, straining on tiptoes, to keep her end from marring the floor. The men set it down gently in the bay window, then drifted back together to examine the effect, their hands on their hips, both frowning.

"What do you think?" Adam said.

"I don't know."

"You don't like it?"

"Oh, I *like* it. I'm just wondering where your table's going to go, that's all. That's good light to work by. Seems wasted on the sofa."

"You're right. Well...switch it back? Sorry about this."

"Hey, no problem. We have to get it right." They hefted the thing again, and James said, "You know, once we rent an office, we can put this back in the window. It does look better there, no doubt about it."

Sophie knew, because Adam had told her that morning, that he wouldn't be working from home for much longer. He and James were going to set up in business together, a little two-man shop, just as soon as James was fired. James explained to Sophie that he was going to wait and get severance pay instead of quit and walk away with nothing. Hell, the firm had exploited him for years; he might as well milk it for what he could get. Sophie asked what he would do if he wasn't fired, but he said not to worry about that, he was doing "little things to help it along," and both he and Adam laughed, an inside joke. Milagros already knew all about their new venture; others probably did, too. It felt strange to Sophie that Adam could take such an important career step and she not be the first to hear about it, or the second, or even the third. But of course that was natural now, just as it was natural for her not to know where the washcloths and the can opener were kept.

When she had emptied the book box, she stood up and dusted off her hands, smiling hesitantly. "Looks nice," she said, nodding at the architect's table now in the bay window, and immediately she regretted it, as it seemed to point out the fact that no one had asked her opinion. "I thought I'd make a little snack for the boys," she said quickly to Adam.

He glanced at his watch. "A bit early. I usually give them something at four."

"Oh. Well. Maybe Milagros needs a hand." She ducked out of the room and went into the kitchen.

"Adam?" Milagros asked, her voice muffled because her head was deep in the cupboard under the sink. "If I see one cockroach, I quit! I tell you that right now!"

"It's only me." Sophie laughed self-consciously, noting that Milagros called Adam by his first name now. And joked with him. "I thought I'd make a snack for the boys, for later. Four o'clock, right?"

"Oh, Adam did that already." Milagros pulled her head free and stood up. "This morning. I'm glad, because it's too filthy here to prepare food. Disgusting. The people who lived here? Pigs."

Sophie snapped open the lunch box and surveyed its contents: two sandwiches neatly wrapped in tinfoil, two apples, two bunches of grapes, some cashew nuts, and a can of sardines in tomato sauce—an abundant and healthy snack, prepared with foresight and care. "I'm not sure how well the sardines will go down," she said with a chuckle.

"They love them! They play they are seals, drop the fish in the mouth by the tail. Then bark, clap the flippers..." Milagros shrugged. "Well, they are only young."

"Wonderful! Omega-3 oil!" Sophie said brightly, snapping the lunch box closed, and she felt relief when Mila gave her a box of little-used kitchen items to carry up to the attic.

"The boys will show you the way. Boys!"

They led Sophie out of the apartment and up the stairs to an attic storage room reserved for their use, a small room with quite a large skylight set into the steep roof and, piled against one wall, boxes of Christmas decorations, a stepladder, skis, camping equipment, and other rarely needed things. "See, there's a tippy window in the roof!" Hugo said with glee, pointing. Obligingly, Sophie craned her neck to study the skylight, an old-fashioned one divided into two panes and hinged in the middle, open a crack for ventilation. "This is our playhouse! Do you want to see our room? Come on!" She laughed and followed them back downstairs.

The real-estate man had described the apartment to her on the telephone, but she got her first view of it all looking left and right as the boys dragged her down the hall to their room at the back. She craned her neck to look into the master bedroom as they passed it. Among stacks of boxes stood all their old bedroom furniture, looking reproachful, mocking, or inviting—she didn't have time to decide which before the eager boys yanked her on down the hall to their room.

"I picked the paint," Matthew said proudly. It was apple green with white trim, fresh and luminous, and in this room, unlike the others, everything had been unpacked and tidied: toys on shelves, beds made up, clothes put away—even the curtains and pictures were hung. There was something else as well: a row of white pegs running the length of one wall, placed conveniently low, for hanging up clothes. Simple but brilliant. And it was thoughtful of Adam to do their room first.

"This bed's mine. That one's Hugo's."

"This one's mine! That one's Matthew's!"

Moving day had made them almost ill with excitement, and they were entering the euphoric stage that precedes total collapse. Each began to jump on his own bed, shouting, "This one's mine!"

"It's a beautiful room," Sophie said. "Shall I put your...?" But they weren't listening, too busy seeing who could jump higher. "Careful, now," she said, unheeded.

She wandered back up the hall. Adam and James were setting up the television and the video and the stereo, crawling around and peering into instruction manuals, black cables stretched everywhere, Adam complaining, "These damned 'universal' symbols—universally incomprehensible!" He took an angry swig of tea, achieving bevel-meter as he did so, had he but known it. Sophie watched him bat the coaster off his mug irritably, feeling like an au pair girl—*with* the family, but not *of* it. Looking around the room for a task, she saw another box of books to put away. "More architecture books!" she called to Adam, making sure she sounded cheerful. "Where do you want these?" But he was engrossed in the problem of cables, studying the back of the DVD player, and he didn't hear her question.

James did. "The shelf in the corner," he said shortly, his mind on the task at hand, but when he realized how abruptly he had spoken, he blushed. "I mean, I guess that's as good a place as any. Near the desk and all."

She fell to the job gratefully, like a shy guest happy to have a little mission at a party, spearing the olives with toothpicks for the hostess instead of just standing there trying to look as if she didn't mind not speaking to anyone. One after another, she pulled Adam's architecture books out of the box, the same books he'd packed when he was planning to leave her and unpacked when she'd left him instead, then repacked to come here. And now it was her turn to unpack them. This, she thought, was how books experienced the triumphs and the heartbreaks of their owners' lives: as trips in and out of boxes.

"There, that's done." She stood and faced the two men. "Well! I guess I'll be going, then."

"I should go, too," James said suddenly. "In fact, hey!" He checked his watch and started violently, poor actor that he was. "Oh, my gosh, I had no idea. I've got to run. Call me tomorrow if you need me." And with a wave, he was gone.

The abruptness of his departure, and his too-obvious intention of leaving them alone together and deferring to Sophie the honor of being the last to go, left them standing awkwardly, not looking at each other, listening to his footsteps recede down the stairs. Then came the distant slam of the front door. Then nothing.

Adam cleared his throat. "Thanks for your help."

"I didn't do much."

"Yes you did. You were a great help. Thanks."

Silence.

"Boys, your mother's going! Come and say good-bye!"

It was a relief when they ran in.

"Can we come, too, Mommy? We want to come, too! We can walk to your house because it's so near!"

"We can go all alone even. I want to come with you and count how many steps it is!"

"Yeah!"

"Tomorrow," she said. "And you know what? I have something to show you at home—a surprise."

"Can we see it now? Can we?"

"Tomorrow. In fact, you're spending the weekend with me, so you'll have a long time to play with it."

"Is it a toy?"

"I'm not saying."

"We want to see it now!"

"All right, now, boys, all right," Adam cut in. "That's enough. Mummy has to go home now." He made an apologetic face, and it struck her that it used to be she who intervened in order to protect him from the children's overexuberance. "Come on, now, bath time."

"No!"

"I'll be right in. You get your clothes off. Go on, now."

They ran off, and he shrugged. "They're just very excited," he explained, rotating his shoulder.

"I realize that," she said coolly.

"I think we've done the right thing, Sophie. Thanks. For finding this place, I mean. They're so happy we're neighbors, it's all they talk about. They want keys to both apartments. Of course they're too young for that, and there's still a street to cross...." He lifted his arm and winced. "Maybe when our businesses take off, we'll be rich enough to pay for our own crossing guard between us."

Milagros popped her head in. "Have you seen the boys?"

"I just sent them in to have a bath."

"Well, they're not there. Now, where...?" She disappeared again.

Sophie gestured to Adam's shoulder. "Have you hurt yourself?"

"No, it's nothing. Well, actually, yes. I did it playing squash, and it's still a little sore. And I guess moving that thing didn't help." He nodded resentfully at the chesterfield.

She looked at it, too, for want of anything to say.

"I may have pulled something. I don't suppose... You couldn't take a look at it, could you? Or is that... not the kind of thing you do?"

"It's exactly the kind of thing I do." She considered for a moment. "All right. How about later, when the boys have gone to bed?"

"All right. Yes. Milagros is staying late tonight to finish the kitchen. That would be fine. But... you won't be... busy?"

"No."

He laughed suddenly. "I've never actually seen your apartment. Do you realize that?"

He had walked her to the door and opened it, and they

stood looking out into the hall in an embarrassed way. "Come around eight, then," she said. "And wear something loose, made of cot—"

There was a scream overhead. Not a movie scream. The electrifying true scream of a woman in terror. Tingling with shock, Sophie and Adam locked eyes. Milagros. Now Milagros was running down the attic stairs, shouting, "Up on the roof! Up on the roof!" Shouting "up" yet running down—it made no sense. Sophie stood frozen, unable to move, unable to think past that ghastly scream. Adam dashed into the hall and up the stairs, two at a time; Milagros rushed down past him, still shouting.

Sophie broke the grip of fear and raced after him, up the stairs to the attic, through the door, panting. The stepladder lying across the floor, fallen over; Hugo wailing, pointing up. The skylight, and Matthew's pale face pressed to the lower pane—*from the outside*. Matthew was trapped out on the roof, hanging by the fabric of his shirt caught on the latch of the closed skylight, his face white against the glass, mouth open, eyes wide in terror. Hugo was whimpering, "The bird was hurt! He was trying to get it!" Sophie saw it in her mind in a series of freeze-frames: Matthew climbing the ladder, leaning out the top opening of the tippy window to reach a bird resting on the pane, leaning too far, pushing the ladder over with his foot, his weight swinging the window up to close and bringing him with it, his shirt catching as he slid out, him pivoting, staring facedown back through the skylight, his feet pointing to the edge of the roof and the ground three stories below, his shirt stretching.

Adam slammed the ladder back onto its feet, raced up it.

"No!" Sophie screamed. "If you open it, he'll fall!"

"I have to break it! Cover your eyes!" And through the

glass to his son, "Matthew, close your eyes!" With sharp raps of his elbow, Adam cracked the top pane until he made a jagged hole. Some glass fell in, other pieces he wrenched out with his hands, working feverishly to clear a hole big enough to lean out of. Glass showered to the floor with a tinkling crash and, among the shards, drops of blood. He worked fast, but—

What happened next would revisit Sophie in dreams. Matthew shrieked as his shirt ripped free of the latch and his head disappeared from sight. "No!" she screamed. Adam abandoned his task, snapped the catch open, batted the window up, and threw his upper body out the lower opening. Sophie listened with her whole being for the sound along the roof tiles that would mean Adam had not caught their son—the scraping sound of the boy sliding off the roof before he fell over the edge into the void. *Nothing else matters,* she thought, with penetrating clarity. *Nothing in life matters but life itself.*

And there it was, the scrabbling sound. Their son was slipping, slithering down the tiles off the roof. "Good God!" Adam shouted, leaning out farther. Matthew screamed, Sophie screamed, and through the open window came Milagros's voice from down in the garden: "I'll catch you, *mi amor*! I'll catch you!"

Then the scrambling noise on the tiles stopped abruptly— and Sophie's heart with it—to be replaced by something yet more hideous: the sound of death, silence. Matthew over the edge…Matthew plunging through the air…

"He's stopped!" Adam shouted. "He's got a foot on the gutter!" Spread-eagle on the roof, his fingers splayed and white-tipped in his effort to grip the flat tiles and brake his slide, Matthew lay looking back up with panicked eyes at his father, just out of reach. Adam eased his legs up and out and lay on his stomach along the roof, holding on by the tops of his feet flexed against the frame of the skylight, reaching. Reaching...

"Adam, no!" Sophie saw now that they were both going to fall.

"I've got him!" Adam cried. "I've got his arms! I've got you, son! You're all right!" A moment's silence, and then with a metallic groan the guttering broke away, and Matthew slipped farther, his legs now over the edge, his waist at the level of the missing guttering. "Sophie!" Adam's voice sounded strained and far away. "Go down and try to bring him in the window directly below!"

"What? What?" Too panicked at first to understand.

"Pull him in through the window downstairs!"

Sophie turned and ran down the stairs, Hugo crashing after her, down, down, and into the room below—a run she would never remember. It was a sash window. Stuck! With frantic fingers she fumbled with the lock, couldn't open it, whimpered with fear, did open it, threw the window up, and leaned out. Above her she could see Matthew's shoes. "I can't reach him!" she called up to Adam. "Lower him some more!"

"I'm stretched full out! Can you get higher?"

"I'll try!" Sophie climbed onto the sill and stood up outside the window, clinging with her left hand to the frame inside, under the fixed top half of the pane. She swayed out over the void. "Help me!" she shouted back inside to Hugo. "Hold me!" He ran and wrapped both arms around his mother's leg, leaning back to throw all his slight weight into the hopeless task of providing ballast for her. He lifted his feet off the floor to make himself heavier.

"I called the firemen!" Milagros yelled from below, her frightened face upturned and framed by her extended palms. "Hold on, Matthew! Hold on! Don't worry! If you fall, I'll catch you!"

Sophie tightened her grip on the frame inside and reached up. She could just touch the boy's knees. "He's still too high! Adam, he's still too high!"

"All right, I'm going to lower him! Sophie, are you ready? We only have one shot at this! Are you ready?"

"Yes!"

"Here he comes!" Little by little, by loosening his grip, then tightening it again, Adam allowed the boy's arms to slip through his grasp until he was holding him by the hands. "That's all I can do! Do you have him? Sophie, do you have him?"

Sophie braced herself to receive Matthew's weight. "Let go!" she called up.

"No!" Matthew screamed.

As the child's and father's fingers separated, Sophie gained a further couple of inches, just enough to clamp the boy's legs above the knee to her chest with her right arm. Matthew grabbed her head with a scream as he came down, yanking her hair, and Sophie swayed out over the drop, unable to see, her fingers slippery with sweat on the window frame inside. She envisioned herself falling, ripped from the window, Matthew in her arms, pulling Hugo out after her: a vision that would recur in nightmares. But she groaned and held on, hauled herself back in against the building, the fingers of her left hand cramping. Matthew slid down her body until he could wrap his legs around her waist and his arms around her neck. Slowly, she bent her legs, clutching Matthew tight to her chest, then swiveled until she could sit straddling the window frame, her whimpering son on her lap. She shook Hugo off her leg and pushed Matthew into the room. He fell on the floor, crying. Safe.

"Move! Get out of the way!" Sophie ordered her sons. She clambered stiffly in the window and ran back upstairs on uncontrollable rubber legs. She slipped on the stairs, smacking her head against the wall, got up, ran on, burst into the attic, panicked eyes upturned to the skylight, afraid she would find—nothing. Afraid Adam had already fallen.

But no, she saw shoes. He was there, still holding on with his feet, only the soles of his shoes in sight. She skidded over broken glass to the ladder, dashed up it so fast it rocked on two legs, poked her head and shoulders out the opening, and locked her arms around his calves with all her strength. "It's okay, Adam, I've got you!" she gasped. "I've got you. I've got you." Eventually she was aware of the firemen's siren, then big boots tramping up the stairs and deep voices next to her, then big men pulling her husband back inside, then someone putting a blanket around her shoulders.

———

Matthew recovered from the shock fairly quickly, his parents less so. Several days later, still feeling shaken and achy, Sophie got a call from Adam asking again for a shiatsu. His shoulder was worse from holding Matthew on the roof, and, he added sheepishly, the tops of his feet were sore from clinging to the frame of the skylight. "Let no drama be without its element of low slapstick," he said ruefully.

"I'll do what I can one-handed," Sophie said. "My left went into spasm, and I still can't open it all the way." She gently flexed her heroic left hand, where shock and fear still resided. In self-defense her mind had rapidly shrouded its memories in translucent layers, but her body lacked the protective mechanism of forgetfulness and it would retain the horrific imprint forever. "Is eight o'clock tonight all right? What about the boys?"

"It's fine. James is here. He'll stay with them. Eight o'clock, then."

The knock on her door came at ten past eight, which is eight o'clock straight up for parents. "A hundred and four steps, I make it," Adam said when she let him in. "Between our houses, I mean." He saw that she was dressed all in white—drawstring trousers, T-shirt, and socks, no shoes—looking modest and businesslike.

"It takes me a hundred and twenty-seven," she said. "Not counting the stairs. Come in. This way." He stepped in gingerly and glanced discreetly around. She led the way across the kitchen, saying, "They have shorter legs, so I calculate it'll take them, oh, two hundred and three. When they can count that far. Look, this was their surprise." She snapped on the light of her former treatment room to reveal the boys' new bedroom. Like their room at Adam's house, this one was neatly arranged and freshly painted, but it was much smaller, with bunk beds against one wall. "They needed a room of their own over here, so I packed up my work space and made this for them. At first I was so sure this room was too small for them that it was blocking my thinking. But it's not, not if they spread up instead of out." She pointed to the wall opposite the bunk beds, filled entirely from floor to ceiling with built-in cabinets, divided horizontally into two sets of closets and drawers by a shelflike platform running lengthwise.

"But how do they— Oh, I see!" Adam laughed and went over to touch the ladder that served as access to the upper level. It slid on a runner, like the kind used in libraries. "This must be great fun."

"Yes, they love it. And look at this. Like Murphy beds, except they're desks. You just unfasten the catch, and the panel comes down—see?" There was one of these on each of the remaining two walls, staggered so that when the boys were working back-to-back, their chairs wouldn't touch. "And when you don't need them, they fold up flat against the wall to make extra play room. Ingenious, eh? I bought it all ready-made, and they came and installed it."

"Brilliant. Who gets the top bunk?"

"They alternate weekends."

He nodded. "They must be delighted. You've made excellent use of this space. But where will you work?"

"Well." She snapped the light off and led him back into the kitchen. "In here for now." She pointed to the futon set up provisionally under the window. "When I get my license, I'll have to rent work space somewhere." Maybe in L's building, or maybe Rose or Jean would know of a place. She would find something, she knew. Problems of that size didn't worry her anymore. "As a wise friend once told me, one problem is just a problem, but if you line up two problems in the right way, they often point toward a common solution. I paraphrase somewhat—my wise friend didn't really understand her own adage, but that's the sense I make of it. In this case, problem one: My apartment, which I adored and didn't want to leave, was too small for both my children and my work. Problem two: Working from home was risky. Solution? Work elsewhere and use that room for the boys. Simple, right? But I was still blocked by two false assumptions. One, I was convinced that the room was too small for both children, and two, I thought I couldn't pay two rents. I solved the first problem with ingenuity and the second...well, that's easy. If I can't work from home—or live at work—then I *have* to pay two rents. I was wrong to think the other option existed, so I adjusted my givens. I'll just have to find somewhere not too expensive. And work very hard to pay for both!" She knelt down to smooth the cotton sheet covering the futon and arrange the flat pillow and few cushions around it. "Anyway, I like the idea of going out to work. As you said, leaving the house in the morning...having colleagues..." She patted the futon. "Take off your shoes and lie down here."

But he was roaming around examining things. He studied the meridian charts, the hairy cactus, the children's drawings on the walls, the titles of the textbooks on her desk. At the glass door to the porch, he paused. "May I?" She nodded, and he stepped out and stood for some time in the moonlight. When he came back inside, he closed the door quietly. "This is a lovely place," he said seriously. "It has a very good feeling. I'm glad you kept it on."

"Yes. So am I."

They stood facing each other for a moment, she looking at ease and he rather out of place. Then she said in a pleasant professional tone, "Have you had shiatsu before?"

"You know I haven't."

"No," she said calmly. "I don't know that. Well, you may feel tired afterward, and you'll need to drink plenty of water to help eliminate the toxins. You may find you have vivid dreams tonight. In any case, take it easy tomorrow." She studied his posture, his tongue, and his pulse, then made him take off his shoes and lie down on the futon faceup so she could diagnose his *hara*. It all confirmed what she had already guessed: weak kidney yang and a need to bolster chi. "All right. Now roll over onto your stomach." He did so gingerly. "Turn your head—that's right."

She knelt beside him, rubbed her hands together gently, favoring her injured left, and began by placing it comfortingly on his back. She moved through the routine smoothly, keeping reassuring contact with the mother hand while the child hand went seeking places of *kyo* and *jitsu*, emptiness and fullness, along his Bladder channel. She kept her *hara* open to his, using her energy to adjust the flow of his. Gradually, he relaxed and grew more receptive. When he turned onto his side, she rotated his arm to ease the shoulder, then hooked her fingers under his shoulder blade and leaned back, lifting it away from the spine. She did the Triple Burner and Small Intestine channels down his arms. He hummed appreciatively, then lay on his back while she did the Kidney channel along the insides of his legs, and finally she wrapped her hands in a silk scarf to work on his face and head. She ended the session by resting her hand on his *hara* and lifting it off slowly. "Now I'm going to ring a bell," she said. "I want you to follow the vibrations for as long as you can." She struck a pair of Chinese cymbals together, and a clear, sweet note lingered a long time in the air. Adam's face looked lined, unshaven and peaceful; he was nearly asleep after another strenuous day. She slipped on her shoes, stepped out onto the porch, and leaned against the railing, breathing in the tepid night air.

It was a mild night in May. The children would be out of school soon. The summer lay ahead with its promise of buckets and spades. The moon was bright, and so were the streetlights in the park, greening the leaves around them. She couldn't quite see Adam's house, but she knew it was there, just off to the left, and she could see a maple lit by what must be light from his bay window. It was comforting to think of her children asleep so close by—yet sad, too. On the other side of the park were Florence, Mercy, and Jean. They formed a triangle across the park: Sophie, her children, and her friends. And another triangle would be formed by Sophie, her children, and her work. Someone had said to her—Florence?—that a three-legged stool is best because it never wobbles. A tripod, three sturdy legs with a good, wide base: home, work, children. Rock solid. The succulent plants in their pots glowed palely, looking prehistoric in the moonlight. She reached out and touched the smooth, spiky-edged leaf of one that looked like a starfish.

And there was Henry.

There was Henry, too. She couldn't think of him without smiling, and she had called to tell him so. He had been out, so she'd left a message: "Henry, my friend, I would like you to meet my children. How about a picnic next week?" Sophie, her children, and Henry; that made another triangle. And looking across the rooftops, she felt sure that she would become more widely and deeply connected over time, with links to more friends, and to her children's friends, to new clients, new colleagues, and their friends, forming a network of interlocking triangles that would spread out over the city. And she would be in its center, safely anchored. A slight breeze wafted the scent of a night-blooming plant through the darkness.

Adam's voice came through the open door. "Good night." There was the slightest inflection in it, the hint of an invitation to stop him from going. "Good night," she answered quietly, without looking around. She heard the door open, then click shut, and she imagined him going along the hall, down the three flights of stairs, out the door, turning right, past two doors, turning left, across the street, and along the end of the park to his door on the left: a hundred and four steps home to where their children lay sleeping.

———

"So what now? I get stuck with the lonely-woman-at-the-top bullshit role? That hackneyed convention? Fuck that." The evening sun shone on the rice-paper shade, and from around its edge yellow rays sliced into the room, striking Agatha's coffee table and making the two glasses of red wine on it glitter. At one end of the white sofa, Valerie sat slumped, her arms crossed over her chest, and at the other, Agatha was curled up in a sympathetic position.

"What's Masterson like?" she asked, thoughtfully sliding a clean ashtray across the table to within Valerie's reach.

But Valerie seemed not to notice. "Oh. You know."

"It's my fault. That ultimatum . . . I should never have made you do that." The words produced a pinprick of pleasure in Agatha, but not the need to indulge in triumphal crowing. She thought her friend was looking thin and drawn and in need of protection.

"No," Valerie said. "It was time I got out of that situation. It was sordid being with a man who went home to his wife every night, pretending I was glad I didn't have to wash his socks. No, I did it because I thought you were right. I still do."

"I'm glad."

Valerie eyed her friend. "Look, it just so happens you were right this time, but it still counts as meddling in my affairs, so now it's my turn. I get to play deus ex machina in your next affair."

"No thanks. You're not screwing up this one."

"What, are you seeing someone?"

"You probably don't remember, but that night you had the crisis in the hotel, ages ago, I had a date?"

"You did?"

"Yeah, but I told you it didn't matter, and instead of going out, I talked to you for an hour to calm you down. You were so upset about Adam."

"So what happened?"

"I called him, but his phone was switched off, so I went late."

"And he was still there?"

"No. He'd left."

"Just proves he didn't deserve you."

"I was an hour and a half late to the restaurant! No one would have waited. I called the next day and apologized. I explained that my friend was having a crisis in her love life, and he said I would do better to look after my own love life."

"The nerve."

"No, I think he was right."

"Oh do you?"

"Anyway, we've been seeing each other ever since." Agatha smiled and sort of hugged herself, looking, Valerie thought, very smug. Or—damn it, why did she always have to be so bitchy?—maybe Agatha was just happy.

"Really? Well, well. You've been keeping very quiet about this. So. What's he like? Tell all. Starting with the physical."

Agatha smiled in that inward-looking way of lovers that excludes the rest of the world. "I think he's cute."

"Uh-oh. 'Cute' is usually code for 'chubby and balding.'"

But Agatha just laughed, invulnerable in love.

"Yes? Come on, more details. Age?"

"Forty-four."

"Married? Divorced?"

"Single."

"Forty-four and single? What's wrong with him?"

"God, Valerie, you might as well ask what's wrong with us!"

"We're not forty-four. Not yet. But okay, I'll rephrase that. Why do you suppose he never married?"

"Well, there are several things. A difficult mother, for one."

"Okay, I get it. A mama's boy."

"Not anymore. Mama died. Wasn't it considerate of her to die while I'm still of childbearing age? Just."

Valerie looked closely at her friend for the first time since she'd arrived. Then she studied the room. There was a "new look" of some kind going on. "So this is serious?"

"I think so. I hope so."

"And your latest gimmick? You're now—what? I'm looking, and I'm noting the roughly woven brown clothing, the wispy hair swept back in rustic combs. I'm registering wildflowers wilting in folksy jam jars—we're, what, tree hugging now? We're talking some kind of Return to Gaea?"

Agatha threw back her head and laughed. "I guess you could say that! What I want now are Real Things. Genuine Things. No doubt this will turn out to be my most superficial phase of all!" Laughing at herself like that, Agatha looked suddenly very pretty.

"Does this guy have an interesting job?"

"Not especially. But I don't mind. What I'm looking for is a kind, intelligent man who cares for me and who's ready to start a family."

"Oh, Agatha, not that! Kind and intelligent are fine, but

what ever happened to sexy, dynamic, and brilliant? And a man who cares for you? What's wrong with adores you? Worships you! Agatha, it's not too late! You don't have to panic and settle for second best."

"But it's not second best. That's what I've come to realize. It's what I want. And it's a lot. Think about it: a kind, intelligent man who really cares about you and wants a family. That's everything! We're not teenagers anymore, to be sitting around dreaming up meaningless lists of superlatives to describe the movie star we're going to marry someday. This is *real. Arthur* is real."

"*Arthur?*"

"This is Life. This is Real. Not just sitting alone in my apartment pretending things, playing to an audience that isn't there. This is what I want. A real man, real love, warm babies to snuggle."

A vision flashed into Valerie's mind of herself as the favorite "spinster aunt" of Agatha's children, thoughtfully included in their family gatherings so she wouldn't spend holidays alone. Funny old Auntie Valerie, bearing gifts, everyone kind to her, the fifth wheel, poor thing, she was once so beautiful. She felt a geographic shift under her feet, like the separation of two continents, their friendship groaning and creaking and slowly drifting in a new direction, she who was once the leader growing caustic and shriveled, passed up by the vigorous wife and mother, glowing with womanly fulfillment. "Am I allowed to meet this paragon?"

"Sure." Agatha took Valerie's hand and squeezed it.

Valerie hesitated, then returned the pressure. "I see. So we're not going to be two gals catting around town this summer, drinking and whoring, now that my affair has ended. What a disappointment. Think about it, Ag—picnics out at

Tanglewood listening to the symphony orchestra, cannoli at the Vittoria, running down to Newport for the weekend…"

"I can cat around town. I'll just pass on the whoring."

They sipped wine in silence, and then Valerie said, "You're not very observant, are you? I spotted those jam jars, but you haven't noticed anything new about me."

Agatha's sharp eyes raked her friend from her haircut down to her shoes.

"No, you're cold," Valerie said. "It's not anything I have, it's something I don't have." Smiling, she wiggled the two first fingers of her right hand. Fingers that were normally holding—

"You've quit smoking?"

Valerie nodded, still smiling. " 'I don't smoke,' is what I say, not 'I quit'—I'm doing this thing right."

"I can't believe it! Congratulations! But my God, *why*?"

"Matthew. He was worried about me, and there's something about a child telling you not to smoke that…" She stopped, laughed, and wiped a tear from her eye. "When even a five-year-old knows it's dangerous and stupid, it's time to act. And hell, I'm almost forty. I'd better start taking care of myself—doesn't look like anyone else will. It was meant to be a surprise for Matthew, but then… Well, I decided to quit anyway."

"I'm amazed! But you smoked like a chimney. Isn't it *hard*?"

"Shit, no. I can do anything." She changed her position on the sofa and also the subject. "I'm happy for you, Aggie. I really am. You and… Arthur." Then she made an unflattering transition in her mind on the topic of "unlikely people who are finding partners" and said, "Oh, big news! You'll never guess who's getting remarried."

"Adam? He's going back to his wife?"

"Oh. No. Not that I know of. Although he might as well. You know, she's probably a very nice woman, actually."

Agatha opened her mouth in delighted disbelief. "Do you mean that?"

"Yeah. But go on, keep guessing. Who's getting married? Give up? My mother."

"You're kidding! That's great! Who's the guy?"

"I don't know. But here's the thing, she's invited my father. So she's known all this time where he was. Wants to rub it in his face, I guess. Not that he'll come to the wedding, of course. Not that I care if he comes or not." She held up her hand to block any comment from Agatha. "And I know what you're going to say. That I have 'unresolved father issues.'"

"I wasn't going to say that."

"Yes you were."

"I wasn't. But...do you?"

"I knew it! I knew you were going to say that. Oh, go on, open another bottle, why don't you?" Valerie rubbed her hand through her hair, ruffling it up. "I don't know, Ag, I guess I'm just drunk and morose and pissed off, but this game of musical chairs...I mean all this finding-a-partner stuff. The music goes on and on, and I'm dancing around, but someday the music is going to stop, and we *know* there are more people than chairs! What's going to happen in the final scramble? God, even *you've* got a chair now. No, wait, I didn't mean it like that. You know what I mean—my best friend, the person I've done everything with up to now."

"I'm not married yet, you know," Agatha said in the voice of a woman already planning Valerie's maid-of-honor outfit.

Valerie searched her friend's face. "What if I get left standing? What if the music stops and there are no more chairs?

For the first time in my life, I'm realizing that could actually happen! To me! To smart, beautiful me!"

"It could happen," Agatha said, and Valerie felt her stomach lurch with cold fear; she had been so sure that Agatha would deny it. "Anything could happen. Your life could take any direction, any day. Just make up your mind that whatever happens, it'll be something good. Convince yourself of that. Right now. Use willpower to decide that everything is going to work out fine."

"Is that possible?"

"Yes, it is. It's an effort, like working a new set of muscles. Very hard to do at first, but gradually you gain control over it, and you can flex it whenever you want. And you know what? You can tell when you're doing it right—because you feel good."

"You feel good."

"Yes. Mentally of course, but even physically. You really do. Sort of...protected and strong and lighthearted. As if something wonderful just *did* happen to you instead of *will* happen. It's amazing the power you have, if you harness it. You can—"

"I can bend spoons by just looking at them?"

"Listen to me. You can bend even Time to your will. If you decide your future will be happy, then the present glows with anticipation. You can will yourself into a new state where things are...well, they're just all okay."

"Oh, *that* state. I know the one. Insanity."

"It's not, Vee. Possibly it's a sister state—but if it is, who cares?"

"I can't just will a life partner into existence."

"No. But you can will yourself into a state where it doesn't matter if one shows up or not."

"Are you saying he's more likely to show up that way?"

"No-o. Because if you thought that, you'd be lying to your-self about its not mattering. It has to be true."

"And if it is true, if I honestly don't care, does that help it happen?"

"Possibly... Because you give off such good vibes."

"I already give off excellent vibes, Agatha. But the fact is, I could end up alone in life. I really could." To guide Agatha's response, she added after a pause, "Not that I think I will, really..."

But all she got was, "Of course you could end up alone. But it isn't about being alone or accompanied, it's about be-ing happy. Alone can be one of the good ways to wind up. Look, you don't know what the future will be, just *how* it will be—good. What kind of good, you have to wait and see. You have to trust in the benevolence of the Fates."

The setting sun was lower now and redder, and its rays had turned the window shade a radiant orange. Valerie blew out a stream of air and tossed up her hand in a gesture of sur-render. "Well, what the hell, I guess I might as well! And if it turns out I'm wrong—no, that *you're* wrong—and the Fates screw me over and my life ends up being a heap of crap, at least I'll only realize it at the last minute, and up to then I'll have lived in a cloud of merciful delusion. I guess that's bet-ter than seeing the shit coming at me the whole way, in 3-D and slow motion."

"It really will be all right," Agatha said matter-of-factly. "That's the point. So you might as well spare yourself the worry."

Valerie turned to the dazzling window and bit her lip, con-sidering that.

Reading Group Guide

Here are a handful of thoughts, questions, and opinions that
led to my writing this novel:

- It has never made sense to me that typically after a divorce
  the woman stays in the family house with the children.
  Especially if she has been a housewife up to then, she has
  a life to rebuild and she needs time and space alone to do
  that.

- I believe in the importance of fathering (where fathers exist), both for children and for men—real fathering, equal
  in time and intensity to mothering.

- It's cruel to speak badly to a child of his mother or father.
  The temptation to bad-mouth an ex-spouse is one we fall
  into too often. Divorcing couples often pay lip service
  to the idea of "putting their children's welfare first." But
  what if a couple were really to do that? How would they
  go about it?

- We would all like to believe that we have a reasonable amount of control over what happens to us, but I think the frightening truth is that we don't. Chance is the main determining factor, and other people, even distant ones, play a bigger role in shaping our lives than it's comfortable to think about. "A butterfly flaps its wings and..."

- There are dreary ideas about "commitment" out there that need debunking. Promises are hot air, and trying to extract them from lovers is pointless and degrading. Relationships shift and evolve, like everything else in the natural world.

- For some single mothers, banding together to form households could be a practical and life-embracing idea.

- There's often no rhyme or reason to who ends up with a partner in life and who doesn't. Therefore that cannot be the seat of happiness.

- Most often in life it isn't so much a question of good guys and bad guys as a matter of casting. Whether you're good or bad depends on what your role is in relation to mine.

- In fiction, I like to come across the kind of observation that is not something I'd ever thought of before in quite those words, but the truth of it is so immediately apparent that I greet it with a shout of recognition, like an old friend.

- There's some comic potential in a difference of register between a rather formal narrator's voice and the earthier speech of the characters.

Those are some of the elements I put together, and *Leaving Sophie Dean* is the result. I hope you enjoy it.

Discussion Questions for Book Clubs

1. How do the various friendships in the novel evolve, and how do they drive the plot?
2. A number of fathers are mentioned in the book, including Adam, Jacob, Henry, and Valerie's unnamed father. Discuss their varying roles in their children's lives.
3. How is suburbia depicted in the novel, and is that image true to your own experience of it?
4. What do you think of Henry's views on "commitment" as he explains them to Sophie near the end of the book?
5. Do you have a favorite moment, character, or line?
6. "It's simplistic and archaic to say that a failed marriage is one that ends in divorce, and a successful marriage is one that doesn't. It's possible to have a good short marriage, and a life-long failure." Do you agree or disagree?
7. Is Milagros an important character? Why or why not?
8. Do you think Sophie's strategy could work? What elements would need to be in place for it to work? Would you do it?
9. What future do you foresee for each of the main characters? Which character do you think "travels the farthest" in the course of the story?

10. Sophie compares loss of trust in a partner caused by infidelity to a crack in a plate, which will still show, even if mended, and still harbor germs. Do you agree with her, or do you think trust can be reestablished?

About the Author

A nomadic upbringing traveling through North America and Europe made Alexandra Whitaker a perpetual "new girl" who developed survival skills of observation and mimicry that would later prove to be useful writing tools. Necessity also made her a keen language learner. She speaks a few languages well, and a few more badly.

Elder daughter of bestselling writer Trevanian, she collaborated with him on various projects over the years. She has settled down at last in southwestern Europe with her British husband and their daughter. She writes fiction and runs a one-room hotel for solitary travelers.

She invites you to visit her website:
www.alexandrawhitaker.com